S. S. BAZINET

WILLIAM'S BLOOD

BOOK THREE

of the

The Vampire Reclamation Project

Renata Press
Albuquerque, New Mexico

Published by Renata Press
Albuquerque, New Mexico
www.renatapress.com

Visit the author's website:
www.ssbazinet.com

ISBN-13: 978-1-937279-14-1

To all of my family,
those special beings who reside in
the physical and the nonphysical.
They are my constant support team!

Acknowledgments

I have so many people in my life who have helped to make this book possible. My appreciation and gratitude goes out to all of my family for their continued, loving support. Regarding the book's content, Laura Christine has been my editing guru and guiding light. Gene has been an invaluable blessing as a copy editor. Anna Marie and Julia Ann have also been extremely helpful with their thoughtful support and additional copy editing. Gabriel is forever cheering me on!

One

William paused and listened. There was usually a hum of computers and equipment in the background of his laboratory. Now the lower level of his London home was too quiet. "Like a tomb," he muttered. He placed a cover over the microscope, put two beakers back in a storage cabinet, and turned out the light in the work area. All his months of research had turned out to be futile. There were no new theories to pursue. Even if there were, he didn't have the strength needed to continue working. His latest blood samples were swimming with inexplicable, crystalline anomalies. They resembled the samples taken from Arel, the person responsible for infecting him.

Arel will be thrilled to know that science has failed.

Arel lived in his own misinformed world. Even seeing William wasting away did nothing to convince the man that they were diseased.

So I wonder how he explains the fact that I'm dying.

He knew the answer. Arel was an idiot who was beyond thinking rationally. But William didn't have time to think about Arel. He tried to take a deep breath and coughed. His lungs were laboring to keep up. With each day that passed, it was getting harder to breathe. That meant that he had to prepare for what was coming next.

He started for the stairs and let out a gasping sigh halfway there. He was too exhausted to make the climb. He turned to his recliner instead. Its soft, leathery confines were a small comfort for his steadily declining state. It was also a place to take notes and record his current observations about his condition. But note-taking was becoming useless at this point. He stared at the dressing that covered his hand. After two months of meticulous care, his self-inflicted wound refused to heal. While Arel was visiting, he had insisted on one last parting ritual, a ridiculous and juvenile blood brother ceremony. William hadn't wanted to slice open his palm, but he'd finally given in. It seemed to be the only way to get Arel to leave. Now, he was being punished for his foolishness. His hand was showing signs of an infection.

He could have been enraged over his condition, but he refused to go that route. There had already been too many rants and ravings on his part, and none of his outbursts accomplished anything. How could they? He knew he wasn't Arel's victim. He was his own man and responsible for his life. If it was totally screwed up, he had to put the blame on his own head. It was a bitter pill to swallow on one hand, but liberating on the other. He had a choice in the moment, and he planned to make it one that served him. If he was going to die, he'd do it on his own terms.

Two

Arel sat on the sofa in the spacious, living room of his ranch style home. Subdued light streamed in from the large, front windows. Its gloomy flavor was offset by the warmth of heated air coming from the heating vents. The two elements came together in the room and created an atmosphere of winter coziness. But Arel didn't notice the room. His attention and a forced smile were directed at his angelic friend, Michael. "Kauai was beautiful, but it's good to be back."

Michael was stretched out in a chair by the window. He was dressed in his usual attire, blue jeans and a white sweat shirt. Unlike Arel, who was on the slender side, Michael had a more robust frame. At six-foot, two-inches, he appeared solid and fit in his human form. "I'm glad you took Carey's advice and got away from everything for a while."

Arel slowly rubbed the nubby fabric on the arm of the couch. His tanned fingers contrasted sharply with the white linen. "Taking Carey along worked out very well. I enjoyed his company, and I think he enjoyed surfing. He's a natural."

"Did I hear my name?" Carey asked as he came out of the kitchen. He was carrying a dessert plate that barely contained his generous slice of apple pie.

Michael's gaze settled on the young man's face. "Looks like you got plenty of sun too."

Carey grinned. "I almost lived on the beach the whole time we were in Hawaii. The water is incredible. Like Arel said, I loved learning to surf. Of course I got axed a few times, but hey, I'm still a beginner." He gave Arel a teasing frown. "Arel should have given it a try."

11

Arel stiffened. "I like the feel of something solid under my feet, but that's just me." He stopped rubbing the sofa arm and flexed his hand. For a long moment, he studied the thin scar on his palm. After his bonding ceremony with William, his hand had been a painful reminder of his visit to London. It finally appeared to be healed except for a burning sensation that wouldn't go away, especially when he thought about William. He glanced up at Carey again. "Could you give us a few moments?"

Carey shrugged as he forked a large portion of pie and waved it in Arel's direction. "Sure. I'll be out in the garage. I want to check on my bike. I'm looking forward to taking it out for a spin."

Arel's brows narrowed. "Do you think you can do something about that oil leak?"

"Yeah, sure." A few crumbs sprayed from Carey's mouth as he tried to answer without swallowing his last bite. "Don't worry about it. I'll work on the grease stain on the floor too."

"Thanks." Arel tried not to sound irritated as he watched Carey exit the room, leaving behind his mark on the white, wool carpet. Arel had lived alone for a very long time and had always been fastidious about his space. When Michael became a houseguest, he was careful to follow Arel's example. Carey was a different matter. He challenged everything without even trying.

Michael shifted in his seat. "Don't worry, I'll vacuum the carpet later."

"Is it me, Michael, or is Carey a bit of a slob?"

"He does seem very comfortable here. But if his actions bother you, talk to him."

"That's just it. I want him to feel comfortable."

"He certainly loves to eat."

"Yes, especially sweets. Thank you for picking up a pie for his homecoming. When I'm shopping, I'm always looking at the desserts. I know they're not good for him, but I keep picturing his face and how excited he is when he's unloading groceries. It's like Christmas when he spies a carton of donuts." He paused. "I want to be a responsible friend, even a father figure, but I end up caving most of the time."

"You're concerned about his happiness, that's all. And when it comes to important matters, believe me, you don't cave in to his wishes."

Arel's smile turned genuine and playful. "I guess I do have my tougher side."

Michael's smile slipped away. "Your face is getting thin again. Is William's situation troubling you?"

Arel's golden eyes flared in Michael's direction, but he quickly looked back at his hand and made a fist. "I've tried to take your advice and have faith in William, but I can't ignore the feeling that he's not long for this world. It's hard not to feel guilty when I know that it's all my fault."

"Your heart was in the right place when you tried to help him."

"That didn't stop me from nearly killing him. Thankfully you were there." He paused and stared at Michael again, letting his eyes soften. "Thank you for always trying to help, for never giving up on me."

"Don't give up on William. Remember that you were nearly a goner when I showed up."

"Yes, but I was indestructible, wasn't I, so you didn't have to worry."

Michael shook his head. "That's not true. You might have felt that way, but—"

"Please, remember how I tried to starve myself to death and never succeeded? I was fine."

"You believed that. You thought you were invincible, however—"

"Oh I see what you're trying to say. As usual, I deceived myself, and you showed up before I did keel over. Of course, your help wasn't foolproof either. Later, in that quaint little churchyard, I did have a fatal heart attack." He let out a weak laugh. "It was a close call."

Michael sighed. "Yes, it was."

Arel's hands closed on themselves, gripping hopelessly at what lay ahead as he contemplated the future. "What are we going to do, Michael? William is headed towards his own churchyard, and you won't be there to save him like you did me."

"Perhaps one of my friends could reach out to William."

"An angel, helping William? That will never happen."

"Why do you say that?"

"He'd spot one of your kind immediately."

"Really?"

"Of course. I can't put my finger on it, but there's something all of you have in common. None of you seem quite as down to earth as a real human is. William would see through one of yours in an instant."

"I thought I blended in quite well."

"Generally speaking, you do, but—"

"Hey, Arel?" Carey called out. He stood in the doorway to the garage, wiping his hands on a rag. "Just wanted you to know that I think I stopped the oil leak."

"Great," Arel called back. "There's some cleaner on the workbench. Maybe you can get the stain up."

"I'll get right on it," Carey called back.

Arel stood up. "I better go out and help him."

"I'm sure he's capable enough."

"I don't know about that. He's still just a kid."

"Is that how you think of him?"

"Carey tries his best, but when it comes to taking care of the basics, I have to say, he's definitely an example of a real human and an immature one at that."

Michael laughed. "No halo or wings?"

"No, just an endless appetite for pie and ice cream."

Three

Peggy put a plate of shortbread cookies on the kitchen table and pulled out a chair to sit down. With baby Sara upstairs napping, she could pay more attention to her guest. She flashed a sly smile in Carol's direction and quickly reached out for a cookie. "You look like you have something on your mind."

Carol placed her tea cup on its saucer and stared back accusingly. "Don't act like you don't already know what's going on."

Peggy giggled. "I'm sorry if I spoiled your surprise. But please, pretend that I'm clueless and tell me everything!"

Carol's face lit up as she smiled too. "It was all so unexpected. I was standing there at the kitchen sink, doing dishes, and Kevin came in. As soon as I saw his face, I knew something was going on. And sure enough, you know Kevin, when he's hiding something he has to get it out." She blushed as she picked up her cup and took a sip of tea.

"Well, don't stop there. Go on!"

Carol didn't look bullied by Peggy's tone. Instead, she glanced over at the infant swing that was located a few feet away. Baby Ariel was contentedly chewing on a teething biscuit. With a rock solid, chubby body and full rosy cheeks, he looked older than nine months.

Peggy tapped her foot, but she forced herself to let Carol tell her news in her own time frame.

"Sorry," Carol said as she brought her attention back to Peggy. "Sometimes, I find myself just staring at the baby. He's so amazing." Her green eyes flashed a little brighter. "And Kevin is a great father."

"But—" Peggy let out a sigh. "I feel like you're holding out."

"But you know that we have had our ups and downs."

"Yes, of course." Carol's simple pronouncement made Peggy pull back. Her frown of impatience was replaced by one of worry. "I know my brother can be a dunce at times—"

"Please, you know I've never liked it when you refer to Kevin like that."

Peggy blinked back a quick apology. "It's an old habit. The fact is that I guess I'm sticking up for him. In spite of his faults, he loves you. He's just so hopeless about expressing it sometimes."

Carol's shoulders relaxed a little. "Well, he expressed it this morning. He announced that we're going to Paris for a week. We're going to take that honeymoon that we never had. He also said that you and Tim are going to take care of Ariel."

"And you agreed, right?"

Carol nodded. "It sounds wonderful. Are you sure you don't mind babysitting for a week?"

"Of course not. Ariel is very easy going. But you don't seem as happy as I thought—"

"I'm sure it'll be great."

Peggy tightened the grip on her fragile, tea cup. She loved family. She loved her brother, and Carol was the perfect sister she'd always wanted. They'd been best friends for a long time. Now, they shared so much more. They were both new mothers. They lived close enough to visit each other almost daily. She didn't want anything to happen to change that. But what control did she have when it came to other people's lives. "So tell me more about going to Paris?"

Carol shrugged. "What can I say? It's a dream come true."

"Carol, if there's anything going on in your relationship, you can always try a marriage counselor."

"Actually, we did."

"You did? You never said anything."

"We only went a couple of times, and Kevin just sat there. I know he tried, but he couldn't seem to open up to the therapist any more than he opens up to me."

Peggy sat up straighter, needing to get everything back on track. "Talk to Arel. He's a perfect counselor."

"We've already burdened him with too many of our problems."

"He loves to help. You know that. Please, Carol, if you throw Kevin out, he'll be miserable forever."

Carol frowned back. "I'm not planning on anything like that."

"Really, are you sure? You did leave him briefly when you were first pregnant with Ariel."

"I just wish we could communicate a little better."

"When you come back from Paris, give Arel a try, okay?"

Carol put her napkin on the table and smoothed it out, carefully straightening the bent edges. "This is so weird. We're going on a honeymoon and listen to me. I should be the happiest person around."

"Couples can go through tough spots, especially when they've never had much time just for themselves."

"I guess you're right. Plus I hadn't dated for fourteen years when I met Kevin. Falling in love so quickly was a bit of a surprise. Then with getting pregnant, everything happened so fast."

Peggy reached over and stilled Carol's hand. "I think a honeymoon is going to be the perfect opportunity for you and Kevin to reconnect, to find that spark that attracted you two in the first place."

Carol smiled. "I do still find him terribly attractive."

"Trust me, it's going to work out. I'm sure it is."

Later that evening, while Peggy made supper, she didn't feel as confident about her statement to Carol. She stood at the sink watching seven month old Sara. Peggy's worries were clearly lost on the baby. Sara sat in her highchair, completely absorbed with the food on her tray. Her intense, dark brown eyes were focused as her tiny fingers targeted her cheerios.

"Anybody home?" Tim called out from the foyer.

Peggy's face brightened as she took off her apron and glanced at Sara. "Want to see your daddy?" she cooed.

The little girl didn't look up from her task. She seemed oblivious to anything but her quest for her cereal. Even when her tall father walked into the kitchen, she barely acknowledged his presence.

Peggy was her opposite. She smiled broadly. "Supper is almost ready. Are you hungry?"

Tim's steel-gray eyes lit up. "You bet," he said as he walked over to the highchair. Sara was happily munching on a bit of cereal as Tim bent down and planted a kiss on her golden curls. "Looks like somebody couldn't wait for supper."

Peggy laughed. "She needed something to keep her occupied while I was cooking."

Tim came over and kissed Peggy next. "How's my beautiful wife?"

"Happy to see you."

Tim stood back and studied Peggy's face. "What's wrong?"

"It's nothing. I'm just kind of concerned."

Tim's brows furrowed deeper. "About what?"

Peggy stared up at him. At six-foot, three-inches, Tim was an inch shorter than her brother, Kevin. Both still had the strong, muscular bodies of college football players. Tim was only six months older than Kevin, but he seemed so much more capable when it came to tuning into a person's mood. He could take one look at Peggy and know exactly how happy or sad she was. "Carol and I were talking this morning, you know, about stuff. Kevin came up."

"Let me guess. Carol isn't happy with him."

"It's not her fault. Kevin's my brother, and I love him but he's a little dense." She pulled back and twisted a button on her shirt. "I'm worried that he's going to ruin everything, his marriage and his relationship to Carol."

"Honey, please, Kevin is taking her to Paris."

"Yes, but that trip wasn't entirely his idea, was it?"

Tim turned and grabbed a carrot stick off of the counter. "I might have made a few suggestions."

"Because you're worried too?"

"No, not exactly. Kevin and I were talking, and he asked for a little advice. He's crazy about Carol. He wants her to be happy."

"How did you come up with Paris?"

Tim chewed a bite of carrot thoughtfully. "Carol has a couple of posters in the house. I noticed the Eiffel Tower in both of them. I figured that she must want to go to France someday."

Peggy snatched up a carrot stick too and snapped off a piece with a scowl. "See, this is why I worry. You notice things. Kevin doesn't."

"He may not see some things, but he noticed that Carol's been unhappy. Otherwise he wouldn't have asked for advice."

"I guess, but I hope he gets it together on this trip. It's an opportunity to let Carol know he can be involved."

"He is involved. He loves Carol. But maybe she's not letting herself feel that he does."

"I just hope they can work things out."

Tim latched on to her shoulder and pulled her into his arms. "Sweetheart, I know you get very concerned, but you have to let them solve their own problems."

"What if I did that with Arel? Do you remember how he pushed us all away at first? Goodness knows what would have happened if I'd let him go his own way. And speaking of Arel, I'm getting some funny feelings about him too."

"What now?"

"He seems distracted. I can't pin it down exactly, but I think it has to do with that friend of his in London. I get a very bad feeling about all that."

"Look, Peg, we don't know what's going on with those two, but again, it's their business."

"I know. I'm just being a friend."

"And I want to be Arel's friend too, you know that. When I thought he needed help, I even made that trip to New York."

"You're right." Peggy glanced at Sara again. The baby was still contentedly going about her task of cereal retrieval. "I need to get my mind off other people and focus on my own life. In fact, I could do what Michael does. He's always reading those flower magazines and planning out his garden. Maybe that's how he stays so calm around Arel."

Tim smiled. "After supper, maybe you can call him and ask to borrow a few."

Four

Michael remained in the corner of William's downstairs living area. He was there to observe Annabel as she acquainted herself with William. Her excitement over a possible assignment was evident. She sparkled brightly, and her energy flared several times. Of course William was none the wiser. Michael and Annabel were in their ethereal forms. Annabel could sparkle like the sun and still go undetected. "So what do you think about William?" Michael asked telepathically.

"Goodness, I might not get a chance to help. He's in a very poor state."

"Yes, but if he's anything like Arel, he won't give up easily on whatever he sets his mind to."

Annabel's energy flared again. "But William's not at all like Arel, is he? Arel can be consumed by guilt and remorse. William seems almost devoid of such concerns."

"William feels that his only sin is that he loved and trusted someone he considered a brother. When it came to the rest of humanity, he never held himself accountable for his actions. He never realized that his hatred of humanity isn't a part of his true nature."

"So he was happy before—"

"Before Arel passed on my blood? Yes, William considered himself very content with what he'd made of his life."

Annabel studied William from different angles. He was resting in his recliner. As he dozed, his pale, hollow cheeks and gaunt features were totally exposed to her scrutiny. From what Michael had said, he was a shell of his former, handsome self. His ailing, compromised body heaved in and out with every breath. "On the surface, his

20

control is evident, but on a very deep level, he's still harboring a lot of negativity."

"William is very analytical in his approach. He believes in keeping his emotions in check."

"Interesting. Even in his dismal state, I sense a courageous presence about him in spite of whatever he's believed."

"He'll need that courage in the days ahead. As you observed, his health is very fragile. He'll have to face the possibility of dying soon. Hopefully, you'll have an opportunity to interact with him before that happens."

"I see." Annabel hesitated. "This time I'll be on my own when I'm in physical form. Do you think that I'm ready?"

"More importantly, are you sure that you want this assignment? After working with a person like Arel, who wants to change, who tries to cooperate, I still find it—"

"A challenge?"

Michael's energy filled with a touch of caution. "Helping William to acknowledge that something exists beyond his small world of solid facts will be extremely difficult."

Annabel smiled. "I've always enjoyed a challenge."

Michael laughed. "You and Gabriel both."

"He's still going by the name of Carey, right?"

"Yes, and Arel is none the wiser about who he really is. I think he's enjoying his role. In fact, we can refer to him as Carey while he's in that role."

"He's a great teacher. When I joined him on that trip to New York with Arel, he helped me to understand how to behave. His instructions were so detailed that I managed to look like I was lost and unable to handle life."

"Carey said that you did a very fine job at playing a homeless girl."

"Thank you, but will I be able to do a convincing job with William? I don't have much experience in the physical world."

"You'll always have support from our side, but you'll have to stay in physical form most of the time. Are you prepared for that?"

Annabel's luminous body shimmered a little less consistently. Some angels had a lot of trouble living within the boundaries of the material realm, especially for extended lengths of time. She looked up at Michael. "You've been in corporeal form on and off for years. Do you have any recommendations?"

"The feeling of confinement and heaviness can be difficult, but there are beautiful compensations." He opened his mind to her, giving her a taste of what he'd experienced. Sweet memories were shared. He loved the feel of the earth and the act of touching the rich loam in his garden. In autumn, he gloried in the crisp, fresh currents of the wind on his face. The first time he'd inhaled the fragrance of a rose had been exhilarating. "To gaze at a sunrise with physical eyes or to hold a newborn is incredible."

Annabel lit up with fresh anticipation. "When I helped out Carey, I learned a lot about laughing in a human sort of way. I know the energy of happiness very well. The tricky part was learning how a body responds to something like a joke. I must say, my physical form made some very loud and surprising noises when I tapped into that aspect of the body."

Michael shrugged. "Arel doesn't understand my humor. He says I'm always using it in an inappropriate way."

"But Michael, your humor is meant to lighten up a situation."

"Yes, but perhaps it's better if Arel sees me as a serious type. It comforts him to know that I understand his plight, that I never fail to realize when he's suffering."

"I see. So you've adjusted how you present yourself to best suit his personality." Annabel glanced at William as he moved his injured hand and moaned. "I have a question. With this situation being so dire, why have you enlisted my help? Aren't there many others who are more accustomed to being in physical form?"

"Yes, but it's because you haven't much experience that you'll be perfect. William despises most of humanity because he sees it as weak, cruel and needy. I believe that he needs an angel who is a little more removed from physicality, one who behaves in a very strong, resolute way."

"Not like a floundering waif?"

"That's right. You'll have to adapt quickly and adjust to his personality, but I think you can handle what he throws at you."

Annabel smiled. "I have an advantage over humans. Even if I assume a physical form, I won't get lost in the emotional moods that govern most people."

"That's correct. Our love and concern can never become so personal that we forget our connection to the truth of who we are. However, it's much harder to maintain that knowing when you're in the physical." Michael paused, opening another inner portal, allowing Annabel to access something that was rarely shared. When he did, Annabel's wispy, bright essence was temporarily diminished. When she was able to comment, her communication was slow and halting. "I don't really understand what I just felt, but it was very disturbing."

"It's what humans call sadness. It's one of many negative feelings that people experience. You won't have to entertain that feeling yourself as long as you stay aware and focused. You can't allow yourself to be drawn into William's turmoil."

"Michael, tell me, how do you know so much about such emotions?"

"I've purposely lowered my energy on certain occasions so that I could tune into Arel's feelings. As a result, my ability to understand and act with compassion has improved."

"But what I just experienced has left me slightly off kilter. What would happen if one of us tapped into that kind of energy for a sustained period of time?"

"I believe I know what you're asking."

Annabel paused. "Could one of our kind lose themselves in this type of assignment?"

"Absolutely, however, we can usually come to an angel's aid before that happens." He turned to William. "In this case, you would have to remain very aware. William is battling to stay in control on every level. His energy is very intense. If you're not very careful and keep an objective attitude, you could get caught up in the chaos too. That's why I want you to take your time in deciding on what is best for you."

Annabel's answer was given without a moment's hesitation. "I've already decided. I want to do this."

Michael nodded. Annabel was a very committed angel. She loved taking chances and trying out new roles. "Remember, William is very entrenched in his attitudes. He'll fight to keep it that way."

"But what if I could help him to open up to other possibilities?"

"He might not allow you to help at all."

Five

The London air was heavy with drizzle and cold as William made his way back home. He'd gone out earlier to meet with one of his connections, a man who could usually get him what he wanted. And William wasn't disappointed with the results. He was returning with a powerful and very expensive prescription antibiotic in his pocket.

Let's just hope this med works.

He'd been careful in tending to his wounded palm, keeping it scrupulously clean and bandaged. Recently it had started to fester in spite of his efforts. His hand was swollen and red. He was also running a fever.

Probably the end of the line for me.

He should have been more upset, but life didn't hold much interest anymore. As a young man, he'd been the recipient of a gift. He'd been given a virus that gave him an extended life span and other grand benefits. But his gift had been snatched away. His wondrous "vampire" days were behind him. He only trudged on because of Arel's promise that he'd been given another gift.

The idiot almost had me convinced until his damnable blood brother ceremony.

Arel did exhibit amazing strength at times. He also had an ability to go from burning up with fever to perfect health in a matter of minutes. Sometimes his eyes appeared to glow like golden flames that could mesmerize a person. Whatever his disease, it was a mysterious one with very weird and potent symptoms and extraordinary side-effects. Unfortunately, William didn't get anything that was beneficial. His body was racked with pain, period. Now, his hand was going to finish him off.

Good, I can finally rest in peace.

He couldn't find a cab, so he was on foot. Normally it would have been an easy walk back, but the pain and infection continued to sap all his strength. A half block from his home, he leaned against a building wondering if he'd make it the rest of the way.

"Are you alright?" A woman called out as she walked towards him. "Do you need help?"

Oh hell, what now?

It was late. The streets were deserted or so William thought and hoped as he stared at the person in front of him. The woman had stopped a couple of yards away. Her face was shrouded in the shadows.

"Are you ill?" she asked sweetly.

For William, her caring, kindly tone was an immediate affront. "I'm fine," he hissed back.

"I just thought you might like a little assistance."

"What I need is to be left alone. So if you know what's good for you, you'll be on your way!"

"Sorry," the woman said as she quickly moved past him.

Her fragrance lingered in the damp air. It was sweet, like her youthful voice. It reminded William of lilacs and his summers as a boy when he still believed that some good existed in the world. For a brief moment, he almost called the woman back, wishing he had someone there to share his pain. That was before his hand delivered a shock of excruciating torment that brought him back to reality. His resolve was reinforced. He'd never trust again, never.

I did you a favor, young lady. It doesn't pay to help someone, I know.

His own selfless act, his singular altruistic attempt to help another person, ended up costing him everything. But what did it matter. Better not to give the past another thought. He'd simply turn into Arel's clone, blaming others instead of believing in himself.

He tried to gather himself up, to find the strength to continue on, but a bout of utter weakness flooded his body. The winter cold penetrated his heavy, wool topcoat and invaded his bones. He began to shake with another bout of chills. Would he have the strength to go on? Or would he die then and there on the street with no one to care that he'd ever lived. The thought was too much. The bottom suddenly dropped out of his world. Dread, that extreme fear, that he'd seen in the eyes of his former victims flooded in. He knew what had horrified them. As their final moments of life were being torn away from them, they understood the true meaning of helplessness, of having no power over anything.

I refuse to die like one of them! I'm better than that!

He gritted his teeth and used sheer determination to stand up. Bracing his shoulders, he staggered a few feet, gasped in more air and kept going.

* * *

Annabel continued down the London street, walking briskly forward. She'd had one chance with William and failed to intercede in a meaningful way. "Sorry, Michael," she whispered to the ethers. She knew her message got through. In fact, Michael's calm energy was instantly by her side. A moment later, he was walking next to her, dwarfing her lithe, feminine form with his own tall, masculine presence.

"You did your best," he said quietly.

Annabel dug her hands deeper into her jacket pockets. "The encounter was so brief. I never got a chance—"

"Getting a chance to help William was a long shot, but we had to try."

As they neared a street light, its glow highlighted Annabel's fine, delicate features and large, emerald eyes. Her twinkling gaze was reinforced by her animated attitude. She gave Michael a sideways glance. "I don't know William very well, but I already like him."

"Of course," he laughed. "As Arel has pointed out, we like everyone. It's our job."

Annabel smiled back. "Arel thinks he has us figured out, doesn't he? When he ponders who we are, we must seem like the Creator's cookie-cutter watchdogs."

"I believe that sums up his perception quite nicely."

"Really, even after all this time that he's spent with you? Hasn't he been curious about learning more—"

"He's usually steadfast in how he views his world, and I can accept that."

"But William is extremely curious about life."

"Yes, he is as long as it's within certain, factual parameters. However, he doesn't believe in us."

"Perhaps if we put Arel and William together, we'd get a more balanced individual."

Michael didn't reply. Instead, he paused and looked heavenward. He seemed to lose himself in the night sky and silent reflection.

Annabel stepped back with a look of concern. "Why are you frowning, Michael? Did I say something inappropriate?"

"No, not at all. In fact, you're very observant. I think that quality will serve you well in the future."

"I hope so. I also hope I get another opportunity to work more closely with humans."

Michael returned his gaze to Annabel and took her arm. "I'm sure you will," he said as they started walking again.

"I'm looking forward to it."

"That's because you're the kind of angel who enjoys helping incarnate souls. Others of our kind, well, they never venture too close to mortals."

Annabel laughed. "I know a few of them. They much prefer a less stimulating existence."

"I can understand that feeling, especially in times like this."

"Arel is very unhappy again, isn't he?"

Michael nodded. "Unfortunately, he's also starting to shut me out."

"Hasn't he learned that you could help him when he's miserable?"

"But that's a problem too. I can't help him if he insists on a course of action that violates another person's free will."

Six

Kevin stood on the street corner in a long sleeved, sweat shirt, stomping his feet. He hadn't dressed properly for the weather. The sun wasn't up yet. A cold, grey sky hung low overhead. He could ignore the weather, but not the dismal feeling that had taken hold of him. The argument he'd had with Carol the night before had been one of their worst.

"Where are you when I need you, old friend?" He checked his watch again. Arel was late. It was probably foolish to think that his friend could help him. He'd tried to change like Carol wanted. He thought he had succeeded in some ways, but Carol felt otherwise. Deep down, he had the forlorn feeling that his marriage was slipping away, and nothing he did could alter that fact.

Peggy's been right all along. I don't have a clue, and I'm going to lose everything because of it.

"Kevin!"

Arel's hail made him look up. As he watched his friend jogging over, he felt a glimmer of hope. "Did you oversleep?"

Arel slowed to a stop and yawned. "Just slow getting started. What's up? When I got your text late last night, asking me to meet you, you didn't explain what you wanted."

"I had to talk to somebody. I know you like to run in the mornings."

"Not lately."

"Aren't you training anymore?"

"I got sidetracked."

Kevin's shoulders slumped. "Sidetracked is one thing. Going off the rails completely is a lot worse."

"I didn't know I looked that bad."

28

"I'm not talking about you. I'm in a helluva mess again. Carol is talking about splitting up."

Arel instantly came to attention. "What do you mean? I thought you two were going to Paris soon."

"I thought so too. Then out of the blue we had a really bad run in."

"You're kidding."

"It seems I'm not measuring up to Carol's standards. It's a real mess."

Arel rubbed his hands together briskly, but his wounded gaze wandered as if he was trying to understand some great mystery. "I can't believe it."

Kevin returned an accusing scowl. "I told you this wouldn't work when Carol first got pregnant, but you insisted that I could make things right. Like a fool, I believed you."

Arel's eyes refocused instantly, going from disappointed to insistent. "I told you the truth. You're a good man, Kevin."

"Tell that to Carol. Tell it to my sister. When it comes to women, I always seem to fall short."

"Don't worry about Peggy. Tell me what happened with Carol."

"It got pretty ugly. I ended up saying things I shouldn't have. Dammit, the one time I open up, I blurt out a bunch of crap." He paused and looked away. "Carol ended up bawling her eyes out."

"What did you say to her?"

"I got mad and told her to stop trying to put everything on me, that she was always acting so needy. That's when she started with the water works. Then she threw me out of the bedroom."

Arel moaned. "I can't believe you did that."

"So how do I fix it?"

"Go home, now. Tell Carol that you're sorry."

"That's not the answer, not in the long run. We both know that."

Arel slumped and let out a sigh. "Maybe you're right. I shouldn't always be handing out advice. I should keep my mouth shut, period."

"Geez, don't give up on me now, old buddy. I'm in this thing up to my neck. I have a family, and I need answers." He reached out and clamped a hand down on Arel's shoulder. "Maybe you should be the one talking to Carol. Tell her that I love her, that I love little Ariel, but I don't know how to give her what she wants. Plead my case for me. You're so much better at explaining things than I am."

"Sorry, Kevin, I think you have the wrong idea about me." Arel began rubbing his palm. "I don't think I'm much better off than you when it comes to handling problems."

"Oh please, Carol and Peggy act like your advice is golden."

"Maybe I've said some things that helped them, but—"Arel grimaced as he made a fist and held it close. "I can't get my life straight either."

"What's wrong with your hand?"

"It hurts."

Kevin narrowed his eyes. "Your pain has to do with that English friend of yours, doesn't it?"

"You're starting to sound like Peggy. She always acts like she knows what's going on."

"Come on, Arel. It's not that hard to put two and two together. I remember your friend's face when he was leaving your hotel room in New York. He'd changed from the night before. He looked like he was running for his life. Do you want to tell me what happened?"

"It's a long story, too long a story," Arel said. His voice was low and despondent, but when he glanced up at Kevin, he offered a weak smile. "Look, if you can just get through the next couple of weeks and go to Paris, I think you and Carol might start to work things out."

"I hope so."

Arel tried to stand up straighter. "I know so."

Arel's words were fervent and determined, but his eyes didn't have their usual direct and forthright gaze. They were defused with some sort of inner turmoil.

Kevin stepped back and crossed his arms. "It's funny, seeing you look and act like hell, makes me feel a little better. Let's go for that run. It might help both of us to get some of the stress out."

"I didn't get enough sleep. I better go home and go back to bed."

"Hold on." As Arel began to walk away, Kevin became the obstinate one. "Hey, I might not know about how to handle relationships, but I know something about exercise. It's good for you."

Arel paused and gave Kevin an irritated scowl. "I told you I'm out of shape."

"Yeah, that's why I'm going to keep freezing my butt off out here. I can see you need some help too. It'll be like before. Remember when I was your coach?"

"Could I forget? The last time you were so devoted, I felt like I was going to need a walker."

"I'll go easy on you."

"Really? You're sure I'm not going to regret this?"

Kevin grinned back. "Positive."

* * *

Carol stood at the kitchen sink and stared out the curtained window. It was still early morning, and the sky was a dark, dismal grey. It reminded her of how she felt. When she woke up, Kevin was already gone. Her first thought was that she'd driven him away with her talk about splitting up. Her threat had back fired on her. When she found his note, saying that he was going for a run, she felt a little better, but not much.

I shouldn't have said all those things. They just came out before I could stop them.

All she wanted was for Kevin to take her seriously, to realize she needed him to communicate, to be there for her in a way that made her feel secure. When she talked about going their separate ways, he looked so desperate. He hadn't replied, but his eyes were full of shock and pain.

I wonder what he's thinking about now. I hope he's okay.

It wasn't like her to be so forceful. She wanted their marriage to work, but the uncertainty of where it was going was driving her crazy. Of course, during the argument, Kevin had said horrible things too, things that made her angry. But maybe he had a point. She threw the dishcloth into the sink with a frown, hating to admit it, but maybe she was too needy.

"Carol?"

Kevin's voice, calling to her from the back door, made her jump, but in a good way. She turned around and stared back at him as he stood in the doorway. His contrite presence filled the space and her

31

heart with new hope, but she couldn't give it voice. She heard herself saying things in an indifferent tone. "I didn't know how long you'd be gone."

Kevin remained mute and unmoving. He didn't seem capable of expressing himself either, but his eyes were wide and imploring, like those of a child chastised and trying to find out why. When he finally spoke, he brought up a more positive topic than their previous argument. "Arel begged me to cut our workout short. He's up to his old excuses again."

Carol wanted to rush over to him. She wanted Kevin to hold her and tell her that everything was going to work out. Instead, she went to the dinette table and retrieved an empty salt shaker. "You did a great job coaching him the last time. Don't give up on him."

"I won't." Kevin walked over to her and took the shaker out of her hand. Placing it on the table, he hesitated, then put his arms around her waist and pulled her close. "I won't give up on us either. You might not think so, but I love you. And I'm sorry about the things I said."

Carol lowered her eyes. "I love you too."

Kevin's next words were delivered with a sense of urgency. "I'll do anything to make you happy. You have to believe that."

Carol laid her head on his chest and listened to the sound of his heart thumping in her ear. It rekindled old feelings. When they'd first fallen in love, Kevin seemed so perfect. He could make her happy by simply holding her. Why didn't she feel that way now? "When I think about us, it frightens me. I don't know where we're going."

He pushed her away just enough to engage her eyes. His own held a fierceness that he rarely exhibited. "I do, if you'll come to Paris with me and give what we have another chance. Please."

Kevin's conviction was contagious. It buoyed Carol up enough to make her nod. "I'd like that."

* * *

Arel was barely moving after his run. When he let himself into the kitchen, his first thought was to sit down. He groaned as he lowered himself into a chair. After two grueling miles on tortured legs, he was ready for that walker he'd mentioned to Kevin. There was an upside to the situation. Kevin looked rejuvenated after yelling out orders during their entire workout. He even promised to go home and apologize to Carol.

But what about tomorrow and the day after?

Michael walked into the room and interrupted his thoughts.

"Getting back into jogging again?" Michael asked.

"I've been engaged in Kevin's training school for the crippled."

"What do you mean?"

"When he's done with you, you need crutches."

"He does seem to have a bit of an aggressive approach."

"Kevin was in bad shape after a big blowout with Carol last night. He needed a whipping boy to get his testosterone moving again."

"I'm sorry to hear about the argument."

Arel stood up, leaned forward on the kitchen table, and gave Michael a sullen frown. "Why bother? Why bother with any of it?" His outburst was fueled by a rising anger, but his legs, wanting to buckle, convinced him to sit down again. "I've tried to help and what good did it do?"

Michael took a seat across from him. "Sometimes you have to allow people to find their own way."

"I thought we're supposed to care about our fellow man. You care about me. I'm following your example."

"We've had this conversation before. You can't manage other people's lives. You can't—"

"I know! But I still don't get it! I had these lofty dreams when I wanted a normal life. I thought that I'd be free and happy. But that hasn't happened. Look at the mess I'm in. William is in London, probably on his deathbed. And Carol and Kevin are ruining their lives. My little godchild is going to grow up without his father being there for him."

"I'm sure that's not the case. Carol would let Kevin—"

"That's not good enough. Those two love each other!"

"Sometimes love is only one of many factors."

"You're right. Kevin won't let go of that damnable past life he had as a teacher. He thinks Peggy and I were burned in that life because of the things he taught us. Now, he refuses to open up and communicate properly with Carol. Why in the hell can't he let go of his guilt and stop feeling responsible?"

"It's not just Kevin who's holding on to the past. In fact, he's addressed it in many ways, but there's another party involved."

"If you're talking about Carol, she was just a six year old child in that life."

"Yes, she was a six year old child who witnessed her brother and sister being burned at the stake. She was helpless to change what happened."

Arel pushed back into his chair. "I guess I forgot to consider how she was affected."

"Patterns repeat, you know that."

"I'll talk to her, I'll—"

"Arel, you also know that it takes more than talking. Everyone has to confront their fears, like you did."

"Sure I faced my fears, but only after I died and you brought me back!"

Michael's eyes sparkled with mischief. "You were a particularly tough case. Not everybody has to go that far."

"No, they just get divorced."

"It's their decision."

"Not if I have any power to change things. I'll do whatever I have to do—"

"Like you did with William?"

Arel's eyes flared in Michael's direction. "Reminding me of William is a low blow. I didn't think angels played that kind of game."

"This isn't a game. You do have power, more power than most humans. Be very careful, please. It's wonderful to want to help, but if you misuse your influence, there could be consequences that you'll regret."

Arel's face was instantly flush with shame. "You and I both know that I wasn't trying to be helpful when I first interfered with William's life."

"Still—"

Arel stood up again. "I need to go back to bed. My head's killing me."

"Taking out your anger on your physical vessel isn't wise. Your body doesn't deserve punishment."

"Maybe not, but from what you've said, my meddling self does."

"I don't believe that punishment is ever the answer."

"Of course not, angels and humans think differently about a lot of things."

* * *

"William!" Arel woke up gasping. He tried to blink away the nightmare he'd just had. He'd been back in London, walking down a dark, lonely street. The fog was so heavy he could barely see an arm's length in front of him. His teeth chattered in the damp chill air as he made his way through a maze of lanes and alleys. He was searching for William's house. He tried to ask for directions, but there were no people around. The city was eerily quiet. He tried to call out to Michael for help, but his voice was useless and mute. He was completely alone and lost. No, not lost, abandoned. When the dream shifted, he was in a cemetery. That's when he realized that William was dead. But it wasn't the William he usually thought about. This time William felt like someone else. His brother, Aldwin, came to mind.

But Aldwin has been dead since I was a young boy.

As he rehashed the nightmare and the idea of losing his older brother when he was a child, a gloom descended on the bedroom. It was thick and heavy, a burden that could become unbearable if he allowed himself to ponder it for long. Deep in his bones, Arel knew that the fateful event was a cornerstone of his life, driving an inner mechanism of grief that he couldn't control. He could deny it for days, months, even years, but his loss would always be there. He would always be desperate to keep it at bay, to keep it from repeating again.

I tried to take his place, Arel, I tried to be your friend, but you pushed me away, you bastard! Now I'm going to die too.

It was William's voice, announcing itself like a news bulletin in Arel's mind. He sat up stiffly and looked around.

"I'm sorry, Will! It's not what I want, but I don't know how to help you." He yelled out the words as if William could hear him. Perhaps he could. At times, they were connected by more than blood. They could connect with each other's thoughts if they both dropped their shields.

35

Yes, that's true, Arel. We can communicate if we choose to allow it. So listen carefully to what I'm saying. Because of your stupidity and need for revenge, I'm another casualty in your life, and there's nothing in this world that can stop me from leaving you.

Arel's response was immediate. "No! I can't lose another brother!" As he began to argue, Arel felt his words bouncing off some invisible wall. William had hung up on him, throwing up his shields in a clean, efficient manner, letting Arel understand the finality of the conversation. William was saying, "Goodbye." It wasn't a nice farewell. It was a bitter leave-taking that left Arel without any options. He prayed that he'd find a way to prove William wrong.

Seven

William's recliner had become his deathbed, a place where he ticked off time with each wheezing breath. He did have one chore left before he departed his earthly life. He steadied a pen in his left hand, grateful that he was ambidextrous as he finished writing out his will. His right hand was useless. The medication he'd taken wasn't helping with the infection. In fact, he was sure he was having an allergic reaction and his end was near. But he wouldn't go without taking care of a final responsibility. When he thought about his collection of art, he was determined to have it go to a person who would care for it properly. It was unbearable to think that his secretly owned Matisse and other rare pieces would be gawked at by hordes of detestable humans in some museum.

"So it'll all go to you, Arel. You're a bastard, but you've always loved beauty. At least you'll know how to appreciate what I've valued."

He signed his name at the bottom of the document and dropped the pen on the side table. Leaning back in his chair, his body sank deeper into a state of weakness, but he smiled briefly. He'd made peace with his enemy. Letting go of any hatred for Arel came as a surprise. He'd kept his feelings under control for a long time, but to actually feel all his bitterness dissolve was unexpected. It was almost as if he'd had a brief moment of enlightenment, a moment when something seemed to be urging him to let it all go. It felt like the right thing to do. Why should he let Arel's ignorant, immature actions spoil his final hours? It was a comfort to know he'd die in peace.

William! You can't do this!

"Oh hell," William mumbled back. He recognized the voice calling to him and realized that in his weakened state, he had inadvertently lowered his shields.

William, are you listening?

William couldn't believe that one of the side effects of his disease was an ability to hear Arel's thoughts, or in this case, his rantings. He let out a weary sigh, wishing he had an icepack to cool his brow. He was burning up.

William!

He moaned out a protest.

Arel, stay out of my mind. I only have a few minutes left, and I want those minutes to be free of your meddling.

A response popped in immediately.

No! I refuse to let you leave this world knowing that I'm responsible.

William laughed.

Sorry, but I'll have to foil your desires, you misguided lunatic. And congratulations, you sound healthy enough. I guess you'll beat this thing that's done me in.

A barrage of Arel's pleas followed, but William was able to tune them out by turning his attention to the art of dying. The quiet around him, the feeling of knowing himself as very special and unique was comforting. Peace, even joy, began to replace the pain in his hand and in his body. He began to drift out of the world. He began to let go of everything but the sweetness of his calm, tranquil mind.

"Help! Don't let this thing devour me!"

Just as William was falling into a fatal slumber, a jarring shout from somewhere in the room broke the silence. It was so unexpected that William was jolted back to a more externalized focus. The cry of a panic-stricken voice was his reward. When he opened his eyes, Arel stood eight feet away, looking not quite solid. Before William could respond, Arel let out another horrified shout.

"Stay back! Please!"

William stared at his visitor. How dare Arel show up on his doorstep when he was taking his last breaths?

Or maybe, this is part of the death process, a few last emotions coming up for disposal.

He tried to blink away the apparition in front of him, but he couldn't help but note that Arel's eyes were wide with alarm. Arel the

Ghost looked like he was seeing a ghost or maybe, judging from his terrified expression, he was checking out the hound of the Baskervilles.

"Will, help me!" Arel begged loudly.

William sighed. "Dammit, this apparition certainly seems real enough."

As the shouting continued, William knew his wonderful appointment with a composed, quiet death would have to be postponed. He couldn't relax with Arel having a fit in front of him. Somehow, goaded on by a need to stop the assault on his nerves, he found the strength to get up, to stumble over to where Arel's ghost was standing. It was his turn to start yelling. At first, his voice was feeble. It picked up in volume as he felt Arel's terror course through his own body. It activated his protective side, the part that had always tried to look out for his "blood" brother. "Arel, you're okay! Quiet yourself!"

After a moment, Arel finally acknowledged William's order. Staring back with wild, blazing eyes, he reached out a shaky hand that passed through William's body. "Thank goodness, Will. I thought I was a goner. These damnable out-of-body experiences never go well. When I got here, I thought I saw a fiery beast."

William was still able to get out a few words. "All that I see is an idiot. What are you doing here, Arel?"

Instead of answering the question, Arel tried to reach out again. "Will, my god, you look horrible!"

William leaned heavily against the wall for support. He tried to get his breath, but his body refused to take in enough oxygen. Every time he inhaled, his chest rattled and heaved uselessly. "There's a reason for my condition, Arel, and he's standing in front of me."

* * *

Arel was still shaken, but he was grateful to be in the lower level of William's home. Like he told William, astral travel was a scary proposition. A person never knew who or what one might encounter. But he didn't have time to think about the monster he'd seen when he arrived. William looked flushed with fever, and he was struggling to maintain his standing position. "You better sit down,

Will. I'd help you, but I'm not quite sure how my body works in this form. As you might have noticed, I haven't mastered astral travel."

William gasped out a reply. "Please, astral travel your ass back where you came from. I'm trying to die in peace here." After a few more labored breaths, he pushed off from the wall, barely able to stagger his way back to his recliner.

Arel wanted to help, but he didn't know how. He silently called out to Michael for advice.

Michael, if I find a way to really touch William, would it be safe to try to help?

Michael's reply was immediate.

Not unless you're sure about your control.

Arel felt his chest tighten. His control was utter crap.

Does it matter at this point? If William's dying, I have to try something.

Michael's voice was firm and unyielding.

Arel, please, he's asking you to let him die in peace.

Astral body or not, Arel couldn't breathe any better than William when he thought about William leaving the world.

No! That's not acceptable!

William coughed and looked up. "Why are you still here? I asked you to go. I even said 'please.'"

"I know, but I can't leave just yet." Arel was on a mission. To accomplish his task, he needed a body that he could manipulate. As he tried to understand what he was working with, he had a brilliant idea. If operating in the astral plane was anything like lucid dreaming, he had to visualize what he wanted.

I have to see myself as real. I'm sure that's the key.

Using his experiences in the dream state as his guide, Arel saw himself having a physical body. As soon as he did, he felt a shift. His ghostly body began to take on a denser quality. After a few more tries, he felt almost as solid as he normally felt. A sense of triumph made him rush forward to where William was sitting. "Look at me, Will! Look at what I can do. Isn't it exciting?"

William stared back with annoyance. "Why me? Why won't you just give me a break?" he wheezed.

"Are you kidding? I've got more power, more control! That means I might be able to really help you."

"Help me how? In case you haven't noticed, I'm dying of an infection and a disease that you gave me."

"I understand, and I want to make it all right again. Just let me see what we're dealing with." Arel reached out and touched William's bandaged hand. Another triumph! He could interact with actual matter. He could feel the gauze. "I'll be very careful, Will," he said as he began to unwrap the layers that covered William's wound.

William gritted his teeth in pain, but he seemed too weak to attempt any resistance. "Stop tormenting me!"

But Arel couldn't stop. He had to see what lay beneath the stained gauze. When he managed to strip away the last layer, he nearly gagged at the sight in front of him. William's hand was red and swollen twice its normal size. His palm was a bed of festering pus.

"Are you satisfied?" William shut his eyes and paused. "Listen to me. I'm talking to my hallucination."

Arel smiled. "That's right, but this hallucination is going to help you." He felt more confident, merging more closely with his new body. In fact, he imagined himself a kind of hybrid angel. But he wouldn't just be a hybrid angel. He'd be the healing kind. He reached out to William. "Now just relax, my friend, and don't worry about a thing."

Before William could reply, Arel took hold of William's hand with both of his own. As he touched his blood brother, Arel willed himself to be a healer who would restore William to health again.

* * *

Michael appeared in William's lower level, ready to help Arel if he insisted on taking on his 'angel' duties. Raphael, a fellow angel, had also volunteered. Raphael had been assisting William on an unseen level before Arel arrived. He'd been successful in helping William to attain a more peaceful attitude. Arel was oblivious to the two angels. With his astral eyes shut tight, he was intent on healing William. William had his eyes shut too, looking dazed and breathing heavily.

"After what happened a couple of months ago, we better be ready for a sizable surge of energy," Michael warned as he positioned himself on Arel's left.

Raphael, appearing tall, youthful and handsome in an earthly body, gave Michael a thoughtful glance as he stood on Arel's right.

"Gabriel or Carey as he's now calling himself, says Arel is not capable of precise energy measurements."

Michael's brows went up in alarm. "Be prepared for more than an imprecise delivery. Arel nearly took out my corporal form the last time he accessed his ability. And with William in such a fragile state, we'll have to divert all but a small amount of the energy Arel channels."

Raphael laughed. "I've never seen you like this before. You look a little—"

"Worried? Maybe I am." Michael smiled too. "Arel hasn't had time to really practice with this sort of thing."

"I understand. In fact, when he appeared in William's room, I was a little unprepared myself. I'd just managed to help William release some of his resentment and anger. The room was quite tranquil for a few moments. But Arel's entrance changed everything. When he saw me in my ethereal form, his fears escalated so quickly. The only thing I could do was retreat."

"Arel has quite an imagination, especially after his first astral trip. He encountered an angel named Grace and thought she was a fire-breathing dragon. The experience nearly frightened him to death."

"But he took a chance anyway. He must be very concerned about William."

"They share some deep and unresolved attachments. Arel also needs to clear a lot of painful emotional issues. They often confuse him when it comes to decisions. As a result, he can react in very impulsive ways."

Raphael gave Michael a nod. "Right, and I think he's going to prove that now."

The next instant, both angels were on the receiving end of a discharge of energy that nearly dislodged them from their posts. The room became a small amphitheater of dazzling fireworks. As the light faded, both angels tried to ignore their own reeling worlds. Both of them attempted to check on the two humans in their care.

Michael looked up with eyes as bright as pale-blue stars. "Arel's disappeared."

Raphael's eyes were bright too, but filled with dismay. "William is dead!"

Eight

William glanced down at his lifeless body. From his lofty vantage point, it lay far below, resting immobile in his recliner. "I'm must be dead, but I still feel like me." His tone held an element of contempt. He hadn't expected to survive death, and he wasn't comfortable with being proved wrong. But he wasn't one to make hasty judgments either. He needed to gather some facts about his new situation. "So what is this place?" He checked out his surroundings with caution and curiosity, knowing the advantage of adapting quickly to new circumstances. The place he was in was definitely unlike anything he'd experienced before. It had a wispy feel with no defined parameters. His next question was more personal. Did he have a form? Taking stock of himself, he saw that his new, non-physical body was a duplicate of the one he'd left behind. There was only one difference. He flexed his hand a couple of times. "Nothing hurts anymore. That's a plus."

He moved forward, feeling very light and buoyant as he observed a sunny area in the distance. When he focused on it, he noted a pleasing sensation in his chest. The feeling reminded him of happy times in his childhood. He'd often explored the woodlands and meadows surrounding his family's home. Their beauty had filled him with the same excitement and pleasure. As he walked towards the light, he smiled. Somehow, he knew he was back where he belonged, in his true home, one where the heaviness of earth would be left behind.

"William, thank god I found you!"

"What the—" William stopped short and turned around. He was shocked to see Arel standing a few yards away. An immediate question came to mind. "Dammit! How did you get here?"

Arel grinned back. "Can you believe it? I was wandering around for a while. Then I realized I could simply state my desire to find you. As soon as I did, I was transported here."

William stumbled back a few feet. "I thought this peaceful little cloud was too good to be true. I must be in hell."

"You don't sound like you're very happy to see me."

William couldn't reply. His mouth was hanging open with disbelief. He knew Arel could be a little dense, but he never imagined how unable Arel was of recognizing his ignorance.

Arel moved a little closer. "Will, say something? This is a momentous accomplishment on my part."

William took a couple of breaths and got his voice back, along with an acute case of irritation. "Oh, I'm sorry. Should I be thanking you for blasting me out of existence?"

"You were dying anyway."

"I might have lived a little longer, you imbecile, but you made sure that didn't happen."

"I did my best! The point is that you have to go back. You don't have to stay here."

"How do you know that?"

"I don't know how I know these things. It's just a very strong feeling that I have."

"I don't want to go back. I have nothing to go back to, remember?"

"Of course you do! You love life, Will. You love it more than anyone I've ever met."

"Right, I did until you spoiled everything."

"I want to make it up to you. Things will be different, I promise."

"Leave me alone. Let me rest in peace. Heaven, hell, wherever I'm at, has nothing to do with you. That's one perk that comes with being dead. I won't have to have you torturing me constantly." William paused and stared hard at Arel. "Unless you're the devil. Is that it? Have you always been the devil, and I didn't know it. Maybe you've been deceiving me all these years."

Arel shook his head. "No, it's not true! I'm not the devil. Besides, neither I nor you believe there's such a thing."

"Just go away."

"I won't go away, not until you agree to go back to your body!"

"No, I won't go back and that's final."

Arel gave him the blinky-eyed look of a child finding out that Christmas had been canceled. "Please, Will, you have to do this."

"Why? What difference does it make to you? You have your own life. Now that you've finally killed me, you're free to play with your new friends or should I say family."

"We're brothers! You're my closest family."

"Don't bring up that subject. I was in excruciating pain because of your insane idea about making me your 'blood' brother."

"If you go back, your hand will heal."

"I suppose you have another strong feeling about that too." William started to walk towards a bright opening he saw in front of him. "Good bye, Arel. Have a great life without me."

"Will, I'm begging you. I can't lose you too!"

William swiveled round. "So that's it. You lost your real brother, and you want a substitute. Do you realize how co-dependent you are? Grow up, Arel! Once and for all, realize that you have to take responsibility for yourself."

"Maybe you're right. Maybe I am dependent, but I know this is wrong. You and I are connected in a way that I can't explain. Remember how you had that vision of us working together?"

"I don't give a damn about that now. I'm dead, and I'm going to enjoy being dead."

In an instant, Arel was standing next to him, grabbing hold of his arms. "No, I won't let you go!"

William felt the world around him shake, as if a small quake had hit his wispy surroundings. "You're scary, Arel. Do you know that? Now take your hands off my dead body."

"No! If you don't know what's good for you, I do. You're going back!"

William tried to wrench himself free. Before he succeeded, Arel's form began to glow. It increased in brightness until he was blinded by its brilliance. An explosive flash followed. After that William began to fall out of the heavens at an amazing rate.

* * *

William woke up in his recliner groaning. His head was pounding. The slightest movement sent stabbing pains through his temples. When he opened his eyes, the room was spinning so fast he felt sick just looking at it. He shut them immediately. As soon as he did, he remembered his nightmare.

I've had some bad dreams, but that was the worst.

He remained very still, trying not to aggravate his headache. After a few minutes, he opened his eyes again. This time his dizziness was almost gone. He could breathe easily. He wasn't wheezing. When he carefully moved his hand, he didn't have to grit his teeth just to bear the pain. It felt much better. Was the antibiotic working after all?

I told you that it would be fine!

He glanced around. "Arel, is that you?" He continued to scan the room, but there was no one there. Still, the more he thought about his nightmare, the more he felt like he'd been violated. A bullying transgressor had enforced his will on him with no respect for William's basic rights. "Oh my god, Arel threw me out of heaven."

Nine

Arel trudged his way out of his bedroom, down the hall and into the living room. Looking around with blank, staring eyes, he barely acknowledged Michael's presence. His head had an empty feeling as if it had been sucked dry. He looked at Michael again. "I feel like a fighter who's gone fifteen rounds with a black hole."

Michael looked up and gave him the once over. "I can see that."

"I don't feel right, and I'm exhausted."

"I'm surprised you're not still sleeping."

Arel closed and opened his eyes a couple of times, but the overwhelming heaviness of the sleep state wouldn't go away. "Maybe I've been sleeping too much. I can't believe that it's already late afternoon. All I did this morning was go for that run with Kevin."

"Sorry, but you went for a run yesterday morning."

"Yesterday?" Arel stumbled over to the sofa and sat down. "Are you saying that I've been sleeping for a day and a half?"

"Not exactly. You were very busy part of the time."

"What are you talking about? I don't remember doing anything?"

"Sometimes, in situations like this, it's best not to try too hard."

"There's something else. I keep getting these strange flashes of light, like the sun's popping in and out in my head."

Michael rubbed his eyes, blinked a couple of times and looked back. "Yes, I'm aware of that effect. It can be quite disconcerting."

Arel frowned, giving the angel the once over. "And what's going on with you?"

"What do you mean?"

"Your eyes, Michael, they're kind of different, like you've been at the beach too long or you've been—" Arel paused. In the midst of his confusion, he saw William's London home. He also saw what looked like a heavenly landscape, complete with misty cloud banks that he could walk through. "Oh hell, I only remember seeing you look like this after you've been helping me. Did something happen that I don't know about?"

"Get some more sleep," Michael said quietly.

Arel tried to clear his mind, but it refused to be bullied into giving up whatever was hidden behind the fuzziness. "You're right. I'm still exhausted. I'm going back to bed." He got up and began to retrace his steps to his room. He barely got to the hall when his exhaustion became almost paralyzing. Unable to move forward, a face broke through his murky thoughts. William was looking at him with fresh hatred and disdain. As Arel stared back, letting William's anger sink in, his mind opened up, offering him clear access to its secrets. He grabbed at the wall for support as the facts revealed themselves. They were so damning that he couldn't speak or move. When he finally got his voice working, his words came out in a husky whisper. "What have I done now?"

* * *

Leaned over the dining room table, elbows splayed, head in hands, Arel wished he was in a confessional. He needed to kneel in darkness, curtained off from the priest, unable to see his face. Instead, Michael was sitting across from him. It wasn't that the angel was censuring him. Angels weren't in the judgment business. The hanging judge lived inside Arel, and he was the one that demanded retribution. His absolute law was so exacting that Michael's loving attitude was grating on Arel's tender, guilty nerves. That's why Arel had to be the prosecutor. In the courtroom that played out in his mind, Arel had to convince an angelic being that he was too forgiving.

"Please Michael, look at the facts. I'm needy. I'm abusive! I use my power to run rough shod over the rights of others. Isn't that true? You have to agree with me on this one." Arel paused and mopped the sweat off his forehead. As he laid out his list of wrongdoings, he might not be convincing Michael to convict him, but the fires of his personal hell were getting hotter. "You can't deny those charges, can you?"

Michael sat very still. He seemed to inhabit an air conditioned space. Except for eyes that still glowed a bit too bright, he looked unaffected by Arel's need for self-flagellation. When he finally spoke, his voice was calm and even. "Of course I hear what you're saying, but I'd like to talk about what you're not saying. Isn't there another side to this issue?"

Arel's inner fires flared hotter, making him pound his fists on the table. "Of course there is! I'm thrilled that he's—" He clamped his jaws shut and finished out the sentence in his mind. *I'm thrilled that William's alive!* In the background, for the briefest of moments, a wonderful sense of euphoria overrode his guilt and self-loathing. "Michael, help me. Tell me what to do. I know I've done something unforgivable, and I'm sorry, but if I think about William being dead, I wouldn't change what happened. I'd rather be dead myself." His eyes widened with his next question. "Is that an option? Could I give up my life for his? I know this sounds insane, but I'd do it. I'd gladly die in his place."

Michael shook his head. "It doesn't work that way."

"It's so weird that I want William alive. When I was a child, my brother's death and the aftermath left me feeling that I deserved my father's abuse. Eventually, all I wanted was to die." He paused and stared at the scar on his hand. "But William refused to let that happen. As a result, he sentenced me to a hundred years of hell."

"He forced you to live against your will. Now you've done the same thing to him."

"But I didn't do it out of hate! I wasn't trying to get revenge. I'm sure of that."

"William didn't give you his blood out of hate either. He tried to give you time to find yourself. Maybe you had a similar motive."

Arel clamped his hands together. "I only wish that were true, but I doubt that it is. I'm a co-dependent, needy parasite like William said."

"Could it be that William has a similar need?"

Arel came to attention, jerking up and staring back. "What?"

"William was the first one to make contact again, remember?"

Michael's words swept across Arel's fevered psyche like a cool breeze, giving him a moment of respite. "That's true. He was the one

49

who wanted to renew our friendship." He got up and started to pace. "Of course it doesn't let me off the hook for all my transgressions, but maybe I'm not alone in how I feel."

"Can you explain what made you follow William into the afterlife?"

"All I know is that there's something between us, as if we're conjoined, like our fates are connected. I think that's why I hate him at times. I can't get away from that connection. It can override all reason. Then I do something crazy."

"Sometimes caring that much is expressed negatively and sometimes positively. Yet, ideally, there comes a time when unconditional love transcends all boundaries. It's beyond feelings. It's a state that frees you from everything, frees you from fear and neediness."

"Transcendent love? Like I'm going to understand that one."

"It's not exactly something you can understand. As I said, it's something that simply exists."

"Thanks, Michael. That's a big help."

"I'm sorry."

"And what am I supposed to do with your apology? I don't have your world to fall back on. All I have is this new hellish mess I'm in. And my human understanding is telling me that I've damned myself."

Michael offered a warm smile. "That's not necessarily so."

"I'm glad that one of us feels that way."

Ten

The deep, woodsy scent of frankincense and myrrh filled the room as William lay soaking in a steaming bath. He was finally beginning to feel himself again. When he'd first contracted Arel's Madness, the name he'd given the disease he was infected with, his world fell apart. No, it was worse than that. His world was torn apart.

His mind and feelings were thrown into total mayhem. He went from being in control of his life, to behaving like a maniac. The memories of those awful bouts of insanity were disturbing. But maybe it wasn't such a bad thing if he put a different slant on it. He thought about the chaos theory.

Evolving elements could seem totally chaotic, but there was an underlying order in the process. Things might seem to make no sense, but they had to be torn down so that they could evolve, so that they could be more than they were before.

If that were the case, perhaps he wasn't just coming back to himself. Maybe something unexpected was happening to him. From the start, Arel had insisted that they were both okay, just going through a change. He said that there was no disease involved with what they were experiencing. He even claimed that they would exhibit new powers when the change was complete.

Maybe I should have believed him. He certainly seemed to display amazing abilities in our encounters.

After Arel snatched him from the throes of his death episode, William had been observing his progress back to health. Physically, he was doing well. His emotional swings were also balancing out. He found himself able to maintain a peaceful mindset most of the time. He stared at the scar on his palm. After dying and coming back, his hand healed almost instantaneously. The antibiotics might have been part of the cure, but no medicine acted that quickly.

He had another disturbing thought. Did he want to be like Arel? He hated to admit it, but his old friend scared the hell out of him. It was a first for William. He'd had an unbearable bully for a father and many a bullying teacher. Yet none of them could bring out the fear that Arel could elicit. And he understood why. Arel was still the child who refused to grow up, but now he was a child with incredible power, like the monstrous kid in an episode of the Twilight Zone.

As a vampire, I experienced power over life and death, but I changed. When I matured, I didn't need that kind of power.

Arel's power went far beyond the world. He could follow someone into the afterlife. But it didn't stop there. Not only could Arel follow a person into the heavenly realms, he could manipulate what happened to them. He could decide their fate.

Arel's dangerous, the ultimate stalker, and he's stalking me. I'm his security blanket. He'll never let me go.

William could hope that his own power would grow and match Arel's someday, but he didn't have any assurance that it would happen. In the meantime, he was at Arel's mercy. He'd been at his mercy since they met in New York. William had simply never wanted to acknowledge it.

He began to list Arel's crimes. First, Arel enticed him into infecting himself. Their meeting in New York replayed in his mind. He'd wanted to leave, to get away from Arel's insanity, but Arel made sure that William first sampled Arel's tainted blood. As a result, the gifts that came from his vampire condition were nullified. His aging gene was turned on and his immune system was put on overload. Secondly, when Arel came to London, he added to William's stressed out condition. William nearly had a stroke. The third strike was Arel's juvenile need for a bonding ceremony which involved slicing open William's hand. The end result of that lunacy was William's death. And he was alright with dying. The other side was beautiful, more beautiful than anything he'd experienced on earth. Which brought him to Arel's latest crime.

He snatched me out of the afterlife with no trouble at all, like he was playing chess, and I was simply a pawn who was in the wrong place!

His heart raced as he relived the sensation of falling back into his body like a misplaced, rag doll.

Dammit, Arel has to be stopped, but I'm not strong enough to take care of the job!

Another person came to mind, someone who might be powerful enough to take out Arel. As he pondered his solution, as he thought about having Arel killed, his throat closed up with regret. In that instant, he knew Arel was the only real family he'd ever had or loved.

But caring about Arel has been my downfall.

He had to push away the horror of what needed to be done. He had to steel himself against any emotions that would endanger him further.

I have no choice.

William had to find the one who had made him a vampire. He had to locate Rolphe.

Eleven

K evin frowned as he watched Tim put his cell phone into his pocket. "I hope calling Arel doesn't backfire."

Tim returned a questioning look. "But it was your idea."

Kevin walked over to the coffee table and grabbed a handful of chips. "Yeah, well I'm having second thoughts. Telling Arel that we've got an emergency might not be the best way to get him over here."

"You said we didn't have a choice."

"We don't. Once again, he's been holed up in his house. Something isn't right."

"Peggy feels the same way. She's been complaining about her bad vibes recently."

"I'm getting some bad vibes myself. Arel's helped me out, and I guess I feel a responsibility to return the favor. Besides, I'm leaving for Paris in a couple of days. We have to do something before I leave."

"Hopefully, the two of us will have more influence joining forces."

Kevin stared at the foyer expectantly. "I'm glad that you told him that it was just a small emergency, nothing life threatening."

Tim laughed. "That'll make no difference to Arel, you know that. As soon as he thinks something's wrong, he imagines the worst."

Kevin looked at his watch. "Yeah, he'll probably be here within two minutes of getting your call."

"We might have an extra minute. He said he had to dress."

"He's not dressed at two in the afternoon? Peggy is right. He is in trouble." Kevin popped a couple of chips in his mouth, gave them a cursory chew and swallowed hard. "Why does he have to always shut us out? Doesn't he know we want to help?"

"You're not usually so tuned in to what other people are doing. What's going on?"

Kevin grunted. "What choice do I have? You know how it is with Carol. You know how touchy she's been. According to her, I better be tuned in or else. Plus, she's been worried about Arel too. How's she going to go off on a honeymoon if she thinks he's not okay?"

"Arel is a bit of a mystery all around. I get the idea that he sees himself as the wise one. Maybe he doesn't confide in us because—"

"He thinks we're the dummies?"

"I'm not saying that he tries to put us down, but he does come off as a little parental."

"Maybe I've put him in that position with all my issues with Carol. In fact, I wonder if I'm to blame for this latest episode he's having. I kind of accused him of giving me bad advice since the get-go. Maybe he took what I said to heart and is blaming himself."

Before Tim had a chance to reply, there was a knock at the door and Arel letting himself in. Standing in the foyer, Arel's eyes scanned Kevin and Tim anxiously.

Kevin waved to him. "Hi, old buddy."

"What's the emergency?" Arel asked as he came forward.

"That was fast," Tim said. "I thought you weren't dressed."

"I was in my work sweats. They were wet. I had to change. So what's going on? Is everyone okay?"

"Everyone is fine," Tim said, gesturing Arel into the living room. "Sit down for a few minutes."

"Yeah, Arel, get your butt in here," Kevin added. "We haven't seen you around for over a week."

"Is that why you called?" Arel asked.

Kevin dusted off his hands and crossed his arms. "Yeah, and don't blame Tim for the little white lie. It was my idea."

Arel stiffened. "I don't understand."

"What Kevin is trying to say is that we're concerned," Tim explained. "You haven't even taken our calls this past week."

Kevin nodded. "Peggy's radar is going nuts. Tim's having a devil of a time keeping her from coming over and giving you the third degree. So I suggest you talk to us if you don't want her getting involved."

Arel glanced around furtively. "Where is she?"

"It's okay," Tim said. "She's out shopping with Carol."

"And both the kids are napping upstairs," Kevin said. "So this is the perfect time for you to spill your guts."

Arel's slender frame was bent as he went to the sofa and sat down. "Maybe you're right. Maybe I do need to talk to someone who might understand."

Kevin pulled an ottoman over to the coffee table and sat down too. He took another handful of chips. "Wow, I thought you'd put up more of a fight. You're usually pretty tight lipped about everything."

Arel frowned. "What do you mean by that?"

Kevin held up a hand as he washed his chips down with some iced tea. "I'm just saying—"

"Never mind, Kevin," Tim said. "Let's let Arel tell us what's on his mind."

Arel paused as he rubbed his hands together nervously. "Well, this is more of a hypothetical situation, okay?"

Tim nodded, but Kevin was busy cutting some chunks off the cheese that was sitting on a snack tray.

Arel gave him an annoyed look. "Of course I wouldn't want to bore you if you're busy."

Tim nudged Kevin's arm. "Kev, listen up. Remember Paris?"

"What?" Kevin's face was filled with surprise when he glanced up at Tim.

Tim gave Arel another encouraging look. "Sorry, Kevin missed lunch."

Kevin's face went red with embarrassment. How did he get off track so easily? What if he did the same thing in Paris? He could lose everything. He sat back and gave Arel his full attention. "I did miss lunch, but don't worry, Arel, I'm all ears."

Arel gave him the briefest scowl. "As I said before, this is all hypothetical, but here goes. Let's say that Person A finds out that Person B is dying."

"Dying?" Kevin asked. "Is person B anyone we know?"

Tim gave him another nudge. "Save it for later."

Arel let out a heavy sigh, but he went back to his story. "Person A feels that he could keep Person B alive, but Person B has already decided that it's hopeless and is ready to die. Don't you think that Person A has a responsibility to help Person B?"

"Is Person B of sound mind?" Tim asked.

"I guess so," Arel said.

Kevin sat up straighter. "What kind of help are we talking about, extraordinary measures or life support of some kind?"

Arel swallowed hard. "I guess you could call it an extraordinary measure."

"Does Person B want Person A's help?" Tim asked.

"Maybe not," Arel said.

Kevin narrowed his eyes with satisfaction. Once he put his mind to it, he could fully engage in Arel's story. It was a comforting feeling as he shot Tim a glance. "I don't know about you, Tim, but when it comes to life and death, I'd like to make my own decisions."

Tim nodded. "I agree."

Arel avoided looking at either man. For a long moment, he rubbed the fabric on the arm of the sofa. When he spoke, his voice was low and measured. "What if Person A helped Person B anyway? Is that really so wrong to want someone to live? Shouldn't life be protected no matter what?"

"I don't know about that," Tim said. "If a person is dying and has the capacity to think clearly—"

"Yeah, Arel, you wouldn't want one of us to do that to you, would you?" Kevin asked.

Arel's eyes lost their beseeching softness when he glared back. "But you did in a way! After we met, I was dying, remember? If it hadn't been for all of you acting on my behalf, I'd be long gone."

"We didn't use extraordinary measures," Tim said. "We just tried to help you get better."

"And you wanted our help after that first visit," Kevin chimed in.

Arel continued to stare at them. "What if Carol or a family member, a brother or sister, were dying? Wouldn't you do anything to save them?"

Kevin's gaze clouded over. Just the thought of Carol leaving him made him desperate to find a solution. "I see your point. That's a tough one."

Tim gave Arel a look of concern. "When I think about losing Peggy or Sara, I don't know what I'd do to keep them on this earth. But hopefully I wouldn't put my needs above their best interests."

"Tim's got a point," Kevin said. "Love can sometimes be a tough one when it comes down to it."

Tim shrugged. "For me, I guess the bottom line is that it takes a lot of courage to always do what's best for the ones we care about."

Arel clasped his hands nervously. "And if Person A is a coward and puts himself first? What then? How does he live with himself?"

"If he did his best that counts for something," Tim replied. "Kevin and I are talking big, but who knows how strong we'd be under certain circumstances."

"By the way, how is Person B? Is he still on life support?" Kevin asked.

Arel let out a heavy sigh. "If Person B actually existed, the news would be good. He's almost fully recovered."

"Has he forgiven Person A for butting in?" Kevin questioned.

Arel looked away. "I'm sure a type like Person B will be unforgiving and never want to see Person A again. However, while Person B is enjoying the life that's been restored to him, Person A will be living with tremendous guilt and the knowledge that he's desecrated the rights of another human being."

"Geez, Arel, maybe Person A should try to go easy on himself," Kevin said.

"How?" Arel's eyes narrowed even more. "Helping people is a thankless job at best, Kevin, and a treacherous one when your help doesn't pan out."

"I'm sorry about what I said to you," Kevin replied with an apologetic voice. "Your advice was great. I love my life with Carol and the baby."

"Thanks, but you were right. I shouldn't interfere. In fact, I'm finished with helping other people." Arel stood up and walked to the door. He paused as he was about to leave. He gave Tim and Kevin a final obstinate look. "After what I've just told you, please don't call me when you have a problem, unless of course, it's an emergency, a real emergency."

Tim stepped forward. "You've been a great friend. Kevin was just upset when he said what he said."

"Yeah, Arel, we all appreciate what you've done," Kevin said.

Arel grabbed for the doorknob. "I'm glad you feel that way, but my statement stands. Now I have to get back and continue with some chores at home."

"What's going on over there?" Kevin asked. "You said something about wet sweats."

"If you must know, I've been vacuuming half the day. I've also been down on my knees trying to get stains out of the carpet."

Kevin and Tim looked at each other and smiled. "Carey?" they asked in unison.

Arel's jaw clenched. "Yes, Carey. The kid must have been raised in a barn." He hesitated. "I'm sorry, I didn't mean to put it that way. I'm sure Carey comes from a very difficult situation and doesn't know any better."

Kevin laughed. "So make him clean up his mess. He'll learn."

Arel opened the door and started out. "Again, I don't want to sound unkind, but Carey doesn't know one end of a vacuum from the other. He tries, but his ability to adequately go over a carpet seems beyond his reach."

* * *

Clothed in her angelic form, Annabel watched as Arel let himself out of Tim's house. Michael had invited her to join him and observe Arel as he interacted with his friends. It was an opportunity for her to know Arel a little better and to understand his motivations. By the time Arel's conversation with Tim and Kevin ended, Annabel had learned a lot. "To say that Arel is having a very hard time, is an understatement. His energy is so heavy and dull."

"Yes," Michael said. "He feels he's done something unforgivable. He won't let himself get beyond his actions."

"I don't know how to comment. I've never encountered anyone who could follow another person beyond the grave and force them to return to earth."

"It's complicated."

"I can imagine it is. But if he's so upset why is he bothering with cleaning his rugs?"

59

"When he's upset, cleaning becomes one of the few outlets he allows himself. When he's deeply involved with a task, it helps him to forget his problems for a bit."

Annabel paused, trying to understand the concept that humans needed many ways to cope with life. It was foreign in her world to have any such needs. Her life was very straightforward and simple, free from human trauma and stress. "People seem so fervent about the simplest of things. For instance, Arel has very definite ideas about his environment and its upkeep."

Michael sighed. "Indeed, he does."

"Unfortunately, our Gabriel seems to lack the skill Arel thinks he needs when it comes to vacuuming."

Michael chuckled. "Arel does have a point. Carey is still a little behind when it comes to proper housekeeping."

Michael's playful attitude was contagious, and Annabel found herself smiling too. "Yes, I noticed that Arel is quite vocal about Gabriel's shortcomings."

Annabel was still smiling when another angel joined them.

"Did I hear my name?" Carey asked enthusiastically.

Annabel quickly adopted a more serious mode. "Sorry, Gabriel—"

Carey interrupted her. "Call me Carey. It helps to keep me in my role."

Annabel nodded. "Yes, I keep forgetting, but I am beginning to know how important it is to play a part appropriately when in physical form."

Carey smiled back at her and at Michael. "What did I miss? I got caught up in straightening out some issues with the garage. I wasn't paying attention to what Arel was up to."

"Arel thinks you were brought up in a barn," Annabel replied matter-of-factly. "Why would he say that?"

Carey's shimmering form dimmed a little. "A barn? He said I grew up in a barn?"

Annabel focused intently on Carey's response. "Yes, I guess he believes you spent your childhood on a farm. Is that a bad thing?"

Michael intervened. "You can't take everything a person says as a literal statement, Annabel. What Arel was actually saying is that Carey doesn't know much about being orderly or taking care of the untidiness he makes in Arel's house."

Annabel turned back to Carey. "Do you have problems with using the vacuum? Are they difficult machines to master? Arel says that you don't know one end from the other."

"Really?" Carey asked. "I think I'm quite competent when it comes to getting the carpets cleaned."

"I'll have to show you how it's done," Michael teased. "I'm an expert after sharing chores with Arel all these years."

Carey hesitated for a long moment. "I think Arel is exaggerating. I went over that rug for ten minutes last night."

"Only ten minutes?" Michael asked. "Those are wool rugs. Very deep pile. According to Arel, it takes a generous amount of time and effort to properly do the job."

"I see. Thanks for the advice," Carey said. "I guess I haven't been monitoring Arel's thoughts about my performance as closely as I need to. Anyway, I better get back to the house and finish my project in the garage. I don't want him to think too poorly about my ability to keep the cement clean."

After Carey left, Michael smiled again. "Carey has no idea about what he's up against."

"What do you mean?" Annabel asked.

"Arel can be a tyrant when it comes to doing chores, a very exacting one. Carey's got a better chance of getting William to do charity work than getting those rugs right." He paused. "Of course, the rugs wouldn't be in such need of attention if Carey were a little more careful when he's eating."

"But Carey doesn't seem like the type of angel that would make more work for a human."

"Carey claims that his actions are part of his plan to get Arel to lighten up," Michael replied. "He also claims that his sloppiness is a great distraction and helps Arel to forget his troubles."

Annabel took some time to digest Michael's explanation. "My goodness, Carey's role sounds rather difficult. And the part about how he uses food is a very complex matter. He must have had to study and observe humans for quite a while to learn how to portray such a sloppy type of individual."

Michael laughed. "Or maybe he was raised in a barn, a big red one in the sky."

"Barn in the sky?" Annabel repeated. "I'm confused."

"It's okay, I was just making a joke."

Annabel felt suddenly tenser than usual. "Oh, Michael, I can see that there's a lot I don't understand about being physical. If I do get another chance to help William, how will I do a proper job?"

Michael smiled. "For starters, don't go the Carey route. Make sure that you're very neat. William is also obsessive about his possessions and the proper behavior of those in his company. If you decide to indulge in eating while you're around him, observe proper etiquette and watch the crumbs."

Twelve

Carol stood in the airport, hugging Peggy goodbye. "If you have any questions about the baby or if he shows any sign of getting sick, please call us right away."

"I promise." Peggy hugged Carol back with teary eyes. "I can't believe you're really leaving for Paris. I'm going to miss you both."

"Not the water works," Kevin kidded.

"Oh be quiet," Peggy said as she attacked him next. After a long hug, she released him with a sigh and a blessing. "Be safe and don't worry about a thing. Tim and I will make sure that little Ariel is happy while you're away."

Carol bit her lip trying to hold back her own tears. "I know he's in the best of hands, but I already miss my little boy." She looked at Kevin. "Are you sure this is something that we should do?"

Kevin put his arm around Carol's shoulder and pulled her close. "I'll miss him too, but I think this will be good for all of us in the long run."

"This trip is supposed to be your honeymoon," Peggy said in her Mother Superior voice. "Please try to act like it. No phone calls except in an emergency. You need your space. We have all your information if we need it."

"She's right. So have fun," Tim said as he grabbed Peggy's hand and began to slowly pull her away. "Now we better get going. I'm sure Carey is doing fine with the babies. In fact they seem to love him, but Sara can get a little fussy about going down for a nap."

Carol waved as they moved towards the walkway. "Thanks for everything!" she called out. A moment later, Peggy and Tim were swallowed up by the crowds in the busy terminal.

When Kevin turned to her, his eyes were bright, and he gave her a broad smile. "I didn't think that we'd ever get a honeymoon. I'm finally starting to get excited, how about you?"

Carol rummaged in her purse. "Sure I am, but I'm getting a headache. I thought I brought aspirin, but I can't find it."

"I'm sorry that you're not feeling well, honey."

Carol looked up and frowned in pain and frustration. She knew that she was to blame for her body being under the weather. "I can't believe I might be getting sick."

"Wait here. I'll go find something for your headache."

Carol noted Kevin's eagerness. In the days leading up to the trip, she could tell he was trying very hard to be more supportive. "That would help. Thank you."

"Be back soon," Kevin said as he quickly set out in the direction of some shops.

Carol called to him before he was out of earshot. "Don't be gone too long. I don't want to leave without you."

Kevin looked back and saw her smile. "Don't worry. You can't get rid of me that easily."

* * *

By the time they arrived in Paris, Carol was more than exhausted. The weather wasn't helping. A steady rain was pelting the city. When their cab stopped in front of their hotel, they had to make a quick dash to the shelter of its striped awning. "What a miserable night," she cried as she hurried forward.

Kevin put his arm around her shoulder and moved her along. "Come on, honey. Let's get you inside. You're soaked."

She huddled against him, grateful that Kevin continued to be on his best behavior. It was the one bright spot in the middle of her physical woes. When they reached the safety of the hotel, she shook with a chill. "That was a brutal downpour at the airport when we were trying to get a cab."

The trip had been long and tedious. Protesting infants on the plane made sleeping difficult. Some of the other passengers were coughing and sneezing with obvious colds. The temperature fluctuated between being overly hot to cold. Kevin had dozed off a couple of times, but Carol couldn't relax. When they finally arrived at the hotel, the beautiful vases of flowers and gorgeous marble floors weren't enough to distract her from her downward slide. Her throat was getting sore and her body was starting to ache.

Kevin gave her a look of concern as they made their way to their room. "I think you overdid it before we left."

"I just wanted to make sure the house was clean. I hate the idea of leaving a mess behind."

But Kevin was right, she'd done more than her usual cleaning. She'd become obsessed with doing the jobs she'd been putting off for months. Bathrooms were meticulously scoured from floor to ceiling. Walls were dusted for cobwebs, and lighting fixtures made to shine again. She'd even tackled the garage which was usually Kevin's job. The last week became a whirlwind of activity that left her falling into bed every night feeling completely worn. Now she was angry at herself. She and Kevin were counting on this trip to renew their commitment to each other, and she had no energy to even think about exploring their relationship. Instead, she felt cranky. It was a trait she disliked in anyone including herself, but she couldn't seem to censure herself.

"What a way to start our honeymoon," she grumbled as she waited for Kevin to open the door to their room.

"Tomorrow will be better." He used a quiet tone, like the one he used when baby Ariel was fussy.

She gave him a weak smile. "You've stayed so positive this whole time. I haven't heard you complain once. I've been the harpy."

Kevin's smile was bright and encouraging. "You're not feeling well."

"Thanks for being so understanding."

Kevin turned on a light in the room and held the door open for her.

"It's beautiful," she gasped. She couldn't help it. She was standing in the most stunning hotel room she'd ever seen.

An 18th century style, classic mahogany bed set the tone for the room. Behind the bed, a satin-damask drapery backdrop added extra flair. A palette of blue, moss, and yellow creams, expressed in curtains, bedding and period seating, created a soft, stylish atmosphere. The light blue walls, accented with gold trim, completed the feeling of elegance.

65

Kevin's smile widened out into a grin. "Very nice indeed."

After a brief inspection of the bath and the living area, Carol turned and put her arms around him. "This *feels* like a honeymoon suite. It's so luxurious."

Kevin kissed her lightly on the lips. "Buying a big-ass TV can wait. I wanted this trip to be special. Now, you better get out of these wet clothes. Would you like me to run you a bath?"

She nodded. "I think that would be per—" She sneezed before she could finish the sentence.

"Are you okay?"

"Just a scratchy throat. I've had it off and on for a couple of days. A bath will help."

Kevin frowned. "It's my fault. I should have made you take it easy before we left."

"No, it isn't."

"Are you sure?"

Carol nodded. Kevin had tried his best to be supportive and help out as they got ready for the trip. Instead of letting him, she'd shooed him away, insisting on doing everything herself. "Yes, I'm sure."

* * *

Kevin was pleased with his choice of accommodations. He found their room to be exactly what he thought Carol would like. He'd been learning more about her preferences. Blue and gold were two of her favorite colors. She also liked a touch of sophistication, and their room definitely expressed that quality. It was only Carol herself that had him worried. She was sneezing a lot, and her nose was getting red. On the upside, maybe it was his opportunity to let her know how much he loved her. He was just getting into bed as she came out of the bathroom. "Did soaking help?" he asked in a hopeful tone.

Carol's face smoothed out into a serene smile. "It was great. I think I'll be able to sleep."

He patted her side of the bed. "Get in here and snuggle up next to me."

Carol sat down on her side of the bed, but she kept her distance. "I'm feeling better, but I think I'm getting a cold. I don't want you to catch it too."

"Honey, this is our honeymoon. The threat of a cold isn't going to keep me from holding you."

Carol let out such a heavy sigh that Kevin came to attention. He studied the way Carol sat on the bed with her shoulders hunched over. "Did I say something wrong?"

"No, of course not. You're being sweet. You're being the Kevin I fell in love with."

Kevin let out a sigh of his own. "That's a relief. I was beginning to wonder if that guy ever existed."

Carol glanced back at him. As she bit her lip, a tear rolled down her cheek.

Kevin threw back the covers and jumped out of bed. "Something is wrong," he said as he went over to where Carol sat. He knelt down in front of her. "Please don't cry. I'm sorry I've been a jerk. I'm sorry I didn't shape up sooner."

Carol started to tug at his arm. "Kevin, please, get up. It's not you. It's me."

He obeyed reluctantly. "I don't understand."

"Neither do I, but I think Arel does."

"Arel? What's he got to do with this?"

Carol sniffled back her tears. "I talked to him before we left."

"You did?" He sat down next to her, contemplating their mutual friend. Arel often acted like their father confessor. "Did you want to talk to him about us?"

"No, not exactly. I went to see him because I was worried about him. He's been such a hermit lately."

"So what did he say? Anything that I should know?"

Carol grabbed a tissue off of the nightstand and dabbed at her eyes. "He said he's out of the advice business. He said he was going to concentrate on working on himself. Maybe I need to do the same thing."

"I think Arel said that because he's got himself into a bind."

"What kind of bind?"

"Seems things didn't go very well with Person A and Person B."

Carol's gaze widened with curiosity. "Who are they?"

"We're not positive, but Tim and I think Person A is Arel and Person B might be that friend of his in London. Anyway, Arel told us some story that involved a person who was dying and who wanted to die in peace. Person A insisted on saving him anyway."

"Why do you think Person A is Arel? How could he save a guy in London?"

"You didn't see Arel when he was telling the story. It was pretty obvious that he was talking about himself. So Tim and I figured his friend had an accident and maybe there were instructions about who to call in case of an iffy situation. Maybe Arel got that call and made a decision that he knew his friend wouldn't approve. Afterwards, the friend survived but resented Arel for interfering. In fact, I think Arel's been shunned completely." Kevin shrugged. "Anyway, we were just guessing."

"Sure, but it would explain Arel's attitude. He seemed very unhappy. At one point, his eyes got very intense. Then he said people should forget about other people and trying to help, that they should stick to figuring out their own problems, period."

Kevin put his hand over Carol's, stilling her fingers. "I think that's his excuse for hiding. He can be like a kid who gets roughed up playing ball and goes home to sulk. But if one of us acts like that, he's all over us."

Carol smiled and grabbed on to his hand. "You mean like the time you were having trouble with the idea of becoming a father?"

"Exactly. When I pulled back, he was instantly in my grill, insisting that I shape up." He laughed. "Of course he was right. When I came to my senses, I knew I wanted you and a family no matter what."

"Do you still feel like that?"

"More than ever!" Kevin realized he blurted out the words in a tone that was a little loud, but he didn't care. He had to make Carol understand that he was committed. As his face went flush, he saw his chance to take more of Arel's advice. "Honey, I love you as much as I'm capable of loving anyone or anything in this world. I don't know if that's enough, but I hope it is."

Carol sniffled again. "Well, that makes me feel better about having this cold. Maybe being together is the only thing that really counts."

"That's right. Who cares about seeing Paris? Let's camp out in this bed." He gave the mattress a couple of bounces. Even with his bulk testing its softness, the mattress remained very firm with very little give. Kevin smiled anyway. "No matter what, it'll be great."

Thirteen

When Michael opened the front door, Peggy stood waiting with her finger poised, ready to press the bell a third time. She had narrowed brows and a sullen expression on her face. Michael smiled anyway. "Peggy, how nice to see you."

Peggy's brows relaxed a little. "Tim's home watching the babies, and I saw my chance to check on Arel. Can I come in?"

Michael hesitated, but finally stepped back. Arel had been uncompromising about his need for privacy. Ever since he'd interfered with William's attempt at exiting the world, he was cloistering himself away. "I'm sorry, but Arel said he was going to take a nap. Can I help you?"

Peggy quickly stepped into the foyer. "Arel doesn't nap unless he's depressed. What's going on?"

"I don't feel comfortable—"

"Michael, it's me, Peggy. I know when something's wrong. So please, tell me why Arel is staying away from us. We're his family."

"I'm afraid that I'm not at liberty to discuss—"

"Remember when we first met? Arel was in trouble. I could feel it right down to my toes, just like now."

"I understand, but he's not well."

"What do you mean? What's wrong with him?"

"He's got a very bad headache. He needs complete quiet."

"I'm sorry." Peggy stepped back and pursed her lips in disappointment. "In that case, tell him that I'm worried about him. I've had some strange dreams about someone wanting to harm him. Maybe it's nothing, but tell him about what I said anyway, please."

"I will. I promise."

"I know you will." Peggy's tone was unwavering as she turned to leave. As she was about to step out onto the porch, she paused and looked back at Michael. "Arel is very lucky to have you as a friend."

"I do my best. In the meantime, try not to upset yourself."

"Besides my Tim, you're the steadiest person I know, Michael. How do you stay so balanced and unruffled with all the ups and downs that Arel goes through?"

"I always believe in Arel, and that he'll get through his difficulties."

"Great attitude," Peggy laughed. "Maybe I should try it. In the meantime, I notice that you like flowers and gardening."

Michael smiled. "Yes, I do."

"I'm thinking about having a little flower or vegetable garden someday. Maybe an interest like that would keep me from worrying so much."

Michael's smile broadened. "Working with the earth is an excellent choice when you need a bit of serenity. If you ever want any advice or help, remember I'm next door."

* * *

Arel sat very still in the dim light of a small lamp. He was trying to deal with a pounding headache. After days of cleaning every inch of his home, the dwelling was immaculate. Now he was left with himself again, thinking about his life. No amount of elbow grease was going to clean up the mess he'd made regarding William.

And I don't know how to make amends, Will.

Recently, Arel had moved back into his windowless, belowground level apartment. The space had once been his retreat when he'd thought of himself as a vampire, unable to tolerate the sun. He'd felt safe there, not only from the blazing orb, but from life and people. Furnished with a mixture of new and old, it had a pleasing quality that was easy on his tender nerves and fragile mindset. Treasured artwork and a few pieces of furniture had been shipped over from England long ago. There were more recent purchases, including a plush, luxury sofa and chairs for the living area. An imposing king-size bed, decked out in soft Egyptian cotton sheets and a matching gold comforter filled a good portion of his bedroom. But Arel no longer needed a space for safety reasons. That part of his life had changed. He sat, anxious and restless, in the semi darkness for a different reason.

Now, I'm the threat!

Arel knew it, and William knew it.

William thinks I'm a monster, and I guess he's right.

When he tuned into William's mind, he was bombarded with anger and resentment. That would have been fine. They were often at odds with each other. The new element in William's makeup was a fear about his safety. It was an emotion that Arel had never felt in William before. Arel had grown up being frightened and nervous. He needed to protect himself from whatever the world might throw at him. William had a different approach. William's father had also been a brute, but he'd never been able to break his son's spirit. William had always been tough when it came to facing life. Unlike Arel, William always accepted whatever came his way with an indomitable resilience.

Until now.

William lived through a hellish childhood and still found a way to thrive, to be happy.

It was his last encounter with me that changed all that. I'm the only one who has managed to ever terrify him.

But Arel hadn't played fair. He'd misused his powers again, and this time he had much more than guilt to deal with. He stared down at his hands. They were trembling as he remembered grabbing hold of William. When he was in his astral form, his body felt real and solid. He'd had no problem using it to hurl William back into the physical world. Or had it really happened that way? He didn't know for sure. He only remembered one absolute, undeniable fact. He had intended for William to go back to his body no matter how fervently William protested.

And I got my way. I'm able to override another person's wishes, even in the afterlife.

How was he supposed to deal with such a power? No person should have that kind of control over another person's fate. It went against everything Arel believed in.

Yet, I wouldn't change what happened.

That was the final nail in Arel's coffin. He had loads of guilt, enough to sink an oil tanker before it made it out of port, but another part of him refused to consider letting William die. It was unthinkable.

He put a shaky hand to his head, knowing that his flawed personality was the problem. He was weak. He was an unsuitable candidate that should have never been allowed to partake in angelic blood.

What the hell was Michael thinking that night in the alley? Was he insane? Am I dealing with an angel gone haywire?

A soft knock brought him out of his contemplative mood.

Speak of the devil!

"Come in, Michael," he growled out. The forceful, three word greeting made Arel's temples explode in pain. He didn't care. Michael's mistake took precedence over everything, and Arel had to express his utter disappointment over the angel's negligence. "I'm glad you're here. I want to talk about my situation."

Michael quietly shut the door behind him. "Peggy stopped by, but I told her you were ill. She's worried about you—"

"Peggy should be worried!" Arel grabbed his head, hoping to keep it on his shoulders as he continued to voice his outrage. "You should be worried!"

Michael walked over to a chair and sat down. "I see."

"What do you see, Michael? Do you see an assault rifle sitting here? Or a rocket launcher? Maybe when you look at me, you see a ticking bomb, is that it?"

Michael's eyes widened, and he shook his head. "No, I don't see any of those things."

"Of course you don't, because those are just toys compared to what I am. If I ever get totally out of control I could be more like an incarnate Satan."

"I don't believe in an incarnate—"

"That's the problem, Michael! Your angel vision is all screwed up. You don't even realize what a blunder you made choosing to help me. With your halo and your pure thoughts, you're incapable of understanding the evil in people."

"Actually, I—"

"Please, I'm sorry to have to take this tone with you, but you need to understand why angels aren't able to properly deal with defective human beings." Arel fell back against the sofa where he was sitting and gritted his teeth. Maybe his head wouldn't explode off his

73

shoulders, but the pain he was in was blinding. He lowered his voice. "Oh god, Michael, what a hell of a mess you've gotten me into. I'm a bumbling, cowardly fool, the last person who should be running around with your blood."

"Arel, if I thought that anything you just said was true, I'd be honest about my feelings, but I don't."

"I know that. You always think the best of everyone, and you were trying to help me when you did what you did. You were such a nice guy, one who couldn't turn down a pathetic loser. I just wish you'd had a little more wisdom in that idealistic head of yours."

"I think you have the wrong idea about angels—"

"Please, I don't have time to listen to what you think. I've got to figure out how to dispose of myself. I can't take a chance on hurting someone else."

"What about William?"

"William?" The name had an instant effect, making Arel more attentive. "Oh yes, Will, my constant victim. After what I did to him this last time, he's sinking into a very dark place. He was serene when he died, but I wrecked everything."

"First of all, you don't have that power in most instances. Think about your friends. You haven't harmed any of them, but with William, it's different."

"What do you mean?" Arel opened his eyes and managed to connect with Michael's steady gaze.

"I think you know what—"

"The only thing I know for sure is that I couldn't let him die— "Arel wanted to add, "not this time!" However, the words didn't make any sense to him. There was only a strange knowing deep inside of him, some mystery within that he could feel but not decipher.

Michael nodded. "And how do you want to proceed with William?"

Arel returned a weak smile. "The strangest part about my feelings is that I don't have to see him again. He can go his way and that's fine with me."

"Excellent, now try to be patient with yourself. It takes time and experience to handle your gift properly. You're still clearing away a lot of your issues."

Arel's fingers dug into the arm of the sofa. "I scare the hell out of myself. While I'm learning how to 'handle my gift,' I don't know what's coming, and I don't want to do more damage. Can you promise me that William isn't just the beginning of the carnage I could leave behind?"

"Arel, I know your life seems uncertain at this point, but I believe in you. I see a much different version of who you are than you do."

"And what about William? He's got your blood too. How do you feel about that? What if he allows his dark side to take over? What if he starts killing people again?"

"You saved him for a reason. You think it's only because you're weak and needy, but I think there's more to it. I think some part of you believes in him just like I believe in you."

"I hope your right. If you're not, we're both going to have a lot of explaining to do when your boss checks out the mess we're in."

"Are you planning to contact William again?"

The question set off a new round of pounding, double-bass pain. "No, in fact I've decided to completely cut off any connection I have to him. No more snooping around his mind. He's sensitive to my energy, just as I'm sensitive to his. Maybe if he feels my complete withdrawal, he'll go back to being his usual, confident self. Maybe he'll forget about me and enjoy life."

Michael got up to leave. "One more item, Peggy said to tell you that she feels that someone is out to hurt you."

Arel waved Michael off. "Yes, I know all about that. William is trying to have an old pal of his kill me."

"And that doesn't concern you?"

"Please, after what we just discussed? Tell Peggy to relax. I'm perfectly safe."

"Arel, are you sure you shouldn't—"

"Michael, at this point I just have to extricate myself from everybody who knows me. Once that's done, I'll move to some desolate island and live out my life in seclusion."

"If that's what you think best, but in the meantime, perhaps you can comfort yourself with the fact that William has a chance at a new life. Secondly, if you want to extricate yourself from your friends, the best way might be to help them to stop worrying about you. If they

75

feel that you're fine and they see you acting normally, their concerns will subside."

Arel relaxed a little as Michael's advice sunk in. "Actually, that seems like a rather good idea. I might give it a try."

Fourteen

William locked his front door, walked down the stone steps and took off at a slow jog. The evening promised to be cold, but he couldn't quite get used to the idea of exercising in daylight. Still, it was great to get out and feel his strength coming back. His body had taken a beating during the past months. That fact would have been more bothersome if his thoughts weren't on other matters. For days he'd combed the internet, posting cryptic messages on every vampire blog he could find, trying to connect with Rolphe. It wasn't the first time he'd searched for the one who had made him a vampire. But in the past, his attempts originated from curiosity, not need. Recently, he'd come up with a new approach. If Arel could reach out to William using mental airways, William could do the same with Rolphe. Deep in his gut, he was sure of it. So every day, he sat meditatively sending mental posts, urging Rolphe to check out the vampire blogs. That afternoon he was rewarded with a message on one of his online email accounts. The message was a one liner: "Are you the little shit that tried to suck me dry a hundred years ago?"

Rolphe hadn't intended to give William his blood. William was simply his dinner. But William always recognized an opportunity, especially when he observed Rolphe. The man had an aura of power that fascinated William as soon as they met. Even as he lay dying, he lusted over Rolphe's obvious command of life. With his last breaths, William had begged Rolphe to share his secret. On a whim, the tall, hulking man had obliged him and given him a taste of his blood.

Now, you'll help me again, Rolphe.

As he ran, he smiled. He had an ally. All he had to do was inform Rolphe that there was a certain person seeking him out to kill him.

And I don't think I'm lying to him.

Arel had hated the fact that he'd been made a vampire. Afterwards, he'd been filled with a need for revenge. It was quite probable that someday he'd punish Rolphe just as he'd punished William.

Sorry, Arel, but your bullying days are numbered.

He noted that the thought of killing Arel didn't bother him as much now. He was succeeding in deadening his feelings of regret. In fact, a sense of power surged through him as he thought about turning the tables on the person who acted like a puppet master, who decided William's fate with total abandon.

He began to pick up his pace until a loose shoelace made him stop. Stooping down to tie it, his attention shifted to a woman walking by. There weren't many people about, and he wondered why she was braving the damp, chilly evening. There was something familiar about her as she paused briefly, looking down at him and then pulling back.

"Oh, it's you."

He was immediately offended by her tone. His response was to jerk upright and stare at her with hard-set annoyance.

She retreated a couple of steps, but after returning an equally irritated look, she continued on her way with a quickened pace.

"Do I know you?" he asked, jogging up to her.

She didn't stop. She increased her pace and ignored him.

His crossness escalated. People had always deferred to him, as if they knew he was their superior. It was very rare to find an individual who could ignore him so completely.

My god, how far have I slipped? First, I have Arel doing whatever he pleases. Now a girl in a cheap jacket treats me like I'm nobody.

He continued to walk next to her. "I asked you a question?"

The woman finally stopped under a bright streetlight. "You're that rude person I tried to assist a while back."

His gaze narrowed knowingly. "Oh yes, and you're the do-gooder. How could I forget?" He'd been ready for the grave on the night the woman had stopped to check on him. It was aggravating to think his memory was slipping too.

The woman did a quick sweep over William's person. "You looked ill on that occasion. I was trying to help, but you seem well enough now."

As the woman spoke, the light caught her emerald green eyes. William was stunned by their exquisite color and clarity. When she blinked, they flashed with a blue-green fire. Their sparkling splendor made something in his chest expand. He had never seen eyes like hers. Suddenly, he needed to stall for time as he contemplated the idea of something new and beautiful in the world. He blurted out an apology. "I'm sorry if my manners were lacking when you stopped to help me."

The woman's face relaxed a little, giving William a moment to examine more of her. She wore a cap, but it couldn't completely contain the richly colored, auburn wisps that escaped around its edges. They were nestled against her flawless, white skin. Her features were delicate and fine with high cheekbones. Her soft rose lips, slightly parted, were naturally full. He found them inviting and imagined himself kissing them, first softly, then with passion as she yielded to him.

"Excuse me," she said, breaking into his reverie. "I have to be going."

Her announcement and the reprimanding look she gave him was embarrassing. He hadn't felt or exhibited such unbridled desire since he was a teenager. He quickly reined himself in. It was his turn to step back. "Could we start over?" He held out his hand. "My name is William."

The woman smiled shyly. "I'm Annabel."

"It's cold out here. Would you like to go for tea?"

* * *

The quaint neighborhood café was busy, but William found a table towards the back that suited his purpose. He needed time to sort out his feelings while he made small talk with Annabel. Why was he so drawn to the young woman? She was beautiful, but he'd known countless, beautiful women. Perhaps he was simply coming back to life more fully after his death experience. There was also the fact that the past months had been spent coping with Arel's Madness. He hadn't had time to think of his physical needs. As he continued to observe Annabel, he was determined to concentrate on something other than the allure of her body. There was something else that drew him to her. "So you're a student. What are you interested in?"

Annabel raised her eyes long enough to take a quick look at him before she returned her gaze to her tea cup. "Aspects of human nature are fascinating. Psychology is a favorite subject of mine."

William noted Annabel's thick, black lashes and found his mind being batted around when she blinked at him. Again, he had to chastise himself. Why was he letting himself be so easily distracted by Annabel's appearance? He went back to their conversation. "Psychology? Not that much to study. A human being is very simple. He's basically a self-centered animal."

"I see," Annabel said quietly. She nibbled at her biscuit and let her lids close in a dreamy sort of way. As she sampled more of her sugary indulgence and swallowed, a smile slipped into place.

William sat back and crossed his arms. "You're certainly enjoying your food."

Annabel's eyes widened in response, like a rabbit being startled by a loud noise and freezing. "Sorry, I love the taste and the way the biscuit melts in my mouth." She sat up, examined her surroundings and quickly retrieved a crumb off the tabletop. She carefully placed it on her saucer. "You were saying?"

"I said that mankind is a bore at best, and a troublesome pest most of the time."

Annabel thoughtfully ran a delicate finger over the gilded edge of her plate. "Your viewpoint seems rather limiting."

"And what's your take on the masses."

"I look for the best in everyone."

"For a person with that attitude, you didn't give me much slack."

"As I said before, you were rude." Her voice was soft and matter-of-fact, but when she took a sip of tea, a little smile slipped into place. After another sip, she replaced the cup back on its saucer. Dabbing her mouth with her napkin, she finally returned her gaze to William. "Just because I'm a do-gooder doesn't mean I'm a martyr."

William didn't know if he should be annoyed or appreciative of her slow deliberate actions. "Thank god for that, martyrs are tiresome."

Annabel folded the napkin and put it on the table. "I should be going."

William's gaze locked on to her eyes. For an instant, he imagined that he was looking at two, steady beacons, two identical lighthouses on a distant shore. They seemed to welcome him in and transport him back to the heavenly landscape he'd experienced when he died. In that ethereal place, he basked in a carefree brilliance. When his head cleared a little and his voice returned, he managed a few words. "The evening is young. I could buy you dinner."

Annabel shook her head. "No, thank you. I have to post a notice before it gets too late."

William sat up at once, shaking out the blissful fog he was in. "What kind of notice?"

"I need a job, just part time, but something to help with my rent."

"Perfect. I need someone to help out. My place is quite a mess after my illness. Do you think you might be interested?"

Annabel hesitated, then smiled. "Perhaps."

Fifteen

Rolphe got up from his desk and scanned the room, drawing comfort from the old world feel of his surroundings. He'd lived in Paris for so long that he could, at times, almost forget his origins. The rich culture of the city gave him solace. Its many museums were favorite places of repose and meditation. As he donned the role of observer and reflected on the beauty that others created, his heart found a bit of freedom. He'd even taken up painting and learned he had an affinity for putting color to canvas. His apartment, with its wood paneled walls, became a gallery for his artwork. His gaze traveled to one piece in particular. The portrait of two boys could have been painted in the Italian Renaissance. Attention to the use of light and shadow, the perfection of the human form, and a feeling of devotion were evident. Yet a hundred, unworthy predecessors had been thrown into the fire. It had taken a very long time for Rolphe to adequately portray his beautiful children. Now their beatific faces looked back at him with all the innocence and purity that he remembered.

He walked over to their painting and put a hand to the face of one of the boys. He fingered his child's dark, curly hair remembering how his son took after Rolphe's grandfather. His careful touch was brief. He pulled his large, grasping hand away, loathing the contrast between an innocent child and what Rolphe knew himself to be. As a young soldier, he'd been called a giant because he was a head taller than most. Even in today's world, at six-foot-five and weighing two hundred fifty pounds, he was considered tall and imposing. But it wasn't the size of him that was damning. To touch such a blameless child with a hand that had taken so many lives was wrong.

With a heavy sigh, he turned and walked back to his desk. He peered at his laptop. The email message he'd recently received was still up, and he read it over again. The first time he read it, his heart quickened. There was a discernable flutter in his chest as he digested the message contents. Two men were alive in the world who carried his blood. It sparked a deep aching desire inside of him. Did he have two sons again, two living beings who were a part of him, family?

The flutter stopped abruptly as reason took over.

They're not sons. They're not family. They're aberrations like me.

He lowered the lid of the laptop ever so slowly as he struggled to make sense of how to proceed. William, the person who sent the email, shouldn't be alive. Yet, Rolphe could envision the man's face even now, after almost a hundred years. It was a handsome face, but also a cocky, persistent one. Even as the man lay dying. William wouldn't give up life without a fight, or at least a reward for the blood that Rolphe had sucked out of him. He begged Rolphe for a parting gift, a taste of what it was like to be a vampire.

I never encountered one like him before. The little shit wouldn't be denied.

In the end, Rolphe shared a bit of blood, knowing that it was a lethal substance for the majority of humans. What chance would a man like William have when he was nearly dead already?

Now my spawn lives on. I've created another parasite. No, two parasites. William said there was a second vampire involved.

Rolphe hadn't pondered the idea of what he was in many years. He didn't think in terms of being a blood sucker. In the evenings, when he sipped at the dark liquid in his crystal stemware, he never thought about its true origin. For him, it came from a procurer, one who serviced his needs as easily as if he'd ordered rare wine.

Now, his mind was being forced back to the truth he'd chosen to forget. But that knowledge of what he was had to be altered by the new information he was dealing with.

"There are three parasites in the world. That's two too many!"

Like his inferior canvases, Rolphe would end up in the fire someday too. Hell would swallow him up as soon as he drew his last breath. He was prepared for that, but he wouldn't have two monsters like himself on the loose. He'd have to deal with the situation as soon as he received more information from William.

Sixteen

Carol stuffed her tissue in her pocket and glanced around at the expansive hall where she stood. The Louvre was at the top of her list of places to visit, and she was thrilled to be feeling well enough to be out and about. Paris was the city of her dreams, a perfect place to rekindle her romance with Kevin. He'd been so helpful in making her feel better about the rocky start to their trip. Now he was doing his best again, trying to appreciate the things that she was interested in. Tickets to the Louvre had been purchased shortly after Kevin had booked their trip. To have missed an opportunity to use them would have been very disheartening for Carol. However, she wasn't so sure that Kevin felt the same way. "What do you think, Kevin, is this place amazing?" she asked.

Standing close to her, Kevin glanced around at the horde of people surrounding them. "I guess you're not the only one who loves this kind of thing. This place is packed."

Carol tugged on his sleeve and nodded in the direction of the Mona Lisa. "I never thought I'd get to actually see her."

Kevin shrugged. "She's kind of a homely broad compared to you."

His openly voiced opinion was loud enough to make a number of people stare at him, then Carol.

"Kevin . . . ." At first blush she wanted to censure him, until she realized what he meant and giggled quietly.

"Sorry," Kevin said quickly. "I didn't mean anything disrespectful." He smiled down at her innocently. "I just think you're beautiful, that's all."

She blushed again. "Thank you."

"I'm glad you're feeling better." Kevin reached out for a bit of her golden blonde hair and played with it for a long moment. "And I'm happy that you're enjoying this place."

When she studied Kevin's eyes, she realized how they could remind her of baby Ariel's eyes. They were very clear and filled with an honest, direct kind of love that resurrected feelings she thought she'd lost. She brought his hand to her chest. "I am better, but—"

"But what?" Kevin's tone was instantly one of concern.

She smiled, wanting to relieve his fears. "We've been here most of the afternoon. I'm a little tired. Would you mind if we go back to the hotel? It might be nice to climb into that wonderful bed for a little while."

Kevin's eyes narrowed as he studied her. "Geez, honey, I'm sorry if you're not—"

"I'm okay, really." She gave him a teasing smile as she tightened her grip on his hand and started for the exit. "There's room in that big bed for both of us."

The light finally dawned for Kevin. His anxious expression was replaced by a playful grin. "Oh, I see."

* * *

Carol lay snuggled up to Kevin under thick, luxurious covers. Warm and content, she was smiling. She felt close to her husband again. In fact, after the way he'd made love to her, putting all his own pleasures aside and singularly concentrating on her needs, she wondered how she could have talked about separating. It was clear that he loved her passionately. He expressed it with every tender caress and adoring kiss.

Her thoughts wandered from Kevin to the fact that they had a son. Little Ariel was such a precious, little boy. When she was single, she had given up on being a mother. Then she met Kevin and got pregnant. It wasn't something they'd planned. Afterwards there was so much confusion and turmoil that it made for a rough start. Kevin doubted himself completely, and Carol almost lost the baby.

"Honey?" She turned to Kevin and put her hand on his broad chest. "Do you think we should call Peggy and check on little Ariel?"

Kevin had his arm around her and pulled her closer. "I'm sure Ariel's fine. Besides, Peggy said that we shouldn't call her, that she'd absolutely let us know if there were anything wrong."

"I really miss him." A sudden stream of tears followed her announcement. A couple of minutes earlier, she was completely happy. Now, a single thought about Ariel's chubby little face smiling at her, sent her over the edge.

Kevin reached for a tissue and handed it to her. "You're going to have both of us bawlin' like babies if you start that. I miss him too."

She sat up and dabbed at her tears. "I know you do. Isn't it strange? We didn't even know how much we were missing before we had Ariel."

"Yeah, life without either of you would feel pointless now."

"I didn't mean to hurt you when I said I might have to leave. I just didn't know what to do."

Kevin sucked in some air. "I guess it really scared the hell out of me thinking that you could make that decision, and I wasn't any part of it."

Carol started to fidget with the tissue. "Yes, I know, but I felt like you made a decision to push me away, and I didn't have any power to change your mind. And it really hurt, Kevin. I didn't feel wanted anymore."

Kevin sat up too and took her hand. "I didn't realize . . . anyway, the bottom line is that I'm a fool. I'm sorry."

"I guess we're both foolish. You said I was needy. I think you're right."

"It's okay. We both get a little squirrelly sometimes." Kevin let out a sudden burst of laughter.

"What's so funny?"

"At least we don't have Arel in the middle of it all. He'd have us on adjoining couches."

She let her gaze travel over Kevin's face. His strong bone structure hailed back to a Scottish grandfather, but his blond hair came from Norwegian lineage. It made for a great combination. "Don't let this go to your head, but sometimes I wonder how you weren't snatched up by somebody long before you met me."

"Believe it or not, I'm basically a shy person."

"I can see that. You really put yourself out there when it comes to things like sports, but underneath, you're skittish."

"Skittish? I sound like a horse."

"I didn't mean it to sound insulting," Carol giggled. "However, you do have quite an appetite, and I think little Ariel is going to be just like you."

Kevin's face flushed as he studied the folds in the comforter. "Wait 'til Ariel is older. Mom told me I nearly ate them out of house and home."

Carol nudged his arm. "So that's what I have to look forward to."

"Yep, I'll have to bring home lots of bacon when he hits the teen years." Kevin glanced up. "What about you? Are you skittish?"

Carol shredded off a bit of tissue. "Maybe I am. Life can be scary."

"Are you scared now?"

Carol shrugged. "Did you ever feel like something is going to come out of the blue and ruin everything? I remember the day my parents sat me down and said that they were going to get divorced. I thought we were all happy. But as I sat there, my whole world fell apart."

"Do you think that's why you wanted to leave? You don't want Ariel growing up thinking everything is alright and then he finds out it's not?"

"I never thought of it that way."

Kevin frowned back. "Honey, I'll do everything I can to make things right with us. But I can't guarantee that our life will be perfect, that there won't be problems."

"Maybe that's it. I do want everything to be perfect. I don't think I could handle years of thinking we're going to be okay, and then find out it was all a lie."

"In your parents' case, maybe they were happy for a long time. Then they grew apart, and their marriage didn't work for them anymore. It happens a lot."

"What if that happens to us?" She paused. "What am I talking about? It already did happen before this trip."

"But look at us right now, we're back on track. I'm crazier about you than ever. Doesn't that mean something?"

"I hope so."

S. S. BAZINET

"We're not your parents. Just because they split up, we don't have to."

Carol tossed the tissue aside. "Living with the past is hard."

"You're right about that." He threw the covers back, grabbed his robe and got out of bed.

"What is it?"

"I was thinking about some nightmares I had. Arel said they were based on a lifetime that he and Peggy shared. It seems I was part of it too. I was an old man who screwed them by teaching them things that the locals didn't like. They died as a result."

"That's horrible."

"Yeah, I know, but Arel insisted on my letting go of it. I thought I did, but maybe I'm kidding myself. Sometimes, I want to talk to you about things, but I feel like I'm going to say the wrong thing."

"You're talking now, and you're doing fine."

"I hope so. Because if I screw up this thing I have with you—" His smile was gone, replaced by a dark scowl as he looked away.

"I'm here."

"But for how long? How long will you put up with me if I screw up again?"

Carol could feel how much pressure she put on him. But her fear was always so close to the surface. It was always in the background telling her that Kevin might be right about failing again, and that they would get a divorce.

Kevin reached out for her hand. "Tell me that you forgive me, that you won't throw me out because I don't measure up. Please, Carol, I love you. I love our child. Doesn't that count for something?"

Carol made herself smile. "Let's try not to think about all that, at least not now."

"But that's why we're here, isn't it? You're not the only one who's scared. When you can't give me a straight answer, I'm scared as hell."

88

Seventeen

Arel sat at his desk in his upstairs bedroom, catching up on paperwork. He couldn't excuse what he'd done in the past, but Michael did give him some options for the present. After careful consideration, he'd decided that Michael's comments about his powers were sound. He had never harmed anyone but William. In fact, he had assisted his friends in some instances. Where William was concerned, Arel would never contact him again. William would be safe. Arel might still have to move to a desolate island someday, but in the meantime, he wouldn't worry his friends any more than need be. For everyone's sake, he had to get on with his life and direct his energy in more positive directions.

"Are you busy?" Carey asked as he stood in the doorway.

Arel looked up, noting the young man's smile, and waved him in. At least Carey seemed happy. Arel had saved the boy's life after an accident, and he continued to help Carey as time went on. At least he could be proud of that achievement.

Carey walked over and sat down on the bed. "I wanted to check in, to see how you are? You've been pretty down for a while."

"We all have our ups and downs," Arel said, trying to sound as unperturbed as possible. He directed his gaze back to some mail that had piled up. "I'm just catching up on a few things."

Carey crossed his arms and gave Arel a puzzled frown. "Is it me? Am I the reason you've been moping around lately?"

"Of course not," Arel said as he glanced over at Carey.

"I know that I'm not measuring up."

"What?" As soon as Arel heard the anxious tone in Carey's voice, he felt his own apprehension rising. Had he been too hard on Carey when it came to unimportant matters like Carey's clothes? The

89

S. S. BAZINET

boy insisted on wearing torn jeans and t-shirts that could have belonged to a homeless person. Arel had offered to take Carey shopping, but the young, independent man always declined. "If this is about how you dress—"

Carey glanced down at himself. "What's wrong with how I dress?"

"Nothing, I just thought—"

"I know I haven't been helping out around here, not as much as I should." Carey tugged at his shirt. "Now I see you have a problem with other things too."

Arel threw a utility bill aside and stared at his visitor. Carey didn't talk about having any family, so Arel tried to be a kind of paternal adviser when needed. But it was a tricky road to navigate. Had he come across as too judgmental? "Carey, please, I care about you, not how you dress. So when I offer to take you shopping or inquire about the idea of going back to school, it's because I want to be a friend."

Carey shrugged. "Okay, fine, but what about the rugs? What am I doing wrong?"

"The rugs? I don't know what you're talking about."

"Give me a break. You don't think I can do a simple thing like vacuum them the right way."

"Did I ever say that to you?"

"No, but it's pretty clear I'm not doing a good job."

Arel's jaw tightened as he remembered the hours spent on getting spaghetti sauce and cherry pie stains out of the living room carpet. "I know that you do your best. That's what counts."

"Is that why you have to go over my work?"

"I'll let you in on a little secret," Arel said as he glanced out into the hallway. He gestured for Carey to listen closely. "Michael isn't much better. I know he does his best, but—"

"Really?" Carey began to smile. "He offered to give me some tips."

"Heaven forbid!" Arel looked at the hall again. "But Michael's very sensitive, so don't let him know I said anything."

"Right, my lips are sealed."

Arel leaned back in his desk chair. He had to give Carey something to boost his self-image. "Actually, I think you're a faster study than Michael was."

90

"You're kidding. Michael looks so capable."

"Yes, but looks can be deceiving. He's always had a devil of a time with simple household chores. And the rugs, forget it. He's still a little deficient when it comes to the exacting care involved."

"My goodness, Arel, I never knew that vacuuming was so complicated."

Arel threw up his hands. "I know, most people feel that way, but there's a correct way to do even the smallest task. Can you remember that the next time you try to rush through something?"

Carey nodded as he got up. "I'll certainly try."

"Before you go, I want to say that I'm proud of you. It was very thoughtful of you to check on me. And about the rugs, I know I'm kind of particular, but they're white. When I bought them I wasn't thinking in terms of—"

"A slob like me? I'll try to be more careful like Michael told me when I moved in. He said you had high standards."

Arel felt his cheeks grow warm with embarrassment. "Sorry, I guess I was raised in a very strict environment."

"Where I come from, we didn't have rugs."

Arel reflected on the statement, slightly amazed. "I had no idea, but don't worry about it. I'll help you with anything you want to learn."

"I appreciate that," Carey said as he walked to the door. "Well, I better get going. I told Michael I'd meet him in the garage. I'm going to show him how to change the oil and check some of the fluid levels on the bike."

Arel cleared his throat. "Remember, I bought a tarp for projects like that."

"Sure, especially since Michael's new at this."

"How right you are." Arel thought about his recent conversation with Michael. In the end, he'd realized a little more about Michael's take on life. Angels were probably great as long as they stuck to heavenly duties. Being on earth was a different matter. Arel had expected too much from Michael all along. He needed to pass on his findings to Carey. "Carey, wait up," he said as he walked over to where Carey was standing. He lowered his voice to a whisper again. "Please, be patient with Michael. Give him time to catch on."

"He seems pretty sharp to me," Carey said with a shrug.

"I thought the same thing. The point is that Michael is kind of special. Things that come easy for us might be a challenge for him."

Carey nodded. "Got it. Thanks for the tip."

* * *

Michael crouched down next to Carey's motorcycle, inspecting the machine. Ever since Carey introduced the bike, Michael found his interest growing. It was enjoyable to learn more about internal combustion engines, gear ratios, and fuel injection. When Arel wasn't around, he even took the bike out a few times. Now, he was looking forward to helping with bike maintenance. When the door to the garage opened, he looked up to see Carey coming out to join him. "How did it go with Arel?"

Carey walked over, grabbed a polishing cloth, and ran it over the motorcycle fender. "He's doing a little better. I think he's trying to take your advice about getting on with life. However, he gave me some very explicit advice about you."

Michael smiled. "Yes, I'm sure he did."

"I'm a bit reluctant to say this, my friend, but Arel has some deep reservations about your competence."

"I know—"

"He told me that you're 'challenged' when it comes to simple tasks." Carey began to laugh. "I'm afraid I won't be able to allow you near the motorcycle until you've proven that you understand the intricacies of a socket wrench."

Michael stood up and gave Carey a sly look. "You're enjoying yourself, aren't you?"

"Just heeding Arel's warning."

"Yes, he seems very pleased with himself when he points out my shortcomings."

"You were privy to our conversation?"

"He's been so busy shutting out all exchanges with William that he forgot to shield his thoughts from me."

"You can't let on. I promised not to damage your ego."

"Arel does try to spare me."

Carey's face took on a puzzled look. "We seem so lacking in his eyes. After knowing how Arel feels, I almost find myself wanting to go over the rugs again, to really make sure I've done a thorough job."

"I've been there."

"You're kidding."

"You forget, I've lived with this situation for a long time. Arel is quite the perfectionist. It helps him to feel that he's in control."

"But none of us, angel or human, was ever expected to be perfect. It limits one's freedom to enjoy."

"I'll remind you of that when I see you working on the rugs."

"It's kind of strange, but I like hearing the vacuum suck up those crumbs I dropped."

"About the crumbs, you might want to ease up on acting like a kid. The last time Arel tried to get all the stains out, he was at it an entire afternoon. He could barely stand up by the time he finished."

"Hey, it was a great distraction. After that cleaning spell, he fell into bed and slept eight hours straight."

"Yes, but I've watched you eat. You're not simply providing Arel with a distraction."

"When I'm enjoying a slice of pie, I forget my manners. The sensory input is amazing. I think cherry might be my favorite."

"I love working in the garden for the same reason."

Carey's eyes strayed. He put his polishing cloth down and stared at the door leading to the house. "Strange, but I'm pulled towards mastering the vacuum. Arel promised to show me the right way to clean the deep down fibers of the wool rugs."

Michael winked at him. "He has you where he wants you."

"Unfortunately, I think you're right. People are so interesting in their approach to the physical. Which reminds me, how is Annabel doing? I was a little surprised by William's offer to hire her."

"She's learning how to navigate in the world of humans rather well."

"I enjoyed working with her. She adjusted quite easily to whatever the situation needed."

"She was quick to notice William's preferences too. He can't abide someone who's too nice. Secondly, he loves beauty. She's adapted by being a strong and independent type. She's also allowed a little of her true nature to shine through. All in all, William was very interested."

"Great. She sounds like she's perfect for the job."

"The real challenge will come when she begins to interact with him. Talented or not, the physical is a very new experience for her, especially when it comes to being around a person as strong and self-contained as William."

Eighteen

William stuffed another load of laundry in the washing machine and slammed down the lid. He couldn't believe that he was cleaning up his home for someone else's benefit. He'd hired Annabel to do the job, but the thought of her seeing the state of his living quarters was unacceptable. He'd really let things go in the midst of his madness and failing health. With Annabel's promise to stop by the next morning, he started his housekeeping campaign as soon as he came home from the tea he'd shared with her.

I'm acting like an immature kid with a crush.

He detested the fact that he could be so juvenile, yet it was an invigorating rush at the same time.

I'm back from the dead. Maybe it's normal to feel so revitalized.

He pictured Annabel's beautiful face and began to imagine what the rest of her body looked like. A surge of wanton lust grabbed hold.

Or maybe I just need to be with a woman again.

But he didn't want just any woman. He was fixated on Annabel, and that fact really bothered him. He'd never felt such a connection before. After all his years of being detached, how could someone affect him so deeply?

He stormed out of the laundry area and went directly to the main bathroom. He'd already cleaned the two other baths. Each one was an exhausting chore after months of neglect. This one was going to be the biggest job. Towels lay on the floor, the sink was littered with shaving remains, and the tub needed definite attention.

Just finish the job.

Getting down on his knees, he began to spray the extra-long, deep interior. Halfway through, the can of cleaner sputtered out its last bit of foam. He knew he didn't have a replacement. He rocked back on his heels, fighting the urge to hurl the empty can at a wall.

Get a grip! It's just a tub!

That's when he remembered that he'd been up working all night. He often pulled all-nighters in the lab. However, that time was spent sitting at a microscope or computer, not scrubbing floors and mending plaster walls. For the past twelve hours, he'd been working at a furious pace, needing to put right the carnage from months of outrage.

With a fixed determination, he went back to cleaning the tub, draping himself over the side with weariness. Thirty minutes later, the bathroom was clean and tidy again, and his only desire was to go to sleep.

My first all night cleaning binge. Annabel better be as unique as she appears.

The thought repeated when he finally climbed into bed. He was so exhausted, it was going to be easy to sleep soundly. He closed his eyes, enjoying the pillow top softness of the mattress as he let out a sigh of contented triumph. He'd done it. He'd cleaned the two levels of his home from top to bottom.

The shrill sound of his dryer brought him out of his two minutes of slumber. His fourth load of laundry was dry and ready for retrieval. "Dammit, I forgot about the clothes." He moaned when the buzzer sounded again, demanding attention. But he knew he had to respond if he wanted any peace. The machine was programmed to repeat its signal every sixty seconds.

He fought his way out of the covers reluctantly. Once on his feet, he was still half asleep as he made his way out into the hall and to the laundry room. Just as his hand reached out for the dryer, the doorbell rang. He froze in mid reach. "Is she here already?"

He went back to his bedroom and grabbed his robe, rubbing at his eyes and trying to clear his mind. As he made his way to the foyer, he began to wake up. As he did, a small thrill of excitement took hold. He was eager to see Annabel's pretty face again. The moment didn't last. When the doorbell rang again, he stopped short.

What the hell am I doing?

He let deep frown lines take over his brow. Why was he letting himself get interested in this woman? He'd already made a huge mistake with Arel. Now he was welcoming a stranger into his home.

Don't answer the door! If you do, you'll regret it!

The warning came from his gut. He'd always trusted that part of himself. It had been a guiding force in times of danger. He needed to heed its advice now. As he turned and started walking back to the bedroom, the warning was reinforced.

Don't make another mistake. Besides, the woman is nothing special.

The words were voiced with conviction, but he'd only gone a few steps when he remembered the feel of Annabel's hand the night before. When she was saying goodbye, he'd taken it in his as if he wanted to cement their agreement with a handshake. Actually, he'd wanted to touch her, to connect with her in a more tactile way. Recalling the rush that flooded his body, he knew he hadn't ever felt so captivated by a woman. He wanted to touch her again.

He stood in the hallway listening, waiting for the bell to ring a third time. When the silence went unbroken and the house suddenly felt too quiet and empty, his breath caught. Was Annabel gone? Did she give up on him and leave? Didn't she care that she'd disturbed him? The questions made him angry.

Who cares? Let her leave. I need my solitude.

He tried to convince himself that he was better off alone, but he hurriedly walked to the foyer anyway. When he got there, the bell rang again. The sound brought a smile to his face. He didn't need her. She needed him. It was a deciding factor that released him from his delusional thoughts of romance. When he grabbed the doorknob and swung the door open, he was about to tell Annabel that he'd changed his mind. He'd send her away and go back to bed.

"Hello, William." Annabel got out the greeting before he had a chance to speak.

"Uh—" William stared at the woman in front of him. For a moment, he thought he saw wings, blindingly-bright affairs that fanned out behind her. Blinking and squinting, he finally realized the sun was shining in his eyes. He retreated with relief that only lasted a moment.

Oh hell, she's even more beautiful than I thought.

Getting a better look at his visitor, he swallowed back an overwhelming desire. Annabel was a lithe, lovely goddess of a girl. Without the cap she'd worn the night before, her hair fell about her shoulders like red silk in the morning light. Her face was youthful, with hints of innocence and wisdom combined.

Annabel gave him a warm smile. "Did I come at a bad time?"

Even her voice sent a small chill through William's body. Her tone was deliberate, but it also had a soft, pleasing quality. It struck a chord in him, a place where desire and an unfulfilled longing meshed. The longing wasn't for temporary pleasure. It wanted more than that.

What am I getting myself in to?

Recognizing the danger Annabel posed, he knew he should slam the door shut, but he had no strength left. He could only hang on to the edge of the door, hoping to stay upright as his fatigue and Annabel's loveliness both took their toll on him. "No, it's not a bad time. Come in."

Nineteen

Tim lay on the cold cement floor, trying to remain very still. Everything was spinning. He'd been working in the garage. While he was taking boxes down from a high shelf, he lost his balance and fell off a ladder. His head hit the corner of an old dresser being stored in the space.

Peggy is going to go crazy if she gets home and finds me like this.

He kept fading in and out of consciousness. He'd only had enough clarity to call Arel by hitting the speed dial number on his phone. Afterwards, the numbers blurred when he tried to dial 911. His message to Arel was short. "It's a real emergency. Help. Garage."

As Tim began to black out and fought to stay conscious, he felt good about Arel coming to his rescue. He'd observed his friend around the babies when they were sick. After Arel's visits, the children were always better. Arel's healing touch reminded Tim of his grandpa. When Tim was a kid, his grandpa had the same ability. He seemed able to perform minor miracles with sick stomachs and colds. Tim didn't question such gifts. He thought everybody had a grandpa like his until he was older.

"Tim! Where are you?"

The sound of Arel's voice, shouted from the door to the garage, brought Tim back as he was fading again. It even made him chuckle to himself. The guy who insisted that he'd never get involved was clearly ready to get involved. "Over here, I had a little accident," he called out from behind some fallen boxes.

Arel was kneeling by Tim's side almost immediately. "Oh god, there's a lot of blood! What can I do? Where's Peggy? Have you called 911?"

"Peggy's shopping, and I can't call for help myself."

"You're kidding!" Arel grabbed his phone out of his pocket and hurriedly punched in some numbers. When he disconnected from his call, his news was laced with disappointment. "I'm sorry. They said there was a big accident on the Expressway. It might take a little longer than normal for them to get here."

"You can help."

"Of course I will. What do you want me to do?"

"If you have a clean handkerchief, press it against my head and try to stop the bleeding."

When Arel stared fixedly at Tim's wound and the blood flowing down his scalp, his face began to turn a slight shade of green.

Tim knew he had to get Arel's attention. "Arel, stay with me."

Arel looked away long enough to retrieve a handkerchief from his pocket. "Sorry, sometimes blood makes me sick."

Tim continued to give directions. "Keep pressure on the wound."

"Yes, I'm trying, but I think the gash is pretty deep." Arel's face was going from green to white. His body swayed as he took short gasps of air. He looked ready to faint.

"Arel, please, I'm barely hanging in here."

"I know. I thought I was getting better about this sort of thing, but I guess not."

"Just breathe, and while you're breathing I need you to do something for me."

"Anything, just ask."

"Use your magic."

Arel startled as if he'd been struck. "What? I don't have any magic."

"You've helped the babies when they were sick."

Arel shook his head. "I don't know what you're talking about."

Tim struggled to keep his eyes on Arel. "My grandpa had the healing gift. So do you. I'm sure of it."

"I'll do anything in the world to help you, but don't ask that. I can't—"

"You're making excuses. Unfortunately, I did the same thing when Gramps tried to pass on his gift to me. But you already have it."

Arel kept looking away, but his tone was resolute when he protested. "It's not an excuse."

Tim could tell that arguing wasn't going to work. He'd seen Arel's stubborn side. Once Arel got his back up, there'd be no convincing him. Still, he was sure that Arel was as capable as his grandfather. Just thinking about the kindly old man made way for an idea. Gramps tended towards a diplomatic approach to problems. That meant that Tim needed to do a little backpedaling. "Sorry, Arel, I didn't mean to put you on the spot."

Arel blinked back another apology. "Believe me, I'd help if I could."

Tim paused. "Maybe, while we wait, we can talk about something that gets my mind off of the pain in my head, like Sara and Ariel."

Arel's face flushed with a little color. "They're like two angels, aren't they?"

"I think you love them almost as much as if they were your own."

Arel's breathing began to slow down. "Yes, that's true."

"Tell me about the last time you and I took them to the park."

Arel shrugged. "I don't remember."

"Try, please. I think it was about a month ago."

Arel's eyes brightened as a hint of a smile began to slide into place. "Yes, it's starting to come back. It was a nice afternoon, and you wanted to give Peggy a break so she could go to get her hair cut. We asked Carol if little Ariel could come too." Arel hesitated wistfully. "I wish I hadn't forgotten my camera. I could have taken a million pictures that afternoon."

"Keep talking. It's helping."

Arel got more comfortable, going from a kneeling position to sitting next to Tim. "Both Sara and Ariel loved the baby swings. They laughed out loud. It's like they live in another world, a world that's so happy and free." He smiled. "If only we could be like that. Wouldn't it be great to simply let go and have fun all the time?"

"Yes, you're right. It would be nice. What else do you remember about that day?"

As Arel began to relate his thoughts about the children and a life that didn't have any problems, Tim felt warmth coming from Arel's hand. It was like the sun's warmth, only it went deeper than the rays of the sun. The feeling spread throughout his body. It was soothing but powerful. As it grew in intensity, the pain in his head began to subside. The room slowly came into focus. After a few minutes, Tim smiled. He reached out to Arel. "Help me to sit up."

Arel frowned back a warning. "No, you need to lie very still."

"It's okay. I don't think we're going to need that ambulance after all."

* * *

Arel came through the front door in a dreamy state of shock. "Michael!" He was filled with so much excitement, he was almost reeling. "Michael, come here!"

"What is it?" Michael asked as he rushed into the foyer.

Arel continued into the living room and collapsed on the sofa. "Something just happened, and I don't know what to think about it."

Michael paused and stared at him, then smiled as he walked over to a recliner. "You helped Tim, correct?"

"Yes, but I didn't plan on helping him."

Michael laughed. "Is there a problem with that?"

"I guess not. I mean, I'm beyond relieved that Tim is okay, but I want to know how it happened. Tim was lying there ready to pass out. Next he's telling me to think about the children. For a couple of minutes I lost myself in picturing how happy they can be. When I looked at Tim again, he's telling me to cancel the ambulance. I took my handkerchief away from his head wound, and it was already closing up. I insisted on taking him to the ER just in case, and they said he seemed fine. There's no sign of a concussion."

"And how do you feel?"

"I feel great. It's just that I don't understand what I did." It was true. Arel's body felt buoyant and light. Yet, in the midst of his exhilaration, a nagging feeling flitted around in his mind, and he didn't know why.

Michael offered his thoughts. "What happened was perfectly natural. You allowed yourself to simply be. You didn't get in the way of your power with negative emotions."

"It's that easy?"

"Yes, but now your mind wants an explanation for something it didn't orchestrate."

Arel held up a hand. "Wait a second. Back up. I just performed a bit of a miracle, and I didn't even try to do it. I sat there with Tim and talked to him about a nice time at the park."

"True, but that didn't negate your good intention to help Tim. It was in the background. And that good intention, plus your positive attitude made the miracle possible."

"Why didn't you tell me all this stuff sooner? Why didn't you explain it before all my disasters with William?"

"I thought I had."

"Maybe so, but obviously I missed something. I nearly killed him a couple of times. Then I did kill him. Then I—" He leaned back into the sofa. "Oh hell, I'm really confused."

"Sometimes, people have hidden agendas that stem from fear based emotions. Unfortunately, that's the situation you have with William. When you use your power around him, that hidden negativity causes a lot of problems."

"Great. So I'm back where I started with him."

"Not necessarily. You're learning about how to find some peace when you think about him. You're letting him go in some respects. In the meantime, William has allowed some help from another source."

"What do you mean?"

Michael's eyes flashed with more sparkle than usual. "William has invited a young woman to help out in his home. He thinks that she's a student, but she's one of ours."

Michael's news acted like a revitalizing agent for Arel. He sat up with a smile. "You're kidding! William is involved with an angel?"

"Hopefully, in time, she'll help him to see life and others with a more open heart."

"I wouldn't bet on it, but I am impressed. I just hope that William never finds out who she is, or he'll blame me for her too."

"Let's just concentrate on what you did for Tim today. I'm sure that he's grateful."

"What *we* did today, Michael. If you hadn't barged into my life, I'd still be hiding from everything."

"I was invited, remember?"

Arel did remember. As a child, he'd often held on to a small glass angel and prayed for a real one to appear. "Did I make a mistake in asking for you to show up?"

S. S. BAZINET

Michael didn't reply. He sat quietly in his seat, but he didn't offer an answer to the question.

Arel waited for long minutes and finally sat back in the silence, asking himself the same thing he'd just asked Michael. When he wanted an angel's help, he was still a child, an innocent who believed in the magic that Tim mentioned. But innocence is often lost by adulthood. When Arel was a young man, he was bitter and hopeless. He tried to escape from life. But he wasn't able to escape now. Michael's blood wouldn't let him. Once ingested, it carried its message to every cell in Arel's body. And that message still repeated every day. The words were always the same. "It's time to look at what you've hidden away in the darkness."

Arel wasn't prepared for what that meant. He had used the darkness for what he couldn't abide in himself. It was a repository, a closeted place where he stuffed away the roots of his pain and anger and blame. Michael's blood turned on the light in his dark, inner cellars. Arel was forced to face his issues. And he did. Kicking and screaming every inch of the way, he finally made peace with his father's abuse. He even came to terms with a past life when ignorant people burned him at the stake for being different. But the price for his enlightenment was steep. His heart gave out. He had a near death experience in a churchyard. But Michael helped him through it all.

What a hell of a roller coaster I've been through. I'm lucky to be drawing breath.

As the reclamation process replayed in his mind, Arel looked at the angel sitting a few feet away.

Michael smiled back. "The bottom line is that you were courageous enough to face your negativity, and no matter what you think, I do know negativity when I see it, Arel. We might experience things differently, but that doesn't mean I'm blind to any of the things that humans think, do, or hide away." Michael stood up. "But if you think you'd be better off if I leave, just say the word."

Arel glared back. "Dammit, Michael, you know I don't want that."

"What do you want? If you could have the normal life you've talked about, what would make you happy?"

Arel rubbed the sofa arm carefully, diverting his eyes. "Do you think there's a chance that someday I'll be able to have a family, you know, a wife and children?"

104

"Of course."

"I'm not too weird?"

"Why would you be weird?"

"Why do you think?" He glanced up and met Michael's gaze. "I have your blood."

Michael blinked back. "Do you think I'm weird?"

"No, you're great as far as angels go. But I'm some kind of oddity, admit it."

Michael sat down again. "I thought I blended in quite well."

"I suppose. Although Kevin said you're . . . oh never mind."

"I'm what?"

"Nothing. He mentioned something about you being a little too stiff."

"Too stiff?"

"Yes, you're too nice. Your halo shines through whether you like it or not. Thankfully, so far I've been able to divert too much attention going your way."

"I never saw myself as being that different. There are lots of nice people around."

"What does it matter? I'm the one who has to fit in, not you."

"That's not totally accurate. It's important that we fit in too. Otherwise, depending on the circumstance, we wouldn't be able to do our jobs effectively. For instance, in Annabel's case—"

"Annabel?" Arel knew a girl by that name. "Are you talking about the Annabel I met when I went to New York?"

"Yes."

"She's an angel?"

"That's right. I thought you needed extra support on that trip so I asked her to tag along."

"I thought she was some homeless waif. Wow, she was believable."

"She's the angel who's helping William now."

Arel quickly went from slouching to sitting upright. "Michael! What are you thinking? That poor thing! William will have her for breakfast!"

"Actually, she isn't using the waif persona now. She's quite capable of holding her own."

"You don't know William like I do. I'd advise her to wear one of those metal mesh shark suits that divers put on when swimming in dangerous waters."

"Don't worry about her. She'll be fine."

Twenty

Annabel's first day on the job was uneventful. There didn't seem like much to do. William's home was clean and tidy. When she told him that he didn't need her services, he appeared to remain calm, but she noted a slight degree of panic in his eyes. There was a long pause before he finally informed her that his book shelves needed organizing. After a few days, she knew it was taking some effort on his part to provide tasks for her to perform. A closet that was orderly on one day, would be in chaos a couple of days later. Newly washed clothes ended up in the clothes hamper.

Annabel's main concern was communication. William remained aloof most of the time, rarely engaging her in conversation. It wasn't that he closeted himself away. As she went about her chores, he was often reading in a central location where he could observe her coming and going, but that was the extent of their association. The situation finally changed on laundry day, when Annabel plopped a basket of clean clothes down on the sofa. She had barely begun to fold William's socks when he looked up from a chair in the corner. Supposedly he was reading a book, but that didn't stop him from making a comment.

"You're doing it all wrong," he said in a crisp tone, trying to avoid looking at her.

Annabel stared back. Maybe she was missing something in the art of sock folding. "What do you mean? It's simple. You take matching socks and put them together."

William shifted uncomfortably in his seat. "Not if you want to do it properly."

107

S. S. BAZINET

Annabel smiled to herself. Carey had discussed Arel's obsession with vacuuming and carpet care. Now William sounded just as picky about his socks. She laughed. "Why make a fuss?"

William put his book down and stood up. Without another word, he approached the sofa, picked up two socks and demonstrated what was needed. He carefully folded the socks in thirds like a tri-fold billfold.

Annabel knew this was a crucial moment. She had to react the right way, the way a strong, modern woman would react. She grabbed a t-shirt and folded it in half. "Fine, I'll do these."

William's brows shot up as he watched her. "Not like that, dearie!" He took the shirt out of her hands. Again, he seemed to have a very exacting way of making sure the piece of clothing resembled something sitting on a shelf in a department store.

Annabel felt the challenge and tried to duplicate his precise folding process. Unfortunately, it wasn't as easy as it looked. When she was finished, her shirt didn't look anything like William's.

William reacted with annoyance. "For goodness sake, woman, you're quite daft, aren't you?"

Annabel had never been verbally criticized before, and she didn't take William's words personally. However, something told her that she couldn't let his remark go. She knew disrespect when she heard it. She immediately moved away from the clothes basket and made an announcement of her own. "I'm sorry, William, but I don't think this job is working out."

William stepped forward with surprise. "I can't help it if you have no sense of how to do things properly. You should be happy that someone is teaching you how to adequately function in your job."

Annabel relied on her angelic instincts and started towards the coat closet. "It's been very interesting working here. I wish you the best."

"What do you mean? You're leaving?"

"As you just said, I'm not doing my job very well."

William crossed his arms, following her with his eyes. "You're being ridiculous, but do as you please."

Annabel slipped on her coat and gave him a final nod as she walked to the door.

"Annabel, before you go, tell me where to send your wages. I don't have your address."

"Never mind, I haven't done very much. I wouldn't want to take your money under the pretense that I'm adequate."

William's face flushed with frustration. "Maybe you're not cut out for folding socks." He quickly walked over to where she was standing. "I could use a lab assistant, but you'd have to be willing to learn proper procedures."

Annabel zipped up her jacket. "What would I do?"

"I'm thinking about some experiments with plants. I'd like to know how they're affected by certain phenomenon."

Annabel smiled, genuinely interested. "I love plants."

"That's not the point. I'm doing a scientific study. You'd need to take care of things in a very specific way."

"I can follow instructions if it's for a reason that seems plausible."

"Are you sure?"

Annabel nodded. "Of course."

William's pale, blue eyes lit up for a brief instant. "Good, we'll start the experiment once I plan it out and buy the supplies we'll need."

Twenty-One

Carol sat at a small, cozy table in a quaint café. It was exactly the kind of little bistro that she'd always dreamed about. With walnut walls and a friendly staff, it bordered a picturesque cobblestone street and was within walking distance of the Eiffel Tower. "It's so perfect," she said, turning her attention to Kevin.

He looked up from the menu he was studying. Dressed in a tan, cable knit sweater, he looked particularly attractive when he flashed his eyes in her direction. "It is perfect. They have some fantastic items to choose from. I especially like the look of the beef tenderloin."

She laughed. "I meant the restaurant itself. Isn't it a slice of heaven?"

Kevin hastily took a look around. "Yeah, it sure is. The smells coming out of the kitchen have me practically drooling."

She reached out and took his hand. "Thank you, honey, for everything. I'm having the time of my life."

Kevin put the menu aside. "Are you really happy, Carol? Because that's what I want." He paused. "I want to be the person you want me to be. You have to believe that."

She knew Kevin was starving after a long afternoon of checking out the sights, but in that moment, he put it all aside. He'd never sounded or looked more sincere as he stared back at her.

She squeezed his hand. "I believe you, and I love you so much. That's why I get so upset. I want to always feel like we feel right now. I don't want that to go away. I don't want you to go away."

Kevin slipped his hand free of hers, only to take it into both of his. He held it firmly. "I'm not going anywhere. Even when you think I've shut you out, the real me is there, underneath all the crap. I just

110

haven't figured out how to keep that part of myself from blanking out, but I'm working on it."

In that moment, she knew clearly, maybe for the first time, the situation wasn't all Kevin's fault. He was sitting across from her, as present as he could possibly be, and yet, she couldn't really feel him the way she wanted to feel him. Maybe, he didn't always blank out. Maybe, she sometimes shut him out.

Kevin tugged on her hand. "What is it? You look sad."

"I'm okay. I'm just trying to stop being so afraid of the future." She smiled and grabbed her menu with her free hand. "But let's forget about all of it for now. I'm hungry."

"Are you sure?"

She sighed. "I think I need some food, that's all."

Kevin's smile broadened into a grin. "You don't know how happy I am to hear that."

Twenty-Two

Carol stood on the private balcony of her hotel room, staring out at the Arc de Triomphe. The majestic monument was commissioned by Napoleon after one of his victorious battles. Its size was staggering, so big that a World War One pilot once flew his biplane through the arch. Its magnificence sent a small thrill through Carol's body as she let it etch itself into her memory. She was leaving that day, and she didn't want to forget any part of her trip.

"I can't believe that we're already going home. This week went by so quickly," she said as she closed the balcony doors and turned to Kevin.

He was gathering up an armful of his clothes from the closet. "It's been great, but I know you miss Ariel and Chicago just as much as I do."

"I do miss our baby, terribly, but—" She grabbed a tissue in case she got weepy. Tears were becoming a regular occurrence, one that she hated but couldn't stop.

Kevin threw his clothes on the bed and came over.

"What's going on? Aren't you excited about going home?"

"I guess I'm scared that when we get back we'll be our old selves." She stared up at him, searching his eyes for the wonderful spark of connection they'd established. Paris had been a perfect place to rediscover how much they loved each other. "It happens a lot after a vacation. People get busy with their lives and routines again, and you know—"

"I guess habits are hard to break."

She watched his eyes lose the spark that had been there a moment before. "Kevin, am I already losing you?"

112

"No, I was just thinking about what you said. I wondered when I started tuning the important stuff out. Maybe it was in college when I played football. It was great until I got some injuries and was off the team. Then I had to watch games instead of being a part of the action."

"That must have been hard. From what Peggy said you were really a good player."

"Yeah, it was tough, but what can you do?"

She sat down on the bed. Staring at the tissue in her hand, she knew it was time to do some soul searching too. "I guess I sort of retreated from some parts of life. Living alone seemed best after my running away disaster as a teenager and a short marital fiasco."

Kevin nodded. "I dated a few women. It never amounted to much, except for some painful times when the gal I was dating pointed out my shortcomings."

"I didn't date. I didn't think I wanted or needed any more relationships. I was happy enough until—"

"Until we met," he said in a playful tone.

She giggled. "Actually, I met Arel first, online, remember? He was so nice. I had a crush on him."

Kevin smiled as he sat down next to her and took her hand. "Then we got together, and Arel was toast."

She blushed. "Yes, I think I fell in love with you as soon as I saw you."

"Now I've made you feel like the other women I went out with. You see me as a guy with a ton of faults."

"No, don't say that. It makes me feel terrible."

He hesitated. "Hey, I just had another thought. People revert to old habits. Maybe, that's what happened to us. As you settled into the daily routine of life, you began to think you'd be safer if you were on your own again. As for me, I'm repeating my past too, feeling like I'm a failure around you."

Carol thought about her worries and how she'd handled them when she lived alone. "Goodness, you might be right. I guess I did feel more in control before we met. But I don't want it to be that way. I want to be with you."

"And you're everything to me, Carol."

"So what do we do?"

113

Kevin pulled her close. "Let's keep trying. Let's promise each other that we'll stick it out."

She wanted to take him up on the promise, but what did promises really mean? She'd already pledged to stay with him "til death we do part." That promise went out the window when her fears took hold. That was the problem. Her fear had a way of blotting out everything else. "I'll do my best."

Kevin pulled back and stared at her. "Don't you believe in us?"

"I don't know if I even believe in me. Here I am, a wife and a mother, but sometimes I don't feel very grown up at all."

Twenty-Three

Tim walked quickly across his yard and onto Arel's property. It was early Saturday morning, and Peggy was in bed, still sleeping. Tim hoped she wouldn't miss him, that he could get back before she woke up. He didn't want to tell her about his nightmare. He had someone else in mind as he pounded on Arel's door. "Open up, Arel, please."

As he stood back, waiting, he noticed that his fist was shaky. In fact, his whole body felt strange.

It has something to do with that nightmare I had.

He'd tried to deal with the terrifying dream on his own, but the vivid images wouldn't go away. He knew they were connected to Arel. The nightmares started shortly after Arel had healed the gash on his head.

He rang the bell a couple of more times.

What's going on with me?

Tim knew he rarely let his emotions take over. He was the steady one in the group. Arel could faint over a couple drops of blood. Kevin could get angry and try to fight his way out of a problem. Through it all, Tim had to remain calm. Yet, as he waited at the door, he didn't feel like himself. He felt like the guy in the dream, the person who was fighting and screaming in the midst of a mob.

He reached for the bell again as the door opened. Michael stared out at him with questioning eyes.

"Tim, is there—"

Michael wasn't allowed to finish his sentence.

"Who is it, Michael?" Arel asked sleepily as he pushed the taller man aside. As soon as he locked on to Tim's face, his eyes widened in panic. "Is it the baby? Is Peggy okay?"

115

Seeing Arel panic so quickly, Tim knew he'd made a mistake coming over. "They're fine."

Arel continued to stare at him. "Something's wrong. You look as white as a sheet."

"Is there anything I can do?" Michael asked from his delegated spot behind Arel.

"It's stupid, but I had this dream—"

"A dream? That's all?" Arel's face sagged with relief. "I'm almost an expert on the damn things. Come in."

Tim proceeded into the foyer. As he tried to steady his nerves, he noticed that Arel had turned to Michael. He was making little shooing gestures in Michael's direction.

"I got this, Michael," Arel said. "No need to get involved."

Michael shrugged. "If you—"

"We're fine," Arel insisted. His tone was tinged with the slightest bit of annoyance.

As Michael retreated, Tim called out an apology. "Sorry for the disturbance."

Arel offered Tim a reassuring smile and directed him into the living room. "Michael doesn't understand these things like I do. As I said before, dreams are my specialty."

"Glad to hear somebody's got a handle on the damn things," Tim said. With Arel looking so confidant and serene, he was starting to feel a little better.

When they were seated, Arel settled back, continuing to display a poised manner in spite of his appearance. His hair was uncombed, with dark, unruly curls hanging over his brow. His beard, normally well groomed, was dark and in need of tending. It gave him the slightly haunted look of a silent film star.

"Again, I'm sorry to disturb you like this," Tim began.

Arel smiled. "Just tell me what's bothering you."

"We both know that Peggy is a great one for having some bad dreams, but mine always fade when I wake up. That's changed." Tim looked up and took a much needed breath. "The night after my accident, I started having nightmares that I couldn't shake. Maybe I bounced my head on the dresser harder than I thought." He clasped his hands in silence.

"Go on."

116

"I'm grateful for what you did, but I think you might have something to do with what's happening. In fact, I think you were one of the people in the nightmare."

"Really?"

"Remember when we all first met and Peggy had that horrible dream about the two of you?"

Arel shifted slightly and crossed his arms. "The one about being burned at the stake?"

"Yes, that's the one. Now I'm having it. Only in my version, I feel like I'm there too."

Arel looked away without commenting. Instead, he sat back again, and made little circles on the arm of the sofa with his index finger.

"What should I do? Any suggestions? You said something about being a dream expert."

"Let it go," Arel replied softly. "You don't realize it, but you're giving the dream too much power."

Tim hunched his shoulders. "I'm not trying to give it anything. But I wake up shaking and quaking."

"Even if your dream was a recall of a past life that we all shared—"

"Is that what you think it is? Are you serious?"

Arel glanced over at Tim and quickly looked away. His voice had an edgy quality when he spoke. "Tim, listen to me. Don't let yourself get caught up in something that has no relevance in your life."

"I agree. I've tried to tell myself it was just a nightmare, but it won't go away. Besides, if there was any truth to what I've dreamed, it was a hell of a life, one that must have been important."

Arel stood up. "I was wrong about what I said. I was foolish telling you that I'm a dream expert. Just try to forget the nightmare."

"What if I can't?" Tim stood up too, glaring back. "I've been there for you, remember New York? I don't understand why you have this attitude. I just need a little help with this fear that's eating at me."

Tim's words seemed to affect Arel deeply. When Arel looked back this time, his eyes were soft and gracious. "You've been the best of friends. Thank you." He put his hand on Tim's shoulder. "And believe me, I want to help you."

Arel's touch was comforting and warm, just like it had been on the evening of Tim's accident. On that occasion, Arel had healed Tim's head wound. Perhaps now, Arel could dispel his fears. Instead, the warmth Tim was enjoying suddenly shifted. The feeling of well-being escalated into an overpowering fiery sensation. At the same time, Tim was thrown back into his nightmare. In an instant, he felt like his whole world was going up in flames.

Arel released him immediately and jerked back, as if he felt the fire too. Happily, he took the nightmare with him. As soon as Arel broke their connection, Tim felt his head clear and his body relax. He didn't feel shaky or afraid anymore.

"That was strange," Tim whispered. In the blink of an eye, the vivid scenes from his dream began to fade. The mob that had been so frightening all disappeared. The screams of their victims went quiet. When he looked up, he knew Arel had worked his magic a second time.

There was only one problem. Arel looked weird. He was staring straight ahead, like some catatonic inmate in a mental institution. Tim snapped his fingers a couple of times, trying to bring Arel back from wherever he'd gone. It didn't work. That's when Tim knew the magician needed help. He called for Michael, the person who usually stayed behind the curtain when things were happening. But Tim suspected that the quiet man had hidden talents. "Michael, the dream expert needs you!"

* * *

Arel was spirited away so fast, he was completely disoriented when the world stopped spinning. It took a moment to understand where he was. He cringed when he realized that he was standing in the middle of a mob. He was surrounded by blazing torches and unwashed faces. Features were distorted with anger and rage. A savage, unforgiving energy battered his body and filled him with dread.

Am I visiting Hades?

As soon as Arel asked the question, he remembered Tim's nightmare.

I'm in his dream!

118

Or was he? Perhaps the place he was visiting wasn't a dream. What if he'd gone back in time? He'd done it before.

No matter what, it's not my reality.

Arel tried to intend himself back to his own time. He started repeating Dorothy's line from the Wizard of Oz. "I want to go home. I want to go home."

His frantic mumbling was lost to the yelling and howls of the crowd. Their shouts rose in a crescendo of malice as a young man forced his way through the ragged throngs. As soon as Arel saw the man, he recognized him. It was Tim, but he looked different. This version was younger, and he had a less robust frame. Noting the man's frantic attitude, Arel froze. A flood of memories followed.

In a past life, Tim's name was Oswyn, and we were best friends.

Arel instantly forgot about going home. His focus was on Oswyn. The man's face was ashen and his expression was one of absolute despair. Arel felt it too. He knew why Oswyn was trying to get to the center of the square, but he still couldn't move.

No! I can't go through this again!

Arel had already relived this scene himself. He knew what was coming. So did Oswyn. The man screamed out at the cheering onlookers who waited for two people to be burned. The young woman who had been condemned was Oswyn's betrothed. The man next to her was Oswyn's best friend. Both people would soon be engulfed in flames.

"You're all murderers!" Oswyn shrieked.

Oswyn's protests were met with instant reprisal. The irate multitude immediately gathered up loose stones from the street. They attacked him with the rocks and with demeaning insults and hateful curses. Oswyn held up his hands, trying to defend himself, but he was attacked from every angle. The stones did their job, battering his head and body. He soon went down, helpless to protect himself.

Outraged by Oswyn's plight, Arel broke loose from his paralysis. He rushed to where Oswyn had fallen. He tried to shield him, but the shower of rock went through his ghostly body, finding its intended target. Bloodied and losing consciousness, Oswyn dragged himself forward. He wouldn't give up.

Arel could feel Oswyn's suffering, his utter torment. Oswyn loved his betrothed with all his heart. Her brother was like a member of Oswyn's family. Soon both of them were going to be set on fire.

There was nothing Oswyn could do to stay the execution, to stop the unthinkable. His anguish and grief encircled him like a great, black cloud of absolute helplessness.

Arel tried to get through to his friend. "You have to let go of this nightmare!"

But the black despair that surrounded Oswyn was too dense. His wretched state was suffocating the life out of him. Arel's only desire was to save Oswyn from his despair. That's when he felt a potent rush. It was a heady rapture that invaded his mind and spread throughout every particle of what he knew himself to be. A powerful force within him began to draw off Oswyn's despair. Massive amounts of the black energy were absorbed in mere seconds. Swirling inside of him, it began to extinguish his own light. But Arel was so caught up by the need to aid his friend, he ignored what was happening.

"Arel! You have to stop!" A stern command emanated from the heavens.

Arel didn't heed the warning at first. As his power was poisoned by what he was taking in, he was losing strength. He was becoming so weak that all he could do was hover over Oswyn protectively.

"Arel! Look at me!"

The voice rang out again, and Arel had enough strength left to glance upward. The night sky was cold and black, but a singular, dazzling star hovered above him. The light from the orb targeted him, like a bright spotlight on a black ocean of doom. He squinted back, unable to look at it for very long. As he shielded his eyes, the name, Michael, weaved in and out of his frenzied mind. He turned to Oswyn, but his friend was still unconscious. Arel was losing consciousness too. Everything was fading into a black void. That's when a second voice called out to him.

"Dammit Arel, you're not going down this easy."

"William?" The sound of the man's voice was an instant slap to Arel's ghostly face.

"Yes, William, the person you threw out of heaven!"

Arel's heavy burden of guilt made him claw his way back from oblivion, to gather up a few shreds of awareness so that he could respond. "You know I'm sorry—"

"I don't want your apology!"

Arel began to tremble. William's voice was so loud, so filled with wrath that it froze the mob scene where Arel was groveling on hands and knees. Everyone around him stopped moving. Even the fires from their torches went into a sort of freeze frame. Arel was the only thing that was animated. "If you want to punish me, Will, you should leave me here, with these ignorant monsters."

"And let you forget what you did to me?" A great laughter shook the still heavens and the frozen medieval scene. "No, you're not going anywhere but back to your body! And you're going back there now!"

William's words were enough to send Arel hurdling through space and time. He felt himself slam into his physical form with so much force that he woke up from the horrific, dream scene.

* * *

When he opened his eyes, Arel was staring at Tim. Or was it Oswyn? Whoever it was, the man was trying to get his attention.

"Arel, are you okay? You had Michael and I worried. You fainted, and we couldn't wake you up."

A very bright light moved into Arel's line of vision and spoke to Tim. "Arel needs to rest."

Tim smiled at Arel. "Maybe Michael's right, Arel. You look like you saw a ghost. You probably need to sleep it off."

Arel's teeth were chattering as he stared at Tim. He was so cold. "I'm sorry I couldn't help with the dream."

"It's okay. I feel a lot better," Tim said as he backed away. "Excuse me, I have to get back to Peggy before she wakes up."

Arel squinted as Tim walked to the foyer and let himself out. After he was gone, Arel tried looking at the blinding light again. "Michael? What's going on? Why are you so bright?"

"Close your eyes and relax for a moment, then open them. You need to settle into your body properly."

Arel did as he was told. When he opened his eyes this time, Michael was his usual self. "Do you know that you almost blinded me when I was in that nightmare?"

"Maybe you shouldn't think about what you just experienced."

Arel sat up, still a little woozy, and tried to calm himself in spite of his chills. "It was just a dream, right?"

121

Michael grabbed a wool throw from a recliner, put it over Arel, and tucked the blanket around his legs. "Yes and no."

Arel stared back, happy for the warmth, but concerned. He knew he'd lost control of himself again. "I don't understand. Please explain what happened to me."

"You projected your energy body into a dream state, and that dream state had validity. In a way, you left this world for a short time. That's one reason why your body suffered."

"But dreams and reality are different, right?"

Michael smiled patiently. "Everything is energy. In that respect, everything is real. When a person becomes very powerful, they have a great potential to alter circumstances no matter what form it takes."

Arel crossed his arms. "Like when I invaded William's experience on the other side."

"Exactly."

"Did I go back in time just now?"

Michael hesitated. "Reality is very fluid. Think of the past, present and future and then imagine that they're all part of an ocean of infinite energy and possibility. Every individual's every thought and every action affects that ocean and what's contained within it."

"Was that a yes or a no?"

"Sorry, I wasn't trying to confuse you."

Arel eyed him reproachfully. Michael was clearly a repository for universal knowledge. Unfortunately, Arel's repository was more like a children's library. When Michael explained one of his concepts, Arel needed a copy of "An Angel's Wisdom for Dummies" guide.

Michael's gaze drifted, as if he was contemplating the merits of such a book.

Arel cleared his throat, bringing Michael's lagging attention back from his ethereal wanderings. "I usually heat up when I pull in negative energy. So why am I so cold?"

"When you left your body and your etheric counterpart became lost in a so called dream, the connection to your normal reality and to your body was weakened. If you hadn't returned to your physical vessel when you did, the connection was in danger of being severed."

"Fat chance with William checking up on me."

"Yes, you ignored me, but you did pay attention to him."

"I guess I should be grateful. I tossed him out of some wispy paradise, and he returned the favor by saving me from hell."

"I'm afraid his motives aren't as pure as they could be."

Arel pushed the cover off of his upper body. His temperature was rising very fast as he thought about his savior. "William wants me dead, but he also wants to be the one arranging my demise. He's getting more vindictive as the days go by."

Michael nodded. "On the other hand, I do have good news about Tim. He won't be having that dream anymore."

"Really?"

"When he was dying in that other life and you were there to comfort him, he felt your kindness and concern. You gave him hope that the world wasn't totally cruel and uncaring."

Arel's spirits soared a notch. "You're saying that I did something good for a change."

"Believe in yourself. Believe that you can have what you've been looking for from the very beginning, the freedom to be who you really are."

"Who am I?"

"Do you really want to have that conversation now?"

"Why wouldn't I?"

Michael beamed back a most heavenly, but mischievous grin. "Where shall we start?"

"Nevermind." Arel had already asked for Michael's blood and gone through hell trying to cope. Did he really want to open up another, potentially catastrophic can of worms? "Right now, I can still function for the most part. Let's keep it that way."

Twenty-Four

William woke up with a start. Rubbing at his eyes, he noticed how fast his heart was beating. It seemed appropriate. He'd just had the most intense dream of his life. It might have been the product of wishful thinking, but no matter what, it was an exhilarating experience. In the dream, he'd encountered a very weak and pathetic Arel. The man who recently acted like some kind of powerful deity, was so feeble in the dreamscape that he was ready to check out. William didn't let that happen. Even if it was just a dream, William was able to call the shots.

What a glorious feeling it was to thwart the bastard.

William stretched, threw back the covers and practically leapt out of bed. It had been a long time since he'd felt so energized. And he was finally enjoying some other bonuses after surviving Arel's Madness. He'd been hyper sensitive to the sun for almost a century. Now, he was able to bask in its warmth again. It had taken a little time to get used to the idea, but he was looking forward to getting out that morning. He wanted to pick up various plant care supplies for the experiments that he was planning. His current studies were based on a statement that Arel had made. Arel claimed they both had powerful abilities. William hadn't believed Arel in the beginning, but now he wasn't so sure. Arel had demonstrated god-like powers. Did William have them too?

I certainly possessed them in that dream!

He thought about Arel's face when the man found out he was William's pawn.

Was that a look of surprise, Arel? Even shock?

As soon as William realized his mind was open to Arel, he quickly shielded his thoughts. He had to be careful not to let Arel snoop around in his head. It was a disturbing feeling to know that

Arel had that capability. On the other hand, William could access Arel's thoughts too as long as Arel wasn't hiding them away in that steel vault enclosure he kept around himself most of the time.

He has an advantage. He's stayed hidden away for most of his life. He's an expert when it comes to the concept of fortification.

William paused, realizing that he was thinking more and more about Arel and how contemptible he was. It wasn't a healthy sign. Becoming obsessed with someone or something outside of himself was a weakness. It was true that he had been abused by Arel, but he wouldn't allow Arel's actions to define who he was. He had to rebuild his self-confidence. He had to return to his previous self-contained state of mind. As he dressed and let himself out of his front door, he continued to enjoy the idea of being a totally, independent man.

No ties, just me again.

The thought put an extra zip in his step as he made his way down the street. He was getting in shape and feeling physically sound. He also felt a lot better about his appearance. With his sandy-brown hair styled short and spiky, it gave his face, with its high cheek bones, a dashing, sophisticated look.

My charisma is coming back too. I'm sure of it.

He immediately tested out his charm on a woman he was passing. He gave her the slightest glance, just enough to let her get the feel of him. She was tall and slender and beautiful. Her red hair lifted off her shoulders as she returned a friendly smile. Inwardly he smiled too, content that his magnetism was working. He quickly forgot the woman herself. He wasn't interested.

But what about Annabel?

He bristled at the thought that he found Annabel enticing. Perhaps, he even found her more than desirable. The deadly 'R' word crossed his mind, but he quickly doused any ideas about a relationship.

Why do I keep her around? I should fire her, send her on her way once and for all! I need to free myself of two mistakes, Arel and Annabel.

He tried to do just that with Annabel. Every day, he vowed to accomplish the simple task. The afternoon before, he'd opened his mouth and pointed to the door. Annabel stared back, waiting patiently for what he had to say. When he was finally able to speak, he asked her to go to the corner to buy a newspaper. It was such a lame request. He flushed red with embarrassment when Annabel went to the side table and fetched the paper he'd been reading earlier. Her smile was playful when she handed it to him. She even called him a forgetful goose.

He should have been furious with himself for being so weak, to allow such an indiscretion. Instead, he smiled back, caught up in the moment and in her sparkling, emerald eyes. There was no malice in them. They were pure and innocent of any ill humor. Afterwards, as he watched her leave the room, he had visions of being with her, of making love in a way that he'd never done before.

Stop it! You can't let yourself care about someone again. You can't let another person into your life.

The thought was followed by something that stirred in his gut. This feeling was cold and callous.

When the time comes, you'll have to really get rid of her, just like the one you thought of as your brother.

He brought himself back to Arel, this time without any emotion. His archenemy was simply a project that needed completion.

Concentrate on business, and soon you'll be free again, with no complications.

Rolphe was visiting London in a few weeks. A meeting was in the works. He didn't know if he could trust Rolphe, but hopefully, the man would become a powerful ally. Together, they could devise a plan that would put an end to the person who could threaten William so easily.

126

Twenty-Five

Paris lay under a stormy night sky as Rolphe sat on his couch and gazed out his living room window. He sipped his supper thoughtfully and leaned back. With his tall, muscular body, he needed an over-sized sofa to feel comfortable. But he couldn't find any comfort when he thought about meeting William.

Why couldn't he stay hidden and leave me be?

Before William contacted him, Rolphe's life was fairly normal. He was involved with a special woman, and he enjoyed painting and playing the piano. As for imbibing a little blood here or there, he didn't let others in on that dark secret. Besides, he purchased his blood supply. He hadn't taken it from the source in many years.

But William's existence proved Rolphe wasn't normal. In his younger days, he'd been a cold-blooded killer. Now he would have to kill again. At first, he dismissed the deed. Getting rid of William, the only one who shared his secret, seemed prudent. He didn't want anyone knowing the truth or exposing him. He needed certain parts of his past to stay hidden, even from himself. But the fact that he was going to kill again meant he'd also have to face what he was. But he wouldn't face it now.

He set his glass on the coffee table, stood up, and walked over to his piano. The ebony, Bösendorfer grand took up a good part of the living area. But he didn't regret its size. The beautiful instrument was an elegant tribute to craftsmanship. Its clean, mellow tones were a delight to his ear.

He took his seat, thinking about what to play. As he pondered his choices, he needed to steer himself towards something good and decent. Family came to mind, and his large, powerful hands took on a life of their own. He opened himself to memories that had to do with love. His hands hovered over the keyboard, trembling with anticipation as he allowed a different past to resurrect itself. There was a gene in him, a unit of heredity that held him fast to ancestors who couldn't deny their feelings, who wept and laughed with every twist and turn of daily life. Thoughts about his family brought the gene alive in every cell in his body.

When his fingers came to rest on the keys, his touch was light and teasing as he began Debussy's *Serenade for the Doll*. It was part of the *Children's Corner Suite*, written for Debussy's young daughter. There was a playful but tender quality to the notes that made him smile. The music prompted feelings of youth and how happy children could be. He knew that the composer and he shared a common love for their families.

For me, there was nothing more precious than my little ones.

He tried to ignore the tightness in his chest as a door from the past swung open, revealing a life far removed from the present. A plump, smiling wife and adorable children were gathered in their small dwelling. They were waiting for him to return home from the fields where he'd been working all day. It was a nightly ritual. He'd walk through the door, and the children would come running. His wife would announce that she'd made fresh bread and soup. How proud he was in those days as he scooped up his little boys and held them tight. Their laughter filled the air with joy as they hugged him back.

Back then, I didn't live alone with an aging tomcat.

As if he knew that Rolphe was thinking about him, Satan came traipsing in. The big tom cat strutted across the carpet, letting out a single meow as he passed by Rolphe. He'd been out all evening. Now, he looked ready for his soft cushion.

Yes, yes, I care about you, old friend, but once, long ago, I had a whole family to love.

His hands paused over the keys as he looked around the flat. It was so quiet. Maybe that's why he needed his piano. He had to drown out the silence around him. He needed his happy boys to be in his arms again.

They made me feel so proud.

His sons loved to watch him play the balalaika. Their eyes were bright with desire, always eager to learn what he could teach them. They inspired him to make plans for the future. He worked hard and saved up to give them a better life than he'd had. His daily existence was simple and good. It took years, but eventually he'd even been able to put the horrors of being a soldier and killing behind him.

But a man's plans are like dust in the wind.

As he considered the depressing statement, he couldn't finish playing the lively notes of Debussy's piece. There was too much sadness wanting to be expressed. His ancestral gene could quickly become a curse when his mood shifted. He began to play Beethoven's *Moonlight Sonata*. Its melody was haunting and filled with a deep melancholy that matched his sudden grief. His family was long gone, victims of a cholera epidemic that swept through their village. But ghostly visions of their passing made him grit his teeth. He'd sat for long hours by his wife's bed, watching helplessly as she took her last breaths. She was the first to die. As the days passed, each child lay in his arms and died too. Only Rolphe was spared.

Death refused to give me the release I yearned for.

As his hands moved effortlessly over the keys, the composition became a homage to those he'd loved. His flawless performance created a mood of beauty and regret. At the end of the first movement, he paused. His eyes grew dark as he cursed the memories.

"God is strange, Satan. He took everything from me. He left me with nothing but pain. Perhaps it was my punishment. I tried to forget how many I killed as a soldier, but the truth was always there, a burden I couldn't escape no matter how much I thought I could leave it behind."

He looked down at the keys and prepared himself for what was coming next. He always skipped the sonata's second movement and went for the third.

"You're lucky not to know the pain of being human. It becomes so unbearable you do things you never thought you'd do."

Satan blinked back at him with a steady, easy gaze. Sometimes the animal's blameless nature was soothing. But it didn't help this time.

How had Rolphe strayed so far from common decency? How did he allow himself to become so cold and uncaring? He didn't have any answers. He could only attack the keyboard again. His fingers flew over the keys in a way that bordered on frenzy. Passion and ferocity were used to still his thoughts about what happened after his family died. But facts were facts.

He became a vagabond, roaming from place to place, drinking and fighting constantly. There was no humor left, only rage and bitterness. He sank deeper and deeper into despair.

Until I met Chessa.

He still wondered if the gypsy woman was a demon or friend. Certainly there was no innocence in her. But there was beauty. Long, thick, raven-black hair. Black eyes. A sensuous body. She drew men to her easily with a look or a gesture. He'd been drawn in too.

I was a fool who didn't take charge of my life. Then Chessa gave me a new life.

He stopped playing, stood up and covered the keys. Again, his hands trembled, but he paid them no heed. He had to get out of the quiet apartment and get some air. He had to find a way to sidetrack his mind and forget the woman who made him into something lethal and cold. He didn't have the strength to face her memory, not yet.

Twenty-Six

Peggy stared out the living room window, watching Tim pull the car out of the driveway. She gave him a final wave and a smile when he looked her way. Once the car started down the street, she left her post and hurriedly ran to the kitchen. Carol was waiting for her there.

"Isn't this fun? Our guys are off to their first swim class for daddies and babies," she said as she went to the stove and grabbed the kettle. "We're so lucky to have such great husbands."

She poured hot water into the pretty, dragonfly tea pot, splashing the water over the jasmine tea leaves that rested in the strainer. "And now that they're gone, we can finally catch up. You've been home for a while, and we haven't had time to really discuss Paris."

A moment of silence followed, making Peggy look up. Carol was frowning. Peggy quickly put the kettle back on the stove and sat down. "Oh no, don't tell me that it was a flop. I thought you and Kevin looked happy when you picked up little Ariel."

"Paris was wonderful," Carol sighed.

"It was? I don't understand."

"I don't either."

"Did Kevin do something again? If he did, I'll sit him down, once and for—"

"No, it's not Kevin." Carol dropped her gaze. "I'm the one with the problem. In fact, I'm a little embarrassed, but I've made an appointment to see someone."

"That's not something to be embarrassed about. It's a good thing." Peggy began to straighten her silverware and napkin. "Is it something you want to talk about?"

131

"I don't know. I feel like I've been holding my breath ever since I came home. Paris was so magical. Kevin and I both felt like we were starting over. But he said something while we were there—"

"Of course he did. The big dope always puts his foot—"

"Peggy, please, why do you always assume Kevin is at fault? Actually, he made a very appropriate observation."

"Really? Kevin?"

"Yes, your brother doesn't say a lot, but sometimes he's very understanding."

Peggy reached out for the teapot and poured a generous amount of tea into each of their cups. "I suppose you're right. I'm just being me, always wanting you two to be happy. I don't want anything to spoil what you have."

"That's why I'm getting some help. I feel like I am going to spoil everything."

She handed a cup to Carol. "So what did Kevin say?"

"He pointed out that both of us seem to have reverted back to being the way we were when we were single. For me, that means that I don't trust being with someone."

"You don't trust Kevin?"

Carol didn't answer. Instead, she pushed back from the table, stood up and went to the back door, staring out with glassy eyes. After a moment, she took a tissue from her pocket and dabbed away a stray tear. "Kevin is a good man. That's why I think it's me. Or maybe it's life. I don't know. I just don't want to get hurt again."

"But isn't that kind of normal? We've all been hurt. We all feel we have to protect ourselves at times."

"But you don't all feel scared all the time. I see myself watching Kevin, tallying up every possible infraction, anything that might make me feel insecure. He doesn't even have to do anything wrong. If he watches TV for more than an hour, I take it personally and get angry. I don't want to live like that."

"Oh, you poor thing." Peggy got up and walked over to where Carol was standing. "You're having a really rough time, aren't you?"

Carol turned to face her. She kept wiping away her tears, but they were quickly replaced by new ones. "Can't you see? I'm not fit to be a wife or mother," she sobbed out.

"That's not true, Carol. You're a great mother and a—"

132

A tapping noise at the door interrupted Peggy's words of comfort, making her pause and look up. "It's Arel!"

"It is?" Carol sniffled in a sob and turned to answer the door. "Arel, what are you doing here?"

Arel's face reddened as soon as he saw her. "I . . . uh . . . wanted to retrieve that ratchet set that Tim borrowed. Carey needs it to work on his bike."

Peggy gestured him forward. She didn't know how to help Carol, but maybe Arel did. Tim sometimes joked about Arel being the 'miracle man.' After visiting Arel, Tim's nightmares were gone. "Come in. I'm glad you're here."

Arel backed up a step. "No, I've come at a bad time. I better go."

Carol reached out to him. "Please, Arel, I don't know what to do."

* * *

As soon as Arel stepped inside Peggy's kitchen, he felt Carol's mood. It was like a desolate island of quicksand, just waiting to swallow him up. But he couldn't resist her plea for help. In fact, he soon found himself hugging her and telling her that everything was going to be okay. He'd said that to her before, and he'd been wrong. This time, he slipped in another ridiculous promise. "Somehow we'll figure this out, okay?"

Carol seemed doubtful. "How? I'm on an emotional roller coaster."

When Carol buried her tear-stained face in his shoulder, Arel instantly tuned into her energy. Its fluttery feeling reminded him of a bird he'd once rescued after it fell out of its nest. After a day of nurturing, it was able to fly away. But Carol's unhappy state was clearly an issue that time didn't resolve. Just the opposite. Her emotional wings were getting weaker.

"Let's go sit down. We can talk about it," he said, mustering as much enthusiasm as he could.

Carol pulled away. "No, I should go home, not burden the two of you with my problems."

When it came to Arel's emotional wings, they were ready to soar at the suggestion.

If you think that's best, dear friend, bye-bye!

He immediately chastised himself for such a selfish reaction. He blurted out the last thing he wanted to say. "You can't do that. We're your friends. We're here for you."

"Arel's absolutely right," Peggy added.

Carol gave Peggy a weepy smile and grabbed hold of Arel's hand. "Thank you both so much. I just don't know how to handle all these feelings I have."

"Arel always makes me feel better," Peggy said enthusiastically.

"I don't know about that, Peggy," Arel protested.

"I do," Peggy said as she flashed him a broad smile. "Now, let's do what you suggested. Let's sit down and talk."

Arel nodded helplessly. He knew from experience that talking wouldn't be the first order of business. Instead, Carol would soon flood the area with her tears. And there was no escape at this point. He had to soldier on. Trying to ignore the vise-like grip that Carol had on his fingers, he led her into the living room. After she sat down next to him on the sofa, he went into an automatic mode of comforting. It was a method he'd learned after being around the babies. He patted Carol's back gently and repeatedly. After a few moments, his mind drifted into his own troubled waters. "Believe me, Carol, I know all about feelings and how uncontrollable they can be." After he made the statement, he realized how disparaging his tone sounded when he was supposed to offer something more inspiring.

Carol didn't seem to notice. She was too busy with a litany of her woes. "It's like I keep slipping into a horrible pattern. I try not to go negative, I really do, but somehow I feel like my marriage is going to fall apart." Her statement was followed by more tears.

Arel had never known anyone who could cry as much as Carol. And every time she cried, he felt powerless to say anything useful. So he offered whatever scrap of encouragement he could come up with. "Don't say that. You and Kevin have made it through lots of tough times."

She answered between sobs. "Kevin tries so hard, and yet I'm always saying things to him that are critical. I hate when I do that."

"I'm sure you're being too hard on yourself."

Carol dabbed at her cheeks. "I wish you were right, but when I hear myself, all I can think is that I'm a terrible person."

"No, it's not true," he whispered soothingly. As he patted her back again, he glanced up at Peggy. She'd taken a seat close by.

"Arel's right," Peggy chimed in. "You're just being too hard on yourself."

Arel offered his best smile to reinforce Peggy's statement. "Carol, I've always thought of you as a wonderful person. Remember how we first met online? No one could have been nicer to me. You were always sweet and helpful. And when I let you down by lying, you forgave me and still wanted to be my friend. A terrible person would never do that."

Carol pulled away from him, sniffled and swiped at her nose. "That was easy. But with Kevin . . . I don't know, it's different. He's the person I truly fell in love with, and everything he does seems to matter more. We've talked about things, and he said that I'm just afraid of my past repeating."

Arel reached in his pocket for a clean handkerchief. As he handed it to Carol, he thought about his own past. He thought about Justina and how much he still missed her. "You always hurt the ones you love most." His version of the old saying came out in a whisper.

Carol sniffled again. "Are you saying that you hurt someone you loved?"

Arel let out a deep sigh. "Yes, guilty as charged, but that was a long time ago. I've finally made peace with it all."

Carol started to cry again. "I'm happy for you. I'm happy that you're not going through what I'm going through now."

"Oh, but I am." Arel let out a cynical laugh as William came to mind. "More recently, I've done something unforgivable." He hadn't meant to confess his latest grievous sin. It just came out on its own.

Carol blinked back. "What do you mean?"

Arel didn't want to bring his own troubles into the conversation. On the other hand, Carol needed to know that her low opinion of herself wasn't deserved. She needed to know how low a person could really sink. He felt compelled to expose his wrongdoing. "I literally barred a person from heaven."

"What?" Peggy barked out the question in her loud, boisterous way.

Arel jumped reflexively, but his confession was on a roll. He lowered his head in disgrace. "It's true."

Carol reached out and reversed their positions. She put her arm around him. "Arel, please, I don't believe it. You've always been thoughtful, kind and caring."

"You wouldn't think that if you knew what I did to a friend." He paused. "No, William isn't just a friend, he's like my brother."

"The person you visited in London?" Peggy asked as she got up from her chair. She pulled an overstuffed footstool over and plopped down in front of him. It was her turn to grab his hand.

Arel tugged at his collar, suddenly feeling claustrophobic. He was trapped by his own guilt and the close proximity of the two women. He was also sharing things he knew he shouldn't share. His transgressions were deeply personal. He tried to back track. "I'm sorry. I didn't mean—"

Peggy's hand tightened on his. "Don't try to carry this burden by yourself, sweetie. Tell us what happened."

Arel's throat started to close with a huge lump of regret. He swallowed hard as he went back to that day in London when William lay dying. They were connected in a way that he still didn't understand. He only knew that a bond existed between them that went beyond his reasoning power. "I didn't want to lose him. I was too selfish to let him die."

"Oh, my goodness, how sad," Carol cried out.

"You poor baby," Peggy added. "Did he have one of those living wills with the 'don't resuscitate' clause in it? Did you go against his wishes?"

Arel nodded. "Yes, I guess that's what I did."

"Is he still living on life support?"

Arel visited William in his mind's eye. William was physically well enough, but there was so much anger in his energy field, even rage when it came to what Arel had done. "No, he's been able to get on with his life."

Carol smiled. "Then you did a good thing. You gave your friend another chance."

Arel shook his head. "You don't understand. He wanted to die, to be free, but I've kept him bound to a hellish existence."

Peggy squeezed his hand again. "I thought you said he was okay."

"All I know is that he hates me and will always hate me."

Carol put her head on his shoulder. "You can't blame yourself for loving someone, for wanting to keep them here."

"Hello? Is anybody home?" A voice called out from the kitchen.

Peggy smiled through her tears. "Carey? Is that you? We're in the living room."

"I'm looking for Arel," Carey said as he joined them. As soon as he saw Arel, he hesitated. "Are you okay?"

"I'm fine," Arel said with as much sincerity as he could muster.

Carey took a step forwards. "I just thought I'd check and see if you have that ratchet set."

"I almost forgot." Arel began to disentangle himself from the women, but he could feel his face flushing with shame. He'd shared too much.

"You look a little strange. What happened?" Carey asked.

Peggy stood up and pushed the stool back so that Arel could get past her. "We were just talking." She gave Arel a quick message with her eyes. She was saying, "Your secret is safe with us."

Arel's face turned a deeper red. Why did he get the women involved with something so personal? Carol needed help, yet he was the one who ended up being coddled. He stood up and looked at her. "I'm sorry. You needed a friend's advice and I—"

Carol's face brightened. "No, it's okay." She paused and shrugged. "I feel better."

Arel knew what she was really saying. He'd accomplished his goal. Carol realized she wasn't as bad off as she supposed when she compared herself to him.

Oh my god, I'm totally pathetic.

He gathered up what little dignity he had left as he moved towards the door. "Please call me anytime, Carol."

Carol stood up and gave him the pitiful look one gave to an accident victim. "And you can always talk to me, sweetie. I'm always here for you, okay?"

"Me too," Peggy chimed out loudly. "You have friends you can count on, isn't that right, Carey?"

Carey grabbed Arel's shoulder and shook it good-humoredly. "I'm always here if Arel needs me. But he can be pretty close-mouthed when it comes to sharing."

Peggy and Carol both responded by coming over and hugging Arel again.

"He's starting to open up," Peggy said as her arms tightened around him. "And from now on, we will insist on him being more forthcoming."

Arel's body went rigid as he tried to stop a panic attack. Once Peggy got something in her head, an animal to rescue, a human she could help, she wouldn't let go. Privacy, that cherished quality he needed so desperately, would become a thing of the past if she was worried about him. As he contemplated her future intrusions, he knew the quicksand of hopelessness wasn't around Carol anymore. It was his own quagmire, and he was going down fast.

As he was leaving, Carol seemed to sense his state of despair. She came up and kissed him on the cheek. "I have a good feeling about William. I think that someday, you two will be the best of friends again," she whispered.

Twenty-Seven

A dozen withering plants sat on William's work table. After a week of trying out his psychic powers on the once healthy marigolds, they were all dying.

How could I be so gullible to think that Arel's Madness has an upside?

Arel swore that they both had special gifts that came with the blood that he had passed on to William. He'd demonstrated what he meant by helping to heal William's leg after an accident.

"And look at how wrong he was about me," William hissed out.

Being the scientific type, he decided to test the validity of Arel's statement. Could William positively affect the growth rate of something living? If he could, it would be a small triumph. At least he'd have something special to hold on to after all that he'd lost. He fingered a lifeless leaf on one of the flowers.

I've got powers alright, I've nearly snuffed out these damnable things in record time.

As a boy, William had an affinity for nature. He often spent long hours in the outdoors, observing plants and animals. He scowled as he thought back on those days. It hadn't paid to watch fox kits grow up, not when their future meant his father's hounds would hunt them down and tear them to bits. After a favorite, young fox was destroyed, he stopped visiting the meadows and manor lands. He steeled himself against the world and the ignorant people who populated it.

Then I was given a true gift, Rolphe's gift. How glorious it was to have the power to punish the bastards who have no regard for anything but themselves.

He sucked in a breath. He couldn't let himself think about the past again. He was getting a handle on his emotions, and he planned to keep it that way. Instead, he snapped up his notepad and began to record the details of the failed experiment.

"The flat of control plants are still healthy. However, all the ones that I handled are dying."

As he pressed pen to paper, his eyes kept going back to the marigolds. They reminded him of everything Arel had taken from him. Not that long ago, he wasn't just a normal human. He was extraordinary, a superhuman who never got sick or aged like the rest of the hordes. Now those gifts were gone. As time took its toll, he'd become old and frail. He'd be like one of the fading plants, left with nothing but Arel's empty promises.

"You lied to me, you bloody bastard!" His arm flailed out in a burst of rage, sweeping the flat of marigolds off the work table. It took flight and landed a few feet away, scattering dirt and tiny, dying plants over the tiled floor.

As he swallowed back the sudden flood of anger, the dark part of him that lived in his gut came alive. It first made itself known when he was a boy raging helplessly at his father. Now, its message was becoming louder and more insistent again, filling his mind with the facts. "It's your own fault. You broke the rules. You let yourself care about someone."

He shut his eyes, knowing it was the truth, hating himself for saving Arel's life so long ago.

I should have let you kill yourself!

"William?"

He jerked around and saw Annabel standing on the stairs. "What are you doing here? How did you get in?"

She froze instantly. "William, please, you gave me a key when I was leaving yesterday."

"I did nothing of the sort!" His tone was harsh and accusing, but he didn't care. In that moment, nothing mattered to him but the searing hatred he had for himself, and most of all, for Arel. The bastard not only took away his gifts, but he kept William's soul earthbound with nothing to live for.

Annabel moved cautiously down the stairs and came over. "Do you want me to clean up this mess?"

He forced his fists to relax and tried to slow his breath. After a moment, he was able to speak in a civil tongue. "No, just leave it alone." He retreated a couple of steps. He wasn't a child anymore.

He wouldn't let himself become some idiot who couldn't control himself. "Secondly, your services are no longer required. I'm shutting down the lab."

"But why? I thought you were investigating—"

"There's nothing to investigate! I've failed!" The words came out in a rush as his fists clenched on themselves again. He was trying his best to remain calm, but his anger was too close to the surface. Images swirled in his head. His father laughing at his childish tears over a dead fox. A young Arel hanging on to him, so innocent, just like the fox, wanting William to help him, to give him a reason to go on living. But the worst image was seeing himself smile back at Arel, thinking he'd do this one good deed. He'd care about another, putting their needs above his own. "I made a fatal mistake, and it's come back to have its revenge."

"What do you mean?" Annabel asked. "What mistake are you talking about?"

She started to reach out to him, and he batted her hand away. "It doesn't matter. Just leave."

"Why are you giving up so easily? That's not like you." She stooped down and picked up one of the plants. She cradled it carefully in her hand. "Maybe your approach has been wrong. Plants are sensitive. They need a loving atmosphere, not someone glaring down at them, insisting that they grow or else."

Annabel was right. William hadn't given the experiment a chance to succeed. Every time he looked at the fragile plants, he saw himself and his life. Realistically, he hadn't believed in any gifts. In fact, he seemed hell-bent on proving that Arel was wrong. He'd let his emotions ruin the scientific part of his research.

Annabel paused and met his eyes. "Talk to me. Tell me why you're so angry."

He almost acquiesced, but he caught himself. There was no way he was going to start sharing his feelings. "It's none of your business."

Annabel stepped back. "You're right, it isn't. But you did want me to help you in the lab. Now give me a chance to prove that I'm right, scientifically, that is."

"What are you talking about?"

"I propose a challenge. I'll take these poor things and repot them. You can start with a new flat of plants. In a week, I wager that my plants will be thriving and bigger than yours or the control group's." Her eyes were bright and hopeful as she gazed up at him. "If I'm able to prove a point, it could really help your research." She reached out for his hand again. "Please, William."

He let himself enjoy the feel of her touch for a moment before he pulled away. But she did manage to challenge his logical side. He was curious to see if she was right. "You have one week."

"Good."

"Fine," he said waving her away as he grabbed his notes.

Annabel looked down shyly. "Oh, and one more thing . . . ."

"What?"

"Please stay away from my plants. I'll put them on the other side of the living area."

His frown deepened. "I wouldn't touch them if you paid me. Now get the broom and clean up this mess."

She reached in her pocket and held out a key on a small chain. "First, let me give you this. It's obvious that you don't really want me to have it."

The key dangled between them for a long moment before he reached out for it. He retrieved his hand just as he was about to take back the key. "No, keep it for now. When I'm working, I don't want to be answering the door every five minutes."

* * *

Over the next couple of days, William found Annabel's challenge to be a perfect form of therapy. As he concentrated on the experiment, logic and reason soothed his emotional turmoil. He began to unwind. Halfway into the experiment, he stood over Annabel's tray of plants. She had asked him to stay away, but he had to check on their progress, didn't he? Nearly every one of the repotted marigolds was standing bravely upright.

How is it possible? They were almost dead.

He thought about Annabel's methods. She smiled at her charges, talked sweetly as she stroked their leaves, and even sang children's songs to them. Not exactly scientific, easily measured procedures, but they produced results.

On the other hand, his plants were turning pale and sickly. He steeled himself, wondering if he could follow her example. His gut twisted at the thought. He had no desire to change his attitude. What advantage was there in being considerate to a group of plants?

His question didn't go unanswered. Earlier that day, Annabel supplied him with a reason. She had plied him with a smile and a suggestion. "Who knows what latent ability you possess? You might turn this experiment around in a day if you really try."

He had scowled at her forwardness.

How does she know anything about me?

Yet, Annabel could be very convincing. As William allowed himself to contemplate her statement, he wanted to believe that he did have some hidden power. He could certainly kill a plant faster than he thought possible. Could he turn that ability around? It was a fascinating idea that hooked his curiosity. But first he wanted to understand Annabel's ability.

She's using sound!

He'd read scientific papers on that subject. But sound didn't usually work so quickly. Annabel's plants were responding at an incredible pace.

Surely I could be just as effective.

He went to his computer and did a quick search for an old lullaby he remembered from childhood. A servant used to sing it as she straightened up his nursery. He soon found a version of it on a website. He thought about the old woman who frequently smiled at him while she was singing and felt his shoulders relax. Dark clouds of resentment about his life parted long enough for him to see the error of his ways.

Why have I been behaving so negatively?

The thought was revitalizing. Could he change his attitude and turn things around? He had to make a quick decision about how to proceed. Annabel would be there in an hour. Hovering over his flat of flowers, he cleared his mind and started off with a basic, logical premise. Singing, without any negative energy, seemed to work. He remembered the servant again, how her song affected him in a positive way. She was the one person that could make him smile as a child. He used the memory to get him started with the simple song.

"Lullaby and good night . . ." He began to croon the song and was well into the second verse when he was startled into silence.

"William! You have a lovely singing voice," Annabel called from the top of the stairs.

He jerked around and glared back. Why was she always surprising him? It was a horribly aggravating trait he would discuss with her. But in the moment, he simply stared back.

Annabel didn't seem to notice his frown. Her face was bright with delight as she came down the stairs and offered an explanation for her timing. "I have to leave early, so I thought I'd come in early." She walked over to where he stood. "I mean it. You're wonderful. Your voice is amazing. It's so strong and clear."

"It comes with training. I was forced to take voice lessons as a boy."

"Please, sing something," she begged excitedly.

"No."

"Please, just one little song!"

"It's not going to happen." He walked over to his lab chair with a small sense of conquest. He had never seen this facet of Annabel's personality. He continued to scowl, but inwardly, he enjoyed his ability to make her plead for something. "I was only singing because I decided to try out your theory. After all, I told you that I have a very open mind."

"I see," she said retreating to her plants. "I'm happy to hear that."

Both fell silent after that except for Annabel happily cooing over her marigolds at the far end of the room. He had to remind himself that it was science in action. With that qualification in mind, her display was no longer irritating. He even found himself smiling at times. That's when he came up with a plan. Later that evening, after Annabel left, he executed it. Perched on a lab stool, he gazed down at his plants and sang. He sang every lullaby and happy children's song he could find on the internet.

If this is a singing contest, watch out, Annabel. You have no idea who you're dealing with.

By two in the morning, he realized that he was sounding a little hoarse. He'd hardly used his singing voice in years. Now he'd stressed out his vocal chords. He was also stiff and sleepy from being hunched over the plants. With effort, he stood up, stretched and went to his recliner, hoping to rest for a few minutes before he went to bed.

***

William came out of a deep sleep, leaving behind a meadow he'd been dreaming about. Annabel was there, but she wasn't herself. She was a beautiful enchantress who was going around casting a magical spell on the flowers, making their blooms triple in size. He woke up just as her wand touched him. As he opened his eyes, she was standing next to him, smiling. For a brief instant, she looked like the gorgeous person in his dream. "Where am I?"

"William, wake up. It's getting late, and I have to leave," she said as she gently patted his arm.

He flipped the recliner into an upright position and rubbed the sleep from his eyes. "What time is it?"

"It's two o'clock. I wanted to say 'goodbye' before I left."

"Two in the afternoon?" he grabbed at his throat, realizing that it was sore from all the songs he'd belted out so enthusiastically. At one point, he'd been in full 'Pavarotti' voice.

Annabel nodded. "I did a thorough clean upstairs so that I wouldn't bother you."

"Fine, whatever," he said as he tried to remember when he'd slept as soundly as he had the past night. He was getting up when he thought about his experiment and his plants. With a sudden burst of energy and curiosity, he was on his feet and rushing to the table where he'd put the tray of flowers. After a moment, he looked up at Annabel. "I can't believe it," he whispered. "They've made a complete recovery."

Each tiny marigold stem was straight and reaching out with new energy and vitality.

Annabel hurried over and examined the plants too. "You're right. They suddenly look so green and healthy."

"Bring yours here, and we'll see whose are the biggest?"

"I don't have time. I have to get going."

"What? You're leaving, at a time like this? We should celebrate. I've had a breakthrough."

Annabel frowned. "So this is all about you?"

He gave her a playful smile before he could stop himself. "Alright, we've both had a breakthrough."

She hesitated for only a moment and then smiled too. "You're right. Let's celebrate tonight, say around eight. I'll wear something nice, and we can go out."

"Maybe," he said as he watched her walk to the stairs.

She paused and frowned again. "That's not an answer."

"Fine, come back around eight."

* * *

When William answered the door that evening, he wore what he'd had on earlier in the day, designer slacks and a charcoal, Burberry shirt. He was prepared to tell Annabel that he'd changed his mind. He didn't want to go out. So what if he had an ability to affect the growth of plants. It didn't really change anything. There was nothing to celebrate. But when the door swung open, Annabel surprised him before he had a chance to speak. She hadn't dressed up either. She had on her everyday coat and jeans.

"Sorry, William," she apologized as she let herself into the foyer. "When I got home, I realized I don't have anything really nice." She unbuttoned her coat and handed it to him. "Except for this top."

She wore a soft, emerald green, cashmere sweater. Its cowl neckline draped beautifully over her shoulders and generous breasts. The rich, vibrant shade picked up the amazing color of her eyes.

William stared back mutely, taking her in.

"Windy out tonight," she explained as she took off her scarf and gave it to him.

Like the Annabel he'd seen in the dream, she wore her hair pulled back. A slender section of her thick, auburn locks was gathered at each temple and bound in a braid. It rested on silky, reddish curls that cascaded down her back. The style exposed her face with its delicate, perfect features, satiny white skin, and lovely rosy lips. When she gazed up at him, he realized that recently, he hadn't allowed himself to think about how stunningly gorgeous she was.

He gestured her towards the living room. "Come in," he whispered. His hoarseness was worse than before. "Excuse the way I sound. Singing might have helped the plants, but it's been hell on my voice."

"Well, I'm sure that your plants are grateful," she said as she walked into the living room. She turned around and gave him a pleased look. "You have a fire going, how wonderful. It makes this room so cozy."

"It can be functional. This room doesn't get as warm as the rest of the house." In spite of the fact that they saw each other almost daily, he felt awkward as he showed her to a chair close to the fireplace. Finding Annabel to be so beautiful again was upsetting the strides he'd made in distancing himself from her. "As you can see, I'm not dressed to go out either. Perhaps we could celebrate here."

She held her hands out to the fire. "I'd like that."

"Are you cold?" He walked over to her, hesitated, and took her hands in his own. They were small and slender. Yet he could feel her strength. It radiated out from her, telling him that she could nurture him too, just like she nurtured everything that came into her world. At the same time, there wasn't an ounce of neediness in her bones. For the first time in William's adult life, the tables were turned. He was the needy one. When he looked at her, it wasn't just her beauty that captivated him, it was the glow of confidence that she put off. She never backed down from anything. She met all obstacles head on. He'd once felt like that. Now, it was as if she'd been sent to help him find that part of himself again. An image slipped in. He saw them in bed together. As they lay close, Annabel would sing to him. Like the dying plants, she'd coax him back to life, to the glorious place where he could find his power and prowess again.

His hands gripped hers more firmly as a surge of lust issued from his loins. But it was more than sensuality that took over. He saw himself making love to her, adoring her, gently caressing every inch of her body. The vision was so vivid in detail, so all consuming, he let out a gasp.

"William? Are you alright?" she asked quietly.

He let go of her instantly, knowing that he was crossing some line that shouldn't be crossed. "Excuse me. You're cold. I'll turn up the heat."

He walked quickly from the living area and went straight to the bathroom. He shut the door behind him as his hunger and what felt like the beginning of love, joined forces. But when he looked in the mirror, he was surprised that neither lust nor love was present in his image. Behind his eyes, there was a dark, brutal side of him scowling out.

What the hell are you playing at? You're doing it again. You're letting yourself care about someone. How did that work out with Arel? Didn't he end up robbing you of everything?

The questions originated in the dark, shadowy recesses of his gut. It was the place where the cold, uncaring part of him, a true monster, lived. This monster was filled with all his hatred and disgust for those who were self-serving, the masses of humanity that he despised. This side of him was growing in power, and it didn't suffer from hoarseness. Its voice was strong and insistent. Again, he felt how it connected him to the past, to a time when he was young and filled with uncontained rage at people like his father. He should have listened to it instead of getting mixed up with Arel.

He glared back at the mirror. "But Annabel isn't like Arel. She isn't selfish—"

Listen to yourself! She's got you defending her. But I'm the one who's saved you, the one who made you strong and uncaring so you could survive this heinous planet. Now you're taking her side against me.

Was it true? Was he losing himself to Annabel?

Memories flooded in before he could stop them. When he was a boy in the hunting fields, he heard his fox screaming in pain as the hounds tore it limb from limb. He'd fallen to his knees sobbing, feeling totally weak and powerless in that moment. That's when he'd promised himself that he'd never feel that deeply again. Caring about something or someone gave others power. Even with Arel, he'd never fully exposed his heart. Yet when he thought about Annabel, he felt a deep yearning to do just that. The idea terrified him. "No, I'm in control!"

The husky voice began to laugh.

Sure you are. That's why Arel could snatch you from heaven's gate. Next, Annabel will snatch away your life here in this world. You'll be some sniveling love lost boy again.

William shut his eyes, trying desperately to find some clarity. But his first thought was about Arel refusing to listen to him, betraying him over and over. What would Annabel end up demanding from him? Sure she seemed perfect now, but that was what love did. When it took hold of a person, that person only saw what they wanted to see.

148

He clenched his fists. "I'll send her away, permanently. I can do it, I promise."

Why are you pleading with me? You and I are the same. Why are you so scared? Could it be that you're lying to yourself?

He opened his eyes and looked in the mirror again. For a brief moment, he saw the innocent child he'd once been. Did he want to go back to being that boy? Did he want his heart ripped out again?

He knew he couldn't do it. He couldn't ever be that vulnerable again as all the pain he'd suffered resurrected itself, punishing him, reminding him of the agony he'd endured when he was naïve about life.

Prove that you are in control, that you can take back what little you have left of your life. Annabel is a test! Destroy her and destroy what she represents.

It was such a dark thought and yet, hadn't William found it easy to kill people in the past? He was planning, with Rolphe's help, to kill Arel. So why was Annabel any different?

The answer came through loud and clear.

The only difference with her is that she represents what's weak and wanting in you! Now stop stalling and get rid of her!

The order made William's knees go so weak that he had to hang on to the sink. Yet he couldn't fight what was stirring within him. It started to take on a life of its own. Fashioned from all his fear and rage, it began to move, twisting and turning in his bowels like a viper coiling itself into a striking pose, needing to use its venom to destroy Annabel.

In an airless bog of cold indifference, it took over his body and directed its actions. He could barely breathe as his hand opened one of the vanity drawers. A switchblade was hidden there. He slowly retrieved it from its secreted place.

As he moved towards the door, a flash of Annabel's blameless face made him pause. He almost called out to her, to warn her off, but his voice was hoarse and wanting as the wrathful, black viper rose up within and squeezed the air from his lungs.

Throwing open the door, he couldn't stop the determined forward movement of his legs as they stumbled out into the hall and made their way to the living room. When he saw Annabel, so pretty and unaware, sitting calmly on the rug by the fireplace, he felt like he was split in two. There was the butcher who enjoyed the power to exterminate at will, who would never bow to anything or anybody.

There was also the man that William was becoming, who was learning to sing again, who recognized that there might be room for one other person in his life. That part of him wasn't nice or even civil towards most of his fellow men, but it did have a very definite desire to protect Annabel.

But regardless of that part, his hand clutched the knife as he came towards her. It was being dictated to by the murderer who knew only one way to express itself. It needed to kill whatever got in its way. And it wouldn't stop until it eradicated the woman who tempted William with her beauty and her beguiling ways.

Too late, Annabel turned to look up at William. With the knife held high to stab her with a killing force, he stood over her.

"William!" she called out. "My William."

As if she didn't see the knife, there was no fear in her voice. When she said his name, she made it sound like a holy word. She filled it with dignity and its true meaning, resolute protector.

As the butcher in him brought the knife down with a horrible vengeance, the man named William became her shield. He guided the blade away from Annabel and into his own body. He plunged it into his gut, targeting the beast that killed without remorse.

The weapon went deep and found its mark. It pierced the monstrous creature, wounding it mortally. And even though William could only gasp in pain as his body felt the weapon enter, the beast let out a bellowing sound of rage that reverberated in his physical vessel, sending out shock waves of fury and obsession. Blackness poured out of his bowels as it thrashed about in a frenzy of surprise and madness, fighting for life and knowing that it was doomed.

William didn't think he could survive the pain as it ripped through his body, punishing him with talons of hate and revenge. He felt like he was being torn apart from the inside out. Only the sight of Annabel helped him to hold on to life, a moment at a time.

William pulled the blade from his body and flung it away from Annabel before he allowed himself to collapse. He landed with a heavy thud, face down on the floor, holding his wound and feeling his life blood pouring from his body. But when he turned his head, he saw Annabel kneel down beside him. For a brief instant, he knew he'd done something right in his life. Her face was as exquisite as an angel's countenance. No prettier or kinder person would ever walk the earth. The insane act of stabbing himself was balanced by a clear

150

understanding that he had preserved something wondrous and unique when he had saved Annabel from the beast.

But he couldn't save himself from the torment that raged inside of him. He could only grit his teeth, trying not to cry out. Annabel turned him on his back and put her hand over his. Her eyes were bright with concern as she tried to give him the courage to hang on. Both their hands were soon covered in blood. It joined them in a strange marriage of brief love as he fought the pain inside and tried to stay with the one person who gave him a reason to live.

There were tears in Annabel's eyes. They ran freely down her cheeks, sprinkling him with their wetness as she bent over him. He had enough strength to reach up and pull her close enough to kiss her. Her lips were warm and a sharp contrast to the cold chill of death coursing through his veins. For an instant, he thought he might have felt her kiss him back. No matter, it was clear that she truly cared for him.

I love you.

The soundless words issued from his heart as her face and the world slipped away from him.

Twenty-Eight

Arel woke up fighting the covers, fighting the hot daggers of pain that stabbed his gut. He knew without a doubt that William was dying.

This isn't my pain, it's his. I'm going to lose my brother after all!

As he thrashed around in his bed, he saw William's pale, blue eyes. They were filled with compassion and kindness, just like the time he tried to save Arel from suicide.

In the end, I betrayed William for his kindness.

The thought was worse than the physical pain. It stabbed his heart and tore it in two.

"You can't think about that now."

It was Michael's voice. When Arel opened his eyes, Michael was standing over him.

"William tried to kill himself," he gasped.

Michael shook his head. "No, he tried to save Annabel."

"I don't understand—"

"I'll explain later, but first, you have to let me help you. Taking on William's suffering isn't what's needed."

"I'm afraid to break my connection to him. If I don't hold on, I think he'll die, and this time I know I won't be able to stop it from happening."

"Hold on to the part of him that saved Annabel, not his pain. Otherwise, you're right about him dying."

"But I have to find a way to help him!"

"Then let go of your guilt and shift your focus."

"How can I possibly do that when I know that William should be in some heavenly paradise, not in the hell he's in now!"

"Do you want William to survive?"

"Yes, of course I do."

"Then find a way out of your own torment."

The concept made sense. If William was drowning, Arel wouldn't be able to help if he was drowning too. "What do you suggest?"

"Try to think about something other than the pain. Think about anything that might make you feel better," Michael instructed.

Arel remembered what Carol had said to him. She believed that Arel and William would be friends again. That possibility buoyed him up enough to change his focus. He was able to take slow breaths and calm his body a little. He even smiled at the thought of seeing William happy and well again. As the pain in his gut began to subside, he held out his hand to Michael. "Help me up, please. If I'm going to be there for William, I have to get moving. Every minute counts."

"What are you planning to do?"

"I'm going to London."

Michael gave him a questioning look. "But William is in a critical state. He's also dealing with a lot of emotional turmoil. Seeing you might not be the best idea."

Arel used Michael's arm to steady himself as he stood up. "I helped heal his body after that car hit him. I can help him now. I'm sure of it." He paused and glanced up at Michael. "But I'll need you there too. Please, Michael, fly to London with me."

Twenty-Nine

William lay in his bed, filled with such agony that even Annabel's presence couldn't distract him from his misery. It wasn't only the knife wound that caused his wretchedness. The beast within had inflicted psychic tears, leaving him in shreds. A black cauldron of hate, housed in his gut, had created the monster in the first place. Now that kettle was bubbling with rage and distrust of everything in life, even William himself. Its contents boiled over, spewing acid on his wounds, searing him and keeping him in constant torment.

He barely registered the sound of the front door bell ringing as he slid in and out of consciousness. When he opened his eyes, he saw a glowing form in front of him. The light was painful too. He quickly closed his lids again and moaned.

"William, it's me."

In spite of the pain, William froze with fresh panic. He was sure that he knew the voice that uttered his name. He prayed that he was delusional. But his lips were soon stilled when the voice came again.

"William, it's me, Arel."

This time the words were whispered, but it didn't help. Their message was as loud and as punishing as a church bell tolling at his funeral. As his head pounded, he moaned again. "I didn't think it could get any worse."

Arel moaned too as he pressed closer. "I'm so sorry. Please, forgive me. I know I was wrong to do what I did. I'll do anything to make up for my mistakes."

William opened his eyes, letting them adjust to the light. "Oh hell, it is you."

"Michael's here too. He's in the other room. We can both help."

154

William was barely able to register Arel's ramblings much less try to resist him. He didn't have any strength left to fight. "Why? Why me?" His questions were aimed at the heavens, but he knew the gates to the kingdom were closed to him now. When the beast in him was allowed to roam again, they were slammed shut against him. He turned his head enough to gaze at Arel whose golden eyes were bright with his repentance. But there was no forgiveness left in him, only Arel's latest betrayal. It added new fuel to the fire in his gut. He bit his lip, trying not to cry out as the pain struck with a new and horrible vengeance. "Get out," he finally managed.

"I can't."

Annabel came in as Arel argued back. "Maybe you should let William rest."

William held out his hand to her. Like the rest of his body, it was trembling. "Yes, make him go."

Before she could retrieve William's hand, Arel grabbed Annabel's shoulders and held her tight.

"Annabel, I know you want what's best for William, but just give me a chance. Don't send me away. William is dying. Let me try to save him. You want him to live, don't you?"

"Of course I want him to live," she announced in a loud, clear voice. She stared down at William. "You know that, don't you, William? You know how much I care about you."

William met her gaze. Annabel's eyes were fluid with concern. "Yes, I know." He had to acknowledge her, to let her know that he cared too. If he was going to die, as Arel said, he might as well admit to himself and to her that she mattered to him.

Annabel took his hand and held it to her breast. "Then let Arel stay, at least for the night, please."

"Annabel, no—" William tried to say more, but his voice faltered.

"Please, William, you told me that he has healing abilities."

William had never felt so weak and unable to respond. Yet a part of him screamed out in vain.

No! Make the traitor leave! Once and for all, get him out of my life!

Of course, no one heard his protest. As he tried to focus, as he tried to instruct Annabel on what to do, the room began to spin, and he faded into the blackness again.

Annabel sat across from Michael, not knowing what to say. She'd never experienced a thing called nervousness before. Now, her body was strangely unsettled, making her take notice of its condition. "I didn't know I could feel this way," she finally blurted out.

Michael looked back at her and smiled. "Being in the physical form of a human comes with many surprises. The body and mind receive information in a way that's new to us. The feedback can be a bit overwhelming."

"No, it's more than that. I'm talking about how William makes me feel. As his angel, I've always cared about his welfare, but not in a personal way. I was there to be a support system, a friend he could depend on. I think that's changed, and I don't know how to handle my responses to him."

"What do you mean?"

"I'm not sure, but when he looks at me, I can feel how much he wants me. I can feel his desire, and it sparks something in me. I'm not sure what that spark is yet, but it's growing."

"What do you want to do about it? At this point, I think we both know that William would be devastated if you disappeared from his life."

Her heart did a little leap, making her clasp her chest with both hands. "I would never think of doing such a thing!"

"I know you wouldn't. I also know you'll find your way through the current circumstances with your usual grace."

"Thank you for that vote of confidence. You told me this assignment would be a challenge. I just didn't know how much of a challenge it would be." She stood up. "Anyway, I better go to bed. I want to be fresh and alert if William needs anything later."

Michael stood up too. "I didn't know you required much sleep."

"I didn't, until now. I've never felt tired like this before either."

It was a fact that angels lived very lightly in their bodies, with very little strain or stress on their physical vessels. Yet, as Annabel started to leave the room, she was beginning to understand what people meant when they said they felt weary.

"Just remember who we are and why we're here," Michael said quietly. "William and Arel both need our steadying hands at this

156

delicate juncture of their lives. And if William does leave the world—"

Annabel stopped abruptly and stared at him. "I hope that he doesn't leave. Earth can be a lovely place. If he recovers, he could still find the happiness that his soul desires. It's my fondest wish for him."

* * *

Night swallowed up the last remnants of light, leaving William's bedroom in shadowy darkness. The glow of a small lamp on his nightstand was the only source of illumination as Arel took up his station in a corner of the room. He sat down in a comfortable, reading chair where he could observe William. His first thoughts were depressing.

He's been unconscious for hours. And his life force is growing weaker by the minute. He may not live to see another sunrise.

Arel had to find a way to help William before it was too late. But there was a problem. Like Arel and most humans, William was shielding himself. Fear and anger kept him walled off and inaccessible to outside intervention. Arel knew he wouldn't go against William's wishes this time. At least he'd learned that much after his last misuse of power. But it was so difficult to sit and do nothing.

Dammit, Will, don't do this! Let me in, please! You want to live. I know you do. I saw how you looked at Annabel.

Michael had filled him in on some details about how William sacrificed himself for Annabel, so he knew that William had deep feelings for her. Even with all the pain, his eyes brightened a little when she was around.

Bloody hell, he doesn't know she's an angel. However, he proved his intentions were chivalrous. If he makes it, I'll help him deal with the angel part too. He can find a real woman to love.

Arel couldn't quite understand Annabel herself. She wasn't as calm and composed as Michael. When she looked at William, her eyes were soft and vulnerable. Her energy had a certain human quality that surprised him.

157

Maybe it's part of her act. Maybe she's trying to be totally believable in her role.

Angels were still a mystery to him. They were always there to help, but their ways could be tricky and unpredictable.

A loud groan from the bed made Arel sit up and take a deep breath. William was coming around. He thought about calling for Michael, but William hated him too. He stood up and went to the bedside, putting his hand over William's heart. It was beating so fast, so fitfully. When he tuned into it on a deeper level, he got a picture of William as a boy. He was running through a field in a blind panic. Arel grabbed his own chest as he felt the boy's terror and pain. He'd never known that part of William when they were friends.

You were always so confidant, so unmoved by anything but your own desires.

He flushed with embarrassment.

Except when it came to helping me. You did have feelings after all. I just didn't realize it.

William's eyes fluttered open. For a long moment, they stared at each other.

"Get away from me." William spat out the words in a weak voice.

Arel pulled back his hand, knowing that he had to shield himself from William's physical and emotional torment. If he didn't, he'd be useless. Michael was right. A person couldn't help someone by taking on their problems. "Sorry, I was just—"

"Why are you here? Can't I finally die in peace?"

"Peace? Will, you're in hell."

"Because of you!" The outburst made William cough, then twist and turn helplessly as his body screamed for relief. When he was able to speak, his tone was thick with bitterness. "It's what I deserve, right? Isn't that what you've always thought? You couldn't bear that I might go to the other place. You made sure I didn't end up there."

"No! You're wrong! I couldn't bear being left alone on this earth. I know how selfish that was, but—"

"Selfish? Is that what you call using your power to damn a person to unspeakable suffering? You're a monster!"

The words hit Arel with so much hate that he fell back several paces and slammed heavily against a dresser. A vase toppled over its edge and crashed on the floor. His first thought was its value. William's home was filled with rare, expensive collectibles. He went down on his knees, knowing all was lost and yet, he had to do something to stop the feelings that he was a fiend, that he had damned William forever. Instead, the facts solidified into a palpable truth that couldn't be denied. They crushed all his good intentions and left him in a black void of hopelessness.

"You're right, Will," he said as the full impact of his actions took over. "I've damned us both! Alive or dead, I'll never be able to trust myself again!" As soon as he'd made the statement, something switched in Arel's brain. William's accusations were joined by flashes from Arel's past. His mother despised him. He should have never been born. His father tried to beat him to death because he was worthless. Justina was screaming that he betrayed her love just before she ripped a razor across her throat. As the images kept coming, a great rage of self-loathing began to blot out everything. He pulled himself up to a standing position and glared at William. "It's all your fault! Why did you save me that night? You're the one who sentenced us both to hell!"

"You bastard! How dare you!" William cried out in a wavering voice.

"I hate you!" Arel screamed back. "And I hate life!"

As Arel began cursing his existence and what it had come to, Annabel and Michael came running in.

"What's going on?" Annabel asked as she rushed to the bedside and put herself between Arel and William.

"The idiot is having a breakdown," William groaned out, "like he always does."

Clasping his fists, Arel didn't feel William's pain anymore. He was seething with an inner fury. Everything that he thought he'd put behind him was fresh and raw again. Yet, in the background, he heard laughter. Another part of him, the part that carried Michael's blood, was gently chastising him.

You can't fight your way out of this. Calm down and be responsible. Pick up the pieces and do whatever it takes to go forward.

At the same time, Michael had stationed himself nearby. He was always a wall of stability and strength. If allowed, his presence alone could put out a blazing building with a glance. Now Michael was staring at Arel, giving him the space he needed to see the truth. He had reached the end of the line. He'd never escape his faults, even the odious ones that he abhorred. His choice was a simple one. He

159

had to surrender to the moment and to who and what he was. If he'd fallen short of expectations, if he'd made terrible mistakes, he'd have to live with them. No matter what, William's life was on the line. Arel had to try to help him.

* * *

The second half of Arel's vigil started off in the worst possible way. William was in agony and there was nothing to be done about it. Like Arel, William couldn't tolerate any painkillers. It was a miracle that he was still alive after all his blood loss and the onslaught of an infection. Arel and Michael were forbidden to come near. No amount of pleading on Arel's part would change William's mind. He wouldn't accept Arel's help. There was nothing to do but watch him suffer. Annabel offered to relieve Arel from his post, but he sent her to bed.

As he sat in William's bedroom, steeling his nerves against the sounds of anguish, there was a pause. It was followed by William mumbling something, calling out for him. Arel quickly joined him at his bedside, staring down at William's pale blue eyes. They weren't clear and certain anymore. Instead, they were glassy with the unrelenting pain. "I'm sorry for what I said, Will. But I'm here for you now. I'll do anything you want. Just ask."

William's breath was short and shallow as he tried to find his voice. Finally, when it came, it didn't sound like it belonged to William at all. Its tone was that of a beggar, pleading for mercy. "Do you mean it? Anything?"

"Yes!"

"Kill me," William gasped. "And I'll forgive you all."

"Oh god, not that! Please don't ask that of me!"

William lifted his hand ever so slightly and winced. His slender fingers trembled as he reached out. "For once in your life, put aside your judgments. Have mercy, please . . . you're my only hope. You're the brother who says he loves me. Help me. Stop the pain. It's unbearable. I can't go on."

Arel stepped back, bracing himself against the request that numbed his mind and enflamed his heart. He couldn't answer. He couldn't swallow or stop the tears that coursed down his face. The

160

nightmare was complete. After all their quarrels and all the ways he and William tried to reconcile, their time together on the earth was at an end. And Arel had to be the deadly instrument that would release William from life. The idea was beyond any horror he could imagine. Yet he had no choice. He couldn't bear the suffering either. All he could do was lower himself across William's prone body. Carefully, ever so carefully, he embraced him, whispering into his ear. "If that's what you want, Will, I'll do it. Let my soul be damned if only I can send yours to heaven."

William struggled beneath him, tortured by any kind of contact. "Not heaven, not this time."

Arel smiled. "Sorry, Will, whether you know it or not, you're the best person I've ever known. You faced the worst demons of this world and won. Now you're going to a place where souls like yours can be free. Believe me, heaven will be proud to welcome you back."

William managed two words. "Thank you."

Arel stood up, regaining his composure. "I need a moment. I have to think about how to do this." Michael's conversations came to mind. Michael said that Arel's powers could be used to heal, but he could also deliver a lethal dose of energy if he didn't maintain complete control. So that's what he'd do. He'd kill William with an overdose of kindness.

William looked up and frowned. "Please, every second feels like an eternity."

Arel's grief was almost as devastating as William's pain, but it was time to prove he was a true friend. "Don't worry, I can do this," he said as he went around to the other side of the bed and started to climb in.

"What now? What are you doing?" William gasped.

Arel glared back. "If I'm going to damn my soul, I want to do it holding you, like a brother on the battlefield. Is that too much to ask?"

William moaned as he shut his eyes tight against the pain. "It's always something with you."

"It'll all be over soon, I promise," Arel said as he lifted William into his arms.

William gritted his teeth to keep from crying out. But he allowed himself to be moved without a sound as if he wanted his last moments to be honorable and dignified. When he was settled against

Arel's chest, his face brightened with a sudden smile. "I know how hard this is for you. You are my brother after all."

"Yes, I am. The rest doesn't matter. In this moment, I've finally found a way to prove myself." As Arel's tears flowed in streams of grief, he put his hand over William's chest, feeling the vessel beneath. The heartbeat wasn't as wild as before, but it was very weak. "Farewell, my dear Will."

William smiled almost peacefully, relaxing enough to let down his guard. "Goodbye."

A strange stillness settled over the room as Arel felt their energies merge. He would always cherish that moment. It was so different than anything he'd ever felt. It was as if he was holding himself. There was no 'other.' William and he were one soul, one being in two bodies. It was a transcendent experience that threw open the doors to his heart's magnificent powers. An inner glow began to grow in his chest. When he closed his eyes, his spirit flew upwards, taking flight in realms of light that were as bright as the sun. Basking in the radiant splendor, he also gave himself to the tranquil scene around him. On the earthly plane, he was sure that his heart's explosive power would do its job, overloading William's body with a fatal dose of energy. His brother would be at peace at last.

* * *

William smiled. He'd never expected to see heaven again. Yet he was floating in an ocean of well-being, rising and falling gently as the waves buoyed him up and down. It was such a relief to be released from his body. The pain was gone. He could breathe in the shimmering mist that surrounded him without wanting to scream. He hadn't expected the transition to be so quick. One minute, he was leaned against Arel's chest, listening to Arel's heartbeat, and in the next instant, a flash of light transported him to paradise.

I have to give you credit, Arel. You're a man of your word after all.

He stretched out, contemplating what he'd do in his new environment. A unique and expansive experience awaited him. For a brief moment, he even contemplated being one of those guides that the metaphysical people talked about. He'd be Arel's guide, reminding him not to toss anybody else out of heaven. Of course that would only be a very small part of what he'd do. He enjoyed beauty. Perhaps he'd create an exquisite home overlooking a meadow filled with deer and fox. Surely, in heaven, you could do whatever you wanted.

But Annabel won't be here to share any of it with me.

A twinge of regret made the blissful waters around him a little bumpier, his first sign that there could be trouble in the ethers.

I have to monitor my thoughts. This place seems to react to whatever I feel.

He missed having his notepad for some reason, wishing he could jot down a list of questions. The waters lurched again as soon as his contentment factor wavered. His scientific side was engaged at once. He needed to understand how paradise worked. What if he had a very negative thought? What then?

What if I thought about haunting Arel? Paying him back for the misery he caused me?

The waves turned into rougher seas. The gentle up and down motions turned into swells that threatened to overwhelm his buoyant position. He heard voices just as the shaking intensified.

"Arel, wake up."

It was Annabel's voice.

"You've been asleep for a long time. Let go of William, my dear. I need to change his dressing."

A sharp pain hit William's gut. He wasn't floating anymore. Everything was shifting. The pain quickly spread out, consuming every part of his body.

What the hell is going on?

He suddenly knew the answer.

Oh no, I was dreaming! I'm not dead. Arel tricked me again.

Thirty

The last rays of afternoon light were weak. The cloudy, London day left Arel wishing he was back in Chicago. The windy city could be gray too, but gloomy London weather evoked despairing feelings that went back to his days as a young man. As he sat down on the sofa in William's living room, he didn't have time for those old memories. He had a fragile situation on his hands.

"I swear, Michael. I tried to kill William. I did exactly the opposite of what you told me. I forfeited all control over my powers. I did my best to blast him out of existence. But nothing went according to my plan."

Michael looked up from the book he was reading. "But it did."

"How can you say that? William is more resentful than ever. He hated me before, now his rage is off the charts."

"But his body is better. There's a chance that he'll pull through."

"Right, and he'll personally come gunning for me. Or maybe he'll blow up my house."

"Try not to think so negatively."

"You'll be thinking negatively if you're blown to bits too. From what you told me, a physical body is a very special gift that angels are supposed to respect and care for. Yours will be plastered all over my walls if William has his way." He paused and rubbed the arm of the sofa. "Or maybe that maniac he's contacted will get us both first. William doesn't think I know about him, but I do. That's the trouble with this so called gift of yours. All the crap is exposed. All the stuff I don't want to think about is always there in my face. What kind of gift is that?"

"Would you rather not know about this person that William has engaged?"

Arel's fingers stilled. "I suppose there's an advantage in knowing. I can prepare myself for what's coming, but—"

"Not just prepare, but create something different for yourself."

"Yes, I know you said the future is fluid, that I can change what happens to me, but this man is going after William too. When I tune into his mind, it's clear that he's planning on taking both of us out." He picked at a small nub of fabric. The material on the sofa arm was smooth except for that one little defect. "How can I keep William safe? If he lives, that is."

"You can address that issue later. For the moment, try to stay focused on what's happening now."

"Fine, but you haven't really answered my original question. What went wrong last night? William should be soaking up the sun in some Garden of Eden right now, not gritting his teeth and growling at me."

"What was your intention?"

"To kill him."

"Look a little deeper."

Arel thought about holding William in his arms and witnessing not only the man's physical pain, but the pain that came from growing up with cruel and clueless people, people who branded a sensitive child's mind, who convinced a young boy that mankind was repugnant. "I wanted him to be happy again. I wanted him to know heaven instead of living a hell on earth."

"And you gave him that chance. Being alive doesn't have to be hell. Trust that he can find what he loves right here."

"I suppose that anything is possible, but what about my power? I didn't have any control."

"Intention is another way of expressing control. When you forget your personal agenda and concentrate on wanting the best for someone, you have perfect control."

"I wish William knew that. Better or not, he's still in a lot of pain and nights are the worst for him. I'm going to be there again this evening, no matter how much William cusses me out."

"I'd advise you to take it easy. You talked about my physical form, but you don't always stay aware of how hard you are on your own body. Last night's session took a toll on you."

"I thought you said my control was perfect."

"But there was a lot of emotional turmoil before that."

"You mean when I was breaking William's precious vase and screaming like a banshee? William has a way of bringing out my

165

worst. It's hard to think about my body when my emotions take over." Frowning, he stared at the sofa arm and tugged at the tiny nub of thread more vigorously, accidentally breaking it off and leaving a small flaw in the fabric. His frown deepened into furrows of panic. "Oh no!" William was as meticulous as Arel. He was also very astute when it came to noticing the smallest of details in his environment. "Quick, Michael, I have a little situation here. Go to the store and see if you can find fabric glue."

Thirty-One

It was nighttime, a time that ushered in William's worst pain. He clawed at his covers, trying to find some small respite from his body as each second barely ticked by. His nerves were exposed, raw fibers of flesh stretched beyond the breaking point on the rack of time. Each second extended itself into an eternity of despair. He cried out for answers. How did he get himself into such a wretched state?

Is this my reward for living a life based on reason and sanity?

He grew up priding himself on his ability to act in a calm and rational manner. Arel complained that William was cold and calculating. In a way, Arel was right. William refused to allow his feelings to run his life. He thought about each act before he followed through. He was aware of his demons and even acted on them when he was still young and still establishing control. But he soon learned to keep them housed away. As a result, he'd never felt guilty about his life or his actions, even those deeds that involved taking the lives of others. His choices were precise and justified. He punished the unconscious, selfish people who defiled the earth, people like his father and a score of hateful teachers.

As he matured and he put his need to punish others behind him, life became almost tranquil. He enjoyed each day. He traveled, added to his art collections, and found his own company to be generally preferable to interactions with others. He enjoyed time spent in the beds of beautiful women, but on the whole, he loved his solitude.

Now, if he was being punished, what was his crime? He'd slain his inner demon, sacrificed himself when it tried to harm the innocent Annabel. So why was he suffering? Then he thought about Arel, and the misery began to make sense.

The moment that I gave another person the power to matter to me, I was doomed.

There it was. Mystery solved.

Caring equals misery! Be it a fox or a person, you can't let yourself care about something outside yourself and expect to go unpunished.

With Arel, he had gone beyond caring. He made a decision to save Arel's life when he knew Arel would hate him for it.

He still hates me for it. He's already had his revenge and infected me with his madness and barred me from a decent afterlife, but it wasn't enough.

William had begged Arel to put him down like you would a suffering animal. It was the humane thing to do. How could anyone see another person in such pain and not try to help?

But would he come to my aid? Of course not! The lying bastard has no mercy in his heart, only a continued desire to dole out his vengeance under the guise of being my brother.

He shut his eyes, trying not to scream out as his rage escalated. It festered inside of him, growing in its power to torture him. Hatred seized his torn bowels and made him whimper and whine. Thrashing and twisting helplessly, he couldn't escape the steel jaws of a vicious cycle. Pain fed his emotions and his emotions fueled his pain. Yet, in the middle of his misery, he heard a voice. It was very polite and unaffected in the midst of his feeble pleas for death.

"I'm going to stay with you again," Arel said as he came over to the bedside.

The announcement couldn't be rebuffed. William's body was prone and powerless. He couldn't even curse Arel. He had no breath left in his lungs to defend himself. What breath remained was given over to the forlorn moans of a creature stripped of dignity.

"I'm going to try what I did before," Arel said as he climbed into the bed. "Something went wrong last night, but maybe—"

"Help me!" William loathed himself as soon as he said the words. But they came out anyway. There was no pride left in him. He was a groveling animal, kicked into submission, begging for some scrap of compassion from a master who could inflict pain or pleasure. The night before, Arel had given him a few hours of respite. William knew that he'd do anything for another few.

Arel nodded as he put his arms around William and began to gather him up. "I'll do what I can."

Every movement made William cry out, not just with the pain, but with sorrow and grief. He'd lost himself so completely. He didn't know how to hold on any longer. A part of him listened to his pitiful blubbering. That part was disgusted at his state, disgusted at how far he'd lower himself for a little relief, but the pain was stronger than the censure. As he rested against Arel's breast, he clung to him like a feeble, needy child.

"Help me . . . ." The words trickled out again.

"I'm trying," Arel whispered back as he carefully placed his hand over William's heart.

Almost immediately, a warm glow began to break through William's pain. Miraculously, it only took a few more moments for the pain to begin to recede. His body began to relax, and some small measure of clarity returned. He even began to forget about his rage. All that he wanted was to find that place where he could float in the waters of bliss again. "Please, don't let me come back to this world."

Arel heaved out a heavy exhalation. "If only I could promise that, but we're both caught up in something neither of us can control."

"I don't understand."

"That's the point, neither do I."

William didn't know how, but he knew that Arel was telling the truth. Maybe the guy lied about a lot of things, but he wasn't lying now.

Arel's gaze was steady and clear. "I know you think I'm your worst nightmare, Will, but I never wanted this."

"But you did!"

Arel let out a great sigh. "You're right. When we first met again in New York, it was so hard. When I saw you, I realized you were a perfect example of a human being who's capable and able to deal with life. I felt so useless, so inadequate in comparison. Before I met you again, I tried everything I knew to be a better man, and yet I failed completely. I blamed you for making me live with myself. I betrayed you. Then I betrayed you again a while back, but not for the same reason." He paused, letting his hand fall away from William's chest.

There was an immediate shift, as if someone turned down the flame on a fireplace where William was warming the chill from his bones. A hint of the pain began to make itself known.

169

"Keep talking," he ordered as he put Arel's hand back where it belonged.

"Sorry, I drifted for a moment."

"Well, stop it. It's obvious that you need to stay focused. Get back to your story."

"Where was I?"

"You were talking about violating my rights the second time."

There was another long sigh before Arel began speaking again. "When I kept you earthbound, it was because I'm such a coward. What would I do if you left the world, and I had to face myself alone? It's no excuse, but it's the way I feel. I wish to god it was different, but I'm still lost so much of the time. Then, last night, I finally found the guts to let go of you. I wanted you to be safe from the pain and suffering, safe in a place where none of that existed."

Arel's tale was such a pathetic one, William almost laughed. As much as he hated the person holding him, he couldn't help himself. No one could compete with Arel when it came to explaining one's shortcomings. "You tried, but you screwed up?"

"Yes, I screwed up."

"I always told you that you're an idiot. It's my own fault for letting you try to kill me."

"I'll try again tonight, but I can't promise anything."

It was William's turn to pause, to reflect on how different he felt with Arel's warm hand on his chest. "I can't believe we're having this conversation. A few moments ago, I felt like an animal, one that hated you from the depths of its soul."

"But you let me help you."

"Maybe, but I also despised you and myself at the same time."

"I know. I felt it," Arel said. His tone was calm and accepting.

"It's strange. I know that deep down my feelings haven't changed, but I can't seem to connect with them now."

Arel let out another sigh. "It's the power we're tapped into. If we allow it, its energy helps us to go beyond our emotions. It's also making me sleepy."

Lying against Arel's chest, William noted that Arel's heartbeat, so strong the night before, was weaker, more flighty. "Are you okay?"

"Of course I am," Arel insisted.

170

"No, you're not." Just like he'd known when Arel was telling the truth, William knew when Arel was being deceitful. The energy they were tapped into was also acting like a lie detector. "Your heart feels weird."

"Whatever."

"Stop feeling sorry for yourself, at least while you have my life in your hands."

"I'm doing my best."

"Dammit, Arel, that's not good enough. Forget your failings and generate some energy. Your hand is getting cold and the pain's coming back."

Arel sat up straighter and took a few deep breaths. "Fine, maybe we should talk about something else."

"Yes, I agree, so get on with it."

Thankfully, the warmth returned as soon as Arel began telling William about a little boy named Ariel and a baby named Sara. William drifted off soon after that.

Thirty-Two

Peggy sat blurry eyed over her cup of morning tea. She was drinking an herbal brew called passionflower. Coffee would have been a godsend, but after her fitful dreams, she didn't want to add the strain of caffeine to her already anxious state. Hopefully, Sara would sleep in for a couple of more hours, and she could go back to bed.

"Morning," Tim said. He was tightening his belt as he walked into the kitchen.

"Your lunch is on the counter. I made one of your favorites, tuna on rye."

"Thanks, with this meeting coming up this afternoon, I won't have time to go out for lunch."

"You sound a little tired. Didn't you sleep well?"

He gave her a playful smile. "Are you kidding? You must have had some really crazy dreams. You kicked our covers off a couple of times."

"Oh, sweetie, I'm sorry. I think I kicked you a couple of times too."

His smile broadened. "You came close, but you didn't kick anything important."

"I seem to have this problem every time Arel goes to London."

"At least he's trying to improve his communication skills. He did call us from the airport before he left."

"Yes, but that doesn't seem to lessen my nightmares."

Tim was about to reach for his lunch when he paused and stared at her. "How bad were they?"

"Don't worry, they weren't so horrible that you have to check on him. In fact, I dreamed about his friend, William, not Arel."

"Again? The last time he was in one of your nightmares, you saw a river of blood and thought this William had something to do with it."

"Don't remind me."

"What'd you see this time?"

"It was really just the reverse. He was a nice guy. Maybe that's because of what Arel said about him the day before he left. He convinced me that William is really quite pleasant. But in my dream, this scary demon was after him. I was there too, trying to help him fight it off."

"By giving it a lesson in kickboxing?"

Peggy laughed. "Yes, something like that. Actually, I was pretty good."

"Maybe I should sleep in the spare room if you think you're going to continue the match tonight."

"No way, I won't be able to sleep at all if my gallant knight isn't by my side. But it's okay, I'll give myself some suggestions before I go to sleep. I read in some magazine that it can help."

Tim came over and kissed her cheek. "Just try to relax. Arel is obviously taking care of his buddy."

"I guess you're right. The last time I got all worked up, Arel came home and told me I was worried for nothing."

"So why the frown?"

Peggy pursed her lips into a pout. "Sometimes Arel acts like I'm some big buttinsky, but I only want his best."

"Oh, please, Peg. He's lucky to have you looking out for him. How many times have you known when he was in trouble and helped him?"

"Yes, but he never seems to remember those times."

"Look, it's not you. Arel is a lot different than he was when we met him, but he's still working things out. He can still be very guarded."

She cradled her cup, trying to let Tim's practical outlook appease her wounded pride. "I suppose I have to take your word for it."

Tim took the cup out of her hands and elbowed her up. "Go back to bed. Get some rest."

"You're right. I'm turning over a new leaf. No more worrying about Arel. He said that Michael is with him, and we both know that Michael can take care of whatever happens."

"I'm glad to hear you say that."

She walked Tim to the garage door, kissed him again and waved goodbye. After his calming influence, she felt better. With a little more sleep, she'd be back to her normal self.

I'm learning. It's taken me a long time to give myself a break, but I'm doing it.

She was about to climb the stairs when Carol and Kevin came to mind.

Carol went to the therapist yesterday. I wonder what she thought of him. Is the guy any good? Will she get the help she needs? I hope so.

As Arel moved into the background, Carol came forward, another person to worry about. She hadn't seen her friend for days. What if Carol was depressed again?

No, I will not go there.

She let out a snort of defiance.

I'm going to bed.

She was almost at the top of the stairs when she heard a faint cry. After a moment, it was louder, more demanding.

Great. Sara's awake. No nap for me.

Thirty-Three

It was still early morning as Kevin walked up the stairs, carrying a plate of saltines and a mug of tea. When he got to the bedroom door, he paused and gave Carol as hopeful a smile as he could manage. It was hard not to let his true feelings show. In spite of their happy honeymoon, Carol was on a downward spiral, and he didn't know how to help her.

"You didn't have to take the day off," Carol said as she sat up and smoothed out the covers.

Kevin put the mug and saltines on the nightstand. "I wanted to. I wanted to take care of my two favorite people in the world."

"I'll be fine. It's just a little stomach bug again."

He sat down on the bed and pushed back a stray lock of blond hair that was hanging over Carol's eyes. Her face was anxious and drawn. "I'm worried about you. You look so tired."

"It's this bug. I thought I was over it, but—"

"Honey, maybe it's not a bug."

"What?"

"You know . . . when we were in Paris . . . that one time—"

"No, I don't think I'm pregnant. My periods are always a little off. That's all."

He reached out and took her hand in his and kissed it. "If you are pregnant, I'd be thrilled. Little Ariel would have a sister or brother. Wouldn't that be great?"

"I guess so." Carol avoided his eyes as she took back her hand. She smoothed out the covers again.

"You don't want another child?"

"That's not the point. I love the idea of a bigger family. It's just that the doctor I saw the other day has already wanted to put me on meds. I think that means I'm a mess, not fit to be a mother to Ariel, much less to another child."

175

"That's not true. I bet this guy puts everybody on meds. Pills are standard issue nowadays. What were they prescribed for?"

"I guess they're for stress and depression. That's what I told him I was experiencing."

"Have you started taking them?"

Carol shook her head. "Just in case, I didn't want to take a chance."

Kevin scowled. "I know I haven't been there like I should have been, but I'm here now. And I'll take off the next month if I have to. I'll do whatever it takes to make sure you know that I love you. Just tell me that you won't give up on us or our family."

"I'm trying. I really am," she said as she stared down at the flowered quilt. A tear made its way down her cheek and dropped on the bedding.

Kevin fingered the moist spot, trying to find something to say that would help. "I have faith in us. You have to try to have some faith too. What do you say to that?"

"Oh no, I think I'm going to be sick!" Carol gestured him back as she started to get out of bed.

Kevin moved aside quickly, giving her a clear path as she sprinted to the bathroom. For a moment, he stood in place, not knowing what to do next. Then he ran for the bathroom too. He had to keep his promise to be there for Carol, no matter what. His only concern was that he wouldn't be able to keep his breakfast down if she started throwing up.

A few minutes later, as he helped Carol back to bed, he was proud of himself. He'd done a good job of taking care of Carol's physical needs. But after he tucked her into bed and stood back, he noted how forlorn and lost she looked. Obviously, the symptoms she'd given the doctor were correct. She looked depressed.

"If only Arel were around, like he was the first time. He'd make you feel better."

She smiled. "You're doing great, but you're right about having Arel around. We both felt like he was a blessing those first months when I was pregnant with Ariel."

It was great to see Carol smile again, and talking about Arel seemed like the ticket to get her mind off of her nausea. "Maybe we could get a banner made up for when he comes back. It could read, 'Welcome home, St. Arel, patron saint of those in need.'"

Carol giggled. "You know, I bet he'd like that. He tries to be modest, but I'm sure he'd appreciate a tangible sign of recognition."

Kevin handed her a saltine and watched her nibble on an edge. "You're great with graphics. You could design something."

"Really?"

"Why not? Arel's our friend. Let's do something nice for him."

Carol shrugged. "I guess I could. If you take care of Ariel when he wakes up, I'd have the time."

"I know this printing company that could make whatever you come up with."

Carol grabbed a tissue and dried her eyes. "Could you bring me my laptop?"

Kevin stood up and started for the door. "I hope Arel's friend, this William fellow, knows how lucky he is."

"I probably shouldn't talk about it, but Arel confided in Peggy and me. He said that William hates him."

Kevin nodded. "Remember when we talked in Paris, and I told you that Arel said something similar to Tim and me? He didn't name names, but Tim and I figured Arel was discussing his dealings with his friend, William."

"That's right, I do remember. But we both know Arel. He's sweet and kind. He must have really cared about his friend to do whatever he did. Yet, he's so hard on himself."

"That's why we'll have that sign waiting for him when he gets back."

Carol's eyes got a little brighter. "I'll do my best to make it very special."

Thirty-Four

In the late afternoon's waning light, Annabel stood next to the bed, watching William sleep. Her fellow angel, Raphael, stood next to her, but not in physical form. "Thank goodness, he's able to sleep. In fact, this is his second nap of the day. You've been a big help."

Raphael's smile was particularly brilliant when he was in his ethereal body. "Thank you, but we both know that Arel is responsible for channeling most of the healing that's taking place. I'm just acting as a backup, when he goes off duty."

Annabel glanced up at him with probing eyes. Raphael was much more experienced when it came to knowing all about humanity. She wasn't nearly as well-informed. Her previous duties had never entailed such a close up look at how humans interacted. "Arel and William puzzle me. They seem to always find a way to fight each other. Yet, when the need arises, they can change their rapport and cooperate for a little while."

"Their relationship hasn't always been that way, but through many lifetimes, they've become adversaries."

"If I was a human, I'd simply want to love the other person. There would never be a reason to hurt another."

Raphael chuckled. "You're saying that because you're looking at being human from our perspective, but from what I've observed, angels who give up their wings don't always feel that way after the change."

"What do you mean?"

"We reside in a type of consciousness that prevents us from forgetting who we are. Humans, on the other hand, usually don't remember their connection to the Divine. They often feel alone and

178

cut off from the love that we know as part of our birthright. When they're hurt by another human, it can leave a scar and make them very wary of each other."

Annabel reached out for William's hand. It was warm, but not as feverish as before. For a long moment, she held his hand in hers. "He never lets me touch him like this. Now that he's injured, I'm allowed to attend to his wound, but that's all. Maybe that's what you're talking about. He doesn't feel safe to bond with someone outside of himself."

William started to stir, and Annabel quickly replaced his hand on the covers and stepped back. "So why would one of us ever decide to become a human?"

Raphael paused and glanced at Annabel and then at William. "Some might choose to have a deeper, more personal experience. You see, humans often feel disconnected, but when they give themselves over to their true essence and open their hearts, the experience of love in a physical body can be unique and quite extraordinary. It becomes what they call passionate."

"I don't understand what you mean. Does the feeling go beyond what we feel?"

"It's a different expression. That's the best way to explain it."

Annabel frowned. "I think I saw a passionate quality in William's eyes just before he stabbed himself. His desire to protect me, no matter what the cost to him, was so powerful. His energy hit me with a force I've never felt before. For a moment, I almost forgot myself, and I did something very strange. I kissed him."

"Remember, he has a version of Michael's potent blood flowing through his veins. Perhaps that's why he was able to affect you."

"Yes, that must be it."

"How do you feel now?"

Annabel shrugged. "Sometimes, when he looks at me in that same way, I get confused. I wonder about the feelings I had when I kissed him."

"Kissed who?" William's lids eased open, and he stared up at her. "Who are you talking to?"

Raphael immediately faded away.

Annabel put her hand to her mouth, not knowing how to answer. She found herself wanting to touch William again. "Sometimes I do that, talk out loud, that is."

179

"You mentioned a kiss. Who did you kiss?"

She couldn't lie. She didn't know how. "I kissed you."

"Oh that," he moaned.

"Are you in pain? Should I get Arel?"

William's brow was deeply etched as he tried to find a more comfortable position. "No, don't get him, not yet."

Annabel couldn't help herself. She took his hand and squeezed it gently, wanting to help him feel better. "What can I do?"

A totally new expression of kindness replaced William's grimace. When he looked at her this time, his eyes were the softest, pale blue she'd ever seen in a human.

"Leave, Annabel, while you can."

"What do you mean?"

"You never asked about why I stabbed myself—"

"That's true, but somehow, all I care about is that you get better and that I want to help you."

"Not a good idea." William pulled his hand away from hers. "You don't want to get even more mixed up in the craziness that goes on here. I was wrong to get you involved in the first place."

"Is that an order? Are you firing me?"

William laughed and grimaced again. "I just want what's best for you."

"I know what's best for me, and if it's alright, I'm staying."

* * *

Arel woke up in the lower level quarters of William's house. There was a sofa in the living area that served as his makeshift bed since Michael was using the guest bedroom. Annabel was in the third bedroom. Arel preferred staying in the lower level. When he needed to recuperate after his healing work, he could escape William's groans and cries. William was getting better, but it was a slow process. The downstairs apartment was a quiet island of refuge where he could get some sleep himself.

"Arel?"

He came fully awake and sat up in an instant. "Annabel? What is it? Is William worse?"

"No, his fever is down a little." Her voice was matter-of-fact, even lacking in any inflection.

"Good, I'm glad to hear that." He blinked away the last vestiges of sleep and stretched out the stiffness in his body. His dreams were intense, leaving his muscles tighter than when he went to bed. "Do you need something?"

Instead of answering, Annabel walked over to a table in the corner. It was empty except for two flats of marigolds sitting there, side by side. She turned on the overhead grow lights, picked up a watering can from the floor and began to tend to each plant with great care. "I don't want to give them too much," she explained as she felt the soil and applied a small amount of water to each section.

"Why does William have marigolds down here?"

"He . . . he was trying to—" Annabel paused and set the watering can down on the table. She stood immobile, not moving or saying anything more.

"What's the matter? You seem—" He didn't know how to proceed. Annabel was acting very strangely for an angel.

She suddenly turned and stared at him. "Do you like being a human being? Would you rather be one of us?"

He scratched his head and gave her a questioning look. "I don't know how to answer that, the second part, that is."

"Do you still wish that William hadn't saved you, that he let you commit suicide?"

"No, not most of the time, only when I've really messed up things. Then I guess I use it as an excuse, something to throw back in William's face. It's wrong. I know that, but my emotions get the best of me. I say things I shouldn't."

"Do you like hurting him?"

"No, not really."

Annabel's eyes grew wider until she gave him a full on display of her powerful, angelic gaze. "Are you sure?"

"I don't want to hurt William. Let me make that clear, but you don't understand what I'm dealing with—"

"I want to understand. Explain what you feel, please."

Arel stood up, put on his robe and walked over to her. "What's this all about?"

"I need to know more about humans and how they feel if I'm going to help William."

"Talk to Michael. He's one of you. I can't say I always agree, but he thinks he's an expert on our behavior."

"No, please, I want to hear what you have to say."

"I'm one person. I don't represent everyone."

"Yes, I know that, but I want your viewpoint anyway."

"You're kind of putting me on the spot. I just woke up. I'm still a little fuzzy—"

"Would you kiss me?"

Arel backed up. "What?"

"It's a simple request. I asked if you would kiss me or maybe just let me kiss you."

Arel moved a little further away. He was sure that Annabel was definitely breaking all the rules of angel etiquette. "I think we need Michael."

"That's fine," Annabel said as she gazed absently into space.

"What is going on with you?"

"I just asked Michael to join us. He'll be here shortly."

"Good idea." Arel reached in his robe pocket for a clean handkerchief and patted down his forehead. "It's a little warm, don't you think?"

Before she could answer, Michael came down the stairs in his usual relaxed manner. He traversed the steps in an easy, fluid way as he called out in their direction. "Annabel says you need to speak to me?"

"Thank goodness," Arel said as he quickly walked over to where Michael was standing. He pulled Michael aside. "Looney alert," he whispered. "You have a hurting angel over there. I don't know what William did to her, but she's gone around the bend."

Michael looked back calmly. "What bend?"

Arel swallowed hard. "Michael, this is serious. Not to be a snitch or anything, but Annabel wanted to kiss me."

Michael looked over at Annabel. "Is that true? Did you—"

"Shh!" Arel slapped a hand over Michael's mouth before he could complete his sentence. "What are you doing? Keep it down."

"Why?"

"I don't want to embarrass Annabel," Arel said through clenched teeth.

"I'm not embarrassed," Annabel said. Walking over to join them, she paused next to Arel. "But maybe you are. Does kissing me embarrass you?"

Arel retreated a couple of steps. "Please, you're crowding me," he objected as he swabbed his brow again. He couldn't quite get enough oxygen. "Where's the thermostat? It's really hot and stuffy."

Michael laughed. "The temperature is fine, but Annabel is right. You're embarrassed."

Arel glared back. "No, I'm mortified. People and angels don't kiss. It's a sacrilegious thought."

Annabel frowned. "You're saying that I've done something wrong when I kissed William?"

Arel gave her a deer-in-the-headlights look of disbelief. "You kissed William? When?"

"When he kissed me."

"That fiend! I can't believe he'd violate an angel."

Annabel looked unfazed. "William doesn't know that I'm an angel."

"Still, you're a complete innocent. He had to know that."

"I think he's in love with me."

"Yes, I gathered as much by the way he looks at you." Arel paused. "Wait a second, I don't understand. Why did you kiss him back?"

"I don't know. That's the reason I wanted to kiss you. I thought I might understand the whole exchange a little better."

Arel scowled and cinched the belt on his robe with a jerk. "Bad idea."

"Maybe I should kiss William again."

"No!" Arel shouted. "That's a worse idea. You'd be leading him on." He looked at Michael. "What kind of training do you give your kind? This poor thing seems clueless."

As Arel waited for an answer, Annabel lunged forward, grabbed his face, and pulled him towards her. He was shocked, but also surprised at how strong she was. He couldn't escape her grasp in time to keep her from kissing him. With her mouth on his, time stopped and so did his brain except for the thought that he'd reached that state referred to as bliss. Then she let him go. He was rendered mute for several moments as he struggled for words to express what he'd felt. "Heaven help us!" he finally cried out with a gasp.

183

Annabel gasped too. "Uh oh!"

Arel's first thought was the unthinkable. He'd corrupted an angel. "I'm sorry, but you shouldn't have done that. Justina told me I'm amazing when it comes to kissing."

Annabel shook her head. "No, it's fine. I didn't feel a thing. It was like kissing an inanimate object."

Arel swallowed back his pride. "Thanks . . . I guess." He tried to sound sincere, but a sinking ship feeling overpowered his voice. Maybe Justina had to say he was great. People who love you say things like that to make you feel good. He glared at Michael again. "What a blessing it is that angels are always so brutally honest."

Annabel smiled wistfully. "We always try our best not to mislead anyone."

"So why did you say, 'Uh, oh'?"

"I was comparing kissing you with my experience with William. It was so different. With William . . . it was so meaningful." She walked towards the stairs. "I better look in on him. I'm sure he'll be awaking up soon."

"You're going to break his heart," Arel said with a sigh.

Annabel paused, giving him a curious, yet virtuous glance. "I would never hurt William. So why would you say that?"

"It's just an expression."

Annabel looked at Michael. "Is there something I should know? Am I missing something?"

"It's alright. Arel is stating a personal concern, but for now, we need to focus on William's recovery. Maybe you better check on him as you suggested."

After Annabel was safely out of hearing, Arel sighed again. "It's a very valid concern, one that you should have considered before you brought in an angel like Annabel."

Michael's gaze was also inquisitive. "She interacted with you on your trip to New York, and you didn't have a problem."

"That's because she looked and acted like a lost, teenage waif. Now, she's very different, one of those glamorous women out of a fancy women's magazine. And she doesn't have a timid bone in her angelic body. Bloody hell, the way she kissed me—"

"I'm sorry about that. She didn't mean to upset you."

"Please tell me that you've never kissed anyone like that, Michael. Otherwise, my nightmares are going to triple."

"I've never had that inclination, but why do you find an innocent kiss so upsetting?"

"It may be innocent for her, but . . . oh never mind."

"Really, I am sorry. Annabel is trying to understand the feelings that can accompany the physical realm and also some possible ramifications of being in a body."

"Maybe she should forget about the possible ramifications and just leave now. William might be able to forget about her if she makes a fast exit."

"Neither of them wants that to happen."

"Great, it's a catastrophe in the making. I know William. He doesn't fall in love. But if Annabel stays, and he does let her into that closed off vessel that he calls his heart, it can only end in disaster when she tells him the truth. Like I said, she's going to break his heart."

"Let's just wait and see what happens."

"Wonderful! If I manage to get William through his present hellish situation, I'll have to pick up the pieces when he loses the love of his life." Arel stumbled back to his sofa bed. "I'm exhausted with all of it."

"You've been doing a lot of energy work. You need to take it easy tonight. Otherwise you could overtax—"

"I can't leave William in the lurch, especially now that I know what's waiting for him."

"Arel, please listen to me. Annabel isn't the only one who needs to pay attention to the physical. Your body—"

"I know, I know. Give me a break, Michael. If you want to lecture someone, go talk to Annabel. Tell her to take off the makeup and cover herself with a shawl or something."

"She doesn't wear makeup," Michael said as he retreated to the stairs.

Arel snorted back. "Of course she doesn't. How ridiculous of me to think an angel needs makeup to be beautiful."

"Try to relax. Maybe you can sleep a little more."

"Relax? Are you kidding?"

Thirty-Five

As soon as William saw Arel's face, he knew something wasn't right. "What's going on now? Why do you look like a puppy that just got kicked down the stairs?"

Standing in the doorway, Arel hesitated and let out a long sigh. "It's nothing."

"Don't make me drag the truth out of you. My gut's on fire. I don't have time for fun and games."

"If you want to know what's going on, it's simple. I'm worried about you."

"Why? I'm getting better."

"Yes, physically, but—"Arel's golden eyes dimmed. "Do you ever contemplate sharing your life with a . . . a—"

"With a what? What are you babbling about?"

"I'm talking about a woman, like my Justina." Arel's gaze lifted and flared, targeting William briefly with two golden orbs of passion. Then they returned to a dull, lifeless state. "Do you think about having someone to hold?"

"Oh boy, here it comes, the sob story of a lonely guy who wants a relationship."

"I'm not talking about me—"

"Of course you are. The moment you mentioned Justina, it was as plain as day."

Arel walked over to the bed and scowled. "Maybe you're right. Now, move over. I have to lay down. I'm completely worn out."

"I thought I was the one who needed help," William complained as he inched over towards the opposite edge of the bed.

"Maybe you are, but I need to relax."

"Fine." When Arel got in a mood, it was best to play along, especially if William expected any help from his supposed healer. "So tell me all. What's eating you?"

"I am lonely, not always, but when I remember what it was like to be in love."

"Love?" With all his physical misery, William hadn't thought about love. Now, Annabel came to mind. Did he love her? He was certainly suffering because of her. He'd cared enough to stab himself. If that wasn't love, what was? "The whole concept is nothing but trouble."

"It's not a concept, Will, it's a feeling."

"Okay, but I don't want that feeling." It was true. Once William was well again, he'd get his life back on track and say 'goodbye' to Annabel. "I want to be clear-headed and enjoy my life without the complications of some foolish, emotional state tearing me apart."

Arel looked over at him and smiled. "That's good."

"You're agreeing with me?"

"Yes, you never needed anyone before, and you don't need someone now."

"I thought you were in favor of love."

"For me, yes, I guess I am, but if you're happy without someone, that's wonderful."

"Why doesn't that make me feel better? Are you saying you want me to be alone for the rest of my life?"

"No, of course not. But you're so capable of being independent and fancy free. It's great."

"Right, it is." As William voiced the words, his future fanned out in front of him. He saw himself alone in a museum, staring up at works of art in a cavernous room that echoed with emptiness. When he attended the theatre, he'd be by himself, surrounded by couples smiling at each other. At the auction houses, he'd buy collectibles to put on a shelf and dust. But no one would ever be there with him to share and admire his beautiful acquisitions.

Alone, alone, alone.

A long moment of silence hung over the room as William stared at the ceiling. Arel finally spoke.

"Will, you're so quiet. What are you thinking?"

"That my life is crap."

"What? When I first came in, you seemed fine."

"When you first came in, I didn't realize that I'm like you, alone and miserable."

"But you're not. You're the guy who's always okay, remember? You're feeling this way because you tuned into my unhappy vibration."

"Hopefully that's true." William's frame of mind did shift dramatically as soon as Arel came in.

"You're fine," Arel said nudging his shoulder.

The gesture shook William enough to send a shooting pain out from his gut. The ensuing misery quickly refocused his attention on his physical woes. As William stiffened with pain, Arel laughed.

"If I were in your shoes, I'd be looking forward to strutting my stuff again. You're a lady magnet, William. You can have your pick of any woman out there."

"Right," William groaned. But why would he want any woman 'out there' when he already had the most beautiful and appealing woman right there, already in his life? Annabel was perfect. And from the way she looked at him, she might want him too. "Changing the subject, are you looking forward to going back to Chicago?"

"Sure, why not?"

"You don't sound very convincing. What's bothering you now?"

"Do you think there's a woman for me? You know me pretty well. Am I prime dating material?"

William hesitated. How did he tell Arel that any woman who got mixed up with him was sure to drown herself after the first month of togetherness? After all, Arel said it himself, his vibes were killers. "Of course, there's a woman for you," he lied. "In fact, there are a lot of women who'll look at you and go crazy." This was a true statement. Arel wasn't lacking in looks. He'd draw women in like a magnet too, then send them into bi-polar disorders they never knew they had.

Arel let out a moan. "I don't know. I wish I could believe it, but—"

William wanted to moan too as he waited for Arel to continue with his dialogue of complaints. When Arel didn't go on, William looked over and saw him half sitting up, clutching his chest. "Are you okay?"

"I'm fine," Arel said through gritted teeth. "Ow!"

"Is it your heart?" William had overheard Michael talking to Annabel. There was mention of Arel's previous heart problems. It

188

seems he'd had a miraculous recovery, but the vessel was still at risk when Arel overtaxed himself. "Should I call for your friend, Michael?"

"No, I don't want him gloating!"

"What kind of a friend would gloat over your pain?"

"Maybe not gloat—" Arel's teeth clenched with another spasm.

"I'm calling him—"

"No!"

"You are so stubborn," William said as Arel fell back on the pillow again. "Is the pain gone?"

"I'm better. Just give me a minute."

William reached over and put his hand on Arel's chest. "You're heartbeat is as erratic as hell."

Arel pushed away his hand. "It's nothing."

"It's weaker than mine, you idiot. What if you die, then what?"

"Then your problems are over, and you can tell your old acquaintance to back off."

"Who are you talking about?"

"The hit man you're contracting to kill me."

William sucked in a breath and winced. He had made every attempt to shield his thoughts from Arel. "I've taken precautions, so how—"

"I can't help it if you're sloppy, Will. Besides it takes a while to completely control stuff like this."

William already knew that Arel had the capacity to read his mind, but he never expected Arel to be so open about it. "So you have no qualms about invading my thoughts?"

"I believe in privacy, so I'm doing everything I can to avoid going there. Some things, maybe important matters, simply slip in when one of us isn't attentive."

William frowned. "So if you know about this guy, why did you try to help me?"

"Because I'm selfish like I said before. I don't want to lose—" Arel grabbed his chest again.

"Another attack?"

"Yes—"

If William had been conflicted over Annabel, he was totally confused about Arel. Yes, he'd contacted Rolphe to kill Arel. He needed to rid himself of the person who had a power that scared the hell out of him. Yet, that same person now demonstrated an amazing ability to help William. In fact, William was probably going to get well. If he did, he could pursue Annabel. At some point, he might even marry her if he wanted.

Maybe Arel isn't my worst enemy.

The thought slipped in, but it was too far a stretch to be seriously considered. Deep down, William still had too much anger to let Arel off the hook that easily.

But maybe Arel could be my guinea pig.

What if William also had Arel's kind of power? What if he could affect more than the growth of a marigold? With Arel moaning and groaning next to him, William had a chance to test his abilities. He turned to Arel and made a decision. "Let me help," he ordered.

"Really?"

"Why not?"

Arel tried to smile. "Only if you promise not to gloat."

"I'll gloat all that I want if I can do what you do."

"Fine," Arel whispered as he tried to catch his breath.

William moved closer to Arel, trying to get as comfortable as possible. When he'd worked with Annabel and the marigolds, she made it clear that he had to have a positive attitude. That meant William would have to call a truce with Arel. He'd have to "white flag" his way into power. But it was hard to put their past behind him. His hand grew shaky as he held it over Arel's chest.

"Ow, ow, ow! Dammit, Will, white flag, red flag, do something or I will have to call for Michael."

William reacted at once. "Stay out of my thoughts!"

"Stop thinking!"

Arel's words hit William in a meaningful way. He had a flash of insight.

That's it. I have to see Arel getting better, then turn off my thoughts.

After a few minutes of effort and careful breathing, William's mind quieted. With his hand on Arel's chest, he felt Arel's heart begin to calm down and establish a steady rhythm. If only William had his notepad, he would have recorded his moment of victory in bold print.

I'm doing it. Arel isn't the only one with a gift.

But there was more. As William was able to relax into a deeper state, he felt a new sense of freedom. His awareness expanded so much that he noted a glow at the foot of the bed. It was so compelling, so completely mesmerizing that he abandoned the world of words and explanations. He forgot about Arel and even his own pain as he watched the soothing light and drifted off to sleep.

* * *

Michael stood next to Raphael, watching William slumber. The man's hand was still draped over Arel's heart. "I think they'll both wake up feeling much better."

Raphael smiled. "I added a bit of my own energy to William's. But he's a natural at healing. Once he let go of his resentment and got into his unbiased, scientific mode, he was excellent." He paused and looked at Michael. "About Arel, you told me that he has a different approach to problems, but I didn't expect this. He's already engaged William's healing abilities. The strange thing is that I didn't think he had a weak heart."

"He doesn't. It can act up now and then, and sometimes Arel really does worry me. But right now, he just needs to rest."

"Did he orchestrate what just happened?"

"On occasion, his body does things for him when he needs it to. It's a subconscious interaction. Arel has no idea he's doing anything. In this case, his heart simply went into spasms." Michael noted Arel's sleeping frown, and how it contrasted with William's unlined face. "They're a strange combination, so different. Arel gravitates towards an almost frantic approach to circumstances."

"And William?"

"I think he'll always be one for maintaining a strong foundation. In fact, if he ever decides that being part of the lighter side of life is okay, he'll excel at holding down the fort, so to speak."

"Do you think he'll get that far?"

Michael smiled. "When this process all started, I didn't know that he'd get this far. But if he and Arel could join forces, they'd definitely keep it interesting for all of us."

"Or they could destroy each other."

"Yes, unfortunately, that's a possibility."

Thirty-Six

Two days after William discovered his healing powers, he slowly limped down the stairs to his lab. He cursed the pain that accompanied his movements, but he was determined to return to his research. He'd given Annabel orders to buy some mice for experiments that he was planning. She was at his side as he navigated the stairs to check out the new specimens.

"Are you sure you're strong enough to be doing this?" she asked in a concerned voice.

"If I have to spend another day playing chess with Arel and listening to his babble, I'll stab myself again, this time in the heart."

"Thanks a lot," Arel murmured as he followed behind them. "And I still say I should be going down in front of you, in case you start to fall."

"Did you hear that, Annabel? The guy who can't walk across the bedroom without half killing me, wants to help me down the stairs."

"I didn't mean to fall on you last night. I tripped on your blasted carpet."

"Excuses. You get distracted. Try focusing when you're walking across a room."

"You're right, I was worried," Arel said.

"Obviously not about me."

"It can't all be about you. I found out my friend is expecting a baby. She had problems with her first pregnancy, and I'm concerned about this one. Michael is going back to Chicago to keep an eye on things."

"Sorry, I hope she's okay." William paused and looked at Annabel. "I want to apologize to you too. I never used to be a complainer. Even Arel will attest to that."

192

Arel shrugged. "It's true, Annabel. He was a lot of things, but a complainer wasn't one of them."

Annabel smiled. "I accept your apology, William, but I think you've faced your condition very courageously overall. Your pain was obviously intolerable."

"Thank you." Annabel's compliment was enough to quiet William's swearing as he climbed down the last of the stairs. He was sweating profusely when he reached the lower level, but he had a renewed sense of triumph as Annabel and Arel helped him over to his recliner. Once he caught his breath, he wanted to get on with his purpose for coming down to the lab. "The three of us are going to conduct a little experiment."

Arel had a puzzled frown. "Annabel mentioned something about mice. What's that all about?"

"We're working with these little fellows," Annabel said as she brought over a cage and set it on a table next to the recliner.

William peered into the cage. "We're going to test our abilities. It's as simple as that."

Arel smiled. "Mine have already been tested. You look like you're feeling much better."

"That's true," William agreed. "And I was able to help you out the other night, but I want to see if we can reproduce the results in a more scientific environment. We'll work with subjects that are not emotionally biased."

Arel stepped closer to the cage and inspected the small rodents that were nestled together in the bedding. "I saw a few of these critters when I was a boy. I never thought of using them in a test."

William smiled back, trying to be patient. Arel didn't have a scientific bone in his body. "You mentioned something about control. We can use these mice to practice."

Arel sucked in a breath. "Control? Oh, hell."

William ignored him. "Here's what we'll do. We have three mice here and also three control mice over there in the corner. There'll be no interaction with those three. Annabel has already weighed each one and started a log. With our subjects, there will be a period each day when we hold them. During that time, we'll try using our abilities to positively affect their growth and health. After a week, we'll see if our mice differ from the control group."

Arel frowned. "A week? I don't know if I'm staying that long."

William should have been happy to send Arel on his way, but instead, he had to grit his jaw as a surge of anger hit him full force. "I see. Well, there's the stairs. Please don't let me keep you here."

Arel back pedaled at once. "Just give me a mouse, okay? I wouldn't want to stand in the way of science."

William was surprised by his outburst and quickly made himself relax. "Fine, you can have the one that just woke up."

"That little tan and white one? It's so small," Arel protested. "I suppose you get the big, white one."

"Of course not. That white one belongs to Annabel. Mine will be the little brown one sitting next to it." William looked up. "Would you like to go first, Arel?"

Arel stiffened. "Why me?"

"They're very sweet," Annabel said as she opened the cage.

"Never mind, let me show you how it's done," William said confidently. Annabel was watching him, and he liked the idea of demonstrating how competent he could be around animals. He even gave her a brief smile as he reached in the cage and tried to snare his particular rodent. He was rewarded by razor sharp teeth that pierced his finger before he could pull back. "Damn!"

Arel laughed. "Feisty little bugger, isn't he?"

"You frightened him," Annabel said as she examined William's finger. "It's just a little nip, hardly bleeding at all."

William's misfortune seemed to spur Arel on. He reached in slowly and carefully scooped up his mouse. Holding the tiny creature in his palmed hands, he smiled. "I'm naming this one Whiskers. He has an extra-long, impressive set."

Annabel went next and carefully picked up her white mouse. "I'll call mine, Squeaky. He seems to make a lot of noise like a couple of people I know."

William ignored her look and made another try at his mouse. This time he was successful in picking it up. "This ferocious beast will be called Wolf, and he'll be the leader of this pack, a true reprobate like myself."

Annabel put her face close to William's. "He's got a mark under his chin."

William held Wolf up and noticed a little diamond of pure white under its mouth. "You're right, and it proves my point. This is a special mouse."

Arel was stroking Whiskers' tiny head. "This one has character. Do you notice how he's cleaning himself? Very fastidious."

William glanced over. "He's probably obsessive. When Annabel first showed me the little buggers, he was doing the same thing."

Arel carried Whiskers over to a chair and sat down. "Don't listen to him, Whiskers. Your tidiness is a sign of mouse manners."

Annabel gave Arel and William each a look of censure. "I thought we were supposed to commune with our mice, not each other."

"You're right," William conceded. "Let's give them our undivided attention for ten minutes." The small creature in his hand was a young mouse, but at five weeks, it was socially developed enough to leave its litter mates without too much emotional stress. It sniffed his hand, including the finger it had bitten earlier. For a long moment, its beady, black eyes were focused on William's. The message was clear. *Do you have a treat for me?* Smiling, William reached in the pocket of his robe and retrieved a shelled sunflower seed. He'd come prepared after reading up on mouse care and telling Annabel what to buy. He'd barely put the seed in his palm when Wolf snatched it up. William smiled again as he watched the mouse sit on his haunches and devour the delicious morsel. When the timer dinged and the ten minutes were up, he was surprised. He'd been so entranced by the mouse, he'd forgotten his pain.

Annabel got up from her chair and put Squeaky back in the cage. "Excuse me, gentlemen, but I want to change William's bed while he's down here."

"Sorry about all the extra work," William said with a frown.

"Do you need a hand?" Arel asked as he put Whiskers back in the cage.

Annabel paused on the stair. "Yes, that would be great."

William cleared his throat. "Annabel . . . uh . . . could you give me a moment with Arel?"

"Of course."

After Annabel disappeared up the stairs, William turned his attention to Arel. "I won't keep you long. I just wanted to tell you something." He ran a finger over Wolf's head. The mouse was sleeping soundly in his hand.

Arel came over and smiled. "Whiskers didn't want to nap. But you're right. He does clean himself a lot."

195

William eased the sleeping mouse back into the cage. "I sent a message to the man you mentioned."

"The guy who wants to kill me?"

"Yes, I told him that circumstances have changed. You don't have to worry about—"

"Your message won't make any difference. The guy wants us both dead."

"What?"

"I tuned in this morning. It's kind of something I do automatically, like checking the weather. He's gunning for us both."

"Why would he want me—" William let out a long sigh as he answered his own question. "He's a loner, easily threatened. My contacting him was a mistake."

"William, listen to me. Sooner or later, I'll be returning to Chicago, but you'll be here. And you're in no condition to defend yourself at this point."

"He doesn't know where I live."

"It doesn't matter. This guy is different. We might have been vampires, but he's also got psychic abilities. He'll find you. I'm sure of it."

"You know all this from simply tuning into him?"

Arel shrugged.

"I'll be fine."

Arel opened his mouth, then shut it. "I better go upstairs and help Annabel."

Thirty-Seven

Rolphe closed the lid on his laptop. He'd read and reread the latest email from William. Each time that he did, Rolphe questioned himself. Should he change his mind and forget about William and his friend? Obviously, William thought that was a good idea. The man explained that he'd made a mistake in wanting his friend killed.

Your mistake was taking my blood, William. Your second mistake was giving it to another. Then you had the stupidity to tell me about it. There's no going back now, you fool.

William might want to call off their arrangement, but Rolphe didn't. William and his friend were dangerous. He could feel it in his bones. As he got up from his desk, he rubbed his hands in thought.

"So how dangerous are these two?" he asked aloud. He was used to talking to his cat, Satan. But the tom hadn't been home in a week.

He's been fighting again. He's in trouble.

It was another burden that Rolphe felt in his bones. Sometimes he hated the gift of "knowing" that Chessa had shared with him. It was hard enough when bad things happened, but to have a vision of them in advance drew out the misery. But he'd be the foolish one if he didn't take advantage of his gift.

He walked over to the window. The moon was full, reminding him of the woman who changed his life. Chessa loved the time of the month when the lunar orb bared herself to the creatures who lived below. It was the time that Chessa welcomed with anticipation and eagerness. The moon's powerful urgings stirred something wild and free in the sensuous gypsy. She put on her colorful, flared skirts and blouses that exposed her smooth, inviting shoulders. She danced wildly around the campfire, unable to contain her desires. Her intense appetites were always more needy when the moon was in its full glory. Chessa often came to Rolphe in the middle of a moonlit night. Her long, flowing hair, the color of raven feathers, framed her striking face, making her look like a beautiful bird of prey.

She brought me out of my despair on many occasions.

But Chessa also used the moon when she wanted to know things. She passed on her knowledge to Rolphe. He was an apt student and quickly learned to focus on the moon's radiance. When he did, he could use the light to enhance his natural gift of sight. In that state, he often tapped into the future, especially those events that held the seeds of danger. He'd even seen Chessa's life coming to a close. He tried to make her take flight, but she said she already knew her time in the world was finished. She'd made peace with the fact, saying she wanted a new adventure. This world was becoming a bore after all the years she'd lived.

Rolphe understood Chessa's feelings of being on the earth too long. But unlike the bold woman, he wasn't ready to let go of his life. He had times of sadness, but for the most part, his life was still good. When he thought about William, he was determined to keep it that way. That meant that he had to know more about the danger that William and his friend posed.

As the moonlight bathed his face in soft light, he gave himself to it like Chessa had instructed. He shut his eyes and allowed the rays to wash over his mind and cleanse it of thought. A perfect moment of stillness followed. In a flash, he was propelled forward. He found himself in a dark place, perhaps an alley. There he saw two faces. He recognized one of them, the man from the email who called himself William. William had referred to the second man as Arel.

In Rolphe's vision, the men stood side by side. A powerful glow, almost like the light of the moon, surrounded them both. But unlike the moon's light, this glow had an ominous quality to it. When Rolphe thought about killing the men, the glow exploded into a fiery orb. It was like gazing at the noonday sun and almost blinded him. He was forced to look away with a pounding heart. As he tried to recover from what he'd witnessed, he was left swallowing back a bitter taste that soured his mouth.

A soft mewing brought him out of his trance state. "Satan, are you back?" It took a few seconds for Rolphe to collect himself. His mind was still scattered as he walked quickly in the direction of the sound he'd heard. He tried to calm himself, but his body was wired and readying itself in preparation for what was coming with the two men. Rolphe's glance into his future was almost as powerful as the one he'd had forewarning him of Chessa's death. Had he just been warned that a similar fate awaited him?

When he got to the kitchen, he turned on the light and glanced at the window. He always left it open so that Satan could come and go as he pleased. Hopefully the old tom had returned home.

"Satan, where are you?" Rolphe's fierce gaze was alert and wary as he scanned the room. Something felt very wrong, and this feeling had nothing to do with the vision that he'd just had. He wasn't prepared for what he saw on the floor. Satan was stretched out on his side. His ears and muzzle were caked with dried blood.

"No, not you too!" Getting down on his knees, Rolphe leaned over the battle worn cat that he'd come to love. Satan stared back with unseeing eyes as the rise and fall of his breath stilled. The tom cat had fought one too many battles.

Rolphe fell back, stroking Satan's rough coat. He began to take heaving breaths as the anguish of loss signaled the end of a long bond. His grief was overwhelming, connecting him to the past and the loss of his family. He thought about his children and how they had been torn from his heart. Death always sought him out. It danced around him, but not in colorful skirts. It wore a black cloak of finality that robbed him of any chance of retrieving what it had taken.

A mewing sound interrupted his heartache. It came from a dark corner close to the chair where Satan liked to sit. Two bright blue eyes peeked out from the shadows. Rolphe swiped at his teary gaze, straining to see what was stirring just a few feet away. When he couldn't get a good look at what was hiding itself, he crawled on hands and knees to investigate. A small kitten tried to run from his outstretched hand. He was fast and caught her easily.

"So, Satan brought me a present." He smiled as he carefully held the creature close. Soon, the small animal stopped struggling and sat quietly in his hand. She was thin and half starved, but stared back at him bravely.

Rolphe smiled at the kitten. "You must have a courageous heart like your daddy's." He ran a large finger over the soft, black fur covering her delicate ribcage and noticed something interesting. Each of the kitten's toes looked like they'd been dipped in white paint. It brought a name to mind.

"I'll call you Dantela."

It was a word meaning lace, and Rolphe thought it suited the way the cat's feet were adorned. The kitten began to purr as if she approved of the name.

Later, when Rolphe gave Dantela a bowl of milk, he thought about the situation with William and the other man. The irony of it all was clear. Death and new life were on opposite ends of the spectrum, and he was the puppet caught in the middle. He was a death dealer who nurtured life. It was a disturbing thought that he quickly dismissed.

Thirty-Eight

It wasn't the "scheduled" time to interact with his science experiment, but Arel was holding his mouse, Whiskers, anyway. Sitting on the sofa bed in the downstairs lab, he held out a piece of oat cereal to the youngster. Whiskers promptly took the food, turned his back on Arel and began eating. Viewed from behind, the mouse's long whiskers twitched contentedly as he hid himself and his morsel of food from Arel.

"Don't worry, little guy, I'm not going to take your treat away."

William wasn't the only one who could secretly sneak food to their charges. Arel had been out walking earlier and found a small grocery where he purchased his own supplies. He wouldn't tell William that he was cheating with treats or the extra attention he was giving the mouse. Why stir up trouble? They were getting along a little better. That was part of the reason Arel needed to do whatever it took to relax.

"William and I are finally finding a way to co-exist almost peacefully," he said to his mouse. "Unfortunately, it's just in time for some maniac to try to snuff us both out."

Arel had saved William's life twice, but if he returned to Chicago, he doubted he'd be able to do it a third time. His anxiety level leaped upwards as he pondered what might happen to William. The man was still very weak. He was in no position to take on a seasoned killer.

Things were also iffy in Chicago. Carol was expecting again. She'd nearly lost her baby the first time she'd been pregnant. Arel hoped she wouldn't have a difficult time again.

The two issues made Arel wonder if he did have a heart problem. He denied that fact to William, but every time he reviewed the possibilities of something going terribly wrong in his world, his heart had palpitations.

"Trouble?"

Arel jerked his head up in time to see a tall man appear a few feet away. He scowled back, wishing that angels gave people more warning before showing up. "We haven't been introduced, but I assume you're Raphael. Michael said that you've been helping with William's recovery."

Raphael smiled. "I'm not the only one. You've been doing a very fine job yourself."

The angel was about the same height as Michael but slighter in build, and he had a more youthful appearance.

"Thanks, but I was trying my best to kill William. It's what he wanted, but as usual I didn't succeed in granting his wish."

"I think he's changed his mind now that he's feeling better. But you don't seem very happy."

Arel stood up and took Whiskers back to his cage. "I've been thinking about something Annabel said. She asked if I'd like to be one of you. On reflection, maybe it's a good idea. Your kind seem to maintain a serene attitude no matter what is going on."

Raphael laughed. "You talk about 'our kind' as if we're aliens. I'm a little surprised. After interacting with Michael all of this time, I would have thought you simply saw us as friends."

"Michael is a friend, but he doesn't have to deal with life the way a human does."

"Do you envy us? Is that what you're saying?"

"When's the last time an angel was torn apart by worry or felt regret?"

"But those are only the negative parts of your world. What about the joy of creating whatever kind of life you want? You could enjoy serenity as a human too, if it was your prime motive in life."

"I don't have time for serenity."

"Are you worried about William?"

"Of course I am. The poor bastard can't win. If the killer who's stalking him doesn't finish him off, one of your kind will."

"Annabel?"

"Yes, little, sweet Annabel. I was hoping to steer William away from her, but as usual, things backfired. Now, he's more interested in her than ever."

"And you don't approve."

"William has gone through enough. And granted, I'm responsible for most of his misfortune, but I never expected an angel to try and take him down."

Raphael walked over to the mouse cage and looked in. "They're such dear little creatures, aren't they? Annabel said hers is called, Squeaky." He looked up, gave Arel another broad smile and reached into the cage. "I'm sure she wouldn't mind if I held the little animal."

"You can't touch that mouse," Arel said as he quickly retrieved Squeaky from Raphael's sheltering hand. With a censuring glare, he placed the mouse back in the cage. "William has strict rules."

"But I thought I saw you holding your—"

"Never mind what I'm doing."

"I'm sorry." Raphael backed away. "We were discussing Annabel. You're afraid that she'll make things worse for William."

"I know she will."

"But isn't that something the two of them need to work out? Why are you involved?"

"Whether he admits it or not, I'm William's only friend. I have to look out for his best interests."

"Why do you think Annabel would do anything to harm William?"

Arel sighed and sat down on the couch again. "I don't think she knows any better."

"What if her interest in William goes beyond the boundaries of what you call 'our kind'?"

"What do you mean? What boundaries?"

"What if Annabel is thinking of her interaction with William in a more personal way."

"Personal? An angel doesn't get personal."

"That's true, but Annabel might want a different experience."

Arel's eyes widened as Raphael's meaning began to sink in. "You're not saying that she's thinking of becoming one of us! She's not contemplating losing her wings, is she?"

Raphael smiled. "She's free to make that choice."

"Bloody hell! She is crazy! You have to talk to her, convince her that she'd be making a mammoth mistake, an enormous error in judgment!"

"Why?"

Putting his hand to his racing heart, Arel felt suddenly weak. But even worse than his physical woes, he had to confront the feeling that he was helpless to change what was happening. "I can see it all now. I'll be getting calls from London constantly. Annabel, the ex-angel, will be crying her eyes out when William reverts back to the cold hearted bastard he really is."

"I thought you said you're William's friend. In fact, you told William that you admired him because he's slain his demons, so to speak."

"Yes, and I meant it at the time, but that doesn't mean that William won't revert back to being cold and impersonal if the mood suits him."

Raphael stared back with a puzzled look taking over his tranquil features. "Can you clarify what you're trying to tell me? You said you're worried about Annabel hurting William. Now you seem concerned about Annabel."

"Look, Raphael, the bottom line is that relationships are hell all around for both the parties involved. My friends, Carol and Kevin, are barely keeping it together. Now Carol's pregnant and goodness knows what that strain will put on their marriage. Then there's poor little Ariel, their son. How will he fare if his parents keep fighting?"

"Arel, don't you think you should calm down a little. You're letting your emotions become so negative."

Raphael was right. Arel's ranting was affecting his heart. It was doing a jig in his chest as he went over all the possible things that could go wrong with all the people he cared about. Now he had to add an angel to his list of worries. "I guess I could become a loner again. I could ignore everyone I care about and do what William did. Maybe I could travel."

Raphael walked over and patted his shoulder. "I'm afraid you know too much for that, dear friend. Solitude is fine for some, but you enjoy having family around you. That's when you're happiest."

"Do angels have families?"

"Yes, of course," Raphael said in a cheerful tone.

Arel blinked back a couple of times and studied Raphael's unlined face. It was as smooth as baby Ariel's. Everything about the angel was peaceful. "Don't ever give up your wings, Raphael. And pray that I find a way to grow a pair. Tell Annabel we can do an exchange."

Raphael's eyes lit up with mirth. "You still have too much fire and passion in your spirit to be an angel."

"I guess you're right. I couldn't leave my earthly life now, not when people like Carol might need me. But I swear, after everyone gets their act together. I'm going for my wings."

Thirty-Nine

William fell asleep in his downstairs recliner after doing some work in his laboratory. In spite of the fact that he tired easily, life was slowly returning to normal. He was just waking up from his nap when he heard Annabel's cry of alarm.

"The mice are gone!"

William opened his eyes, found the bright, overhead light objectionable, and shut them tight again. "What did you say?"

Arel came running down the stairs. "What's the matter?"

"It's our mice!" Annabel pointed at the cage. "They've escaped."

William sat up in the recliner, winced and steadied himself. "How could they be gone?"

Annabel went down on her hands and knees, peering under the table. "The cage door wasn't properly locked. I think they climbed down the cord from the lamp on the table."

Arel hurried over, looking paler than usual. "Oh hell, maybe I didn't latch it earlier."

William glared back at Arel. "Earlier? You were handling the mice this morning?"

Arel answered in a hushed tone. "Maybe, what's the big deal?"

"Dammit, Arel." William stood up slowly. His movements were on par with a ninety year old senior, but at least his mind was clear. He held a hand to his gut, trying not to aggravate it. "You've invalidated the whole experiment."

Arel scowled back. "Come off it Will. You've been doing the same thing, and you know it."

"Just help me find them, please," Annabel said as she crawled across the floor.

WILLIAM'S BLOOD

William gave the floor around his chair a quick scan and let out a low whistle. "Wolfie? Do you want a treat?"

Arel got down on his hands and knees too. "He's not a dog, Will. He's not going to come when you call him."

William didn't argue, but he knew his mouse was already learning how to respond to his voice and certain sounds.

"I've found two of them," Annabel announced in a happy tone. "They're hiding next to a pillow on the floor. It's Squeaky and Whiskers. They look okay."

"Good, that only leaves Wolf." William continued to call softly as he limped about the room. When he leaned over enough to peer behind his large, oak desk, he was hoping to see his mouse staring back at him. Instead, his worst fears were realized. A small, brown body lay on the tile. He swallowed hard as he held in a sudden spasm of sadness. How could he care so much about a mouse? But he did. The last time that he'd reached into the mouse cage, Wolf had quickly responded. He didn't hesitate to leap into William's outstretched hand. The creature's beady eyes had been so bright and expectant.

He was a smart, little fellow.

"William, did you find the missing one?" Annabel asked as she came over to where he was standing.

"I found Wolf. I think he's dead."

Arel was immediately on his feet and rushing over too. "No, it can't be." He paused only long enough to check on the mouse's whereabouts. "Move back, Will. I have to get behind the desk." He grabbed an edge and tried to lift it. "Dammit, this thing is heavy."

"I think it's too late anyway," William sighed.

"Maybe not," Arel insisted as he continued to use all his muscle in an effort to shift the heavy piece of furniture.

"Just stop, your face is turning beet red." William paused, trying to keep the emotion out of his voice. "Your heart . . . you're going to—"

"I'll help," Annabel said as she joined Arel. She grabbed the edge of the desk and began to tug it sideways.

Together she and Arel moved it out from the wall far enough for Arel to scoop up the small escapee. Gasping, he studied the mouse anxiously. "He's still alive, but barely."

William knew what the problem was. "He must have eaten the rat poison the exterminator put down a while back. Bring him to me," he ordered as he limped over to his recliner. He held on to his injury as he sat down.

Arel did as he was told and put Wolf into William's outstretched hand. "Maybe I can help him."

"No, you've already over-extended yourself."

"What are you talking about?"

"Your energy is screwed up! Feel your pulse."

Arel blinked back in a bewildered sort of way as he put his fingers on his wrist. "I can't believe this. My heart is going haywire again."

William shut his eyes. "So sit down and let me concentrate. Wolf isn't going to last much longer." After quieting his thoughts, he could feel the animal's life force, just as he could feel Arel's. Wolf's heartbeat was very faint. The poison was moving swiftly through his tiny body. William had to set his intention at once, willing some part of himself to extract the poison out of the animal's body.

Arel seemed to understand what William was doing. "No, stop it. You're going to poison yourself."

William shot back a stern look. "I'll be okay."

Annabel grabbed William's arm. "Please don't do anything risky."

William waved them both away and shut his eyes again. With great care, he curled his fingers protectively over the mouse and held it close to his chest. It was so small, so fragile in his grasp. But he didn't allow himself to concentrate on anything but giving himself over to whatever it was in him that had power.

Let this innocent creature be spared.

After his plea was offered to the ethers, he slipped into a light trance state. For a moment, he experienced a brief episode of dizziness. The next instant, he felt peaceful, even serene. He seemed to float in a blissful dimension that felt like a dream. He could have remained there forever if someone wasn't shaking his shoulder.

"William, come back to us," Annabel called out.

William had a hard time waking up. When he opened his eyes, he didn't know how much time had passed. Then he remembered his mouse. "I hope I helped Wolf." As he spoke, a small paw stretched out from the confines of his partially closed fist. Then it was withdrawn and a black nose took its place as Wolf sniffed the world beyond the hand that had healed him.

"He's okay," Annabel said with delight. "You did it, William!"

"Yes, I guess I did." He stared gratefully as the little animal lightly tested his teeth on a finger and realized that it wasn't food.

"You're a greedy, little ingrate," William complained as he handed the small creature to Annabel. He gestured Arel to come over. "I'm going to be sick."

Arel quickly took William's arm and helped him out of his chair. "And you call me an idiot," he said as they made their way to the bathroom. "You really took a big chance for a little mouse."

William's stomach lurched, but the nausea was worth it. "And you're telling me you wouldn't do the same for Whiskers?"

"Oh course I would, but I have more experience, and I'm not already ill."

"Listen, Cardiac Poster Boy, experience or not, I'm doing pretty well. I just have to survive what's next. I have a feeling that my gut is going to go ballistic when I throw up."

Forty

Villiam laid back in his recliner, enjoying the icy compress that Annabel had applied to his head. He was still recovering from saving Wolf. "The cold really helps."

Annabel smiled. "You have more color in your cheeks. You seem better."

"Thanks for your help."

"Arel was worried about you. I'm glad he got that call from his friends. It'll help to get his mind off of things."

"He needs to go back to Chicago. The longer he's here, the worse off we both are."

"I thought you two were getting along a little better."

"Have you looked at him lately? The dark circles under his eyes? That nervous foot tapping thing he does? He's a wreck, and he's driving me batty. I can't believe I asked him to stay for the mouse research."

Annabel pulled a chair over and sat down. "I think you wanted to share something nice with him after he helped you."

"No, I wanted to prove to myself that I'm as gifted as he is."

"You have to be very proud of yourself. Little Wolf is almost back to normal."

"I'm going to padlock that cage and give you the key. Promise to keep us both away."

"It was a very good thing for you and Arel to interact with them. Holding an animal can be an excellent way to relieve stress."

"Or, like I said, Arel could pack his bags. That would bring my stress level down to zero."

"Can I ask you something?"

"What do you want to know?"

"I don't understand why you and Arel fight all the time, and then the next instant, you're concerned about the other's welfare."

"You think I'm concerned about him?"

"William, please, you know you are."

"Arel has this weird way of sucking people in. I swore I'd never let that happen again. Then the other night, he tells me that we had a life together a very long time ago. I laughed and told him he was delusional."

"What did he say?"

"Nothing, he gave me this forlorn look and walked away. Next thing I know, I close my eyes, and I'm hallucinating. I see these two boys, twins. And everything is as real as the chair I'm sitting in. Our clothes, the dusty road where we're walking, the scene was so vivid I could smell the fresh air. When I looked down the hill, I saw a town that had to date back to ancient Greece or Rome. It was like a movie, but I was in it."

"That's extraordinary."

"That's Arel's Madness."

"What do you mean?"

"I mean that Arel is a menace. Ever since I had that damn vision, I find myself worrying about him, like we really were brothers. But it was all an illusion, a suggestion that Arel managed to plant in my mind."

"Or maybe you two were twins in another life."

"You don't believe that nonsense, do you?"

"I believe that there's more to life than people realize."

William took the compress off and handed it to Annabel. "Like what?"

Annabel dipped the cloth in the bowl of ice water. "My opinion doesn't matter."

"I never thought of you as a person who suffers from low self-esteem."

Annabel laughed. "I don't have worthiness issues. I simply respect other people's opinions as valid."

"Could you talk to Arel and explain your reasoning. He has no idea about respecting anything or anybody."

Annabel replaced the compress. "He's very passionate."

"Do you think of me as passionate?"

"I suppose you are, at times."

"Do you find Arel attractive?"

Annabel pulled back. "What do you mean?"

"Oh come on, Annabel. He can be . . . what's the word?"

"Nice?"

"No."

"Considerate?"

"Considerate? You mean like a baby rattlesnake? Okay, that's being a bit harsh. Arel does usually announce his presence before he strikes."

"I think he's sweet."

"Sweet? Are you using that adjective to mean something that's pleasing, something that brings a person a bit of enjoyment?"

"Of course."

"My goodness, Annabel, I'm disappointed in you."

"Why?"

"Because you have no discernment."

"Could you explain what you mean?"

"I'd be happy to do just that," William said as he gave her a satisfied smile. "That quality called sweetness that you bestow on Arel, is not what you think it is. It's his secret weapon around women. He pulls them in with those blinky, pathetic eyes, then he destroys them."

"What?"

"I'm just warning you. Arel even admitted it. A woman had the misfortune to fall for him, and his uncaring behavior made her kill herself."

"William! I'm surprised at you, telling tales. I'm sure Arel never wanted that."

William shrugged and leaned back. "I'm just giving you the heads up."

Annabel laughed again. "Are you jealous?"

William snatched the compress off his head and glared at her. "Me? Why would I be jealous? I could have any woman I desired if I wanted a relationship."

"And you don't want a relationship?"

"Absolutely not." William surprised himself with his inflexible statement. Even though he'd had thoughts about giving up his solitary status, when questioned by Annabel, he suddenly found himself needing to deny it.

"Really, you'd never consider the idea of being with someone?"

After his vehement declaration, William made sure his tone was even and indifferent when he answered. "I might consider a brief fling with someone, but all in all, I enjoy my solitude."

Annabel studied him for several moments. When she stood up, her face relaxed into its usual composure. "I better go. I have some laundry I need to do."

Annabel's sudden desire to leave made William less sure of the path he'd just taken. "But we were having a conversation."

"I'm sorry," Annabel said as she turned and walked towards the stairs. "I'll send Arel down after he gets off the phone. He can help you back to bed when you feel up to it."

"Ask him about Justina," he called after her. "You'll find out just how sweet he is."

* * *

Sitting in the living room, Arel put the phone back in his pocket and let out a sigh of relief. Things in Chicago were running smoothly for the time being. Carol was in bed, taking it easy. Kevin was there to help out with baby Ariel and house chores. The young man had arranged some time off from work, and according to Carol, he was doing a splendid job at home. The thought made for a cozy picture in Arel's mind. Perhaps if the couple spent some relaxed time together, they could work out the bumps in their marriage.

I guess I can relax too.

He continued to go over his conversation with Carol and how the baby had another tooth coming in. He wasn't paying attention to the fact that he was scratching at the sofa arm again. Luckily, he caught himself before he dislodged the tiny bit of fabric glue he'd put there after his earlier mishap.

"Arel, are you busy?"

He looked up and saw Annabel coming in from the hallway. "No, do you need something?"

Annabel took a seat across from him. "You might want to go downstairs in a bit and help William back to his room."

"He's better?"

"Much. In fact, he was quite talkative. We haven't had many conversations since you arrived."

"I wish I had that problem. What were you discussing, if I may ask?"

"A lot of things, including the fact that he'll never want a relationship."

Arel sat back, relaxing his shoulders. Maybe William wouldn't get his heart broken after all. Things weren't just looking up back home. London felt suddenly lighter too. Then he saw Annabel's face. An angel's expression usually projected a sense of calm or tranquility. Hers was blank. "How do you feel about that?"

"I don't know. Should I feel something?"

"Let's approach it from another angle. When you think about William, what's the first word that comes to mind?"

"He's . . . confusing."

Arel's shoulders stiffened. Angels didn't get confused. "How is he confusing?"

"Remember? He saved me when he was in a rage."

"Yes, he was being gallant, a surprising gesture for him, but one which I truly admire."

"Is that all it was? I heard his thoughts. They were very loud and forceful. He said he loved me."

"Was this after he stabbed himself?"

"Yes."

"Well there's a perfectly good reason for what you heard. He thought he was dying. His heart opened enough to admire the world one last time, and then he saw you. You're a beautiful angel, Annabel. What's not to love about an angel?"

"Oh, I didn't think about it that way." She paused. "That would explain it."

"So, tell me, do you feel better now?"

"I don't feel much of anything except for—"

"For what?"

"I feel like humans hide things from themselves."

"You think William is hiding his true feelings?"

"No, when he said he didn't want a relationship, I knew he meant it. He's very afraid of opening his heart to anyone."

"That's why I was a little worried when you seemed affected by him."

Annabel gave him a puzzled look. "Affected?"

"Yes, remember how we talked about your feelings once before?"

"Oh yes, you became very upset when I kissed you."

"No, that's not what I'm getting at." Arel frowned, scratching at the spot of glue. "If it's not William, who is hiding from themselves?"

"You are."

"Me? You're joking. Do you know how much purging I've done since Michael gave me his blood?"

"Yes."

"So why would you target me? I'm not the one who stabbed himself."

"I'm not trying to upset you. If you don't want to hear my thoughts, that's fine."

Arel crossed his arms, hating that people and angels alike always wanted to give him advice. True, he often needed it, but he just wished he could get beyond the feeling that he would never measure up.

Annabel reached out to him. "Arel, I think you're doing a great job measuring up. It's just—"

He stiffened even more. "Yes, go on."

"You're using everyone else's situation to keep yourself occupied."

"So what?"

"William needs you to be an example. He's having a hard time, and you're the person who can show him what it means to have an open heart. You can show him what it means to really make peace with one's self and be happy."

Arel's frown deepened. "Right, then he'll want you."

Annabel's bright, green eyes widened in surprise. "I didn't think about it that way. From my point of view, I simply thought it might help to solve both your problems. But you're saying that if William accepts himself, he'll also want me in his life. Is that correct?"

"No, absolutely not." Arel uncrossed his arms and shook his head. "Please, don't jump to conclusions."

"But—"

"I just blurted that out. Forget it."

"But Arel, I can't forget it. Thoughts are vibrations that remain—"

"If you can't forget it, think about something else."

"I don't understand why you're getting upset?"

The first sharp pains of a headache shot through Arel's brow. "Look, I'm trying to help you. Stop trying to think so much. It's a very dangerous habit that humans have gotten into. Be your angel self. Go read a garden book like Michael does. Let yourself float around in bliss for a while."

"And what about you?"

He stood up and gave Annabel his most sincere look. "I'm going to get William back to bed. Afterwards, I promise to concentrate on my own life. Maybe I'll plan another vacation. In fact, you can help me. Forget about William. Make me your project. I'll do everything you tell me. I'll find a way to open my heart and be that good example for William. Then both of you can get on with your separate lives. You can be your beautiful, winged self, and William can slowly come to grips with his ability to be balanced and whole."

Annabel smiled. "No matter what William said, you are sweet. Thank you for trying to look out for me."

Arel sat down again, clasping his hands. "Not that it matters, but maybe I should ask you something before I go down to see William. Does he have a problem with me?"

Annabel hesitated. "I'm not quite sure. Do you think he might be jealous of you?"

Arel laughed. "Please excuse my language, but there's not a chance in hell of that. Every woman who sees the guy practically throws herself at him. Sorry, but maybe he has that effect on angels too."

"I guess you're right, but he did get a little defensive when I said some nice things about you."

"Nice things?" Arel felt his heart lift a little. "I know this is silly since you're an angel and all that, but it's reassuring to think that you see me in a favorable light. After you kissed me and made that blank face, I wondered if someone of the feminine gender would ever want—" He stopped himself and picked at the glue again.

"Arel, as you just said, I am an angel, but I've observed lots of people and I know how difficult some people can be, but in your case, I think you have a wonderful, giving nature. If you can begin to see that in yourself, you'll attract the perfect person for you."

Arel returned a timid smile. "I hope you're right. I won't go looking for anyone for a long time, not until I get my life straightened out, but someday, I think I'd like to have a woman in my life."

Annabel nodded. "I'm glad you have that attitude. It might take a while for you to accomplish that goal."

Arel stood up again. "Thank you. I can always count on your candor, can't I?"

Annabel frowned. "Did I hurt your feelings? If I did, I didn't mean to. With William, I can be so forthright."

Arel started for the hall, but he paused and looked back at Annabel. "Allow me to let you in on a little secret about William and all men, Annabel. When it comes down to it, we all like a bit of coddling now and then. In my case, with my nerves strung out like harp strings, I can use a more sympathetic approach. Please remember that when you decide to be blunt."

* * *

Rolphe noted Myra's warm smile as she welcomed him into her apartment. He usually brought along a bouquet of flowers or some pretty bauble he'd found for her. On this occasion, he was clutching a cat carrier.

"Is this the kitten you told me about?" Myra asked.

"Her name is Dantela."

Myra took the carrier from him and ferried it to the coffee table in the living room. As soon as she opened it, she cooed happily. "I love kittens, and this one is so pretty."

Rolphe seated himself on the red and yellow, flowered-print loveseat. The thick cushions sagged under his weight as he got comfortable. "I appreciate your offer to care for her while I'm gone."

Myra held the small, black kitten close to her chest as she sat down next to him. "Look at how adorable she is. She's already purring."

"Satan was a good friend, but this one is even more determined to worm her way into my heart."

"I'll love having her, but I hope you're not gone too long."

"I have to find an old associate in London. I lost track of him, and it's very important that we connect again."

She leaned over and snuggled against him. "I'll miss you."

Rolphe's hand dwarfed Myra's small face as he stroked her cheek. "I'll come back as soon as I can, I promise."

"Good. I'll put on my prettiest dress, and you can take me dancing."

Rolphe's gaze filled with desire as he studied Myra. Tall and slender, she'd been a model in her younger days. Now, with a little age, she had matured and was more beautiful than ever. She responded to life and to him with an openness that almost frightened him. "I'm lucky to have someone who loves life so much."

"We make a good pair. You're the artist, and I'm the poet."

He looked over at the nude painting he'd done of her. "I hope I'm more than just an artist to you."

Myra's dark brown eyes sparked. "You're also a rascal, but I can never resist your charm."

He caressed her face again, this time with more fervor. "I am your devotee, Myra. You inspire me to search for more than I know myself to be."

Myra smiled back. "Enough words. Dantela is ready for a nap, and so am I."

Rolphe stared at her knowingly. It was such a natural thing to make love to Myra, not like the many women in his past, but with real longing. He yearned to fill his heart with the excess purity that flowed from hers. If only he could consume her goodness and let it eradicate the sins from his soul, he'd be saved. "Do you believe in redemption, even when we go on sinning throughout our life?"

Myra's eyes melted into deep-set pools of warmth. "Yes, my love. I believe the Creator knows that we are misguided children, children who will someday leave behind their folly."

"I wish I had your faith. But maybe I've seen too much evil to believe that we're worth redeeming."

Forty-One

Sitting in his bedroom, William put his book aside and listened. The house was too quiet. Annabel had gone out for a paper, and Arel was down in the lower level. After praying for solitude, he realized that he'd actually gotten used to having people around. That would soon change. After serious consideration, he'd decided he needed things to go back to the way they'd been. Even thoughts of being with Annabel had been shelved. Complications were something he didn't need. He'd stabbed himself once. That was enough. If he resisted Annabel and temptation, his life would be perfect again, just like it had been for years.

In the past, he'd spent so much time seeing the world, admiring all the beauty, and collecting artwork. Some of his treasures were displayed in his bedroom. The painting across from his bed didn't have much monetary value, but it was very pleasing. The woodland scene featured a family of fox. He'd commissioned the artwork when he was a young, university student. The crystal, Lalique vase on the side table was a stunning piece, purchased recently. It wasn't as exquisite or as costly as his favorite, the Tourbillons vase with black enamel etching. Arel broke that one.

William sighed.

I suppose it's the price I had to pay. At least I'm getting better.

But he knew that there were also extra, unseen costs involved. Visions about the twin boys were becoming commonplace. His dreams were also being hijacked. The one he'd had in the early morning was particularly disturbing. A blond, pregnant woman latched on to his arm, pleading desperately for his help. He was sure he'd picked up on one of Arel's nightmares. Arel pretended that he had banished his worries.

219

But we both know that's a lie.

Happily, after a call to Chicago, Arel confirmed that his friend was fine.

And Arel is leaving in a couple of days.

Smiling at the thought, William grabbed his book and began reading again. Two pages later, there was a hard knock at his door, the latch being turned and Arel appeared.

"William, you were right!" Arel cried out. "Carol's in the hospital. She was fine when I called, but a little later she started having pains."

"I'm sorry to hear that," William said. It was a truthful statement. In the dream, he felt strangely drawn to the blond woman, almost as if they'd met before. Maybe he was picking up on Arel's feelings. "Are you going back to Chicago?"

Arel clung to the door jamb, staring at William with the wide-eyed stare of a traumatized, accident victim. "I'm getting the first available flight out," he said in a weak voice.

"Good idea."

"I want you to come back with me," Arel blurted out.

William humored Arel with a smirk. "You're kidding of course. You don't want me anywhere near your friends, remember?"

"I've changed my mind. I think your dream was telling us something. Carol needs you."

"I don't even know the woman."

"I realize that, but I have this gut feeling that you can help her."

"You're the one that flies around the world rescuing people. Go home and perform your magic on this Carol person."

Arel let go of the doorjamb and took a step into the bedroom. "Do you think I'd ask you to help if there was any way around it?"

"Sorry, but I'm not changing my mind."

"I knew you'd be this way." Scowling, Arel came forward wearily, making his way to the side table by the wall. He used it as his new crutch, leaning on the table like a parched man coming out of the desert. "I'm asking nicely. Fly back with me."

William noted that Arel's trembling hand was only inches away from his new Lalique vase. "Arel, please."

"I know, I know. You think I'm crazy."

"No, I just think you should come and sit down over here where we can discuss this calmly."

"Calmly?" Arel straightened up and glared back. "I'm worried as hell about Carol losing her baby!"

"Yes, I can see that you're under a strain."

"This isn't about me!"

"I want her best too, but—"

"I don't believe you!" Arel pounded the side table with his palm, making the table shake and the crystal vase wobble precariously. "You could care less about Carol!"

"Arel, please—" William grabbed his cane and stood up. Keeping an eye on the vase, he slowly advanced towards the side table. "Tell me why you think I can help."

Arel rubbed at his face and sighed. "I hardly slept last night, and my heart is racing. If Carol needs help, I'm going to be totally useless in my present condition." He sagged more heavily on the table. "I think that's why you had the dream. Maybe you can do something."

William approached Arel slowly. "I'm sorry that you're exhausted."

"Are you sure about that?" Arel's left eye twitched as he worked his fist open and closed.

"You've always worried a lot. It's sapped your energy." William put a hand on Arel's shoulder to steady him. "Come and sit down."

Arel fired back a wounded look. "You're one of the main reasons I'm like this."

William noticed the change coming over Arel. At times, when Arel was really upset, his eyes transformed into pure, golden orbs that were twice as bright as normal eyes. "What do you mean? "Why would you worry about me? I'm getting better."

"That hit man you contacted is coming to London. That's why I've stuck around this long. He plans on hunting you down like one of those foxes you used to love."

The statement hung between them for a long moment. Finally William looked away, limped over to a chair and took hold of the back. It was his turn to steady himself, not because of the news about Rolphe, but because Arel's gaze reminded him of his vision of the twin boys. Arel was the smaller of the two, but his eyes could be bright as fire in that life too. He had a fierce temper and fought like a possessed demon if he thought William might be in trouble. William was just as protective. "Let it go, Arel. I've always been able to take care of myself. It's you that needs looking after."

221

Arel turned his attention to the vase and began to trace its flowing lines with a shaky finger. "I know it's my problem, but I can't live with the idea that someone will take you out, Will. So here's the deal, come back with me to Chicago. Help Carol. Afterwards, you can recoup at my home. When you're better, and I know you can handle this villain, you can come back to London."

William's hands tightened on the chair. Arel looked like hell, but he still had the determination of a hungry bear going after beehive honey. Besides, there was something about the woman in William's dream that affected him on a deeper level than he wanted to admit. "If I do this thing, will you forget about me, once and for all?"

Arel nodded. "Yes, I promise."

"Got anything more reliable than a promise?"

"I wish my word was enough. I hope that someday I'll earn your trust again." Arel stopped fingering the vase and picked it up to examine it more closely. "This piece has exquisite form, doesn't it? Sorry about breaking the other one. I'm looking for a replacement."

"Good luck, I searched for years. Its color made it very rare."

"Years?" Arel jerked around, nearly dropping the vase as his eyes went wide with concern.

"Careful," William whispered as he returned to Arel's side. He retrieved the vase, holding it firmly to himself, out of harm's reach. "Now go and do what you have to. Buy me that damn ticket to Chicago."

Arel's face became that of a choir boy caught drinking the communion wine. "Uh . . . I've already purchased it. We leave in a few hours. I better help you pack." He went to the closet, was about to open it, but hesitated. "And about your sofa and that little place on the arm . . . the fabric glue seems to be holding."

William squinted back. "What are you talking about now?"

"Hello! I'm back."

Annabel's voice called out from the foyer, interrupting William's thoughts. Just hearing her voice made his day seem brighter, especially when he contemplated a trip to Chicago. Being away from her was another reason to agree to the trip. The old saying, "Absence makes the heart grow fonder," would be put to the test.

Forty-Two

Arel breathed a ragged sigh of relief as the Mustang pulled up to the curb at the airport pickup area. Carey was at the wheel, and he offered a broad smile when he parked the car and got out to help with the luggage. Arel was too rattled to smile back. If he thought his nerves were bad before he left London, he was wrong about how stressed and panicked he could feel. The plane ride alone nearly finished him off. Not only had William suffered after being forced into traveling, he'd relapsed into a terrible state, gritting his teeth, trying not to cry out. Arel tried to help, but his own body was in a useless state. Worry about William and Carol had muddied and tainted any miracle waters he might bestow. His heart, that place that held explosive, healing light, was shrouded over by an ominous, black cloud. He was sure some terrible fate awaited William and Carol. Of course, there was the possibility that his feelings of doom were a result of his negative imagination. When Carol was in labor with baby Ariel, he'd been despairing too.

"Arel, what else can I do?" Carey asked after he'd stowed away their bags.

"Help me into the car, young man," William moaned out.

"Yes, help William," Arel said as he came back from his dark musings. His fingers were clutching at the handles on William's wheelchair so tightly that he had to consciously focus in order to let go of them. At least the chair was one small blessing that helped with William. Arel had been able to procure one without too much problem. He'd also had help with their luggage. Carey was another blessing. He seemed very competent when it came to transferring William to the back seat of the car. After he fastened William's seatbelt, he turned to Arel again. His eyes were bright and encouraging. They conveyed a hopeful message that was potent enough for Arel to find the strength to climb wearily into the front passenger seat. "We better take William home before going to the hospital," Arel said to Carey once the car was in motion.

"No, I said I'd help, and unlike some people, I keep my word," William replied gruffly.

Carey glanced back at him. "It's nice to meet you, sir. I'm sorry you're so ill."

"Arel has pronounced me well enough to travel. That's good enough for me," William groaned.

"Please, Will, I couldn't leave you in London. Now I'm taking you home."

William shook his head. "No, I'll see this thing out. If my dream means anything, maybe I'm supposed to help."

Carey frowned as he weaved his way to a lane that was moving faster. "Arel, I have some bad news. Carol isn't doing well."

Arel had been avoiding tapping into Carol's energy field. He didn't want to invade her privacy. But just a quick glimpse at the condition of her aura told him that his fears were grounded in reality.

"And, of course, Michael hasn't done a thing to help." Arel blurted out the statement without thinking. His panicked state was triggering his anger. As always, Michael was an easy target. He'd become Arel's substitute father, a figure with unlimited patience whose shoulders were broad enough to put up with Arel's need to vent.

Carey shot Arel another glance. "Michael's been at the hospital the whole time. He's doing all he can."

Arel narrowed his eyes into slits of fixated temper. "I just wish it didn't always come down to me having to find a way out of every mess."

Carey looked over again. "I'm sorry—"

"What good is it to be sorry?"

William let out a gasp. "Stop being a bastard to your friend, Arel. This situation isn't his fault."

Arel knew William was right. He was taking his anger out on Carey too. He rubbed at his face, hoping to clear away some of the fear, but his gut was telling him to prepare for the worst. "Sorry, Carey, I'm really beyond rational at this point. Carol's been in a very tough place recently. With this pregnancy and possibly losing the child, who knows how she'll react."

"I get that," Carey said. "But why are you angry at Michael?"

"That's an easy one," William groaned again. "Arel is at war with anybody who threatens that little reality bunker he calls his life."

Arel tightened his jaw, trying to keep his tone in check. "I want the people I care about to be safe and happy. When one of them is in trouble I get upset."

"So you take your lousy attitude out on the rest of them?" William asked.

"You're one to talk. You don't have any friends to care about." As soon as he said it, Arel knew he was doing exactly what William said, striking out like a madman. The more he heard himself, the more he started to worry about his own mental state. "I didn't mean that, Will. You've always tried to be there for me. As for my part, I am trying to help. Please believe that."

"I believe you, Arel," Carey chimed in. "You saved me that night I had an accident, and I was a complete stranger."

"And now you're his chauffer, right?" William asked.

Carey beamed back a smile. "Arel's been great. He took me to Hawaii."

William let out a barely audible laugh. "Lucky kid, I got a first class ticket to Hades."

Carey gave the rear view mirror a quick check. "I don't understand."

William laid his head back and closed his eyes. "Pray that it stays that way, young man, or you could end up like me."

Arel clamped his jaws shut. What more could he say? William was right about everything he was telling Carey.

Forty-Three

The last time Kevin sat by Carol's hospital bed, he was smiling with pride. He'd been holding his newborn son and was awestruck by how perfect little Ariel was. When Carol got pregnant a second time, it was a surprise that quickly turned into an opportunity. Kevin took time off to make sure that Carol could rest. They continued to talk frequently, like they had in Paris. They began to dream again, to imagine how wonderful another child would be. Ariel would have a little brother or sister. All was going so well until earlier that day when Carol came out of the bathroom and announced that she thought she was losing the baby. Still, she fought so hard to hold on to the new life within her womb. When she failed, she cried just as hard, blaming herself for their loss.

Kevin wanted to bawl too. As he clasped empty hands together, he knew he'd never get to cradle his second child. Not only that, he didn't know how to help Carol. Earlier, when he looked at her, she stared back like she was totally lost in her sense of failure and grief. After all they'd gone through, trying to learn how to relate to each other, there was a new barrier between them, and Kevin didn't know any way to scale it. If the wall between them was a physical obstacle, he could batter it down. But how could he batter down something as intangible as Carol's sense of failure?

"Hi, Kev," Peggy said as she tiptoed into the room.

Kevin returned a little wave. "Carol finally fell asleep," he whispered.

Peggy's bright eyes dimmed when she looked at Carol, but she continued over to where Kevin was sitting. She put her arms around his shoulders. "Tim and I came as soon as we could. I got a neighbor's daughter to babysit the kids for a little while."

"Thanks, I appreciate both of you trying to help out."

"Again, I'm so sorry." Peggy's usually animated voice was subdued and quiet.

"I guess it wasn't meant to be, but how can I get Carol to believe that?"

"It's tough, I know."

"Why does it have to be this way? Why does Carol have to do this to herself?"

"I don't have any answers, Kevin. I wish I did, but I do have a surprise. Arel is here. He's in the waiting room."

"Arel? I thought he was in London."

"He flew back as soon as he heard the news."

"That was nice of him."

"He wanted so much to help. He was deeply saddened by the news."

"Kevin?" Carol's eyes fluttered open, immediately searching Kevin out and targeting him with a helpless stare. "I was afraid you left."

"Of course not. I'm here for you," he said. He quickly stood up and took Carol's hand. "Do you need anything?"

"No, it's just I can't really sleep very well when I think about—"

"Honey, please," Kevin pleaded. "Try to rest."

Peggy moved to Carol's other side and kissed her cheek. "Kevin's right, but when you're feeling up to it, Arel wants to see you."

"Arel? He's here?" Carol asked.

Kevin smiled at her. "He came back as soon as he heard you were in the hospital."

"Really?" Carol's eyes brightened a little.

"You know how much he cares about you," Kevin added.

Carol sniffled and pulled his hand closer. "He cares about both of us."

Kevin smoothed back a lock of Carol's blond hair. "There's no rush, but when you're ready—"

Carol frowned. "I had the strangest dream a night or two ago. I want to ask him about it."

"A dream?" Peggy asked.

Carol sniffled again. "Yes, I dreamed about Arel's friend."

Peggy's brows arched. "You're kidding. Arel brought the guy back with him."

Carol let out a little gasp. "He's here too? I want to see them both."

Kevin remembered Arel's friend from New York. The man was okay, but there was something strange about him that Kevin didn't quite trust. On the other hand, Arel was extremely protective. He would never do anything to hurt any of them. "Are you sure, Carol? Are you up to seeing them now?"

The little spark faded from Carol's eyes. "What's there to lose at this point? I've already lost everything."

"Honey, please," Kevin pleaded. "You haven't lost Ariel or me."

Carol bit her lip. "I'm sorry. I know you're right, but—"

"It's going to take time, okay?" Kevin said. "But if you want to see Arel, I'll go get him." Arel had been the one person who seemed able to get them through challenging times in the past. Kevin hoped that Arel could find a way again. He started to let go of Carol's hand.

Carol hung on to him. "No, stay here."

"Of course, I will." He looked at Peggy. "Would you go get them, sis?"

* * *

William sat in the waiting room, cursing the fact that he'd agreed to come. The trip had taken a horrible toll on his body. It was begging for relief from the constant pain in his gut and the pounding in his head. Arel seemed to understand and tried to help, but his energy was so low, he was totally ineffective. Happily the waiting room was empty except for their party. William had been introduced to Tim, a tall, robust guy whose shoulders were wide enough to hold up a small building. Now Tim had the job of talking to Arel, trying to help him to relax.

Good luck with that one, you poor soul.

Michael and young Carey were sitting quietly on the other side of the room. Both were reading. Carey's young enthusiasm was barely contained as his grey blue eyes scoured the page of a travel magazine. Michael was the solid, mature one. He had stayed in the background while he was at William's London home, rarely coming anywhere near. He seemed to have the same attitude now, except for

228

isolated moments when he'd glance up at Arel with a sparkling look of concern.

Arel says he's an angel. Maybe so.

At this point, Arel's Madness had taken hold so completely, William believed about anything. As soon as he had the thought, Michael's eyes lifted. As William stared back, Michael's mesmerizing gaze held the moment suspended long enough to ease some of William's pain. He also experienced a strange feeling that his mind was being disengaged, that he might lose what little control he had left.

The hell with that!

As soon as he looked away, the connection was broken and the pain flooded back. It was a price William was prepared to pay. What was left if one's mind was lost? As he shifted his weight, trying to find some small comfort, the red haired woman named Peggy came back. She went directly to Arel and grabbed his arm. Arel winced, tightening his jaw as he struggled to appear composed.

He's wound up tighter than a Christmas clock.

After a short bit of whispered conversation between Peggy and Arel, both of them looked at William.

Oh hell, it's show time.

The thought of having to see the unhappy woman from his dream, combined with a sudden stabbing pain were too much. William's mind blanked out as another vision took over. This time he wasn't in Greece or Rome. He was a little boy again, but not Arel's twin. In this life, he was dressed in rags, and he stood in the middle of a mob scene. A little girl, sobbing uncontrollably, was next to him. Her dirty face was streaked with tears as he tried to console her, but they both shook with fear and anguish. Misery hung in the air, punishing both of them with a sense of hopelessness as they clung to each other.

All is lost!

The words were still echoing in William's mind when Arel shook his shoulder. He jerked upright and stared at the waiting room. "Where am I?" he mumbled. He tried to orientate himself, but his mind was slipping back and forth between two worlds. He couldn't keep the waiting room in focus. He kept seeing the angry mob, hearing their vicious shouts and slurs. He kept seeing the little girl's desolate face as he tried to escape the pain in his gut. Her sadness intensified the grief that the little boy felt. The children were in some hellish situation. It was so intense that it drew William in, grabbing hold of his psyche with dark, malicious tentacles. He tried to stay focused on his present reality, but the mob and the darkness became a consuming force that overrode his rational abilities. The pain in his gut exploded and became so excruciating that it threatened to overwhelm everything he knew himself to be. In the middle of his ordeal, Arel was trying to get through to him.

"William, what's going on?" Arel asked.

William looked up at Arel with eyes that belonged to the ragged, pathetic boy in the other world. They were pleading, fluid orbs, filled with the knowledge that the man in front of him was a traitor, an evil agent who was responsible for the torture that was waiting for him.

Arel stared back with an acute concern. "William, talk to me!"

Arel's demanding tone was enough to bring William back to the waiting room for the briefest moment. "I hate you!" he blurted out. The statement couldn't be contained any more than the rage that burned in William's gut. His trip into the past had given him a clear understanding of who Arel really was and what he'd done to the little girl and boy. He tried to stand, to confront the person who destroyed both of them. "Hell is too good for you!" he cried out as his legs buckled and he began to fall.

Arel reached out to help, but William's journey back into a past life happened too fast. The world exploded in flames. Fire surrounded him. He couldn't escape the flames or the smiling demons who watched him suffer.

Forty-Four

Rolphe had barely arrived in London when he decided to return home. His targets, William and his friend, must have taken a trip of their own. He knew it as soon as he set foot on English soil and tried to tune into their energy. When he returned to his flat in Paris, he closed the door on the episode with disappointment and relief. Killing was a job, and a tiresome one at that.

I'll give it some time and try again later.

In the meantime, he'd go back to doing something he loved, painting. He'd indulged in applying color to canvas for years. His expressions were varied and included many styles. The hall leading into his studio was a small gallery of his efforts. He paused in front of his wife's portrait and touched the raised layers of soft pinks and beiges. The Mona Lisa had been an influence, but he turned to cubism for his actual presentation. The background included a garden, something she loved. He'd broken up her smile into triangular sections, one being markedly lower than the other.

"We live in two different worlds, you in the heavens and me down below. Even if I die someday, there'll be no beautiful gardens for me, not after all the sins I've committed."

The next painting, another of his children, had a Titian softness. There was no room for the angular when it came to his boys. "My little angels," he said as he stopped for a moment to kiss their faces.

The third work of art on the wide corridor was a modern piece. An all-black background displayed only minimal color and expressed exactly how he had viewed his beloved cat, Satan. A small, faded Cheshire smile and two large, soulful eyes looked out from the canvas. He sighed as he realized how much he missed the big tom. "You and I understood each other." They both had their battles.

They were both soldiers of sorts. "But in the end, we wanted to come home to a warm fire."

He reached down and picked up Dantela, holding her close, enjoying the loud purr she made. She was always on his heels, following him from room to room. "You're not as aloof as your father, are you?"

When he reached the studio, he deposited the kitten in a wicker basket. It was something new he'd picked up just for her. Satan never bothered with the studio, but Dantela was different. She insisted on always being next to him. A soft, plush cushion made the basket a perfect cat bed. He figured it would keep her content while he worked. He was wrong. He was about to sit down at his easel, when she meowed in protest and jumped out of the new accommodation.

"You wicked little pest," he hissed as she came over and stared up at him. He bent over and scooped her up. He held her high over his head. "What now?" Some kittens would have been afraid of such an elevated position, but Dantela seemed to think that he was paying her the due that she deserved. Her clear, blue eyes closed and opened in her usual relaxed way. "Yes, I am extraordinary," she was telling him. When she finally meowed, it meant, "Now hold me close. Pet me and adore me."

He laughed as he nuzzled her softness and the kitten rubbed her face against his cheek. "You petite little shit, I can't believe you're sleeping in my bed now. You are the first animal to achieve such a triumph. And for good reason! I could have one of my nightmares and kill you." He frowned. "Now I have to stay aware in my sleep so that I can keep you safe."

He walked out of the gallery and made his way to the kitchen. "Are you hungry?" He sat the kitten down on Satan's cushioned chair and retrieved some fresh, ground rabbit from the refrigerator. Dantella watched as he portioned out a bit in her feeding dish, but she had manners. She waited for him to pick her up and take her to her special bowl, one that Myra made in her pottery class. When she ate, her bites were small and she often stopped to glance over at him as she enjoyed her favorite food.

Rolphe sat down at the table and watched her. The kitten was a reminder of what he liked best about himself. He enjoyed taking care of those he loved. Long ago, bringing home an extra chicken for the family soup pot had warmed his heart. But caring wasn't always an option. Again, his mind went to William and the other man he was hunting. "What a wearisome chore I have in front of me, Dantela."

But chores were part of life, and Rolphe accepted that fact. That meant that he'd have to take time each evening to tune into William's whereabouts. Now that he'd already accomplished that feat, it would be much easier to locate him. When the man returned to London, Rolphe would make his move.

Forty-Five

The lower level of Arel's suburban rancher was quiet except for William's delirious moaning. His fever had been raging for two days.

Why is he so sick again? Why did he get so angry at the hospital?

The questions repeated over and over in Arel's mind. Michael was sympathetic but wouldn't comment. As usual, he wasn't allowed to interfere with explanations.

But I need answers.

Arel wrung out an icy compress and held it on William's head. He'd tried his best to help, but neither he nor Michael could put out the inferno that burned in William's body and soul. The condition was so serious that Arel knew William couldn't take much more before his body gave out.

A soft knock intruded on Arel's thoughts and made him glance at the door. Who was his visitor? Peggy had come over several times. Perhaps she was back. He loved her dearly, but her visits could be draining, especially when she tried to help out by fussing over him. He had to remember that she meant well as he put the cloth in the basin and let out a sigh of resignation. "Come in."

The door opened enough for Carol to peek in. "Michael said it was okay to come down and check on you and your friend."

"Carol!" Arel dried his hands and stood up. "It's so good to see you. I'm sorry I couldn't visit at the hospital." He went over to hug her. "How are you? Should you be up and about?"

"I'm okay, physically that is. I'm still pretty depressed about—"

"I know. I'm so sorry that I couldn't come back from London sooner."

"There was nothing you could do. Kevin keeps reminding me that sometimes things like this just happen. He says we have to make peace with the ups and downs, but it's not that easy."

Arel glanced at William. "You're right. But why don't we go upstairs and talk. I can get Michael to sit with William."

"If it's okay, could I just stay here for a little while?"

"Are you sure you're up for that?"

"Yes, please, just for a bit."

"Of course, but I have to warn you, Will calls out in his sleep off and on. He's in a lot of pain."

"I know, Michael explained his condition. It'll be okay. I had a grandfather who was in a bad way when I was a teenager. I sat with him on a number of occasions. But you could do something for me."

"Anything."

"Could you get me a cup of tea?"

* * *

As soon as Arel left, Carol went over to where he'd been sitting and pushed back the chair. She wanted a closer look at William.

Oh, my goodness!

Her throat tightened. The man lying on the bed was a flesh and blood version of the person she'd dreamed about. She smiled as she continued to study him.

He's very handsome.

With sandy brown hair and pleasing angular features, William had a distinguished look that could have belonged to gentry or to an actor playing James Bond.

But how could I have dreamed about him before I met him?

Peggy was the one who had premonitions and vivid dreams. Was it Carol's turn now? She sucked in a deep breath and then boldly reached out for William's hand. Her fingers hovered inches away from his.

Stop it! You don't really know this person.

An inner voice was forever telling her what she couldn't do. Tears immediately blurred her vision. The voice told her that she couldn't hold on to her baby, that she was too weak to fight the unseen powers that governed life. She'd fought the cruel declaration.

She tried to save her unborn child. But in the end, she failed. Now, she hated that voice.

I won't listen to it anymore!

She flicked away the tears and grabbed William's hand, clasping it to her chest.

Oh god, you're so hot. You're burning up.

Her blouse was a useless barrier against William's fevered limb. Heat penetrated the clothing and her body, searing her heart as William's plight and a vision of her lost baby merged. Would William's life be snatched away too? She gasped at the idea and clung more fervently to William's hand. Pondering another death was too much, especially when she thought about her dream again. The man in front of her was a friend. She didn't know how or why she felt that way, but she knew it was true. He also acted as her ally in the dream.

"And as your friend, William, I want to be here for you!"

Her words, issued in a loud whisper, made something unfamiliar, almost foreign in her makeup resurrect itself. It was a strong and powerful part of her that she'd let slip away when her parents got divorced. Somehow the event stripped her of her courage. Ever since then, she'd allowed life to frighten her, to beat her down whenever she needed to believe in herself. As she let the feeling of courage and strength seep into her cells again, she made a silent vow.

I'm going to be tough from now on. I have to be.

The thought was restorative, making her throw back her shoulders. Somewhere, she'd read that love was stronger than any dark forces. The concept fell on barren ground when she was losing her baby. Her walls of hardened fear hadn't allowed the light of love to penetrate her misery. But what good did her fear do? The baby was gone.

But this man doesn't have to die too!

In the end, she knew that fear was a weakening agent, and she wouldn't give in to it this time. She put William's hand back on the white linen sheet and reached for the cold compress. She had to pause when an idea slipped in unexpectedly. What if she took over William's care? What if she could help him in a very tangible way? Maybe she could be William's nurse. The idea made her smile. "I won't let anything happen to you," she said as she put the cloth on his forehead. As she held it in place, she imagined what William must have looked like when he was a boy. "I bet you were sweet like my

Ariel. If my second child had lived, he or she would have been sweet too. I'm sure of it."

Her words were barely out, when Arel came back with her tea. She looked at him and shivered. She had to swallow back a lump in her throat.

Arel seemed to notice her reaction. "Carol? Are you okay?" he asked as he came over to where she was standing.

She moved back a little, wondering why she felt nervous being around him. Arel had always been a good friend. So why did she want him to leave? She didn't know the answer, but his presence made her frown.

Arel hesitated. "What's the matter?"

She pulled back her shoulders even more, rooting herself to the spot. No matter how Arel made her feel, she wouldn't leave her post. "I'm fine."

"Of course, you are," he said in a soothing voice. "But why don't you sit over there in that comfortable seat that Michael likes. I'll take care of William."

She made herself step forward, putting herself between Arel and William. "No, I think you should stay away from him."

"What are you talking about?"

"Remember what you said to Peggy and me about hurting your friend, William?"

"Yes, but I didn't mean—"

"Please, don't hurt him again." Her plea came from some deep inner well of mistrust and danger. "Please, Arel."

"I don't intend to hurt—"

"He's suffered enough!"

"Carol, you know me. I only want what's—"

"Please!" Her voice became loud and insistent. She grabbed William's hand again as his moans and heated gasps were joined by flashes of her unborn child and how quickly that child had been lost. "He's helpless. Can't you see that? Was he helpless before?"

Arel put the tea on the dresser and stared back. "I don't understand why you're acting this way."

"Because you need to stay away from him!"

"What are you trying to tell me, Carol?"

"For once in my life I know that I have to find a way to take back something I've lost."

"I think I should call Kevin. You must be tired. You need to go home and rest."

"You'd like that, wouldn't you? Send the crazy person away. But I'm not crazy. Admit it. William is here because of me."

"What?" Arel paused. "He did have a dream about you, but—"

"I knew it!"

"Please Carol—"

"I know what to do now."

"What's that?"

Carol took a deep breath. She wasn't going to cry anymore. When she looked at William, at how much pain was expressed in his tortured face, she knew what was needed. "William and I are going to fight the darkness together."

"What darkness?"

"The one that took my baby. The one that's trying to take William."

"Carol, my dear, you're—"

"Anybody home?" Peggy's voice called out from the upstairs foyer. "Hello!"

Arel jerked around in the direction of Peggy's voice.

Carol let out a sigh of relief. Another ally had arrived. "We're down here!" she called out.

* * *

When Peggy let herself into Arel's house, she thought she heard voices coming from the downstairs level. Happily, Carol answered her greeting in an enthusiastic tone. Arel wasn't always as welcoming. Of course, Peggy accepted his shyness. It was a sign that he wasn't coping well with life, and she had to tread carefully.

"Coming!" She started towards the stairs and quickly rounded the wrought iron banister. She'd had a nap while Sara slept. Now, Tim was at home babysitting, and she felt energized as she skipped down the steps. Before going into the bedroom where William was staying, she paused, fluffing out her hair and straightening her sweater. She also reminded herself to keep her voice down. On her last visit, William moaned out loudly every time her volume rose above a whisper.

He's very sensitive for a person who's unconscious. He's probably a lot like Arel.

"Carol?" She used her softest voice as she continued towards the room. She also put on her nicest smile in case Arel was there too. When he was in one of his moods, he needed all the cheering up that she could muster. When she walked into the bedroom, Arel was there, and he looked worse than usual. His sagging shoulders and wounded eyes reminded her of a puppy who'd been left on the street to fend for itself. Carol, on the other hand, had never looked more formidable. With her head raised high and her eyes narrowed and hard, she looked the part of a blond, warrior princess ready to lop off the next interloper's head. The tension in the room was so thick, Peggy went on instant alert. "Hey, guys, what's going on?" she asked.

Arel leaped to her side and quickly took her arm. "I need to talk to you upstairs!"

"No! Stay here!" Carol shrieked.

William added a third voice. It was weak and imploring. "My god, my head is splitting in two. Stop yelling, please!"

The sound of William's voice affected both Carol and Arel at the same time. Each one became even more animated. Carol quickly retreated to William's side, snatching up his hand. Arel ran to the opposite side of the bed.

"Will, you're awake! I'm so relieved!" Arel gasped.

"Don't worry! You have a friend now!" Carol cried out.

Peggy moved closer and stood at the bottom of the bed, observing the three people in front of her. Arel was hardly breathing as he hovered anxiously over William. William looked like he was ready to pass out again. Carol stood over him like a mother bear, but she was gripping his hand so tight, her knuckles were white.

Peggy blinked back at the group. It was a good thing she came over when she did.

* * *

William knew without a doubt that he'd visited hell. The horrific stories he'd been told as a child were true. There were demons waiting in Hades. They threw him into a flaming bonfire. The pain was unbearable, but the fiends laughed at his suffering.

Or was it a dream?

The sound of voices pulled him from the fiery scene. His head was pounding, and he was still hot, but he wasn't in the midst of flames anymore. There were people, not demons, around him. Arel was on one side of the bed. The red headed woman from the hospital stood at the bottom. He thought she was called Peggy. A third person, a petite blond was holding his hand.

No, she's not just holding it, she's crushing it.

But at least he wasn't in hell anymore.

I can't let myself fall asleep again.

As soon as he began to drift off, he saw the flames reaching out for him. He recoiled, trying to keep his eyes from closing. The bone crushing grip on his hand helped. It kept him focused on the real world, but he didn't need more pain. He grimaced at the woman as he tried to pull away from her clutches. He was so weak, he couldn't manage it.

"Carol, I think you're hurting him," the red haired woman cautioned.

"Oh, I'm sorry." The blond lady frowned contritely and let him go. She quickly grabbed a cloth from a basin and wrung it out. "My name is Carol," she said as she placed the cold compress on William's head. "I'm so happy that you're awake."

For a moment, she reminded William of Annabel. Both had green eyes. Annabel's were darker and more beautiful, but this woman's were filled with a similar concern and kindness.

William put his hand on the compress. "Thank you, Carol."

"Tell me what I can do. What do you need?" she asked.

"Don't let me fall asleep. I don't want to go back to that horrid place of torment."

Carol glanced across the bed and gave Arel a scowling look. "Don't worry, I won't let anyone hurt you anymore."

William saw the commitment in her fierce gaze. Was it true? Could this small woman keep the fire and the demons away from him?

Arel leaned in. "I'm here, Will, I won't leave you."

As soon as their eyes connected, William felt so weak it was hard to keep his eyes open. But the worst part was that he was incapable of fighting the person who was responsible for his recent trip to hell. He could only gasp out a few words. "Leave me alone."

Arel's eyes dimmed. "But Will—"

"Please listen to him, Arel," Carol said. "He needs to rest, and you seem to be upsetting him."

"Maybe she's right," the red headed woman said as she quickly moved to Carol's side. She stared at Arel. "You're tired too. Let Carol and I take over for a while."

William was relieved to see Arel back off and excuse himself. Perhaps the two women were going to be helpful. He'd never been able to get Arel to leave so easily. The thought that someone had power over his nemesis made William's breath ease a little. When he blinked up at the women, they smiled back. Carol took up his hand again, but this time she held it carefully.

"Remember me? I'm Peggy," the red head said.

He'd never liked the concept of "nice" people, but he needed all the assistance he could get if he wanted to foil the designs of devils and stay out of the nightmarish place he'd just left. "I'm William. Welcome to my world of insanity."

Peggy laughed. "Don't worry, I know that world very well, William."

"It seems I'm its newest inhabitant," Carol sighed.

William tried to sit up, but he didn't have the muscle for it.

Peggy saw his problem and immediately ran around to the other side of the bed. "Let us help you," she said as she and Carol each took an arm and helped to shift his position.

"Better?" Carol asked.

"Yes, much better." Just having Arel leave the room seemed to lift some invisible burden from William's psyche. After a few moments of basking in peace, his lids weren't as heavy. "Can I ask you both something?"

Carol beamed out a wide smile. She seemed very eager to please. "Anything."

"Is your craziness connected to Arel in any way?"

Both women blushed.

"He did kind of turn my world upside down," Peggy said. "But I love him dearly."

"He's been wonderful." Carol's gaze dropped as she hugged her arms. "It's just that I don't think he's always been there for you."

It was an earnest, but understated comment, delivered in such an innocent tone, that William let out a bark of laughter. His head protested with a new bout of sharp pain as he looked at Carol with the solemn eyes of a tormented soul. "Let's just say I was a happy, contented individual before Arel and I got reacquainted."

Carol bit her lip. "And you're going to be happy and contented again if I have anything to do with it."

Peggy stared at him with the same sorry look that you gave a dog that was still alive after being run over by a car. "I'm sure that Arel doesn't mean to hurt people, William. You have to believe that."

"He doesn't mean to hurt people?" A flash of hell in all its fury reminded William of why just hearing Arel's name made him cringe. He needed to explain a few things to his two Florence Nightingale companions. "I'm sorry, but I can't believe that Arel is wonderful or well meaning, not after what I've gone through." He paused and looked at each of them. "Carol, Peggy, let's get something straight. If you want to help me, you'll keep Arel as far away from me as possible. Otherwise, you can both leave too."

Forty-Six

Michael sat waiting in Arel's upper level bedroom. Within a few minutes, Arel came in, but barely acknowledged his presence. "I think we should talk about what happened," Michael said quietly.

Arel slumped down on the bed, staring at clenched hands. "It's no use, Michael. This time there's nothing you can say or do that will convince me that I'm not a monster. No wonder William hates me. I just tapped into his thoughts. After what I saw, after what I learned about myself, I truly qualify as one of life's cruelest bastards."

"He's caught up in the past, in a life that he lived a very long time ago."

"Yes, I know! It's that damnable life when I was burned at the stake. I've barely made peace with what happened to me and Peggy. Now I realize I'm responsible for getting William burned alive too." He glanced up for a brief instant. "He was just a child, a mere boy, and the thugs in the crowd tossed him on the flames like a piece of kindling!"

"Yes, that's right. Others were responsible for what was done to him."

"But he wouldn't have been there if it wasn't for me. I was his hero, the person in the village that he followed around. He tried to stop them from burning me, and they killed him too! It was so brutal! I can see every detail. I can hear him screaming as he burned!"

"How could you stop what happened to him when you were being burned too?" Michael stood up, went over to the bed and clapped a steadying hand on Arel's shoulder. "Why are you taking this on yourself?"

"There's more to it! I left him behind. When my soul finally escaped my body, it flew upwards into the void. I never even looked back at him. I was so consumed by my own rage that I left that little boy to burn alone. He was screaming for me, and I ignored his pleas and kept going. I had no concern for anyone but myself."

Michael pulled over a chair and sat down in front of Arel. "Look at me, dear friend."

Arel averted his eyes. "No."

"Please, it's very important. Do it for William."

Arel lifted his gaze and stared back. His golden eyes were hooded over with shame and disgrace. "Why do you want to look at a selfish coward? How is that going to help William?"

"Do you trust me?"

"I guess I do."

"Then listen carefully. You just told me that you were consumed with rage, correct?"

"Yes."

"It's the only thing you had left, wasn't it?"

"What else is there when your sister is burning beside you and you're both screaming for mercy and no one answers your pleas? I know you tried to help, Michael. I know you couldn't get through my despair, but—"

"You tried your best, Arel. You tried to save your sister when they arrested her. You put her welfare above your own safety, remember?"

"But I couldn't save her!"

"I know. In your mind, all the things in life that you cherished were destroyed by people who hated you. You gave up on life."

"It's true. I didn't want to exist anymore."

"Before you abandoned that boy, you abandoned yourself. But it's different now. You took another chance on life."

"But that boy looked to me for help!"

"Help the man that he is now."

"I've tried, and I only make things worse."

"Yes, I know, but what if you shift your attention to another memory?" He shook Arel's shoulder again, gently, playfully. "You and William have been having flashbacks to that life when you were twins."

A weak smile spread across Arel's face. "Yes, at least we had one life when we were happy. Even as grown men, our families were close. We celebrated everything together. The bond that we shared felt like having one, great heart between us."

"And in the life when you were both burned?"

Arel hesitated, but his gaze brightened at he grabbed on to Michael. "That heart was torn in two! When I lost faith in myself, I lost faith in both of us."

"You weren't the only one who lost his way. You cursed at god and William cursed at you. You both wanted to blame someone outside yourselves."

Arel scowled as he let out a little, contemptuous laugh. "We were won over to the dark side by the trauma and ignorance we experienced at the stake."

"And now?"

"When I look at your eyes, I see the light again. That's how you've helped me, but William doesn't want that light. And if I have any of it in me, Carol doesn't seem to see it either."

"Remember, you've known her in other lives too. She saw both you and William burned at the stake. She was a child too. She felt helpless."

"So much has been happening. I keep forgetting about that."

"Yes, but now it's time to remember."

"Carol said something about fighting the darkness. How can I help her?"

"This is something she needs to do for herself. In the meantime, you can believe in her and in William, and most of all, you can believe in yourself."

Forty-Seven

Carol swapped out babysitting time with Peggy. That way, they could each spend time each day watching over William. Peggy took the mornings, and Carol took the afternoons. They compared notes on how William was doing. They both agreed that he was already much better by their second day of vigil. His fever still came and went, but overall, he was completely lucid and in much less pain. Now, he sat across from her in an upholstered bedroom chair. He seemed to enjoy her reading to him. She put the book in her lap and arched her brows in his direction. "Tell me, why did you want a book on the history of antique glassware?"

William barely moved, but his eyes flickered in her direction for a brief moment. "Why not?"

"It's rather boring, isn't it?"

William smiled. "You're learning about how beautiful objects came to be. How could that be boring?"

"I never thought of it that way."

"What kind of books do you read?"

"Since having little Ariel, I mostly read parenting stuff. But I used to enjoy a good mystery."

"A 'Who done it?' Wouldn't it be better to solve a bigger mystery, like what makes life go round?"

"Life? That's a pretty big issue to tackle."

"When you don't tackle the big issues, you end up like Arel. You said he was pretty messed up when you met him."

Carol blushed. "I shouldn't talk about him behind his back, but the first time we met, he nearly jumped out of his skin. He was very frightened."

"Unlike me, Arel chose to solve his problems by closing himself off from everything. His love affair with his negative emotions was the only thing that he entertained. When you do that, you're bound to end up batty."

"I might not be doing much better. I have all these crazy moods."

"Why do you assume your moods are crazy? Perhaps if you understood that most people are products of their parents and society, you'd think you're doing quite well."

"But I don't want to be a product of anything or anybody."

"Then stop acting like one, Carol. Don't let your feelings run your life like Arel does."

"What do you mean?"

"You're much stronger than you think. Stand up for yourself like you stood up for me."

"I try. I get so angry because I don't know how to—"

"How to what?"

Carol studied the book in her lap. Its beautiful glossy cover featured an exquisite, turquoise vase. She ran her hand over the smooth paper. "You enjoy learning about how people make beautiful things, like the glassware in this book. And I've enjoyed being creative with graphics and art. But I don't know how to make my life beautiful. I try, but I seem to always fall short of the mark."

"You're making excuses. If you can confront Arel, you can do anything you want."

"He's easy."

William's jaw tightened. "No, he's not. He's a pushy bastard, but you stood up to him, and he listened."

Carol placed the book aside and steadied her gaze in his direction. "Just sitting here with you makes me feel better. Thank you for believing in me."

William's pale blue eyes flashed bright for an instant, a tiny fireworks of summer blue. "You'll be fine."

"Do you really think so?"

"You'll waver, but you'll make it. It just takes time to learn how to create something beautiful. Be patient."

Carol studied him for a long moment. He was a very attractive man, but what drew her to him was his strength. Even though he was still recovering, he exuded a tangible aura of control, a control that came from confidence and self-assurance. "You're very kind, William."

"No, I'm not. I don't believe in kindness. I believe in facts. So don't trust me or Arel for that matter. Neither of us warrants it. But if you had to choose, you might pick me. At least I'll always be honest with you."

"You sound bitter when you talk about Arel."

"When you put your faith in someone, and they keep letting you down, you often fall prey to resentment. But I have to blame myself for that shortcoming, that deficit in my character that went outside itself and allowed Arel's ignorance to take me down."

"So why did you come to Chicago with him?"

William lifted his chin, letting his eyes wander to the ceiling and back to her. "I had the feeling that I'd be needed. In other words, I broke my own rule about staying out of other people's problems." He laughed. "Now look at me. I'm sitting here like a delicate house plant needing your TLC."

"I'm glad you came. I'm glad I got to meet you."

"Yes, now take my advice. Put your faith in yourself and forget the rest of humanity."

"I can't be like that. I love my friends. I know they want my best, even if they don't always know how to go about showing it."

"Fine, but don't say I didn't warn you."

* * *

After she said goodbye to William, Carol went next door to Peggy's house to pick up the baby. Tim answered the door and invited her into the living room. With both of the children still napping, he suggested that she sit down for a few minutes. She took a seat on the sofa, happy to get a chance to talk to him. Tim often reminded her of a rock, that balanced human being who always seemed at ease. "What are you doing home this early?"

"I thought I'd take a couple of hours off this afternoon. I think Peggy needs some help now that she's playing a nursemaid to Arel's friend."

"That's sweet of you. Kevin took quite a bit of time off before and after I lost the . . . before I had the miscarriage. He wants to take more vacation time, but I told him to spread it out. I'm getting back to a kind of normalcy. At least I'm not crying all the time."

"I'm glad you're feeling better."

"It's easy to just sit there at William's bedside. It gets my mind off of everything. He makes me feel like I can help, that I'm not a complete failure."

"Of course you're not. Please, believe me when I tell you—"

"I know what you're going to say, that I shouldn't blame myself about what happened. I want to believe that, and maybe I'm beginning to let myself see other possibilities. Everybody, including Michael, has been so caring and supportive. He and I talked a couple of days ago. He believes that a child is never 'lost' in the truest sense. I'm doing my best to understand what he means."

"It takes time, Carol. Give yourself that time to heal."

She let her eyes drop. "I guess, but sometimes it's too painful to think about any of it. Maybe that's why William is a good thing right now. He helps me stay focused in the present."

Tim gave her the kindest of smiles and changed the subject. "How's William doing? From what I heard, he was pretty bad off after he arrived."

"He's better, much better."

"I never quite got the full story on what happened with him and Arel when Arel went to London the first time."

"I don't know much myself, except that William doesn't want Arel around. That first day when I went over to visit, William was extremely ill and very agitated. He really wanted someone to stay with him. It was strange, especially now that I've gotten to know him. He doesn't seem like the type that gets afraid."

"Afraid? Of Arel?"

"Yes, it's a mystery."

"Maybe not. When I first saw William in New York, he looked like he was on top of his game. After a visit to Arel's room on the second night, he was a changed man, tripping over his own feet."

"Really? But you and I both know that Arel is kind and caring."

"Right, but something's going on. Of course, ever since we all met Arel, life has been a little weird."

"He's had his moments, but he's also been there when any of us needed help."

"He's been in the trenches. That's for sure." Tim leaned back in the recliner and laughed. "When Peggy was first pregnant with Sara, she was over at his house every morning, baring her soul. Arel gave her tea and tried to bolster her confidence. It wasn't an easy job. Peggy can be very insistent about things when she doubts herself, but Arel helped."

Carol gave him a playful glance. "Thank goodness that I don't normally have that issue."

"I'm just glad that you're looking better too."

"William has that effect on me. He says that I'll come through what's happened with flying colors, and for some reason I've started believing it."

"Good. Hold on to that feeling."

Forty-Eight

William could count on Carey when it came to having a nighttime nursemaid. After Peggy or Carol went off duty each evening, the young man volunteered to step in. It wasn't a difficult task. Carey slept on a cot and was available if William needed something. William tried to explain that he was fine on his own, but Carol insisted that someone stay with him at night. Carey wasn't William's only companion. Every night, as he began to drift off, a glow at the foot of the bed appeared. It was just like the soft glow he'd seen when he was recovering in his London home.

Now it's time to confront my mysterious visitor.

William turned off the light in anticipation. "Alright, whoever you are," he whispered. "I know you're around. I can feel you." It was true. He noted a slight shift in his body, a ripple of excitement, just before he saw the glow. "Don't be shy, show yourself."

An area next to the bed shimmered as a pale green light came into view. A form began to take shape. William almost changed his mind about meeting his visitor as he watched the shape solidify. He wasn't used to ghosts, much less ghosts who took on a physical form, but his curiosity won out. "I'm waiting."

"You wanted to see me?" The question was voiced by a tall, slender man who appeared a few feet away. His face was both youthful and mature, handsome and beautiful at the same time. "Let me introduce myself. I'm Raphael."

"Oh hell," William sighed. "You're like Michael, aren't you?"

The man smiled. "We're friends."

William was instantly sorry that he had such an inquisitive nature. The last thing he needed was another so called angel. According to Arel, Michael was the one who started all the misery. If it was true, angelic blood was serum that had to come from the

251

S. S. BAZINET

bowels of hell. "I'd still be my happy, normal vampire self if it weren't for your kind."

When William voiced his sentiment in a loud and bitter tone, Raphael glanced over at Carey.

William laughed. "Don't worry, we won't wake him. Carey could sleep through a Kansas tornado. He's supposed to be my little assistant, but God help me if I needed something."

Raphael laughed too. "That's why I'm here. On a number of occasions, you called out when you were in pain."

"A slip of the tongue in a desperate moment."

"Do you want me to leave?"

"Why would I? My life is already totally screwed. You might as well stick around and answer some questions. Supposedly angels can't lie."

"Why would we?"

"Just give me a straight answer. Can you lie, yes or no?"

Raphael walked over to an upholstered chair and sat down. He clasped his hands in his lap and smiled. "I'll answer your questions truthfully."

"Do you all have that attitude?"

"What do you mean?"

"You remind me of an old schoolmaster. He wasn't cruel like some, but he had a superior way of looking at people."

"Sorry, but we're very fluid in nature. When people look at us, they try to categorize who or what they're seeing. They often project images they feel appropriate." He chuckled. "One lady thought I was her dead cat."

William squinted back. "A cat that glows, right? Can you tone back the sunshine? I have a headache."

In spite of being in a physical body, there was still a bright light around Raphael, and his eyes were as dazzling as dark blue sapphires.

"Sometimes it's hard to gauge exactly what people are comfortable with," he said as his glow dimmed.

"I'm not comfortable with any of this mess."

"You're still very angry with Arel."

"Besides infecting me with something I never asked for, something that eventually resulted in my death, Arel still wasn't content. Right now, I could have my own wings. I could be relaxing on the other side with your kind, in some plush paradise. Instead, I've been visiting hell."

"Not exactly hell. You've been caught up in a past life."

A flush of heat went through William's body. "I was beginning to suspect that's what it was."

"A very harrowing life, I'm sure."

"If this fever is connected to a past life, why is my body still reacting this way?"

"The physical vessel stores memories, especially traumatic ones."

"I've begun to see faces in the crowd that tormented me. At first they all looked like devils. Finally, I realized that they were demons, but the human kind."

"And you took some of their lives this time around when you were a young man."

"Yes, that's true. I didn't know the reason I hated them so completely, but it all makes sense now." He directed his hard gaze at Raphael. "I have no regrets. In fact, I was merciful. Their end came fast. Mine didn't. When they threw me on that bonfire—" He stopped himself, but not soon enough. His body flushed with a sudden fever. "I want these damn memories to stop."

Raphael stood up and came over to the bedside. He put his hand on William's brow. "Let them go. It's that simple. Make peace with what happened. You're not that boy anymore."

Raphael's touch was cool. A calming rain of energy settled over William, dousing the fires and bringing him a kind of relief he hadn't felt since the nightmares started.

"Maybe I can let go of those bastards who burned me. They were part of ignorant hordes that still roam this earth. They were sheep reacting to whatever they were taught. But Arel was different. And he's still tormenting me."

Raphael stood back. "You want to be free, don't you, William?"

"Yes, more than anything."

"Than find a way. Let go of the anger you feel when you think of him."

"How? I'm used to what people are capable of. But I trusted Arel. Then I find out he's like the rest of them, a bastard with his own agenda."

"But he wasn't responsible for you being burned."

"He didn't give a damn about what happened to me!"

253

"He was—"

"I was just a poor, peasant boy, and I loved him. I worshipped the ground he walked on!" William remembered the man that Arel had been. He looked a little like he looked in this life, only younger. "I followed after him, worshipping him because he was kind. He always found some bit of bread for me, even when he was starving himself. But that night, everything changed. He never even noticed when the mob got hold of me!"

As William recalled being wronged by Arel, the room exploded into a horrific scene from the past. He was the child again. Rough, calloused hands tore at the thin rags he was wearing. Soon, he was nearly naked as they clawed at him for being a friend of the man they were burning. He cried out for pity, begged that they would let him go. When they saw his terror, they laughed, enjoying his dread. It fed their need for punishment. He was lifted high in the air. Skinny and small, he became another piece of tinder for the fire. With a violent effort, he was thrown into the flames. His screams were drowned out by the roar of the crowd as they shouted out in triumph. Another sinner was burning. His hair and skin crackled and blistered. The pain was unbearable. He'd been abandoned by everyone, including the man he loved. While the man's soul flew upwards, into the heavens, he was left behind. He was totally alone with his burning flesh filling his nostrils. He writhed in an agony that went on forever. "Come back! Don't leave me!" He tried to scream out, but he was choking on the smoke. His cries were hoarse and useless.

Someone called out to him. "William! Stop!"

"Help me!" he screeched.

A hand reached into the flame and shook him. He saw Raphael standing next to him. The angel shook him again.

"It's a nightmare. It's not real!"

The angel's words were a lifeline in the fires that were consuming him. He grabbed hold of that lifeline as Raphael pulled him out of the flaming past. For a long moment, he lay on the bed, falling apart, crumbling ash on the white, smooth sheets. There was nothing left of him. Yet, he was still alive. He kept coughing, trying to take in shallow breaths until his lungs began to clear. His mind reached out, trying to hang on to anything that might help him fight his way back to reality. Slowly, he started to gather up bits of himself, small remembrances of his present life. One of the first bits was

Annabel. He remembered her kiss, her soft lips lingering on his. It was a small exquisite gesture of sweetness that stirred something inside of him. The charred remains of his heart felt a small respite, a tiny hope that life could be good and pure.

When William opened his eyes, Raphael was sitting next to him. His gaze was gentle, with no hint of the malice that he'd just witnessed in the mob. Their eyes were fired by hate and ignorance. Raphael's peaceful, blue gaze held only care and concern.

"You're safe, but you have to let go of what happened," Raphael whispered. "Your rage at Arel is what's keeping you tethered to the past. It's time to let it go." He reached out and put a hand on William's chest.

William shuttered at first. But when he shut his eyes, he could feel what was lodged in his heart. It was a glowing ember of pain, resurrected from a time when a young boy lost everything. Raphael's touch began to sooth the spot, to cool it with his healing energy.

"You never have to feel like that little boy again," Raphael said in a firm, steady voice. "Hold on to the person you are now."

William nodded as he felt a heavy burden lifting. The memories and the pain he'd just experienced wanted release. It was time to let that life go. When he could catch his breath, he stared back with determination. "You're right. I'm going back to London and putting all of this behind me."

A singular thought followed. It was calming to William's body and his soul. Annabel would be waiting for him.

Forty-Nine

Annabel nearly panicked as she tried to hold all three mice on her lap at the same time. Wolfie and Whiskers were both looking over the edge of her apron. As they got older and bolder, these two were especially adventurous. She used a cautioning hand to push them back to safety and quickly gave all three mice a treat. As each ate their sunflower seed, she put them back, one at a time, in their cage. "You little scamps should follow Squeaky's example. He's content to stay close and be petted."

After securing the door, she picked up the cage from the floor and carried it back to its station on the table. She paused to observe Whiskers. After he finished eating, he went straight into his cleaning routine. He often enjoyed tidying up his cage mates after he was satisfied with himself. Squeaky usually slept through the careful preening sessions, but Wolfie sometimes squeaked out a warning. He'd do his own tidying up, thank you. "My goodness, you two are just like your owners. Maybe you picked up on their energy."

"They seem to be flourishing," Raphael said.

Annabel looked up to see him standing a few feet away. "They're wonderful little creatures. I love having them around."

"So how is the experiment going?"

"With the mice?"

Raphael chuckled. "With you."

She smiled. "Oh, you mean my idea to dispense with my angelic abilities while William is away."

"It's an interesting concept. Are you enjoying the experience?"

"It's . . . uh, very different, and in some ways, very limiting."

"I understand that you're not using your ability to communicate telepathically."

"That's right. At first, it was a bit of a shock. When Michael visited, he had a wonderful, but silent, conversation going, and I just stared back at him with a blank expression. I quickly began to understand the narrow field of awareness that humans occupy."

"Maybe your experiment could be added to our training curriculum."

Annabel laughed. "I don't think that many of us would find this kind of experience easy. It would have to be an upper level course."

"But you seem to be managing."

Annabel glanced around the large space. She noted the lab area where William loved to work, but her attention quickly wandered over to the living area of the room. She walked over to William's empty recliner. "There's something else that I don't understand. I seem to focus a lot on one subject."

"William."

"Yes. Everything I do reminds me of him, whether it's cleaning the mouse cage or dusting the furniture. I keep wondering how he is. I hope he's doing well."

"You're his angel. It's only normal that you're concerned about his welfare. Would you like me to bring you up to date?"

"No, please don't. I wouldn't have access to that information if I was strictly human."

Raphael didn't comment. Instead he walked over to the mouse cage and peered in for a long moment.

Annabel ran her hand over the top of the recliner and broke the silence. "Of course, I assume that you and Michael and Carey are taking care of my duties now, right?" She frowned after she asked the question. "My goodness, listen to me. Did you notice that my voice has a slight tremor?"

Raphael opened the mouse cage. "Yes, I did notice," he said as he reached in and slowly ran a finger over Wolfie's tiny head. The mouse had been busy arranging some of the bedding material, but he stopped his activity and closed his eyes, seeming to enjoy the attention he was getting. Still petting the mouse, Raphael glanced up at Annabel and smiled. "You really like William."

Annabel walked over to where he was standing and sighed. "I've never felt like this before so I don't know what my feelings mean."

Raphael withdrew his hand from the mouse cage and locked it again. When he turned his attention to Annabel, his face was bright and searching. "What if William decided to transition to our side of things?"

Annabel didn't know how to respond to his question. Instead, she took off her apron and folded it carefully. She placed it on the back of the chair and smoothed out a wrinkle. "You mean, how would I feel if he died?"

"Yes."

She returned to William's recliner and sat down. "If that happened, William wouldn't need me as his angel anymore. I suppose I'd go on with my duties with someone else."

Raphael smiled. "Yes, I suppose you would."

Annabel frowned. "Is that a possibility? Does it seem probable that William's going to transition?"

"Is that something you're comfortable with?"

She gripped the leather arms of the chair and took a deep breath. Suddenly the room felt a little too warm. "I find everything about William and his future confusing."

"Really? I think you'd be disappointed if William left this world."

"Disappointed? I know the word, but I'm not familiar with the feeling of disappointment."

Raphael took a seat on the sofa and sat back. "Let me see if I can explain what I'm trying to say. Human beings often have expectations about life. For example, you might ask yourself if you're happy about the prospect of seeing William again."

"Yes, I'd like that very much."

"On the other hand, what if you found out that William crossed over?"

"He didn't, did he?" Annabel sucked in a breath. "Goodness, my heart feels like it's beating faster and my muscles feel tighter."

"Exactly," Raphael said in a confident tone. "The physical body is designed to help a human being get in touch with their feelings."

Annabel knew Raphael could be an excellent teacher, but the information he provided needed clarification. She put a hand on her chest. "But all these physical reactions can be distracting."

"True, but the body can be a powerful ally. When you feel your physical vessel getting upset in any way, it means that you're not in tune with your wellbeing."

Annabel studied her hands and the way they were gripping each other. "I know that being in a body offers the soul an opportunity to experience life from an entirely different perspective, an individual perspective. However, up until now, that was simply a concept. I didn't know how much was involved."

"Yes, I agree, but—"

"Raphael, please!" Annabel cut him off without thinking. "I'm getting bombarded by constant, physical feedback! It can be overwhelming. And when I think about the time William kissed me—"

"Yes?"

She let out a heavy sigh and sank back into the recliner. "It was wonderful. I never felt like that before." She looked around the room again. "You're right. I would be disappointed if William never came back. Without his presence—"

"Are you saying that you wouldn't consider giving up your wings if it weren't for your feelings for William?"

There was a lump in Annabel's throat that she found difficult to swallow. "I really don't know how to answer that."

"I think you need a little more time to think things over."

Annabel nodded. "I do."

Raphael's eyes sparkled brightly as he came over and patted her hand. "Maybe this will help relieve some of the feelings that you're having. With Arel out of the picture for the time being, William's let his guard down. I've been able to help him. He's getting better, much better."

Fifty

Peggy stepped back, holding open the door. She smiled as she welcomed Arel into the kitchen. Her smile was part of her peace offering. Arel hadn't been happy for days, and she knew it had something to do with Carol and her taking care of William. "So glad you could come over."

Arel took a seat at the table, but his expression was grim, and his body remained rigidly alert.

"How are you?" she asked as she sat down too.

Arel's eyes were hard and accusing, as if she was going to offer him a cup of hemlock.

"I don't know," he muttered.

She reached out for his hand. "Before we begin, I hope you realize how much I care about you."

Arel jerked back from her touch. "You don't have to sugar coat what you want to say, Peggy. Just tell me why I'm here."

"Arel . . . sweetie, are you angry with me?"

He hesitated. "I can't get past the feeling that you think I'm unfit to be around William. Maybe you think I'm unfit to be around any of you."

"It's not true—"

"Then why am I barred from the lower level of my own home? When you come over to change shifts with each other, why do you and Carol scurry past me like I'm some kind of evil overlord, to be avoided at all costs? You two watch over William like you're his body guards."

"I guess I didn't think about our behavior that way, but I understand how you could get that impression. It's been awkward."

Arel crossed his arms and stared at the floor. "I'm worried as hell about William, and neither of you seem to understand that.

260

Before the two of you stepped in, I never left his side. I sat there by his sick bed for two days. But the minute he woke up, you two threw me out!"

"We didn't throw you out. Please, sweetie, we asked you to leave because it was what William wanted. He's been so sick. We thought it best to honor his feelings."

Arel stood up quickly. "Fine, if that's where things stand——"

"But I don't want things to be like this." Peggy stood up too and went over to him, taking hold of his arms. "Look at you. When did you sleep last? You're as pale as a ghost except for the dark circles under your eyes. You haven't shaved or even brushed your hair, have you?"

"Thank you for making me aware of how irresponsible I've been about my appearance. I'll go home and try to make myself presentable."

"Arel, stop it! You're not being fair!"

His eyes glared as he pulled back. "Fair? Life isn't fair. It's not fair that I find out that I'm a bastard in this life and in others. Michael says it's not true, but most of the time, I feel like it. William hates me because . . . because——"

"Because you kept him out of heaven? Remember, that's what you told Carol and me."

"Yes, there's that too."

"There's something else?"

Arel moved to the table and leaned both hands on its surface. Staring down, his fingers clenched at the wood. "William was there. He was with us in that horrible life when we were——"

"When we were burned at the stake?" Peggy's knees went weak at the memory of what they'd shared as brother and sister in a previous life. She backed away and sat down again. "What an awful thing to think about."

"William was just a child, and they murdered him because he was my friend. It was all so brutal, but I didn't help him. I didn't even think about him. I was too . . . too damn caught up in my own——"

She thrust up a warning hand. "Don't you dare say another word about all that! If you do, you'll condemn us both!"

Arel gave her a sidelong glance. "What do you mean?"

"I'm the one who screamed out your name. I'm the person who told the inquisitors that you were my conspirator. If it wasn't for me, you wouldn't have suffered the unspeakable horrors you went through."

"Peggy, please, you were little more than a child yourself. You were being tortured—"

"It doesn't matter! If you're guilty, so am I!" She had a flash of being held down by hooded men. She shivered, trying to stay calm, but she couldn't stop the images. "I wasn't strong at all! But I remember you. You were so innocent and gentle, a loving brother that was blameless. Then they got hold of you!" She started to cry. "I try. I really do, but sometimes I can't forget what they did, how they destroyed you."

"No, please, Peggy, don't go there!" Arel was instantly down on his knees in front of her. "I'm so sorry I burdened you with all this. I didn't mean to . . . I never meant to—"

She pulled him to her, rocking him and herself, trying to keep them both from remembering. "Please, please don't talk about it anymore." Her voice was thin and ragged as she pleaded. "We already made our peace with that life. It's not who we are now. We both have to let go of it."

When Arel looked up at her, his face was pale and drawn. His voice was barely a whisper. "But what about William and Carol?"

"Carol?" When Peggy heard her friend's name, it helped to snap her out of her crying spell. She swiped at her face. "What about her?" she asked as she helped Arel off his knees and back into his chair.

"She was a child too, a child who watched us burn. She was helpless to change anything. I think she often still feels like that about life."

Peggy managed a weak smile. "At least that's changing. You haven't had a chance to speak with her, but I have. Being with William has done her a world of good."

Arel blinked back. "Really? That's great. I only wish I'd been able to do something more for her. Maybe she wouldn't have lost the baby."

"Stop thinking like that. You're not responsible for Carol or any of us."

"But I am. I know it. Deep down I know I started this string of miserable lives. I did something that put things in motion, and now I don't know how to stop it."

"That's ridiculous." She grabbed a tissue from her pocket and dabbed at her nose. "And I'm sorry to say this, but it's a little demeaning for the rest of us. You're always acting like we're a bunch of kids you have to look after."

"I apologize. I never meant to put you down in any way." He frowned as he stood up straighter and stared out the back window. Its clear panes gave access to the back yard. The sky was layered in heavy, gray clouds. Rain was in the forecast.

Peggy stared out too. "I know you mean well."

He let out a laugh. "William says I'm an arrogant bastard."

"Please, stop with the 'bastard' talk. I love you like a brother still. I can't stand it when you start using words like that."

Arel's eyes went hard again. "But what if he's right? What if none of you know the real me, and I am a fiend?"

"A fiend? Did William call you that too?"

"He's sick. He can't help what comes out of his mouth."

"He's much better."

"I'm sure he hasn't changed his thoughts about me." He leaned forward on the table again. When he glanced at her, his eyes were anxious and bloodshot. They were also questioning, plying her for answers as if she might have a key that could unlock some burden he carried. "Do you have any suggestions about how to handle this mess I've made?"

"Maybe things will work out on their own."

Arel shook his head. "You don't know how stubborn William is."

Peggy's smile broadened into a grin. "Oh, I think I can imagine. You two have quite a bit in common."

"What? We're total opposites."

"So you say."

Fifty-One

William took in a panicky breath. Carol and Kevin were visiting him, but they weren't alone. They brought along their little boy. Ariel was both vocal and energized the moment he set eyes on William. The child's intensity had a strange effect on him. He felt compelled to distance himself and immediately took sanctuary in the middle of his king-sized bed. The little boy seemed unaffected by William's need for boundaries. He continued to reach out in William's direction, squirming so vigorously in his father's arms that Kevin did the obvious thing and placed Ariel on William's bed.

"You don't mind, do you?" he asked as he let the baby slip out of his arms and unto the mattress. The rosy cheeked cherub was fair like his parents, with blue eyes. But he had the sturdy body of a tiny, sumo wrestler. With a sloppy, drooling grin, the child seemed delighted to be set free. He made William his immediate target. The soft covers were quickly traversed as the baby set a course on his hands and knees. When Ariel reached his goal, he latched on to William's shirt and pulled himself up into a standing position. He weaved unsteadily on chubby feet as they stared at each other, eye to eye. William's alarm escalated when Ariel let out a squeal of triumph and delivered a body slam to William's shoulder. The squeal was followed by Ariel cuddling up to William, putting all his weight against the man's body. William tried to maintain his position, but it was a hopeless task. He was just getting some strength back. He was in no shape to be pitted against the solid, enlivened bulk of a feisty, muscular child. He ended up listing to one side as he glanced at Kevin. "Quite a little handful, isn't he?"

"I've never seen him take to anybody like he has to you," Kevin said. "Of course, there is one exception. He's crazy about his godfather, Arel."

William nodded, hoping that Kevin would see the desperation in his eyes. No such luck.

Kevin looked uncomfortable too. After he sat down in Arel's favorite, antique chair, he scowled. The tight fitting seat wasn't sized for a bruiser like him. After a few failed attempts to get settled, Kevin gave William a thoughtful look. "Do you want children?"

"Children? No." What a ridiculous question to be asked when he was barely surviving baby Ariel's attack. He tried to readjust his body, to fight his way back to a more upright position, but the boy only leaned in harder, sucking his thumb contentedly and securing his place by holding on to a patch of William's pajamas with his free hand. William sighed out a breath of resignation. "You must be a proud father."

Kevin straightened up with a broad smile and shifted his weight, making his chair's mahogany timbers creak out a protest. "He's not even a year old, and he already weighs over twenty two pounds. But it's not baby fat, he's solid."

"And Arel is his godfather?"

"Yes, indeed."

William had to stifle a gasp of disgust. It passed quickly as he realized the price that Arel paid for such an honor. With his slender, fine-boned English body type, his mettle would certainly be tested when he tried to wrestle the hefty child in and out of car seats and prams.

Better him than me.

Carol came into the room carrying a large mug of coffee and handed it to Kevin. "Here you go."

Kevin flashed back an expression of gratitude. "Caffeine will be great for this headache."

Carol leaned over and kissed his cheek. "Love you," she whispered.

It was obvious that Carol was feeling better too. When William first met her, Carol was protective but very edgy. Now, it was nice to see her with her husband, looking more relaxed. William hadn't forgotten that she was the woman in his dream and also the little girl in his vision. It was strange, but like Annabel, Carol brought out his chivalrous side.

Carol's eyes sparked. "I heard you two talking about Arel. We call him the 'baby whisperer' because he has such a way with infants."

William felt a bout of weariness coming on. "Unfortunately, his talents aren't always extended to his old friends."

Carol's smile waned. "I'm sorry, I forgot about your feelings concerning Arel. But I know he's sorry about anything he did to hurt you."

William's eyes became slits of remembered outrage as all the pain of Arel's many faults flooded back in. He had to take a couple of deep breaths to return to the moment. "Of course, that's how Arel is, always the contrite sinner after his crime."

Kevin's eyes widened in surprise. "Did you say crime? Arel told us that he saved your life when you wanted to die."

Carol gave him a censuring look. "Kevin! That's not our business."

Kevin twisted in the chair. "Sorry. I should keep my mouth shut. It's just that Arel was a good friend when I really needed one." He reached out for Carol's hand. "I think he saved our marriage. We might not have little Ariel if he hadn't been there for us."

Carol dropped her gaze and nodded. "It's true."

William attempted to right himself again and failed. "I envy you. You're a lucky man."

Kevin stared at him with the eyes of a curious school boy who can't help himself. "I have to ask if it's true. Are you still among the living because of Arel?"

To admit that he was happy to be alive, especially when he thought about Annabel, made William's weariness deepen. "Arel is responsible for my being here, but in no way does that excuse him from overriding my wishes."

"You're right, of course," Carol said, "but I'm glad you're here with us."

Kevin nodded. "Carol told me all about how helpful you've been." He paused and studied the carpet. "Recently, we've faced some really tough times. Carol said you've been there for her."

"I don't think I did anything," William protested.

"Oh, but you did!" Carol said. "You made me feel that I could make a difference. I was so depressed after—"

Kevin put his arm round her waist and pulled her closer. "Honey, be very proud of yourself. You've been a huge help to William."

"Kevin is right, Carol," William chimed in. "You've been a true friend." He wasn't one to be overly demonstrative, but Carol had been there for him in a very dark hour, now he had to return the favor. "I'm grateful for all you've done."

Carol blinked back with questioning eyes. "Really?"

"Yes, I mean it." William tried to move his arm, but the baby clenched his fist tighter, holding fast to William's night shirt. "However, I'm very tired."

This time Kevin took the cue. "Right, we should get going." He quickly drained the coffee from his mug and set it on the nightstand. He started to stand up, but he had to use the arms of his chair to disengage his body from the tight fitting seat.

"Are you sure I can't do anything more?" Carol asked.

William shook his head. "No, I'm much better. Hopefully I'll be able to return to London soon."

Carol bit her lip. "You'll be missed."

"Come along, my boy," Kevin said as he began to gather up the baby. The little boy went from placid to frowning to letting out a cry of protest.

William tried to assist Kevin, but Baby Ariel wasn't letting go of his shirt. "He's got quite a grip."

Kevin smiled as he pried Ariel's fingers from the clothing. "He'll make a great running back some day."

Carol hurried over to a chair in the corner where she kept her supplies. She retrieved a bottle of juice from the diaper bag.

"Here you go, my little pudding," she crooned as she handed it to the baby. The bottle caught Ariel's attention and soon silenced his cries. Settling down in his father's arms, he sucked it as greedily as he'd sucked his thumb earlier.

Carol smiled as she was leaving. "Little Ariel is going to miss you too. We have two baby whisperers in the family now."

William's eyes narrowed as he watched her leave. Had he heard her right? Did she say the word, family?

Arel sat at his desk in his upstairs bedroom, listening to Carol and Kevin as they went to the front door and said good-bye to Carey. Whenever the young man was around, he took care of the coming and going of guests. Afterwards, he frequently stopped by for a short report. Today was no exception. He appeared at the door, looking his usual cheery self.

"I sent everyone on their way. They all looked happy, including the baby," Carey said as he came over and sat on the bed. "My gosh, he sure loves that bottle."

When Arel first met Carey, the young man was thin as a rail and from the look of his clothes, very down on his luck. He didn't seem to have any close family to count on. "How do you do it, Carey? I'm sure life hasn't always been easy for you, but you have a great attitude in spite of it. What's your secret?"

Carey beamed back a smile. "I met you of course. Now I'm living in this great house, with tons of great food. I have my bike, and I can do what I want. Why wouldn't I be happy?"

"I guess that's all very nice, but most people seem to need more."

"Like what?"

"Don't you ever think about your past, the way people might have let you down?"

"Why would I? I like what I'm doing now."

"You make it sound so easy."

"Yeah, I guess it is for me."

Arel tossed his pen on the desk and stood up, grabbed his chest and sat down again. The pain he'd had in London was back. He was sure that he didn't have a heart problem, but the vessel was definitely acting out his angst.

"Hey, are you okay?" Carey jumped up and came over. "What's going on?"

"Unlike you, I can't seem to let go of what worries me."

"If you're worried about William, he's doing much better. I have a feeling that he's going to be just fine."

"Yes, Peggy thinks so too."

"Will you miss him when he goes back home?"

268

Arel's heart grabbed again, making him square his jaw against the vessel's pain and his abysmal failure to convince William of his good intentions. "My opinion doesn't count."

Carey stared at him with concern. "Arel, what's going on? You two have barely seen each other in days."

"I know. William thought he'd be better off if I stayed away."

But Arel knew that not all the lifetimes he'd had with William were like that. Visions of when they'd been twins were becoming his daily fare. Scenes slipped in at the oddest moments. While he was showering that morning, he'd found himself at a dual wedding celebration. Two brothers stood shoulder to shoulder, toasting their good fortune as they gazed at their new brides. It was a simple, joyous event that made him smile until he tapped into William's current thoughts. William didn't shield them from him. It was quite the opposite. He aired the fact that he wanted to sever all their ties, permanently.

Carey picked up the pen that had been tossed aside. He clicked and unclicked the instrument several times as if it needed testing. When he seemed satisfied that it was working, he frowned. "Arel, spill your guts? You look kind of miserable."

"Ignore me. Instead of enjoying life like you, I'm being a fool."

"I don't believe that. You're one of those people who feels everything deeply. And I think you're going to miss your old buddy."

"Would that old buddy be me?" William asked. He was leaning against the door jamb with his arms crossed. "Carey, can you give us a minute?"

"Sure," Carey said as he put the pen back on the desk. Before he moved away, he leaned in closer and whispered some parting words. "Listen, Arel, go easy on yourself. You're a great guy."

Arel smiled weakly as he watched Carey walk out of the room and down the hall. In the meantime, William took a seat in a white, slipper chair. When he looked at Arel, his face was calm and serene.

"Did you want something?" Arel asked as he went back to studying a bill.

"I wanted to let you know that I'm leaving tomorrow. I think I'll be well enough to travel."

Arel sat back in the desk chair, forcing himself to offer up a relaxed smile. If William could look tranquil, why couldn't he, at least on the surface? "Sounds good. I'm sure Annabel will be thrilled to see you."

"Really? Do you think she likes me?"

"Of course she likes you." His clipped tone helped him maintain his pretense of ease while he envisioned William's plane taking off.

I'll never see my brother again.

He fought the furrows that were trying to spoil his smooth brow and pressed on bravely. "Annabel is very nice."

William's eyes flared for an instant. "She's extraordinary. I never thought I'd meet someone like her."

"Yes, she is quite perfect." Arel felt himself drifting as he imagined the London bound plane. In his mind's eye, it was gaining altitude and soon disappeared from view. All that was left was a door to the past, and it was swiftly closing on whatever bond he'd ever had with William. The two of them weren't twin boys anymore. They weren't even real brothers this time around. And William had always been fine on his own.

I'm the needy one, the real bloodsucker. It's always been me.

It was a fact. Just a short time before, he had pressured William into traveling. The man was still very ill, but Arel pressed on anyway. By the time William got to Chicago, he was in real trouble. Carol and Peggy feared William wouldn't make it.

They had to throw me out before I sucked him dry.

The thought took the last bit of air from Arel's lungs. He had to sit up and take a deep breath.

William snapped his fingers. "Arel, have I lost you?"

He swiveled his head in William's direction. "No, I was thinking about how happy I am for you."

"Thanks." William inhaled deeply too. "I can't say that I forgive you for all the hell I've been through since this nightmare started in New York, but I want to put it behind me."

"Good idea." Arel ran his hand over the slightly ridged desk surface. Wood had a very pleasing quality, one that gave him strength when he felt things flying apart. But when he lowered his gaze, he noticed that the patina on the desktop was dull. He'd been negligent about closing the curtains again. Now the sun had dried out the wood. He felt an immediate need to rectify the situation. Where had he put the furniture oil?

270

William continued on. "When we part company, we'll go back to the way it was before we met, with you in your world and me in mine. Only now, you have people here that care about you, and I have—" He smiled. "I might have room in my life for another person."

Arel managed a nod. "Annabel."

"Perhaps."

"Great." Arel clamped his jaw shut on the word, trying to make its meaning fill his mind long enough to get through the meeting. But the sound of children's voices barged in. The past was back and invading his thoughts. He saw the twin boys again. Their pitched, excited cries of joy filled the air as they raced each other down a dusty path.

William stood up slowly. "Well then, I think I'll go downstairs and pack."

As Arel watched William limp out of the room, reality continued to shift back and forth. The past seemed so real. The sight and sound of the boys was as tangible as the desk where he sat. But they weren't on the path anymore. They were standing next to him. Their excitement was gone, replaced by puzzled faces. They looked up to him for answers. What went wrong? Why had he and William become so estranged?

Arel didn't know what to say. The young boys were depending on him to fix things, but he couldn't. He'd never been able to fix anything when it came to brothers. He'd been no older than the boys next to him, when his real brother, Aldwin, was killed. Horror filled the big manor house that day. At first, he didn't understand his mother's screams. Afterwards as she began to quiet, he stood on the staircase above the large entry hall and peered downward. His brother lay bloodied and still on the massive receiving table below. But Arel couldn't make sense of what was happening. Or maybe he didn't want to understand. Instead, he crept down the worn stairs ever so carefully, avoiding the creaky places like he always did when he didn't want to draw attention to himself. When he reached the bottom, he tread across the cold, stone floor, furtively glancing at his parents as they continued to grieve. When he reached the table where they had laid his brother, he didn't hesitate. He grasped Aldwin's hand in his own. It was so cold. That's when he couldn't deny what was happening. Still, he begged his brother not to leave him. But it didn't bring Aldwin back. It simply ignited his father's wrath. Leaping from his chair, the man exploded into a rage, blaming Arel for being the child that lived. His father's cane came down on his back over and over.

Now William is leaving me too.

He was losing another brother, not a real one, but one he'd substituted for Aldwin.

But it's all in my mind. I can't replace Aldwin. And that past life, when Will and I were twins, is ancient history. Yet I've been refusing to let go of any of it.

He'd been the same when he was a child. It took a very hard blow across his back to wrench him away from Aldwin. For a boy his size, his grasp was surprisingly strong. It had to be. Once his brother's hand slipped away from his, he knew all would be lost. His life from that day forward bore out that fact. How many times after Aldwin's death did a servant save his life when his drunken father started beating him?

But my father's not beating me anymore. He's dead. I'm the true source of my misery.

Clarity hit home. He sat very still, trying to put the pieces of his current mental state together. He'd always had an active imagination, but this was so much more serious.

My visions of children are just fantasies that I've manufactured because I wanted a connection to William.

Why didn't he concentrate on what Michael had been telling him all along?

"You don't need other people or the past to define who you are, Arel. The trick is to take a chance and let go of everything. Once you do, once you discover who you really are, you'll be free."

Arel's frown deepened.

Of course, as usual, Michael's right.

But it wasn't an easy task. He'd had the strength to hold on to dreams and stories he told himself. Now he had to believe he had the strength to let go and embrace what was real.

William has moved on, and so can I.

Everything brightened as soon as he made the decision. For the first time in months, he noticed what he hadn't lost. He'd been in such a state of turmoil that he'd forgotten to see what was right in front of him. Like Carey said, he had a great home and a great life if he wanted it. Outside the paned windows, the gray skies were clearing, allowing the sun to peek through.

I've hardly given any of it a moment's notice.

A brilliant ray of sunlight flickered over the papers on his desk.

When was the last time I enjoyed a sunny day?

Still, he'd close the curtains just enough to save the desk from further damage.

Which reminds me—

He was about to get up and search for the furniture oil when he remembered one last detail that hadn't been addressed. When William returned to London, an assassin would be waiting for him. That particular detail wasn't in the past. It was looming over William's future. But it didn't have to.

It could be fun to sleuth out the villain. Arel could secretly fly to London, find the guy, and put a stop to his plans. It would be his parting gift to William.

Fifty-Two

Annabel put the phone down and smiled. William was coming home. Recalling the sound of his voice sent a thrill of anticipation through her body. "What a delightful feeling!"

She put her hands in her pockets and began to pace back and forth in the lower level of the house. It was her favorite place to spend time since Arel and William left. The mice were there, and she loved watching them. Whether they were playing or eating or simply sleeping, they seemed to enjoy being in the physical world. Would it be a good experience for her too? Raphael was a wonderful advisor, but now she needed a different take on things. "Michael, can I talk to you?"

When she turned around, he was standing next to the mouse cage, picking up Whiskers. "They've grown a lot in a very short time." He glanced over at the control mice. "But they don't seem any larger than the three over there."

Annabel smiled. "I hold all of them, but don't tell William."

"I think he'll know. He's quickly developing some intuitive gifts."

"Like Arel? They both share a little something from you."

Michael's eyes were playful as he rubbed behind the tiny mouse's ear. Its black eyes closed contentedly for only a moment before it came out of trance, grabbed its tail and checked it with great concentration. "Humans have a capacity for many things they consider extraordinary, but for the most part, their gifts are dormant."

"I know. After only a short time of being without my normal abilities, I have a lot more empathy for the plight of humans."

"By the way, these little fellows are getting quite rotund."

Annabel walked over and watched her mouse, Squeaky. He was sniffing at his food dish. After passing on a food pellet, he found a stray sunflower seed. Sitting back on his haunches, his whole body quivered as he enjoyed his delicacy.

"I might be giving them a few too many treats. They enjoy every morsel so much."

Michael gave her a knowing glance as he returned Whiskers to the cage and locked the door. "The physical has many temptations. Even a mouse can overindulge. Unfortunately for people, they can over indulge in their emotions."

Annabel watched Whiskers run over to Squeaky. He took note of the seed his cage mate was eating and began burrowing in the food dish for one of his own. "Am I being foolhardy wanting to be human?"

"It'll be quite a transition."

"I understand, but with William gone, I've had the time to give the matter a lot of thought."

"Have you considered what you'd be taking on?"

Annabel surprised herself when the answer came so easily. "I love William, and I want to be with him."

"Well then, I'm very happy for you. And I'll do everything I can to help."

"Will I need help?" It was a strange concept after knowing the steady bliss and innocence of being what she was. Her world was always safe and unchanging. "Sorry, what a silly thing to ask. After observing Arel and William, I should know better."

"About William—"

"It sounds like he's much better."

"Yes, he is."

"Hopefully, he'll be fully recovered soon."

"Yes, but—"

Annabel saw the concern on Michael's face and put her arms around herself. She'd discovered the gesture helped to sooth her body if she had thoughts about William's ill health and the possibility of him dying. "You think I'm making a mistake, don't you?"

Michael stepped back and smiled. "I don't think in terms of mistakes, do I?"

"No, of course not." She felt her face flush with what she knew must be embarrassment. She laughed nervously. "I can't believe the things that are coming out of my mouth. This process is very strange."

"Taking off your wings, so to speak, for a short period of time is good practice. But it's not the same as being a real human. I think you'll find things get much stranger when you dive into the full experience."

"My mind is racing with questions. It must be what a child feels when they go off to school for the first time."

"You know that you can't count on William to be there, not at this point. Once he finds out what you really are, he—"

"Do I have to tell him?"

"I thought—"

"He's not very fond of angels. Why should I upset him if it's not necessary?"

"Annabel, my dear friend, I think he's going to know something is very different about you if you make this change."

Annabel put her hand on her chest. Her heart, once so steady and at ease, was getting more erratic, especially if she felt something wasn't quite right in her environment. "Will I forget everything?"

"It's a gradual process. As you become part of the human world, your attention will be drawn to your experiences. Those experiences will activate emotional responses, including fear. People grow up being very familiar with that emotion. In your case, it could be very difficult to adjust to, especially if you begin to depend on William being there for you."

"Why wouldn't he be there?"

"Even if he accepts and loves you completely, a human's physical vessel is a fragile thing. Both Arel and William seem to be testing its limits regularly."

"I could help him, just like I do now, as his angel."

"Are you sure?"

Annabel frowned, wondering why the thought of William's mortal existence sent a chill down her spine. When she considered the possibility that he could perish at any time, her knees felt shaky. She made her way to the table, grabbed a chair and sat down. "Oh Michael, after this conversation, I'm not sure about anything."

It was true. It wasn't just her knees that were shaky, her entire world felt unsteady. It took all of her concentration to slow the pounding in her chest. She'd been looking forward to William being home again. Now, she wasn't so sure.

* * *

William stood stiffly in the airport terminal, patting down his brow as he stared back at the crowd gathered around him. It had taken two cars to get everyone there. Arel, Michael, and Carey accompanied him in the Mustang. Kevin drove the second vehicle, a big SUV that was large enough to accommodate two baby seats, plus Carol, Peggy and Tim. "I'm flattered that you all came, but it wasn't necessary," William said with a slight tremor in his voice.

Peggy returned a teary smile. "We had to come. You're family now. Remember that, okay?"

Tim was holding baby Sara, but he put an arm around Peggy and pulled her close. "Take care of yourself, William. Stay healthy."

William was giving Tim a quick nod of appreciation when Carol came forward and hugged him.

"You're a very special part of the family, and we love you," she said. "Please come back."

Without thinking, William found himself returning her embrace. "Thank you for everything."

Kevin planted a large steel-grip hand on William's shoulder and shook him. "Glad we finally got to meet." He leaned in with a wide smile. His tone dropped to a whisper. "Next time you need a little help, bypass Arel and call Tim or me. We're easier."

William nodded again, trying to manage his panic. What had he gotten himself into by coming to Chicago? "You've all been very gracious, I—"

"Uh! Uh!" Baby Ariel threw his bottle on the floor and stared at William with a troubled frown. Carey was holding the baby, but he had to redouble his efforts when little Ariel threw himself forward in William's direction. The baby let out a loud squeal. "Da!!!!!"

What could William do? The child's demand was impossible to ignore. He went over and put a hand on Ariel's blond curls. "Be a good boy."

"Dada!!!!"

The second time the little boy addressed William in a fatherly way, his chest tightened. He'd never considered having a child, but even that seemed a remote possibility when he thought about Annabel. He backed up quickly. "My plane is leaving soon. I better get to my gate."

"Have a good flight," Michael said with a friendly smile.

Carey handed the baby to Kevin and stepped forward to grip William's arm. He grinned in his easy going way. "I might show up in London one of these days. You can show me the sights."

"Of course."

Arel extended his hand. "Goodbye, William."

Arel's tone and his eyes said much more than his words. Something had changed between them. Arel was pulling back all the energy that had brought them together. Their bond was finally dissolving. William didn't expect it, but his chest tightened even more as he gave Arel's hand a quick shake. "Goodbye."

An hour and a half later, as he sat on the plane, he tried to understand why he was sweating. The plane was a little warm, but there was something else, the scene at the terminal.

Peggy's words about being family echoed in his mind. It seemed like such a foreign concept. It was reinforced by Carol. He could still feel her heartbeat against his chest as she voiced one of the most misused words in the English language. She'd spoken about love. Then there was the baby. Little Ariel addressed him in the same way that he addressed his real father.

Quite a clingy group you have there, Arel.

He grabbed his handkerchief and swiped at his brow again. The group hadn't been thinking about Arel when they saw him off. They made it clear that they cared about William. And if it hadn't been for Carol's dedication, he probably wouldn't be going back home. Instead, Arel would be scattering his ashes around the windy city.

As for Arel himself, at least that chapter in William's life was finally over. His wish had been granted. He was free to be on his own again.

So why don't I leave it at that? Why should I start something with Annabel when I can go back to my own way of life?

Every woman he'd ever met or been interested in, ended up wanting something. That one fact kept him a confirmed bachelor.

278

Of course, Annabel has never been like that. She's different. I don't have to worry about another case of neediness.

He put the handkerchief back in his pocket and began to relax. As the plane climbed high into the heavens, his life was starting over. With Raphael's help, his health was rapidly returning, and he had a beautiful, gloriously, independent woman waiting for him.

Fifty-Three

When William walked through the front door, looking his young, handsome self, Annabel was ready for him. Her halo was dusted and her wings were securely fastened once again. Her decision to remain an angel was well thought out and pure. Maybe her heart was the part of her that helped turn the tide when she considered becoming human. It always beat too fast when she thought about giving up her wings. It sent out a warning, letting her know that the transition she'd been contemplating was a dangerous one. Of course, she didn't know exactly what danger it portended, but she did know her body didn't feel right when she contemplated giving up the serenity that she normally felt. When she went to greet William at the door and he stared back at her with a sparkle in his eye, she gave him a friendly, welcoming smile, nothing more. She was there to assist him as his angel, period. After hanging up his coat in the hall closet, she left him standing in the foyer. She had laundry to attend to.

William noticed her attitude immediately. As she stuffed clothes in the machine, he came into the laundry room with a puzzled look on his face. He asked her if everything was alright. She let out a relieved sigh and closed the lid on the washer. "Everything is perfect," she answered. And she meant it. It was a tremendous relief to be her angelic self again.

How could I ever have considered becoming mortal? What an impossible idea that was!

When she'd taken off her wings, she didn't have interactions with other people or circumstances. Yet she'd nearly panicked just contemplating what life could throw at her. Later, Michael informed her that her little trial run was nothing like being an actual human. She hadn't had to meet the true challenges that people experienced every day. That's when Annabel realized how lucky she was to have her wings.

I don't understand how people manage the emotional load they carry.

She did have a new respect for what people were able to shoulder. But she didn't want that challenge. She'd end up disappointing herself and William. It wouldn't be fair to either of them.

I'll stick around here just long enough to ease my way out of William's life. Then he and I can both return to normal.

Fifty-Four

Arel grabbed his travel bag from the closet, tossed it on the bed, and glanced up. Michael was reading by the window. He'd moved his chair into the narrow section of sunlight that was allowed in. Sporting a bulky white sweater, his broad shoulders looked wider than ever. His blond hair, glistening gold in the sun, was loose for a change. It was usually pulled back in a low, pony tail. Now it graced his broad shoulders, making Arel aware of how angelic Michael could look. "For a guy with heavenly ties, you really enjoy reading those seed and flower magazines, don't you?"

Michael looked up from a rose catalog and smiled. "There are so many choices."

Arel let out a small sneer. "We both know that no matter what you plant, your garden will be something spectacular."

Michael put the catalog down. "Thank you, but I'd like to talk about—"

"My plans for London?" Arel unzipped his bag and flipped it open.

"You just dropped William off at the airport yesterday. Now you're leaving this afternoon."

"Yes, that's right."

"Are you sure you should be doing this? The man you'll be pursuing is very dangerous."

"What choice do I have? I can't let him kill William."

"But there's more to it. You seem to be enjoying this venture."

Arel tried not to smile, but he knew Michael didn't miss anything. "And what if I am? You're always advising me to lighten up."

"This isn't the movies, Arel. This man has killed many times. He's very good at what he does, and he won't think twice about taking you out of the picture."

"He's not going to get the chance. You'll be there, acting as my sidekick. We'll be partners."

"Being a partner doesn't always work out. In the past—"

"Michael, for goodness sake, do you think I'm going to shut you out when I'm facing a murderer?" He offered up his most earnest face. "I promise you, I have no desire to die at this point. Just the opposite. That's why I look excited. I'm finally ready to live. My ties with William are a thing of the past, and I'm finally able to pursue my own agenda."

"Isn't this person you're going after William's problem?"

"Hey, the guy wants me dead too. That makes him my problem."

"Nothing I say is going to make you change your mind, is it?"

Arel turned away and went back to the closet. "Believe me, I take everything you say very seriously. And you can be my advisor every step of the way."

"Good, then as your advisor, I'm advising you to reconsider."

As Arel reached out for a set of slack hangers, his hand stilled in mid grasp. Michael's words made his jaw tighten. Suddenly Carey's need for freedom made more sense. Or was he being obstinate and irresponsible like the younger man could be? "I hear your advice and appreciate it, Michael—"

"But?"

Arel's hand closed on the hangers. "But we need to check a few things out. We'll go to London, get a bead on what the guy's up to, and we'll take it from there."

"We?"

"That's right, you and me." Arel put the clothes on the bed and picked a piece of lint off his favorite, grey wool slacks. After William's comment about bringing his wardrobe up to date, he'd found the pants featured on a stylish, Italian website for men's clothing. "What do you think? Do you think a half dozen pair will be enough if we're there for awhile? Never mind, if I take too many what difference does it make?"

Michael stood up and walked to the door. He paused in the doorway. "I suppose it's settled then."

Arel could feel Michael's eyes drilling into him, forcing him to stop and turn around. "Anything else?"

"After your brother issues, I know you're trying to be totally independent, but—"

"Can't you see I'm doing everything I can to remain positive, to do something that doesn't involve my guilt or an emotional slide into hell?" Arel crossed his arms and let a frown settle in. "It's not easy for me to look at the bright side, but I'm giving it my best. Support me, Michael. Don't try to find fault with everything I'm doing."

"I am trying to support you. And I'm happy that you're feeling more positive, but pursuing a killer—"

"Gives me purpose! And it also gives me a chance to prove to myself that I'm not just a self-centered jerk."

"I hope you meant it when you said that I'm your partner."

"Your blood is in my veins. If that doesn't make us partners, what does?"

Fifty-Five

Rolphe sat at his easel and caught a glimpse of himself in the mirror that he'd purchased for Dantela. She liked to play with her reflection. But when he saw himself, he had to still his brush. His face was anything but playful. He'd been told more than once that he looked like an oversized, syndicate boss when he scowled. His reflection bore out the statement. His brows were hooded. His mouth was downturned and there was a coldblooded, ruthless quality to his eyes. "Holy mother, I scare myself," he scoffed as he threw his brush in a container of turpentine.

The canvas in front of him was disjointed and chaotic. The colors were muddied. There was none of the flow he wanted and needed. It was his fifth attempt at painting that week.

Another piece of shit.

He stood up and steadied his gaze. How could he concentrate on beauty? His mind was at the planning table, mapping out concrete details on how to kill two men. His soul was in hiding.

Where the hell are the bastards?

He quickly walked out of the studio, shutting the door behind him. Dantela was asleep in her basket. He'd make sure she stayed there. As he traversed the long hall, he avoided the portraits of his family. What would his wife say about what he was doing? She had never understood any kind of violence, not even taking the life of a chicken. Killing was always his job.

And I want it over and done with.

He was tired of the whole business, but he couldn't let it go. William started the mess. He was the one who opened up Pandora's box.

Sorry, William, but it's the end of the line for you and your friend.

When he got to the living room, he stretched out his body, trying to release the tension from long hours at the easel. Waiting felt like such a waste of time.

The longer his life was on hold, the more difficult it was to be patient. But he had to calm himself if he was going to find his quarry. He sat down on the sofa and lit a candle. It was time for his nightly ritual. At least it was easy to tune into the information he was seeking. He didn't even need the moon at this point. Once he cleared his mind and focused on London, he intuitively knew whether or not William was there.

He stared at the flame, watching it flicker, letting it draw his thoughts to that still, clear space where his usual perception fell away. He was just starting to achieve a state of calm, when a face from the past appeared. He gasped in surprise. "Chessa, is it you?"

It had been so long since he'd seen the woman from his past. Shortly after her death, Chessa appeared to him in his dreams. Like a kind mother, she encouraged him not to despair, but the dreams stopped after the first couple of years.

"My child! My dearest child." Now Chessa's voice was edged with anxiety.

He blinked back with alarm. It was true. He was her child of sorts. She'd suckled him with her special blood. But she only addressed him in that way when there was trouble.

"What is it? Why are you here after so many years?"

Her dark features were almost lost in shadow, but there was a feeling about her. It was troubled and sad. "Be careful, Rolphe! The men you're looking for can hurt you! Be especially aware of the one with golden eyes!"

He smiled. "They're both back in London, aren't they?"

"Yes."

Fifty-Six

After William got back to his home in London, he wasn't prepared for the new Annabel. He liked the idea of an independent woman, but something had changed between them. When he'd been ill, Annabel had hovered over him with concern. Now, she barely noticed him. In the days that followed his return, he was treated like just another fixture in the house, something to dust and put back on the shelf. His silver vase got more attention. As he watched Annabel carefully rubbing its surface, he would have settled for a little polishing, a little smile of encouragement, or a hand reaching out in a gesture of simple friendship.

Did I misinterpret the look in her eyes before I left, the way she touched me and let her hand linger? When I spoke to her on the phone, she was so excited about my coming home.

His homecoming was still a sore point. It was dismal, a quick and polite hello, followed by a scurrying movement in favor of laundry. After that, things didn't improve.

Annabel's communication was strictly practical. That afternoon, her total conversation was delivered in one sentence. "Do you need your shades drawn?"

William would have appreciated something along the lines of, "My, you're a handsome man, William. Do you know you take my breath away every time you look at me?"

Okay, that was asking for too much at this stage, but he could hope it was a future possibility, especially when he was doing all the things he needed to do to show her his intentions. After withholding any sign of affection in the past, he now gave her a full demonstration of how pleased he was to see her whenever she passed by. He smiled at her and even tried to make conversation about the weather.

The weather, for god's sake! How pathetic is that?

As time passed, he'd become bolder and more obvious. When she came out of the bath, he told her how beautiful she looked. He even waited for her to reply, like some moony-eyed teenager. But her 'Thank you' had as much appreciation as a phone recording that told you the person wasn't home. The words had a flippant, dismissive quality that repeated in his mind every time he thought about her lovely, smooth skin or her gorgeous body. She kept that covered up too, wearing baggy, dreary clothes that she must have borrowed from her overweight granny while he was gone. Where were those pretty slacks that she wore with the lime green blouse? At least those clothes allowed some evidence of a shapely woman instead of an aged resident of a retirement home.

What the hell is going on with her?

The question repeated over and over, but there were no answers, just lingering days of growing desire on his part, and total neutrality on Annabel's.

Fifty-Seven

It was Monday night and the pub was quieter than usual, just as Kevin hoped it would be. He nudged Tim who sat next to him at the bar. "Thanks for getting me out for a drink. I needed to talk to somebody." He took a sip of beer, then glanced at his watch. "Do you think the girls will mind if we're gone more than an hour?"

"No, they looked happy to get rid of us. They enjoy their 'girl time.' But what's going on? You seem a little jumpy."

"Me? Carol is the one who's a bundle of energy. Now that William is gone, she needs a mission. In the meantime, I'm left holding the bag."

Tim's brows arched. "What kind of mission?"

"I don't know. I don't think she knows either, but she better find something soon before she blows a gasket."

"She's usually so quiet."

Kevin drained his glass and sagged down on his stool. "The old Carol is gone." He swallowed hard. "You know that I'm not one to discuss, you know . . . bedroom matters, but she's become—"

Tim gave him a sideways smile. "Your face is turning red."

"Don't laugh. This is serious."

"Does she want to try for a baby again?"

"No, she says she wants to . . . oh hell, forget it."

"What?"

"She wants to 'experiment.'"

"What does that mean?"

"Hell, I don't know. I've kind of been putting her off. I'm not a prude or anything, but I don't feel comfortable with the way she's acting. That outfit she bought was . . . well it was definitely *not* Carol."

"Maybe you're more of a prude than you realize. There's nothing wrong with a bit of fun."

"I agree, but a person doesn't just suddenly change. Carol's always been conservative."

"Maybe you're over reacting. When you two came over on Saturday, she looked fine. In fact, we ended up having a nice conversation about that old Harley I used to have."

"Yeah, I know. And when we got back home, she told me she might ask Carey to take her out for a spin on his old junker. That's not *my* Carol talking. She's afraid of speed."

"She's just pleased with herself. William made a real turnaround after she started taking care of him. You should be proud of her."

"I am, if it stopped there. But what if she keeps changing, and I can't keep up?"

Tim clapped Kevin on the back. "I have my old helmet in the garage. Maybe you'll have to show Carol that you can keep up."

* * *

Carol sat in Peggy's living room. Little Ariel was enjoying himself nearby. He sat on a blanket on the floor, very preoccupied with his task of retrieving tiny bits of apple from a plastic bowl in front of him. Every once in a while, he'd look up at her with bright blue eyes and a face that expressed pure contentment. She sighed quietly. "Our babies are growing up so fast."

Peggy smiled as she put Sara in the playpen with a bottle of juice. "I know. Sara's crawling skills are amazing. She was out of the bedroom before I knew it yesterday. I swear, I folded two shirts, and she was gone. Thank goodness for gates."

"And thank goodness that Kevin went out for a beer with Tim. He hasn't been himself."

Peggy giggled. "Look who's talking."

"What do you mean?"

"Don't you know how different you've been since William was here?"

"No." Carol looked down, pleased with herself even though she'd just told a lie. It was so nice not to have to be agreeable all the time. Still, she didn't want to be difficult. "I mean, I guess I'm a little different."

Peggy laughed again as she sat down on the loveseat and tucked her feet up next to her. "I think it's wonderful."

"You do?"

"Every person should enjoy life. And I think that's what you want to do."

"Kevin doesn't say anything, but he looks at me like I've run amok. When I showed him a sexy, black teddy I found at the mall, he just stared at me with his mouth hanging open. It was embarrassing."

"Kevin is always behind the times. Don't pay him any attention."

"Maybe it was too much, too soon. When we were first together, I guess I was the one who was a little reserved. I hadn't done much dating, and I didn't always feel comfortable with—"

"With what?"

Carol sighed. "You know me, Peggy. I've always been the type that colors inside the lines. So anyway, I thought that Kevin might like it if we tried something different in the bedroom. Nothing too extreme, just something that might be a little more exciting for both of us. So I showed him this book with some pictures—"

Peggy's eyes flared. "Pictures? Really? Did Kevin go nuts and ravish you?"

"No, he just sat there and got very quiet. When I put the book aside, he got up and asked if I'd like some hot chocolate. I think I scared him."

"Just don't stop what you're doing. It's good for both of you. Life gets very stagnant if you never try anything new. Kevin will come around."

"Do you think so?"

Peggy gave her a playful look. "I know so. Tim and I had to go through a similar stage a couple of years ago. Now we're much more comfortable with each other."

"That's good to know."

"So why do you think you're making these sudden changes? Does it have anything to do with William?"

"Maybe. Once he was feeling better, we talked. He spoke with so much confidence when we discussed things like the places he's visited and things that he's done. Just being around somebody who has so much courage to live life with so much enthusiasm was inspiring. But there was something else, something I learned about myself."

When she hesitated, Peggy leaned forward. "What? Tell me."

"After the miscarriage, I was so down on myself. Then I felt this connection to William, like he was a friend I forgot I had. And when I thought about him dying, I knew I couldn't let that happen. Something in me rallied. I was determined to hold on to him no matter what."

"And you did! Be proud of yourself."

"You helped too."

"But I was more on the sidelines. When it was my turn to keep watch, William would wake up and keep glancing at the clock, waiting for you to take over. He never verbalized it, but I know he needed you more than me."

Carol felt her cheeks warm with embarrassment. "Why? Why would he want me there?"

Peggy smiled. "You don't know how strong you are, do you? But William felt your strength. I'm sure of it."

"That's good."

"It's more than good, Carol! Your strength helped William find his way back from a very dark place."

"I don't know what to say."

"Say that you're proud of who you are."

Carol paused and looked at baby Ariel again. The fair haired tot was still eating and banging on the bowl between bites. "I love my family, but I've had so many doubts. I guess I felt capable enough before I married Kevin, but afterwards, I slipped back into some old patterns. I was afraid I wasn't up to being the wife and mother I wanted to be."

"Well, I hope you see things differently now."

"I'm beginning to. I have hope that life can be better for all of us. Maybe that's why I bought the teddy and the book. I wanted to prove that I can move on. I can be a person who's not stuck in the past."

"You have moved on. I can see it in your face and hear it in your voice." Peggy giggled. "But you'll have to wait a little for Kevin to catch up. He's kind of slow when it comes to change."

Carol laughed too. "Maybe I'll hide that book for a little while."

"Yes, perhaps you should, but don't be surprised if he doesn't go looking for it one of these days."

Fifty-Eight

Arel looked out of the window of the upper story, London hotel room. The street below was a sea of umbrellas and dreariness. He hated the weather, and he hated waiting. Michael didn't seem to have his problem.

The tall angel seemed oblivious to the weather. Instead, he always found something to keep him occupied. Currently he was focused on a large arrangement of fresh flowers the hotel had placed in their room. Arel had to clear his throat a couple of times to get his attention. "Foul weather and a killer on the loose, what a nice combination we're facing here in London."

Michael walked over and stared out the window too. "How do you feel about everything now that you're here?"

"The weather isn't helping, but I'm used to gloom. It's Rolphe's mind that bothers me."

"You're able to tap in?"

"Yes. He's wide open. I guess he's not used to dealing with someone with abilities like mine. And I don't think he has to. I feel like he's a loner for the most part."

"What bothers you about him?"

"He has a hell of an attitude. There was passionate rage behind William's kills. For this guy, it's a job." He rubbed his temples. "He's also depressing."

"How so?"

"I think he's been around for a long time, a lot longer than Will or myself. He's still living in the past. I thought my background was dark, but he's seen a lot of misery."

"That doesn't make him less dangerous."

"No, just the opposite. He soldiers on, burying the pain, and doing whatever it takes to protect himself. Thank goodness I'm here.

William's too preoccupied right now. He would have never seen the guy coming."

Michael frowned. "You're still monitoring William's thoughts? I thought you said—"

"I know what I said, but with this killer on the loose, I have to keep an eye on what Will is doing. What if he goes out and this Rolphe guy is waiting?" He crossed his arms and walked over to a chair to sit down. "But Will doesn't have to worry. I'll be at the place where they were going to meet originally. I copied the address off of the email that William sent him."

"You looked through his email?"

Arel narrowed his gaze and scowled. "You know I did. You know everything. We only have these conversations so you can bug me."

"Not true. You asked me not to invade your privacy. Would you like to change that instruction so I can be that partner you talked about?"

"Fine, but I doubt that you'll discover much of interest. There's not much rattling around in my head right now, except what I can do to protect William."

"And what about you? How do you plan on protecting yourself?"

Arel examined a small scratch in the dark-walnut arm of the chair. "That's where the partner part comes in. You'll take care of me, right?"

"I think you need a better plan. What if something happens and you end up shutting me out again? You have a way of throwing up your shields—"

"Michael, listen to me. As I told you before, I don't want this maniac to kill me. I've allowed him to feel my presence here in London, but when we actually meet, the only shields I'll be using are with him. I'll have to keep him out of my head, but I have no desire to shut you out again."

"And what if you panic? Or what if you have a hidden agenda? You were completely unaware in New York."

"Why would you ask that?"

"Because a block is already there. A part of you refuses to allow me access."

Arel's mouth went dry. "I don't want that. I swear I don't."

"I know that's how you feel on the surface, but deep down a part of you is hiding something."

"But why? Do you have any ideas?"

"One thought comes to mind. Rolphe is the one who's ultimately responsible for what happened to William and then to you. You've had a lot of anger connected to that situation. You had your revenge with William. Perhaps you have hidden plans for Rolphe."

* * *

William observed Wolfie's steady breath as the tiny animal lay asleep in his hand. His man to mouse communication skills were improving rapidly. It was a small, but satisfying feat to sooth the little rodent's active mind with his own, to watch small beady eyes go dreamy with drowsiness. He wasn't just a baby whisperer, he was a mouse whisperer as well.

"Looks like you're using what we've been discussing," Raphael said as he appeared next to the mouse cage.

William looked up and smiled back. Raphael had been advising him on the use of his gifts. "You've been helpful. I appreciate it."

"You're a quick study. You have a natural talent when you interact with living things."

William fingered Wolfie's tiny paw, examining the delicate nature of the little beast. "I suppose you're right. Arel used to tell me I could charm a nun out of her rosary with one look. But I never tested the theory. I was never interested in nuns or rosaries."

"But I think you're interested in Annabel."

"Yes, well, I've given it some thought."

"Can I be of any assistance?"

William smiled as the sleeping Wolfie batted at his whiskers. What did mice dream about? A field of ripening seed? Finally, he looked up at Raphael. "What's your idea of people and love?"

"Love? Many times it's a most misinterpreted subject. It probably has as many meanings as there are people."

"I don't care about that. What is the ideal love that two people can share?"

"I'm probably not the one to answer such a question. As Arel pointed out, I don't think like a human."

"But I thought that angels are known for being loving."

"Of course, but I have a very different take on life and people. Take you for instance, I don't think in terms of your personality or your perceptions. I see you from a different vantage point. You're a unique facet of the All, the Creator if you prefer."

"Sounds pretty boring. Everyone is just a nice snowflake that you have to appreciate, right?"

A broad smile creased Raphael's face. "Not exactly. You're a creative being with all the potential that a divine facet embodies. It's wonderful to see you live up to that potential. I'm cheering you on, so to speak, like a friend. You see, in some ways, we are the best of friends, but you've forgotten that. It's part of becoming human."

"And how far does that friendship extend?"

"I'll do whatever I can to help you remember yourself."

"And what do you get out of it?"

"Don't you like seeing a friend find his way back to happiness?" Raphael pulled out a seat and sat down by the table. "But I'm already blissful in my perception of reality. I don't have to find my way back. I know who I am."

"I see." William stood up and carried Wolf to his cage. Before placing him inside, he used a piece of dried apple like smelling salts and the mouse came to life. Stretching and sniffing simultaneously, it only took a moment before Wolf snatched the delicacy with his tiny paws. After he was in the cage, Squeaky and Whiskers rushed forward to examine his treat. There was a bit of a scuffle until the two other mice got treats of their own. When peace was restored, William shut and locked the cage door. He turned back to the angel. "And when I remember who I really am, do I become one of you? Because that doesn't sound very appealing."

"Of course it doesn't, and it shouldn't. You have a different agenda. People are typically bolder souls who love to push the boundaries, so to speak. They create situations that we angels sometimes find a bit extreme. However it's because of your boldness that the Creator can experience something new and expanded. Take love for instance. As I said, your version and mine are different. I'm sure you find your version much more appealing. You enjoy picking and choosing who you'll love. You have a set of criteria for desiring another human being."

"I have to. I don't want to end up with someone who'll sap the life out of me."

"Nice choice of words," Raphael chuckled. "There's some wisdom there, but the only way someone can take something from you is if you forget who you are or you try to change your pure essence to accommodate someone else."

"Don't worry," William snorted, "I'm not planning on anything of the sort."

"Good, but be careful. Falling in love can make you do things you'll later regret."

"Am I hearing you correctly? Are you discouraging me from the idea of loving someone."

"Perhaps I'm not making myself clear. For me, love is a constant. Nothing you do can change my love for you, nor diminish the love I have for who I am. Your definition often deviates from that concept. Words like sacrifice come into play. I never sacrifice because I never have anything to lose. I can never forget my magnificence. Unfortunately, most people never even know how amazing they are to start with."

William lifted his chin and gave Raphael a winsome smile. "Well then, I suppose we share more than I thought. I've always known I was splendid.

* * *

Annabel stood at the top of the stairs, listening to the conversation between William and Raphael. William's comment made her smile. She thought he was splendid too. Perhaps that's why she'd been tempted to give up her wings. He wasn't an ordinary man. Raphael spoke about how humanity had forgotten so much about who they were. William had never totally lost himself. He had the capacity to embrace so much of life, even small creatures like the mice. When he looked at her, he was ready to embrace her. But unlike many men who looked at women, William didn't want to possess her. He wanted her as a partner. He didn't want to change her. He wanted her to expand the adventure that he made out of life.

Maybe I still want that adventure too.

The thought surprised her. She had convinced herself that a decision had been made in favor of staying an angel. Yet, she was eavesdropping on a private conversation for personal reasons. That wasn't exactly angelic. And when she passed the hall mirror, she was smiling, not because of some serene inner peace. She was smiling because William's recent comments were swirling around in her mind. He'd said so many sweet, complimentary things to her lately. She hadn't wanted to acknowledge it, but she'd enjoyed every one, not as an angel, but as a possible future partner for William.

Oh my, I've been deceiving myself!

Fifty-Nine

Rolphe moved quickly along the ill-lit street. He'd chosen not to get a cab. He needed to prepare his mind for what he was going to do. A sudden shower was making his walk more miserable. Rain came down in sheets that splattered the pavement and soaked his trousers. His jacket wasn't doing a good job of repelling the wet either, but he'd forgotten to bring along an umbrella. He cursed softly. He'd never wanted to come to London in the first place. Now the lousy weather was an added depressing ingredient to the situation he was in, hunting down two men who should never have made themselves known. He wanted to go home, back to Myra's bed. He kept thinking about how much the woman meant to him. He fingered the gun in his pocket, wishing that things could be different between them. Why couldn't they have a normal life and just love each other like any man and woman? But he wasn't just any man, and he certainly wasn't normal. He tried to forget that fact when he slipped into Myra's life for those close moments of intimacy. It felt so good to feel her against him, nestled in his arms. The beautiful woman was all kindness and soft heart. How could he go back to her and pretend he'd been away on a business trip? How could he terminate two lives and go on as if nothing had happened?

I have no choice. I have to do this thing.

He swiped the rain out of his eyes and hunkered down to his task. He had to stay focused. Like the soldier he'd been in his youth, he had a responsibility to do what was called for. The thought made him quicken his pace. After he'd gone a couple of blocks, he glanced up at a street sign and knew he was very close to his destination.

Damn, I hope William and his friend are at the pub. I need to finish this thing once and for all.

He stood very still and scanned for a familiar energy. His effort resulted in a sigh. William wasn't anywhere near. Yet, his bones told

300

him not to give up. He sensed that this was a special night, and that he was sure to find at least one of his targets if he remained patient. When he arrived at a little pub, the original meeting place that William had suggested, he even smiled. The dimly lit tavern felt very familiar. Rolphe had seen the place in a recent vision. He made his way past a few tables. Customers were talking and enjoying their drinks. When he found a corner table near the back, he sat down. From his location, he had a clear view of anyone coming in or exiting. As he sat quietly, he felt his body start to tingle with anticipation. It told him that he didn't have much longer to wait.

"So this is the night," he said trying to smile as he realized that victory would soon be his. But he couldn't manage any happiness. A part of him was so ready to execute his plan. Another part was saddened by it all. He'd long ago lost his lust for killing. The anger and rage of losing his family had finally been extinguished by sheer exhaustion. Negative emotions weren't his natural way. He had once loved life because his desire was to experience joy, not pain. When he'd become a vampire, a part of him had fought the need to satisfy himself at the expense of another. In the end, the battle between his terrible creature needs and his true nature had ended in a truce. He drank the blood, but it was purchased. He channeled the rest of the feelings through his music, his art, and even his physical regime of working out every day.

"Perhaps it was the women who saved me," Rolphe mused as he swirled the contents of his glass with his large, powerful hand. "How can you be unchanged when they hold you to their breasts, when you experience their softness, their nurturing natures?"

Sometimes he even questioned his masculinity. He could feel so much of his feminine side in his art and when he'd had a family. How he had loved his children! When they were babies, he'd kissed every toe. Later, when they fell and hurt themselves, he was faster in rescuing them than his wife. He'd kissed their scraped knees. He'd kissed away their pain. That was his true nature.

Fresh tears cascaded down his face just thinking about it all. Yet his boys had been dead for so long. Why were their memories still like branding irons on his heart? He didn't understand it. Their bones were long in the ground, yet he could still see his children so vividly. In his mind's eye, they still had rosy cheeks and blameless smiles.

He wiped his eyes with a quick swipe and reminded himself of why he was in London, in this little pub. "Pull yourself together," he whispered to himself. Looking up, his glistening eyes caught sight of someone who had entered the pub. It wasn't William. It was the other man, the one Rolphe had seen in his vision.

Rolphe sat up very slowly. He stared at his prey and almost cried again. "He's beautiful," he sighed quietly. A little shorter than William, this man was pale skinned with dark, thick, wavy hair. He had classic features that included the most incredible eyes that Rolphe had ever seen. "They're like dark, liquid gold," he gasped. When the man moved, he displayed an elegant grace that told Rolphe he was from a noble line of humankind. Yet there was also power under the cover of gentility. It radiated out from him, as if it wanted to clear a space for the extraordinary being that he was.

Rolphe knew that most people wouldn't notice this man. But Rolphe had the heart of an artist. He observed the flower growing in the crack of the sidewalk. He was aware of the exquisite bird that landed on a branch outside his bedroom window. He also had heightened psychic senses that told him when someone was very special.

"Dammit, I have to get some other perspective if I'm going to snuff him out." Rolphe shut his eyes, trying to rein in his feelings. He had to pause and think about something other than the amazing being he'd just observed. He had to close down his artist's heart. When he'd finally accomplished his goal and looked at the man again, he felt something that he'd missed. The man had Rolphe's tainted blood, or at least Rolphe thought he did. The only thing that he knew for sure was that there was a definite connection between them. "Just as I thought, you're linked to me," he mused.

A group at a nearby table were getting up and putting on their coats. Since Rolphe entered the tavern, many of the patrons had left. The place was almost empty. Even the bartender had disappeared into the back. Rolphe quickly stood and joined the people who were headed for the door. Lowering his head, he hoped he wouldn't be noticed. Once outside, he moved into the shadows of the alley next to the pub. He'd wait there for his chance to finish what he'd come for. He put his hand in his pocket and made sure that his revolver was ready.

WILLIAM'S BLOOD
✳ ✳ ✳

Michael remained in angelic form as he observed Arel. The rain had stopped and his friend was making his way to a pub. It was the place Arel believed he would meet the man who wanted to kill William and him. Thankfully Arel wasn't shutting Michael out. In fact, Arel was silently communicating his thoughts, steadfastly informing Michael that he intended to stick to the plan. Michael readied himself for the unexpected. It was becoming the norm whenever Arel had deep convictions about something he should do.

Arel, the man you're looking for has already arrived and is waiting for you inside the establishment. He's sitting at a table in the back.

Arel replied telepathically.

Yes, I know. I could feel his presence growing stronger as I got closer to the place.

Are you sure that you're ready for what might happen?

I think so. In fact, I feel quite calm. Anyway, I'm going into the pub now and hopefully the situation will be resolved very soon.

Michael's form pulsed more energetically.

Are you sure you're not aware of any hidden agendas?

Arel's answer was filled with conviction.

I swear, Michael, I simply want to let this guy know that he isn't going to be allowed to harm William. Period. Besides, what's the worst that can happen? I'll die and join you guys on the other side.

Michael watched Arel take a seat in the pub.

Arel, please, don't talk about dying.

Why? Your kind seem happy, and William was thrilled on the other side.

Michael noticed Arel's eyes. They sparkled brightly. He had also adopted a discreet smile that he was barely able to contain.

Arel, are you listening to me? I don't think leaving the world would be very wise at this point. You're just learning how to live again.

I'm listening, Michael. But I have to confess that my mind is so clear. Do you think that's strange? I've always been nervous when I've been in dangerous situations.

As soon as Arel announced his feeling of ease, Michael felt his own senses jump.

Arel, you told me that I'm your advisor. So take my advice. Abandon your plan. I'll make sure that you get away safely.

Arel returned a silent laugh.

Calm down, Michael. You're being overly dramatic. It's your turn to have a little faith. Anyway, I'm in the pub, and I see the guy I'm looking for.

Michael waited as Arel took a seat and ordered a drink. A short time later a group of people got up to leave. The man named Rolphe got up too.

Arel, this Rolphe person is on his way out the door.

I know. I saw him try to blend in with some other patrons. How foolish of him. First of all, he's a giant. Secondly, his energy is pulsing out so powerfully that I thought my circuits would overload as he passed by me.

Michael readied himself.

I think it would be better if I join you physically. Just stay put, and we'll decide on how you should handle the situation together, okay?

Arel stood up.

We don't have time for that, Michael. Besides, I need to talk to this guy alone.

Before Michael had a chance to assess Arel's rash decision to leave, Arel was out of his seat and swiftly heading for the door. His eyes were glowing brightly as if he was suddenly overcome by fever. That's when Michael knew Arel was being propelled forward by a need that eclipsed his conscious wishes.

Arel! Stop!

If Arel heard Michael, he didn't heed Michael's command. Instead, he exited the tavern and stood for a moment on the street. Michael knew it was a mistake. He had to act quickly. Using a powerful blast of energy, he slammed Arel's body sideways. It was the best Michael could do under the circumstances, but he knew that his timing was slightly off. As Arel's body took flight, the sound of gunfire shattered the quiet. After Arel landed on the sidewalk, he lay stunned and unmoving. There was a small hole in the arm of his jacket. It was located between his shoulder and elbow. Within moments, blood began to saturate Arel's clothing.

* * *

Rolphe aimed at his target's heart and fired. It was an easy shot, but something went wrong. The man he was aiming at moved just before Rolphe's bullet did its job. It was a dramatic type of movement that the man didn't initiate. Another force was involved. Another unseen power hurled the man out of death's path. It was a phenomenon that Rolphe would have to contemplate at a later date.

Dammit, I think I only wounded him.

Rolphe quickly raised his gun and took aim a second time, holding back long enough to steady himself. With his victim immobilized on the ground, Rolphe decided on a head shot. His finger was on the trigger when his gun flew out of his hand. Rolphe gasped in shock and disbelief. What was he dealing with? He'd seen a lot in his time, but he'd never witnessed an invisible force moving people and objects around. And the power that was being employed was impressive. Rolphe's gun arced heavenward and then landed in some bushes in the park across the street.

Mon Dieu, this man is truly a different and unique kind of creature.

Numbed by the spectacle he'd just observed, Rolphe couldn't move. Only his mind was racing, trying to come up with an explanation. As he stood peering out of the shadows, his thoughts were interrupted. He heard himself being summoned.

"Come here!" The hoarse demand came from the wounded man. The man had regained some measure of himself and was looking in Rolphe's direction.

Rolphe still couldn't move. He could only stare at his victim and note that the man's golden eyes were glowing even brighter than before. The starlit orbs were so mesmerizing that Rolphe gazed back with a gaping mouth.

The man called out a second time. "Come over here and help me!"

Rolphe's paralyzed limbs slowly came back to life. He resisted moving out of the dark alley, but his legs began stumbling forward on their own. Some compelling force was making him close the distance between himself and the man he'd been hunting. With every step, he felt like he was moving towards some inescapable fate. He should have heeded Chessa's warning, but it was too late to think about that now. His heart was jumping about wildly in his chest, letting him know that the tables had been turned, and he was in danger. It was a sensation he remembered when he was a young, unseasoned soldier who was going into battle. Only this time, he felt defenseless. On this field of battle, the man who was calling to him had all the power.

William woke up with a start from an evening nap. "Arel! What the hell are you doing?" He shouted out the question in a panicky voice. He'd just had a nightmare that left him gasping for breath. As he rubbed the sleep from his eyes, he tried to understand why he felt so shaken by a dream. He was still trying to calm himself when he heard a soft knock at his door.

"William, are you okay?" Annabel asked. "Has something happened?"

William quickly got out of bed and went to the door. When he opened it, Annabel looked up at him with bright, inquiring eyes.

"Sorry about the yelling," he said as he began to come back to himself.

"William, what's wrong? Are you sick again?"

"No, it's not that. I had a nightmare."

Annabel reached out and put her hand on his chest. "Dreams can be scary," she said in a quiet, comforting tone.

Annabel's touch made William flinch. He wasn't used to anyone making his heart flutter with excitement, but that's the effect that Annabel had on him.

Annabel started to pull away. "I'm sorry if I overstepped myself."

William grabbed her hand before she could retrieve it and held it to his chest again. How could this woman affect him so deeply? He'd been touched by countless women throughout the years, but none of them could do what Annabel did with the simple gesture. "You didn't do anything wrong," he said quietly. "I'm just a little jumpy after the dream I had."

He realized how much he enjoyed the connection he had with her. Not only did his body come alive, but emotional barriers dissolved into a feeling of bliss. Did Annabel share his feelings? She had kept her distance ever since his return from Chicago. At first, he thought it might be what he needed too. If he had some juvenile crush on her, he wanted to banish it. He told himself that Annabel was wise in distancing herself. Now, he wasn't sure about his feelings. Could he be falling in love?

Annabel put her other hand over his. "You're so pale. Maybe you should tell me about the dream."

"Dream? Oh yes, I almost forgot." William scowled and slipped his hand out from between both of hers. Stepping back, he let his mind return to the nightmare he'd had. Its sharp details made his scowl fade into an expression of concern. "Arel was sprawled out on a sidewalk. He'd been shot."

"That is a frightening nightmare."

William hesitated as his mind reached out to the man he'd vowed to forget. When he communed with Arel's mind, all he felt was pain. "Oh hell, Annabel, I don't think it's just a dream. That idiot has done something stupid again. I'm sure of it."

* * *

Arel lay on the cold, wet sidewalk, trying to keep his focus on Rolphe as the hulking man walked towards him. Arel had called out to Rolphe, but his directive came from a deep, secreted place he hadn't chosen to acknowledge. Now it was too late to change what was happening.

Oh great, Michael was right. I do have a hidden agenda.

The idea angered him, or at least he thought it did until he probed his feelings more thoroughly. There was something he wasn't addressing, an underlying feeling of smugness. When Rolphe dropped to his knees next to him, Arel's first thought was that everything was working out perfectly. He silently stared at Rolphe with a sense of triumph. It was followed by a question.

Why am I feeling like this?

Arel didn't have time to find any answers. Rolphe was asking his on question.

"Who are you?"

"My name is Arel."

Arel had sensed Rolphe's spirit many times, but to actually study the man who made William a vampire was strangely fascinating. Rolphe was a throwback to a different era. He was dressed like a man of the times, but his features and his bearing were more like something out of a Tolstoy novel. He wore an expression that was a mixture of sadness overlaid by complete obedience to whatever ruthless duty he was assigned. For a moment, Arel felt sorry for the man. The moment quickly passed. "Help me up," he ordered.

Rolphe hesitated. "Maybe you should lie still. You're hurt."

Arel grabbed hold of Rolphe's arm and tried to pull himself upright. That's when he realized that his own arm was in bad shape. Pain fired through his flesh and made him grit his teeth. Finally, he managed some control. "Let's get out of here before we're noticed."

Rolphe gave their surroundings a furtive once over. "You're right," he said as he helped Arel to his feet.

Arel pointed across the street to a little park that was poorly lit. "We can talk in private over there."

Rolphe looped an arm around Arel's waist and practically carried him to the appointed area. Once they were hidden in the shadows of a large, overgrown hedge, he looked at Arel for further instructions.

Arel felt like he was dazed and bewildered, but another part of his mind remained sharp and totally capable of making decisions. "I need to sit down," he stated in a stern voice.

Rolphe didn't hesitate. He immediately ferried Arel another ten feet and deposited him on a bench. His brows were furrowed when he looked at Arel's bloody hand. A steady stream of blood was trickling down from his wound. "How bad is it?" he asked.

Arel looked away when he felt himself getting nauseous. "I don't know how bad it is. I've never been shot before."

Rolphe let out a small laugh. "Don't worry, I have. In fact, I've cared for many a wounded comrade." He began to remove Arel's jacket. "Let's get this off so we can stop the bleeding."

Arel tuned into Rolphe's thoughts. The man was very confused and didn't understand why he was helping the person he wanted dead. Arel was confused himself. What was going on? He had discarded the plan he'd had in the hotel, and he didn't have a new one. He was just observing what was going on and trying to deal with the pain he was in.

"You're lucky, I think," Rolphe said as he checked out Arel's arm. "The bullet went through without hitting bone."

Arel's curiosity was caught up by Rolphe's attitude. The man sounded genuine in his concern. When he glanced at Arel, his green eyes were almost fatherly. In that moment, it was hard to believe that the man was a predator, a vampire, a person who had a virus that turned him into a creature of the night. Yet Arel had judged this fellow human and labeled him evil.

Just like I judged William. And I know how that turned out. Now I'm making the same mistake with Rolphe.

Why hadn't he listened to Michael? Why was he always letting a baser part of himself have its way? He could have avoided getting shot. He could have met Rolphe in a different setting if he'd really tried. As he argued with himself about his rashness, he wasn't watching Rolphe. In fact, when he finally brought his attention back to what the man was doing, he had an acute moment of panic. Rolphe clearly had two distinct personalities. One seemed like the compassionate, fatherly type. The other part of him was unfeeling and bloodthirsty. Arel knew it was true because Rolphe was staring at Arel's bloodied arm like a starving man stared at a steak dinner. The man hadn't slain him with a bullet, but the vampire giant was capable of killing Arel by draining him dry. Arel clenched his jaw as he thought about his choices. Should he use his power to fight back? He could do it. He'd demonstrated that fact repeatedly with William.

Or maybe I should let him finish me off. Then I can finally find some peace and join Michael's side.

Arel realized how tired he was of making mistakes and suffering the consequences afterwards. When he considered making another blunder, he didn't have the strength to face the aftermath. He'd had his revenge with William and had to face a mountain load of guilt as William wasted away. Did he want to do the same with Rolphe? Deep down, he knew that's exactly what his own shadow side wanted. Or he could rise above that old pattern and forge a new one. There was a third option. He could leave it up to Rolphe. He could give Rolphe the facts and let him be the one who made the decision and faced the consequences. If Arel died, it was on Rolphe's head.

"You don't want to do this, Rolphe," he insisted. "I'm warning you, if you take my blood, you'll pay the price. And it's a very heavy price indeed. It could mean your life."

* * *

As Rolphe stared at the blood that trickled from Arel's wounded arm, he felt a desire that went beyond any he'd ever known. It was a hunger that lived in his soul and one that he connected with when he painted. Yet, he'd given up on satisfying that needy part of himself, until now. Something new and satisfying had presented itself in the form of a man, a man with golden eyes. But Rolphe knew that he wasn't simply looking at a man. No, Rolphe was acquainted with the world of men, and this person who called himself Arel, wasn't like them. A special creature lay before Rolphe, one that was both beautiful and terrifying. Beautiful because Rolphe could see all that was holy and blessed beaming out from the being's eyes. Terrifying because there was also a hidden darkness that lived in the man's body. Between the two parts of the creature, lay the most sacred feature of all, the being's heart. It was heavily shielded, but Rolphe could feel its power. And it was speaking to Rolphe now. Instead of the moon, the sun reached out to him, asking Rolphe to be open to new possibilities. Just as some wizards could transform base metals into gold, this being's heart could transform lives.

Rolphe paused, trying to clear his head, trying to understand what he was dealing with.

Am I truly hearing a special creature's heart?

Or was it the man himself who was speaking to Rolphe? If so, Rolphe tried to focus on what was being said. As he did, the words, "You'll pay the price" were clear. Yet, Rolphe knew he'd pay any price to drink this man's blood, to take the substance into his own body and feel his own heart lift again. It had been a cold, lifeless thing for so long. If he had to pay the price to change that, so be it.

At first, he tried to be reverent about taking the man's blood, but in the end, he let himself go. After all that he'd lost, his need for something to heal his wretchedness was overwhelming. He became an animal who couldn't live with famine any longer, not when a feast was waiting to satisfy his emptiness. He attacked Arel's arm, not biting it, but sucking it like a child at the tit, the way William had sucked his blood. At first, he couldn't even appreciate the taste. He simply had to swallow up as much of the stuff as he could manage. In the background, he could feel the man struggling against his appetite, but he didn't care about anything but filling himself.

* * *

As soon as William realized that his dream wasn't just a dream, he forgot about his feelings for Annabel. Arel was dying. It was a cold, hard fact that he found acutely upsetting. But why was he having that reaction? Why was he suddenly enraged by the fact that Arel was exiting the world. Shouldn't he be celebrating?

"That bastard, Arel! He's always sticking his nose in other people's business," he cursed aloud.

His shout made Annabel jump back a little. "What do you mean?" she asked.

William stumbled over to his bed and sat down. "I mean he's in real trouble."

"I'm so sorry to hear that, but I know the two of you have a problem with each other."

William glanced up and sneered. "Of course I have a problem with Arel. I have a problem with vicious attack dogs too."

"Is that how you see Arel? I thought he tried his best to help you when you were suffering."

"Yes, that's the worst problem with Arel. When a person is at his lowest, Arel has a way of making that person need him."

Annabel came over and took his hand. She placed it over her heart this time. "It takes a long time for people to be strong enough to have faith in themselves. Along the way, they need others to help them keep that faith growing."

"I've always had faith in myself until I got mixed up with Arel again."

"I'm talking about a different kind of faith."

"Dammit Annabel, I don't have time for this discussion. I need to think."

"Of course you do." Annabel let go of him and turned to the door. "If you need anything, I'll be in my room."

William watched as Annabel closed the door behind her. He could still feel her heart beating under his hand. It was a strong, giving vessel. For a moment, just the thought of what it would be like to explore that part of her filled him with desire. He pushed the feeling aside reluctantly and brought his attention back to Arel. As soon as he did, he remembered his own death and his brief shot at heaven. He remembered Arel appearing next to him and forcing him to return to earth. Usually, the memory brought up his vulnerability and rage. This time he didn't feel either emotion. A lot had happened since then. Raphael had helped him in Chicago. William was able to clear away a lot of unwanted baggage. After that, he didn't feel helpless when he thought of Arel. In a very strange and unexplained way, he knew it was his turn to snatch someone from the jaws of death. "But how? Arel will be dead before I get to him."

Before he had a chance to ponder the problem further, Raphael appeared by the door. He smiled. "There is a way, William, and I can show it to you."

* * *

When Rolphe attacked and began feasting, Arel's body had its own ideas about such a violation. Arel found himself thrashing around, trying to get free of the great bear of a man who held him down and consumed his blood. Yet, as Arel grew weaker, as his body began to go limp, he knew that Rolphe wasn't the only one who made a decision earlier. In that moment when Rolphe chose to attack, Arel saw his opportunity, his chance to leave the earth. After all his mistakes with those he loved, including Justina and William, he was being given a way to go home. Once he died and was safely on the other side, he wouldn't be a mortal being who was always making terrible mistakes. He wouldn't have to feel guilty anymore.

At long last, I can leave this world behind.

But his decision didn't go unchallenged. He could feel Michael trying to get through to him. Arel knew the angel was making a last ditch effort to counter Arel's death wish. Michael's energy was intense as he bolstered the idea of finding happiness in being alive, but Arel ignored him.

Sorry, Michael, thank you for all the ways you've tried to help me, but this life is finally over for me.

As Arel began to relax into the darkness that was closing in, he felt a second attempt to change his mind. This one had none of the loving, peaceful elements of Michael's energy.

Dammit Arel, don't you dare think you're going to leave this easily!

It was William's insistent voice that yelled out in Arel's mind. Arel opened his eyes just enough to see William a few feet away. His form was wispy and glowing. Arel realized that William had learned astral travel too.

Will! I'm surprised!

William's form solidified a little as he continued with his threats.

312

After all that I've been through because of you, don't you dare take the coward's way out.

Arel gasped in a shallow breath. A very small quantity of air was all that his lungs could take in. Rolphe was insatiable in his feeding, and Arel's body was barely able to maintain consciousness. But William deserved an explanation.

I'm sorry, Will. I'm so sorry for everything. But you don't have to worry about anything now. Rolphe took the bait. With my blood doing its job, I don't think he'll be hunting for you anymore. As for me, I'm doing as I promised, leaving you in peace. You'll finally have your life back.

As he worded his message to William, Arel felt his heart soar a little. At least William was safe now. It was a brief moment that was interrupted by William. He didn't seem to share Arel's viewpoint.

That's the biggest bunch of crap I've ever heard, Arel. If you consider me a brother, you'll stop being a victim and do what I'm telling you.

Arel sighed contentedly.

Too late, I'm dying.

William's tone changed.

Please, Arel, don't do this. I saved you long ago because I believed in you. Don't squander that gift.

William's plea sent a discordant ping through Arel's heart. No matter how happy he was to leave a painful, guilt-ridden life behind, he knew William had a point. The man's intention, just like Michael's intention, was to give Arel a chance to find a way beyond his narrow, hellish path.

But I don't know how to be brave like you, Will. I wish I did. Even with your strength to help me, I'm hopeless.

William's voice was even louder when he responded.

Hopeless? Is that what you call your need to suffer? If it is, you have to get off that wheel of woe. It doesn't serve you or me.

Arel's eyes opened wider as he felt his own anger surfacing.

There is no you and me, William! You hate me, remember?

William's form brightened even more.

Maybe I do hate you, and that hatred prompted me to contact Rolphe, but it's not what I want now.

Arel felt so weak, he could barely think, but William was determined to keep him earthbound.

What do you want from me, Will? Why won't you let me die in peace?

William's glaring eyes softened.

I suppose I'm admitting that I'm happy you snatched me out of heaven. I can see that now.

William's confession brought an unexpected surge of joy to Arel's entire body. He had resigned himself to William despising him forever. After all, he had behaved unforgivably when William was on the other side.

William continued to plead his case.

Listen to me, Arel, I want to return the favor. I never thought I'd have that power, but I think I was wrong about that too.

Arel blinked back with more relief when he realized what William meant. Michael's blood had done its job a second time. Enough darkness had been cleared, and now William was coming into his own power. After a moment of initial relief, Arel wanted to respond with a huge, "I told you so, Will." Instead, he sent out a short congratulations.

I'm happy for you, Will.

William sighed.

I know I can help you. Say the word and give me that chance.

Arel tried to smile, but his body was out of energy.

Really, do you mean that?

There was a loud explosion of William's laughter inside of Arel's head.

Heaven help us both, Arel, but yes, you idiot, I mean it.

Arel managed a weak nod of acceptance. As soon as he did, Rolphe was dislodged from his feasting. Somehow he was thrown backwards, and ended up sprawled out on the ground. His eyes were dark and bewildered as he got to his feet and started to run. After that, Arel knew he couldn't hold on any longer. The last thing he registered before blacking out was Rolphe disappearing into the night.

* * *

William had had an out-of-body experience when he died, but he'd never had one while he was alive. It was a new and wondrous feeling to travel to Arel's side via his astral body. With Raphael as his teacher and guide, it was a quick and dizzying trip. He didn't know how to control his movements or what was happening to him. It was only the sight of Arel lying so still on the bench that brought him out of trying to understand what he was experiencing. But he did succeed in having a conversation with his old friend. After that, Arel gave William permission to intercede. That was just before Rolphe stopped feeding and Arel blacked out.

"Oh hell, Raphael, is he dead?" William asked as he tried to touch Arel. His hand passed through Arel's body.

"Not quite," Raphael replied. As he spoke, the tall angel focused intently on Arel. "He still has a chance if you can connect with him on an energetic level."

"But I haven't a clue about such things."

Raphael pointed to William's chest. "If you love this man, connect your heart to his."

"Love?" William felt his energy body diminish a little. "I don't know if I love him or not. After what I've been through—"

Raphael's voice was soft but stern. "Make up your mind quickly or he'll die."

"Dammit! I can't believe he's put me in this spot. I—"

Raphael's glowing form moved closer. "I know this seems unfair, dear friend, but his spirit is leaving his body."

William responded at once. "Oh no it's not!" On some level, he refused to allow Arel to give up. "He's going to stay here and learn how to be responsible, once and for all!" As soon as he made the statement, he felt a small explosion in his chest. A bright stream of energy burst out of his heart, reminding him of a laser. The brilliant ray immediately attached itself to Arel's heart. As soon as it did, William felt a shudder go through his astral body. He could feel his own life force weakening.

Raphael put a glowing hand on William's shoulder. "It's okay, William. What you're feeling is Arel's energy state, not yours. As long as you stay out of fear, you'll be fine."

Michael suddenly appeared and joined them. "Arel's shields are down. I'll be able to help too."

William had to protect his eyes when he tried to stare directly at Michael. He'd seen the angel in physical form on many occasions, but he'd never witnessed Michael in his true splendor. Biblical descriptions of magnificence applied. Tall, commanding and encased in the most dazzling aura of blue and white light, Michael could truly be called a warrior of sorts, one who seemed intent on engulfing Arel with his impressive glowing radiance.

Raphael smiled at William. "Sorry if he's a little too bright, but he needs to stabilize Arel's energy field."

Gazing out of half-closed eyes, William continued to be amazed at both his own contribution and that of the angels who were helping out. He was watching a very impressive and otherworldly spectacle. "All of this because Arel is being an obstinate bastard, right?"

Raphael let out a hearty laugh. "From our perspective, this is quite common. Every human is loved deeply and every one of our kind is dedicated to helping whenever we can. The problem arises when we're shut out by the negative attitudes that humans hold onto. Happily, in Arel's case, you were able to convince him to choose life instead of death. With that change of heart, we are allowed to assist him."

* * *

Rolphe had never known true terror before. He'd thought he'd been scared as a young soldier going into battle, but this was so much worse. Some unseen force was at work. First it had thrown the man known as Arel out of the path of a lethal bullet. Then it had dislodged Rolphe's gun from his hand. Afterwards, he'd come under the spell of the man, Arel.

Once the man's golden eyes grabbed hold of him, Rolphe felt trapped. His mind wasn't his own. It belonged to the man. Yet the man had later given him a choice. When temptation got the better of him, Rolphe chose to drink the man's blood. Once he started, he couldn't stop. He felt like he was in control until he was thrown aside like a child's plaything. That's when his fear grabbed hold, and he started running. He had to get away from whatever it was that could wield so much power. As he ran, he remembered what Chessa had told him.

"Be careful, Rolphe! The men you're looking for can hurt you! Be especially aware of the one with golden eyes!"

When she spoke to him, he'd felt more than her fear for him. He'd felt something much more ominous, an impending doom. He'd quickly pushed it away, thinking he knew enough to survive whatever came his way. He always had managed to best those around him. Now, as pain began to spread throughout his body, he knew he'd made a fatal mistake.

Sixty

Williiam woke up with a groan. When he opened his eyes, he realized he was in his bed.

"Just lie still," Annabel said in a quiet voice. She was sitting next to his bed. "Give your body time to recuperate."

"Don't worry, with my pounding head ready to explode, I have no intention of moving."

Annabel got up and kissed his cheek. "Be proud of yourself. Because of you, Arel is alive."

"Arel, I forgot about him. So he's alright?"

"Not quite."

William sighed and mumbled the first words that came to mind. "He's the reason I'm in this condition."

Annabel nodded. "I guess that's true. You did a wonderful job tonight."

William blinked back at her. "How do you know what I did?"

Annabel blushed. "Michael is here with Arel in the guest bedroom. Michael brought him here and explained that you helped in some way. Afterwards, you must have been so upset about it all that you passed out. I was afraid you'd had a relapse after your recent illness."

William shut his eyes tight as he remembered what he'd been through to help Arel out of another mess. "I don't want you mixed up in what's going on here, Annabel. It would be much better for you to pack your bags and leave."

Annabel laughed. "You've given me that speech before, remember? I'm happy here."

William blinked open his eyes and stared back. "Really, I couldn't tell. Ever since I came back from Chicago, you seemed rather aloof."

318

Annabel took a step back. "That's because I've been trying to shut you out."

William slowly sat up. "Why is that? Did I do something?"

"No, that's not it. I tried to shut you out because I was afraid I might love you."

William scowled. "I guess the thought of loving someone with my track record would scare you, but thank you for being so honest."

"You don't scare me, William. I just never expected to feel the way I feel. It was a bit of a shock to think I could want to be in a relationship that was so personal."

"What other kind of relationship is there between a man and a woman."

"That's just it," Annabel said as she clasped her hands. "I'm not just a woman."

William laid his head back against the headboard to steady himself. "What do you mean by that?"

Annabel stiffened and started for the door. "You don't want to know the answer, really you don't. So I'll go pack my bag and get out of your life before this goes any further."

"Annabel, wait!"

Annabel looked back briefly and then continued to the door. "I can't, William. I love you too much now. I don't think I could stand it if you hated me."

"Annabel, please, why would I ever hate you?"

Annabel hesitated at the doorway, but she didn't reply.

William blinked back, trying to remain as still as possible. "Listen, I'm barely able to think right now. Do me one last favor. Stay put for just a little while, okay?"

"I'll be in my room until you're better," she said.

William thought about the sadness in Annabel's voice when she voiced her concerns. "I'm losing her," he mumbled. As soon as the words were spoken, he knew he had a choice. He could let Annabel leave, or he could face whatever she thought would make him hate her. Something in his gut told him that either decision would change his world forever. Knowing he was in no shape to face that situation, he'd check on Arel instead. Forcing himself out of bed, he made the short journey to the guest room. When he opened the door, he saw Michael sitting next to Arel's bed.

"William, come in," Michael said with a welcoming smile.

319

William walked over to join him and looked at Arel. The man was white as chalk and still as a corpse. In fact, Arel's inanimate body would have looked perfectly natural if it were lying in a casket at a funeral viewing. It was only when William noticed Arel's chest rising ever so slightly that he took a breath himself. "Annabel said that Arel will live."

"Yes, but he's lost so much blood."

William smiled. "I can help with that. I have a couple of frozen pints in the lab freezer. It wasn't easy convincing Arel to donate them for research, but as usual, I was right to insist that he did."

"They'll definitely help."

William let out a sigh of disgust. "I hope he's not brain damaged after this. He was barely able to function when he had all his faculties. If his mind's worse than before—"

"No, his mind will be fine," Michael said. "But I understand how hard this situation has been in your case, William. I'm sorry."

William noted the kindness in Michael's face. "You and Raphael have a lot in common. I hope Arel appreciates what a friend you are."

Michael put his hand on Arel's chest. "He's done his best. I can't ask for more than that."

"At least he hasn't killed you. Thank your lucky stars that you're an angel."

Michael's blue eyes sparkled playfully. "Being what I am does have its perks. On the other hand—"

"Yes, I know. Raphael has explained the limitations your kind face when dealing with humans."

Michael turned to William and hesitated. "Arel didn't mean for so many things to go wrong between the two of you. His heart is in the right place most of the time."

William walked over to a chair and sat down. "You better get that blood out of the freezer downstairs. It's labeled with a capital 'I' for idiot."

Michael stood up and returned a puzzled look.

William laughed and had to grab his head again. "I'm kidding. Arel is Subject B."

* * *

Annabel sat on a chair in her room and stared at the little suitcase that lay on her bed. Finally, she glanced up at Raphael. He stood a few feet away. "Oh Raphael, I don't know why I told William that I love him. It just seemed so natural when I said it. Now I don't know what to do about it. I've failed him, and I don't know how to undo the damage I've done. Do you have any suggestions?"

Raphael walked over to where she sat and put his hand on her shoulder. "You could stay with him."

"No, I can't." Annabel tried to make the statement in a calm, relaxed tone, but she couldn't get her bearings. Nothing felt stable. She'd always been an angel, yet it was so easy to slip into the world of humans when she thought about being with William. Still, that world was unfamiliar and filled her with a sense of inadequacy. She didn't know how to navigate in an environment where emotions could quickly override all sense of wellbeing.

Raphael's hand tightened a little on her shoulder. When she looked up at him, she saw how much he wanted to help.

"My dear friend, why can't you do what your heart wants?" he asked.

Annabel stood up and went to the window. She was determined to maintain her normal perception of who she was. "My heart isn't important. I was given this assignment because Michael had faith in me. He felt like I could assist William as he went through the difficult challenges he'd have to face."

Raphael sat down in the chair Annabel had occupied. "Mission accomplished. From what I've observed, William is doing very well with everything. He's proven himself with both the internal and external difficulties that tested him."

Annabel turned to face him. She could feel herself crossing some invisible line. It was a line that an angel never crossed. She felt her emotions taking over, making her voice louder than usual. "Yes, and I'm very pleased about that, but I know him, Raphael. William will never accept me as a partner once he finds out I'm an angel."

The door to the bedroom opened before Raphael replied. William looked in from the hallway. His face was expressionless, as if he'd just witnessed a crime and was in shock. "I thought I wanted to talk to you, Annabel, but you'll have to excuse me. I don't feel very well." He backed up a step and closed the door behind him.

Annabel stood by the window for a long moment. She could hardly make her lungs take in air. She knew that William had overheard her confession. "He knows what I am," she gasped. Just as she had feared, William looked betrayed by that fact. In the brief moment when their eyes had met, his face was stricken with disbelief and the horror at how he'd been deceived. "I've ruined everything," she said as she started for the door.

Raphael got up and followed her as she let herself out of the bedroom. "Annabel? Where are you going?"

Annabel didn't answer. Instead, she started running down the hallway towards the front entrance. When she got to the door, she managed to open it. Without a look back at what she was leaving behind, she exited William's house, ran down the stairs and kept running. She could hear Raphael calling after her, but she knew she wasn't part of his world anymore. She didn't feel like a human being either. She was lost in some no man's land with nowhere to go. Her only choice was to accept the truth. She'd failed William in the worst kind of way. She'd damaged his connection to his heart when he was just starting to trust that part of himself. Her own heart felt hollow and wanting, but she couldn't let herself think about that. It was better to let a comforting numbness grab hold.

* * *

William barely made it back to his room. Once inside, he had to pause to get his breath. He couldn't think clearly after what he'd just heard. As he took several gasping breaths, he noticed Raphael's raised voice in the room next to his. The angel sounded upset.

"Michael! It's Annabel. She's in trouble." Raphael's words came out in a rush.

When Michael responded, his voice was edgy too. "What are you saying?"

"Annabel's gone. She ran out of the house and kept going. I called to her, but she's so confused, she wouldn't listen. She's shut me out completely."

The news snapped William out of his stupor. His mind was still reeling after finding out he'd been misled, but he had to ignore his own problem. Annabel, the person he thought he loved a few

322

minutes earlier, was in danger. Raphael's statement was confirmed by William's growing ability to connect to other people. If he went deep enough within, he could actually feel Annabel's panic as if it was his own.

Stop! Don't let yourself be pulled in again. Forget about her.

He immediately began to distance himself from caring about Annabel's welfare. Yet, he couldn't content himself completely. He had to talk to Raphael and get some answers. His face was lined with anger and fatigue when he walked into Arel's bedroom. "Raphael, what do you mean Annabel's shut you out? She's one of you, right? She can't do that."

Raphael turned and looked at him. "She isn't one of us anymore. She loves you on a personal level, William. She's given up her wings."

William walked over and grabbed Raphael's shirt. "Angels can't do that. An angel is always an angel."

Raphael stiffened a bit. "That isn't true. They're free to choose a different path."

William's hand was shaky. "You mean they can become one of us?"

"That's right."

William let go of Raphael and backed up. He felt his exhaustion deepening as he thought about the newest calamity that he faced. "I can't believe any of this, but let's say an angel does forfeit its wings, what happens to them after that?"

Raphael sighed. "Hopefully, they'll learn to adapt to the human world, but many times they don't know how. It can be a very perilous transition. Annabel could quickly lose her will to live. If she dies in that state, she won't have any other life experience to fall back on. It could take many lifetimes as a human for her to find her way back to any kind of happiness."

William walked over to the wall. Laying a fist against the surface, he wanted to nurse the anger that was fast replacing the shock he'd had when he learned about Annabel's true identity. It was a righteous anger. Annabel had lied to him. The whole time she was with him, she'd misrepresented herself. "Dammit, no wonder she seemed so perfect. She wasn't human!" he shouted.

Neither angel responded. They stared back, but they didn't attempt any conversation.

"I see," William said as he continued to glare at them. "First I'm saddled with Arel. Now, I'm supposed to care about one of you, correct? Well you can just clean up this mess yourselves!"

Raphael walked over to where William stood. "I wish we could clean it up as you say. With all my heart I wish I could help her, William. But Annabel gave up her wings for you. If you could let her know that you forgive her for misleading you, it might help her to let us in. Otherwise—"

"Otherwise what?" William growled.

"Like I already told you, if she loses faith in herself, she'll have to bear some very severe consequences."

"I don't understand."

"When a person trusts in the power of love and feels that trust has betrayed them, they go into a very dark place."

It was taking all of William's willpower to hold his emotions in check. He might have asked for full disclosure from Raphael, but now he knew too much. "Bloody hell, I can't believe it!" As he was feeling the burden of another life added to his shoulders, he glanced at the bed and noticed that Arel had a little more color in his cheeks. The IV was helping. He was getting some much needed blood. "My god, I'm the one that should have wings, not you two. I'm the bloody idiot who has to save everyone."

Michael came over to where William was standing. "We'd be very grateful if you could help Annabel," he said in a strong, affirmative tone.

William recognized a leader when he saw one. Michael personified the role. With steady, crystalline eyes, he exuded a powerful energy that could definitely inspire even the most hesitant of followers. William wasn't a follower, but he did have a definite sense of what was needed in the situation. First, he had to put his anger aside and temporarily let go of his own agenda. Next, he had to find Annabel. On reflection, he knew he was putting too much blame on her. In truth, she was an innocent at heart. Her only crime was that she cared too deeply about the man she was trying to help.

She cared too much about me! The misguided creature forfeited her wings. Now I have to keep her from throwing her life away too.

Once that task was accomplished, William would detach himself from any more thoughts of love and partnership. Annabel would serve as his final cure, one that set him back onto a course of solitude and sanity.

Taking a shaky step forward, he addressed Raphael and Michael with narrowed eyes. "Here's the deal. If you want me to go after your little darling, you better zap me with some energy before I keel over. I'm running very low after last night's rescue mission."

Raphael smiled. "You're in luck. I'm well versed in energy restoration."

"I can help you too," Michael added. "People who run off when they have a problem have become a specialty of mine."

William thought about what Michael had to endure as Arel's official guardian and felt even more exhausted. "I could try to imagine what you go through, but if I did, I might blow out the last of my working circuits."

Sixty-One

A sudden panic grabbed hold of Annabel when she realized that William overheard her conversation with Raphael. An overwhelming surge of alarm fired through her body. She bolted from her room and kept going. She couldn't stop and face the man she loved. She couldn't bear the thought that William would look at her with hate-filled eyes. Yet, no matter how far or fast she ran, she'd never escape her fate.

What have I done? What have I done?

Breathless, she stopped and braced herself against the hard brick of a nearby store front. Again the question repeated. But why did she bother to ask the question when she knew the answer. She'd fallen in love with a human. No, it was more than that. She hadn't just fallen in love. She had made her love for William more important than anything else, including being an angel. It happened so gradually that it was a shock when the truth dawned on her. Earlier in their relationship, she'd been sitting by William's sickbed, opening her heart to him as he slept, wishing that she could lie down next to him and that they could hold each other forever. In that quiet moment, in that still point in time, as she entertained thoughts of love and the joining of two hearts, she had set events in motion. On a deep, hidden level within, she was already preparing for the final step. Today she'd taken that step and given up her wings.

Raphael and Michael had informed her of what that meant. But their words were just words. Even experimenting with the feeling of being a human wasn't like the real thing. As she forced herself into an upright position and began walking again, reality set in. She hadn't just made a decision. With each step she took, she moved further into an existence where there was no certainty. Total faith and conviction were left behind as a heavy fog began to cloud her mind.

326

She had exchanged her blissful knowledge of who she was for the unpredictable world of earth life. Feelings ruled this world. She'd seen Arel in the steely grip of fear many times. Would it become her new master? Had she given up her beautiful wings to don a cloak of dread?

She didn't want to know how these negative forces worked, but she didn't have that option now. Her mind and body were already responding to her new role as a human. The light that she'd always known was fading, as if she was going blind. She had a gnawing feeling in the pit of her stomach.

She paused again, this time in front of a small restaurant. When she looked through the plate glass window, she recognized the tea shop where she had first talked to William. But that bright moment was behind her now.

I can never go back to my old life.

She opened the door to the café, knowing that she had to calm herself, at least for a few minutes. Once inside the restaurant, she made her way past an elderly man. He looked up at her with a face that was heavily lined from pain. As he reached out for his cane and tried to stand up, his shoulders were bent. He managed a smile anyway. She tried to send him some love to help him on his way, but her heart felt frozen and stiffer than the old man's knees.

How can he still smile when he's so sick?

The thought was a difficult one as she felt her legs getting heavier with every step? As an angel, she lived very lightly in her body. Now, the physical part of her felt dense and stagnant.

It's because I'm letting myself think of what can go wrong.

The idea seemed simple to understand when she had her wings.

I have to stop this downward spiral! But how?

She found a table towards the back of the sunny room and tried to breathe. She didn't have to wait long for her tea and scone, but as soon as she tried to take a bite of the pastry, she balked. She didn't have an appetite like she did when she was there the first time. Just the thought of William made her stomach go queasy. She'd never see him again. The thought was almost unbearable.

Why is there a great longing inside of me? No matter what, I can love William, even if we're apart. I'm sure that he doesn't have to return that love in order for me to be happy.

But when she tried to push William out of her mind, she felt empty.

And rightly so! I don't have anything in my life now, no purpose and no guiding hand from those who have always surrounded me.

That was one point she hadn't considered before. While she was directing all her attention to loving William, she hadn't contemplated her own place in the scheme of things. She didn't have to when she had wings. She was a part of a greater system. She was like a flower in a vast garden of the Creator.

Until I gave up my place in that garden.

She knew that everyone and everything were part of the Divine, not just angels. The difference was that angels never forgot that fact. Humans did. It was part of the game they played. A veil of forgetfulness shrouded the fact that they were always connected to one source energy. Even if she reminded herself of that truth, she was losing her ability to feel it.

She looked around the eatery. There were several other single patrons. Each one was caught up in a world of their own.

Soon I'll be just like one of them. All my memories will feel like dreams that never happened.

Where would she go when she left the restaurant? What would she do? Maybe she'd have to wander forever, another homeless person on the streets of London. The thought stopped her breath. Her lungs stalled for a moment when she imagined what lay ahead of her.

I don't belong anymore!

She tried to stand up, but her legs were unsteady. What was wrong with her body? Why couldn't she get enough air? As she tried to understand what was happening to her, she heard someone call out her name.

"Annabel?"

The sound jarred her. She'd already slipped into her own small space. In this fragile place, anything unexpected, even a noise or her name being called out, scared her. Her fingers clasped the arms of her chair. When she looked up, her lip was quivering. "William?" When she heard herself, she knew something was wrong with her voice too. It was as weak as her legs.

"Annabel, are you alright?" William asked.

He wore a scowl like the one she'd seen so often when he was annoyed with Arel. She tried to make her face smile back at him. It sometimes brought him a bit of comfort. But she couldn't manage a smile. Instead she heard herself saying something that made her feel even worse. "You shouldn't be here. Go away, please."

William pulled out a chair and sat down. His scowl was replaced by a heavy sigh.

She noted his forced patience. "I'm sorry, William," she blurted out. "I don't want it to be this way either, so leave!"

"Listen, Annabel, I've come with a message from Michael and Raphael. They want to help you, but you have to let them in. Do you understand?"

She swallowed the bitter taste in her mouth as she realized she didn't understand what he was talking about. The idea of Michael and Raphael didn't compute anymore. They were beings that lived in a different realm. "William—" She tried to reach out to the one she loved, but her hands were still grasping the arms of the chair. The feel of the wood was the only solid thing in her life at that moment. No matter, she had to give William a message. "I want you to be happy." Again, she tried to add a smile, but her eyes went blurry. That had never happened before. It was another clue that her body was truly broken. But she couldn't let William in on her condition. He was just finding some peace in his life. Somehow she had to stay strong for a little while longer and convince him to forget he'd ever met her. She looked down at the table cloth, hiding herself from William's probing gaze. "I have only one request. Make the time we had together mean something."

"I'm grateful for all you did," he said quickly. "Now, let me take you back home. Give yourself a couple of days to get this mess sorted out. Things will get better, I'm sure."

"Better? Is that what you think?" She started laughing at the ridiculous thought, but she knew her laughter was offensive because William looked back with irritation. "I'm sorry," she quickly apologized. "You're trying to help."

"Yes, Annabel, I am. Now stop being foolish and come back with me."

Annabel didn't know her mood or her physical vessel could shift so quickly. Suddenly, she was on her feet and rushing for the exit. "I don't need your anger, William. I don't need anything from you," she yelled as she reached the door and let herself out. She was halfway down the block when she understood that her body wasn't broken after all. Her voice worked and so did her legs. Her breathing was fast. She was taking in more oxygen. Her ears were fine too. She heard William calling out to her, but she refused to listen to anything he had to say. She was on her own now.

* * *

William exited the tea shop. Looking down the street, he watched Annabel running away from him. He didn't follow her. He couldn't. He had too much on his plate already. His thoughts went to Arel. The man was laid out prone and barely breathing in his guest bedroom. From what Michael had said, Arel's physical and emotional recovery could be a long and difficult one.

William took in a gasping breath at the thought.

I'll never escape that idiot or his needs! And I can't let myself be tethered to another helpless person.

He didn't have the strength. His body was worn and tired. His mind was worse than his body. The night before, it had been blasted by an explosive energy that he didn't know how to control.

I refuse to add more problems to my life!

But in spite of everything, he couldn't stop staring after Annabel. She seemed to be running blindly, bumping into people as she continued to put distance between them.

What will happen to her?

That very morning, when he opened his eyes and saw her smile back at him, his heart skipped a beat. The only thing in the world that he wanted was to reach out and hold her in his arms, to kiss every part of her. He knew without a doubt that she wanted him too. Her eyes were filled with a fire that he'd never seen in them before. They held the same passion that he felt. The two of them were a match in so many ways. Annabel wasn't just passionate. She was capable, straightforward and responsible. She knew how to stand up to him without being rude. She was reasonable and witty.

But that's changed now. I can see it so clearly. She's so afraid.

He didn't only see it and feel it, he understood it. When Raphael had done some fast healing work on William, the angel had also imparted knowledge about what Annabel was going through. She was being thrown into a world she didn't know how to navigate. At least human children had grownups to care for them and to teach them the ways of being on the earth. But Annabel was an exquisite and unique creature who didn't have that background. She had about as much chance of making it in the world as a toddler who stumbled out into heavy traffic.

She'll never survive.

The thought hit William at his core. No matter what his mind told him, if he didn't reach out now, he wouldn't have another chance. The one woman he'd opened his heart to would be that child who rushed into a busy street without looking. This time he was struck in the chest. The vessel within, the heart that pumped blood and nourished his body, nearly stopped working. Whether William admitted it or not, he'd given himself to Annabel the moment he stabbed himself instead of taking her life. After that, he'd played his cards so close to his vest that he'd hidden the truth from himself. Until now.

How much worse can it get than stabbing myself for her?

He started to run too. At first, he didn't think he'd get very far in his condition, but the more he thought about losing Annabel the more his body responded. It came alive in a powerful way that would have astounded him if he wasn't concentrating on catching up with Annabel.

Dammit, she's quite the sprinter.

She was nearing a busy intersection, and she wasn't slowing up. What if he didn't have time to close the distance between them? She was almost at the crosswalk. Why wasn't she stopping? She literally was a child walking into a lane of fast cars. "Annabel, no!" He shouted out the words as he watched her starting to step off a curb. She paid no attention to the oncoming traffic that was speeding across the lane. She was clearly in a state of shock. If she didn't come out of it, she was going to kill herself. "Annabel, please wait! I love you!" He also called out to Raphael. *Help me! Help Annabel, please!*

Annabel must have heard him because she looked back. Her foot was in a forward position, but she paused for just a second. It was long enough for a tall passerby to grab her arm and pull her back to safety.

"Raphael! You do have your moments," William whispered to himself. He was still running and his lungs were heaving. But he didn't let up. He wouldn't slow his pace until he got to the woman he loved. When she was within his grasp, he skidded to a stop. "I almost lost you," he gasped as he pulled her into his arms.

"What happened?" she asked in a trembling voice.

William could feel his own body shaking too, not because he was out of breath, but because he'd never been so relieved. He began to kiss Annabel's face. He anointed her lips, her cheeks, and her forehead with tender demonstrations of affection. His heart was free in that moment, free to expand and cherish the wonderful gift that he held in his arms. "Promise that you'll never run away from me again."

"I promise," she said. After a long pause, she asked a question. "Is it alright if I love you, William?"

Annabel's voice was returning to normal. When she looked up at him, her eyes were filling up with tears, but her smile told him that they were happy tears.

"Yes it is perfectly alright, my beautiful angel."

"But I'm not an angel anymore," she said, lowering her head.

William tipped up her chin and let her see what he'd hidden from everyone he'd ever known. The one exception was a young and struggling Arel, but no other person on earth had been privy to William's complete devotion and dedication. It was something he reserved for those whom he held sacred. "You'll always be my angel, Annabel. Nothing will ever change that."

Sixty-Two

Raphael took a seat on the downstairs sofa and looked across at William. The man was still recuperating from his exploits in helping Arel and Annabel. However, he definitely appeared to be in much better health as he sat in his recliner. He was holding Arel's mouse, Whiskers. Raphael gave William a look of concern. "The little fellow doesn't appear to be very happy, does he?"

Whiskers was curled in a ball in William's hand. His body shivered a little as he dozed. William ran a finger over the small rodent's head and let out a sigh. "It's Arel's fault. His energy is so low that he's affecting this poor creature."

"Really? Why do you say that?"

"Oh come now, Raphael, you know that I'm right."

Raphael smiled. "Yes, but I wondered how you came to that conclusion."

"I'd have to be dead not to feel Arel's low vibes. They've settled over this place like a shroud. And Whiskers is very connected to his owner, so it's doubly hard on him. Of course, I suppose I have to take some responsibility too. I'm the one who asked Arel to interact with the mouse. I should have known better than subject a living creature to someone like Arel."

Raphael's smile broadened. "On the other hand, Arel was very helpful when you were in pain."

William glanced up. "Yes, he was. I have no trouble admitting that he can surprise me in a good way. I simply wish he'd get his act together once and for all."

"You know him very well. Why do you think he holds on to so much negativity?"

"Arel explained it himself. He's afraid of making more mistakes. And let's face it, he has made some very bad choices."

"But in spite of everything, you didn't want him to cross over."

William let out a huff of disgust. "Don't remind me."

"Do you regret what you did?"

"Absolutely not. After all that I've been through with him, Arel is going to stick around until we finish what we started."

"So you haven't given up on him?"

William closed his eyes, letting his thoughts drift to all the beautiful creatures he'd known as a boy. Visions of fox and deer and even field mice came to mind. Then Arel's face appeared. It was as innocent as that of a fox cub. "I guess I still believe in him, just like I believe in this little creature that I'm holding."

As William spoke, Whiskers woke up and looked at him. His beady, black eyes were steady for a long moment as he connected with William's bright gaze. William sat back, concentrating. Slowly, he let his energy expand and caress the little mouse, surrounding the animal in a cocoon of wellbeing. Whiskers responded almost at once. He stopped shivering and shook himself. In the next moment, he began to explore William's hand, sniffing around for a treat.

Raphael stood up, walked over to the food canisters and retrieved a large pumpkin seed. "Is this what he's looking for?" he asked as he handed the seed to the little mouse.

William smiled as Whiskers sat back and began to savor his treat. "Don't worry, Whiskers. No matter what your owner is up to, he's not alone anymore. I'm learning to use what he gave me, and someday, we're going to get to the other side of things. And when we do, Arel is going to find a way to be happy, once and for all."

The story continues in book four, BROTHER'S BLOOD!

Thank you for taking the time to read *William's Blood*, the third book of my series, THE VAMPIRE RECLAMATION PROJECT. If you enjoyed it, please consider telling your friends. Word of mouth is an author's best friend and much appreciated. – S. S. Bazinet.

www.ingramcontent.com/pod-product-compliance
Lightning Source LLC
Chambersburg PA
CBHW020905200626
46814CB00001BA/183